JUDGMENT OF THE BOLD

BOLD TRILOGY #3

JAMIE MCFARLANE

FICKLE DRAGON PUBLISHING LLC

PREFACE

Sign up for the author's New Releases mailing list and get free copies of the novellas; *Pete, Popeye and Olive* and *Life of a Miner*.

To get started, please visit:

http://www.fickledragon.com/keep-in-touch

PROLOGUE

Judgment of the Bold is the third book in the Privateer Tales Bold Trilogy and has been written in a manner to be read independent of the other books. That said, one of the difficulties of writing a long running series is getting people back up to speed with characters they may have forgotten. I have two resources available for this. The first is a glossary at the end of this book. In this glossary, I have descriptions of the major characters. The second is on my website at fickledragon.com/privateer-tales-characters. And, don't worry, neither resource is required. I'll introduce each character as you run into them, just like you'd expect.

Happy Reading!

Jamie

Chapter 1

SPARK

"Captain, sensors are picking up a derelict at one hundred thousand kilometers," Jonathan announced.

Unable to sleep, I'd relieved the watch, preferring the quiet an empty bridge afforded. And while being accompanied by the collective of fourteen hundred thirty-eight sentients we called Jonathan was hardly solitude, it was comfortable. The two of us spent enough time together that we were content in the companionable silence.

"How far off our nav-path?" I pulled my feet from the forward bulkhead and dropped them onto the deck. While on watch I preferred the pilot's chairs as they allowed the widest field of view through *Hornblower's* forward armored glass screen. I focused on the vid-screen, now visible where my feet had rested only a moment before.

We were still under a hard-burn, which meant our sensors were limited in their ability to pick up long range objects, and with a few exceptions, we couldn't communicate ship-to-ship. That said, Jonathan had plucked what to most would look like static from those sensors and had made a positive identification of wreckage.

"We will pass within twenty thousand kilometers," Jonathan answered.

Accompanied by an Abasi cruiser from House Perasti on our way back to Tamu from the Picis system, we'd already run across three derelicts. In the previous three cases, the ships had been violently disabled and their crews murdered.

My AI projected a plan that would allow a close flyby. If this ship were Abasi, then Moyo, Perasti Tertiary, would link with the ship's systems and learn of the crew's fate. If it were anything else, we'd have to rely solely on our sensors as we made a fast pass at a hundred kilometers or so.

"*Hunting Fog* has altered course," Jonathan announced.

"Match course correction," I answered. So much for a quiet watch.

I stood and straightened, stretching out the kinks caused by slouching in the chair, then grabbed my coffee from where it was magnetically affixed to the chair. Before I'd taken two steps, a whistle sounded at the bridge door. On my HUD, Ada Chen, *Hornblower's* lead pilot and a good friend, appeared with her hand on the bridge security pad. As third in command, her security clearance was such that I didn't need to acknowledge her entrance. The hatch popped back and slid into the wall.

"I was having the best dream," she grumbled as she swept onto the bridge, the long tails of the coat she'd taken to wearing trailing behind her. Ada had fine features and a willowy build. Today, a wrinkled-pillow pattern was etched along her high, left cheekbone.

"Morning, Cap." Marny James-Bertrand, my number two, jogged in behind her. The two women could not have been more different. Physically, where Ada was slight, Marny was well-muscled. As leaders, where Ada was instinctual, often making decisions in flight without knowing immediately why, Marny was strategic in every move. Both women were formidable. To be honest, if I had one super-power, it was to recognize their value and make a place where they could both thrive.

"No need to be chipper," Ada grumbled again and slid into the chair where I'd just been sitting. "Thanks for warming up the chair though, Liam."

"Good morning, Marny. Appreciate you two rolling out," I said.

"Six minutes ago, Jonathan detected a new derelict. We've adjusted course for a flyby."

Ada made a show of wiping at her vid screen with a nano-infused cloth. "Did this derelict put its dirty derelict feet onto my pristine, new vid-screens? If not, I'll thank whoever it was to keep their big clods on the deck where they belong."

With the heat of Ada's stare at my back, I rerouted to the sideboard where the ship's steward kept hot coffee, water and snacks. "*Hunting Fog* has already altered course," I said, refusing to acknowledge Ada's complaint. I poured hot water into a thermal cup and filled a small, silver bell with tea before dropping it into the water.

"Looks like the same signature," Marny observed, standing in front of a video panel on the portside. "Am I seeing this right, Jonathan?"

I smiled as I handed the hot tea to Ada. "Hungry?" I asked her.

"Both circumstance and the mass we've measured lead us to the same conclusion," Jonathan answered.

"No. And this doesn't let you off the hook. I don't want my screens all scratched up," she said, tilting her head in an attempt to convey annoyance. I smiled and tried to look innocent. She was a light touch and returned my smile.

"Another cutter?" Marny asked.

Green ready lights illuminated next to both engineering and fire-control status indicators on my HUD. Roby Bishop, a native of Zuri and an extremely bright engineer, and Sendrei Buhari, the powerful, albeit gentle former Earth Naval officer we'd rescued from a Kroerak-controlled planet, had also been pulled from their warm beds in response to the status elevation caused by the wreck.

"That is correct," Jonathan answered.

"Is it just me?" Roby chimed in on the ship's tactical channel. "Or do we *only* find these things on the graveyard shift?"

"It's not just you," Ada agreed.

I wasn't big on chatter during a crisis, but Roby was merely checking in.

"Sendrei, what's our ordnance level?" I asked.

Hornblower was equipped with both blasters and projectile weapons, which made it a rather unusual configuration. The labor involved in simply moving the 400mm, 250mm and 75mm projectiles around made them expensive to carry. It was a cost Marny had been willing to bear for the rescue mission *Hornblower* had just undertaken, but that cost outlay was something we'd have to reconcile over time. The fact was, projectile ammo was as devastating as it was surprising to those we ran into, outperforming the blaster weapons by two or three times in both range and damage.

"We have eighty percent of our four hundreds, sixty-five percent of our two fifties and the seventy-fives are at twenty percent," he answered.

"*Hunting Fog* has cut engines," Jonathan announced.

"All hands, hard-burn desists," Ada announced, having adopted the Felio speech pattern.

My stomach lurched as the engines spooled down and the inertial and gravity systems switched from redirecting the crushing force of acceleration into a 1.5g downward force to space-normal 0.6g.

"Incoming comm, *Hunting Fog,*" Nick, my best friend and business partner, announced from beside me. I hadn't seen him come in. He'd likely been busy with his and Marny's infant son, Peter, who shared the name with my deceased father.

"On bridge," I answered. Having dropped from hard-burn, our sensors transmitted a higher-resolution image of a wrecked Abasi cutter that sailed with the colors of House Mshindi. "Go ahead, *Hunting Fog.*"

"Bold Prime," Moyo answered, her always well groomed, orange furred face appearing on my holo projector. "We have located a communication device that was activated twelve hours previous."

"Oh?"

Nick was furiously swiping at his display. He nodded affirmation.

"House of the Bold has authorization to decipher this message, but I will convey its contents for your interpretation," she said. "I propose that we mate ships that we might meet whiskered. My gunjway has prepared morning entrails."

I had turned off my AI's interpretation circuits. I'd learned enough of the Felio language that I was able to interpret for myself. My AI showed 'raft-up' and 'face-to-face' as substitutions for 'mate' and 'whiskered' on my HUD. I smiled at the translation of entrails to refreshment. I was definitely missing a lot by allowing the translator to work.

"See you in ten," I answered. "Bold desists."

"Catchy phrase, isn't it?" Ada quipped. " I don't care if it *is* morning, I will never be up for entrails."

I grinned but didn't respond. "Tabbs, can you meet us at Deck Three airlock?"

My fiancée, Tabitha Masters, having taken the last watch, hadn't been summoned by the general quarters call. She was below Ada on the chain of command, though they were both excellent pilots. Tabby's real talent was as a warrior, which translated better to small ships and situations requiring hand-to-hand combat.

"On my way," she answered. "What's on that transmission?" I wasn't surprised she was following the events unfolding on the bridge.

"Ship name was *Tracks in Snow*," Nick said. "Smart captain too. After being attacked by three Strix-flagged sloops, she realized there was no escape and dropped the communication devices. *Tracks in Snow* was coming to warn us."

"About what?" Tabby asked.

"Strix, Golenti, and Pogona nations have all broken from the Confederation of Planets," Nick said. "They're targeting Abasi ships."

"That might explain why we've seen so few ships," I said.

The route we'd taken from Picis back to Tamu had been nearly devoid of other ships. It was to be expected on the Picis side, but we were a single jump from Tamu, the home of the Abasi, and still saw absolutely no traffic in a normally very busy area. "Nick, you're with me. Marny, Ada, hold down the bridge. We'll keep comms open."

"Aye, aye, Cap," Marny answered, taking my position in the captain's chair.

"What about Zuri?" Ada asked. "Did they say anything about Petersburg or Silver?"

Nick cut me a worried look. We hadn't talked much about the fact that my mom had gone completely incommunicado at roughly the same time the second fleet of Kroerak were due to arrive at the planet Zuri.

"I'm still parsing," Nick said as we jumped onto the elevator and dropped to Deck Three, "but it doesn't look good. There's information about casualties on Zuri and details about how the Confederation fleet has been devastated."

"Confederation?" I asked. "I thought Abasi seceded from the Confederation."

"Not sure," Nick answered. "That's all I can gather for now."

"If you don't mind," Jonathan interjected, "we've fully parsed the transmission. It is incomplete, but much can be inferred. There are sufficient references to Confederation fleet activities to indicate that the Strix, Pogona and Golenti departure from Confederation rule was accompanied by a return of Abasi to the Confederation. We're also concerned for the safety of the inhabitants of the York settlement and of Petersburg station. Significantly, there has been loss of communication between the Tamu and Santaloo systems."

Nick and I caught up with Tabby in the hallway on Deck Three. While eighty-five crew sounds like a significant complement, we were running with about a third of what we needed, and the ship felt abandoned. I placed a hand on the narrow of Tabby's waist as we joined her in front of the airlock. She'd heard our approach and turned into me, smiling as she felt my touch. She had the lightest little freckles on the top of her cheeks. Her hair was the color of copper, and a single, long braid had been pulled over one shoulder. Misjudging her very feminine form had been the mistake of several in the past. Even before she'd had her legs, right arm, and a good portion of her lower spine and several ribs replaced due to horrific injuries, she'd been a scrapper. After the surgery, her synthetic muscles and nano-crystalized-steel-reinforced skeleton had turned her into nothing short of a force of nature.

"Why the in-person confab?" Tabby asked, giving me a quick peck on the lips.

"We're not sure what we're going to run into when we get to Tamu," Nick said. "It sounds pretty grim though. I'm sure Moyo wants to have a plan."

Tabby nodded at the window in the airlock door. "Catwalk is here."

We were met on the other side by none other than Moyo, captain of *Hunting Fog.*

I tapped just below my solar plexus with my open hand. It was a Felio greeting that, best as we could tell, was derived from a gesture that meant we were satisfied and not looking to start a fight because we were hungry. Moyo returned the gesture.

Felio, including those in command, wore what most humans believed to be overly skimpy clothing. The Felio body was entirely covered in fur, but their uniforms resembled bikinis with high boots and long gloves. According to Semper, the only Felio aboard *Hornblower*, most vac-suits ended up being too warm unless they were cut out as described. Tabby had a different take on it, believing the female-dominated culture proudly flaunt their lithe bodies, knowing most males of the same species could never take advantage of them. I'd caused myself trouble more than once by paying too much attention to 'innocent' uniform failures.

"Does House of the Bold stand firm with Abasi?" Moyo asked, after closing the door to a conference room.

I was startled by her question. Truthfully, I'd been checking out the array of food, which was definitely all non-entrails related.

"Of course we do," I replied. "Bold Second, Marny James-Bertrand and Nicholas James-Bertrand committed the company previously known as Loose Nuts to this agreement. Not only was it in their power to do so, but I believe it was to the mutual benefit of Abasi and Loose Nuts."

"So far the benefit has been primarily one-sided," Moyo shot back. She was not perturbed as much as she was direct. "As we have discussed, Abasi invited House of the Bold to join our great nation.

As part of this agreement, House of the Bold agreed to utilize their resources in the defense of Abasi. It is this commitment that I wish to confirm."

"I believe there was also a discussion of the Mhina system," I answered. "Are you asking if we're going to run when we see a thousand Kroerak ships on the other side of the wormhole?"

"Only one moon in the entire Mhina system is productive. You negotiated for less land than would have been granted to your house on the planet Zuri where taxes would have been immediately available to House Bold." Moyo gave me a hard look. "But that is not the important part of my query."

"We are first and foremost human," I said, watching Moyo stiffen as I said it. "Unlike Felio, there are many human tribes. Our original tribes were that of Mars and Earth. While we would do whatever is necessary to aid the tribes of our youth, we are now Abasi. In two spans, when we transition from Preish to Tamu, we will defend our new home planet of Abasi Prime as if we had been born upon it. We will defend our sisters as if we had grown from our youth with them. Let there be no mistake in our resolve. We will drive Kroerak, Pogona, Strix, Golenti and even those little gnats that get in your fur from our home. We will drive them into the star. We will drive them into the dust of the dead moon. We will drive them into the deep dark where none can find their bodies."

As I spoke, Moyo's lips curled back, showing her elongated fangs. "You speak as a Felio. We are indeed kindred. Mshindi Prime's faith in House Bold will be vindicated even as we die gloriously in defense of our home."

"Bilge scum," I said, spitting on the floor. "There is no glory in dying. There is only glory in living. We've translated the transmission. As Abasi, we also have access to the same encryption as you. The Kroerak are slow in their strategy. They see every problem as a nail, so they only know how to use a hammer. I'm telling you, we just need to make sure those bugs don't see any boards. Are you following me?"

The confused look on her face was evident. "I will follow House Bold to combat. I do not understand nails and boards."

"What he's saying is that Kroerak only know how to fight one way. They line up for a lance wave attack and fire. They don't even mind if they hit each other," Nick said. "We believe it is because many ships are controlled by a single central figure. An important difference between Kroerak and human command structures is that when we separate our attacks, we're able to perform independently."

"You would have us attack this central figure?" she asked, still off-balance in the conversation.

"If we find where the commands are coming from," I said. "But my point is different. You see a thousand ships; I see one leader struggling to send orders to a thousand ships. We need to be unpredictable and use their swarm configuration against them. Sure, if we find that central ship, we take it out, but I don't think that's necessary."

"Unpredictable. Like a leaf on the wind?" Moyo asked.

I smiled. It wasn't the right moment to geek out on ancient science fiction. A kick to my shin affirmed that Tabby felt my moment and wanted me to let it pass.

"Exactly right, Moyo," I said. "What were you able to retrieve from House Mshindi's ship? Were any left alive?"

"Like before," she answered. "All aboard were killed simply by a single shot to the base of the neck. The engines were disabled and atmosphere removed. I have witnessed this behavior while on patrol. The pirates will return to retrieve the ship as salvage."

"*Hunting Fog,* this is *Hornblower*. We will transition in twenty seconds," Ada transmitted.

My heart was beating fast in anticipation. If Kroerak surrounded the wormhole exit in Tamu, we were in for a bumpy ride. Everyone was in the right place, however. We had a seasoned fire-control crew, an excellent pilot, and a weapon that was literally the finger-of-death to whatever ship it reached out and touched.

While sailing, we'd drilled different simulations to confound the attacking Kroerak, using their numbers as much to our advantage as possible. The most effective tactic ended up looking like a complex dance: we drilled a line of ships, used their husks as cover and patiently edged around to chew away at every ship we got near, one after another, until they were gone. After repeated practice, our average rate of fire was one shot every three seconds. With two ships and a perfect line-up, it would require more time than I liked to take out the combined Kroerak fleets sitting in the Tamu system.

"I have five ships on sensors," Nick said.

For whatever reason, I'd always been slow to recover from wormhole transitions. I fought against the fog and peered intently at the holo projection.

"Target acquired," Sendrei barked.

"Hold for identification," I ordered, my heart hammering against my chest.

"Make that twelve." Nick upgraded the number of ships around us as Ada laid into *Hornblower's* massive engines and we started to dig out of the hole caused by coming to a relative stop when entering the wormhole.

"That's too many," Tabby warned.

"Steady!" I ordered.

An Abasi transponder signal fired and for a nano-second, I thought it was *Hunting Fog* as she transitioned at almost that exact moment. The audio cue arrived just before my holo projection updated, showing that we were surrounded by a small fleet of Abasi ships.

"Friendlies!" I ordered. "Cease fire. Communicate friendly status to *Hunting Fog.*"

A triple shot of 75mm cannon fire stitched through space and tore into the side of Mshindi's once proud battleship, *Thunder Awakes.*

"Cease fire! Cease Fire! Blue on Blue," Marny yelled into the comms.

"Hail *Thunder Awakes,"* I ordered, watching as the battered yet still majestic and terrifyingly massive battleship turned slowly seeking a broadside with *Hornblower*.

The Felio who appeared on my screen was a ghost of the once-mighty Mshindi Prime I'd come to know and respect. Having lost substantial weight, her eyes were sunken within their sockets and she looked at me with grim determination. "I would recommend a larger load, given the circumstances," she rasped.

"My apologies, Mshindi Prime," I said as soon as she stopped speaking. "The cannon fire was due to an over-zealous crew."

"Never have I been fired upon and been so delighted," she replied, with a familiar spark in her eyes.

Chapter 2

FISH IN A BARREL

"Thirty ships, Cap." Marny answered my unasked question. "Four battleships, eight battle cruisers, ten if you count *Hunting Fog* and *Hornblower*. The rest are frigates or support craft. They look like they've all taken quite a beating. Intel from Abasi military data-streams show eight hundred Kroerak ships in-system."

I nodded, not yet breaking eye contact with Mshindi Prime. "Adahy, is this what remains of the Confederation Fleet?" I asked, using her given name as a gesture of familiarity. The loss in her eyes told me the answer. We'd all seen the destruction wrought by the Kroerak to the once-proud Earth fleets. If anything, I was surprised the noble Felio hadn't sacrificed themselves to defend their planet.

"I am unable to raise Busara or Imara." Moyo's image appeared on the holo projection next to Mshindi.

"When the Kroerak broke the fleet, many were lost," Mshindi Prime answered. "Moyo, it is you that leads House Perasti. You are Prime. Your mother and sister defended our home with honor and did not flinch in the face of death."

Moyo's expression hardened as she received the news; her eyes narrowed and tail twitched with agitation. "Why are you cowering next to the Tamu-Preish gate? You would run as cowards? Bold Prime, we will set course immediately for Abasi Prime. Our homeland, my sisters, my family *must* be avenged! I am not a coward!"

"You *dare* call us cowards?" Kifeda Prime, the only male head of house I was familiar with, popped onto the projection, joining the conversation. Like Mshindi, his face was sunken and his once-proud mane of fur lacked fullness and luster. "We have lost more than you can know. We fought with honor while you were away. It is you that lacks honor."

The comms erupted in chaos as the final house, Gundi, joined in. Lindia, previously Second, attempted reconciliation, but the hot-blooded Kifeda Prime and distraught Moyo had found sinks for their anguish. I wasn't overly surprised by the explosion of anger. Felio were as passionate about nobility of purpose as they were about the honor of belonging to their respective houses.

Mshindi Prime had taken a seat on the bridge of *Thunder Awakes.* She was much smaller looking than I recalled previously, as if the toll of war had pulled the life essence from her. Seeing that I hadn't joined the fray, her eyes quietly pled with me. I nodded. Words would not be enough.

"Sendrei, fire a burst from our Iskstar cannon over the bow of Kifeda's battleship, *Plays in Tall Grass,* and Gundi's battle cruiser, *Sundrenched Cliff,*" I said, not bothering to mute my order on the Abasi fleet channel.

We'd been away from home for an entire Earth standard year in search of a weapon that could defeat the Kroerak. While the cost had been high, we'd not only found the weapon, but saved an entire species from the Kroerak's evil clutches.

"Aye, aye, Captain," Sendrei answered from fire-control.

A surprised Kifeda Prime turned to me just as the warning shot creased the space between our two ships. His battleship, while ravaged by combat, was more than a match for *Hornblower*, especially considering six of the ships within the fleet were of his house.

Gundi Prime, Lindia, quieted as the second shot crossed her bow. She looked at me with less challenge than Kifeda, but it was clear she was ready to turn her cruiser on me if the moment required it.

"What is the meaning of this? I will tear you to shreds!" Mzuzi, Kifeda Prime screamed at me, momentarily forgetting his argument with Moyo and Gundi Prime. His bloodshot eyes and dripping fangs made me wonder just how close he actually was to the edge.

"I understand your rage, Mzuzi," I said calmly. "My home was destroyed by Kroerak." The words were a bit of a stretch. Earth had very nearly been destroyed by Kroerak, but I'd never considered it my home. "Would you fight your Abasi brothers and sisters instead of Kroerak?"

"But," he spluttered. "It was you that fired upon me!"

"*Hornblower's* weapon did not strike *Plays in Tall Grass*," Mshindi Prime observed almost casually.

"The gunjway is *not* Abasi," Kifeda Prime demanded, winding up again.

"Ask Mshindi why they're at the gate, Liam," Nick whispered, having come up beside me to observe the interaction. A smile tugged at the corner of Mshindi Prime's lips, but didn't quite reach her eyes. She nodded almost imperceptibly at Nick.

"Mshindi Prime, Moyo has a legitimate question. Why has this fleet not defended Abasi Prime? There is no honor in fleeing from battle and I know that House Mshindi, House Gundi, and House Kifeda are all most honorable." My pronouncement took the wind from Moyo's sails and temporarily mollified Kifeda Prime.

"When the Kroerak attacked, our blockade at the Tamu-Mhina gate held for only five spans," Mshindi Prime responded. "The Kroerak fleet cared not for its own survival and plowed a path through our mine fields, racing over the corpses of their own so that they might come at us. But hope was restored when, in that sixth day, allies from the Confederation of Planets arrived and reinforced our numbers. Musi, Chelonii and Aranea warships came to our aid, swelling our ranks to almost three hundred strong.

"For a time, we held the Kroerak in Tamu. But our joy was short-lived as we learned of a second Kroerak fleet that attacked the planet Zuri. As Abasi, we knew that to split our own fleet to protect Zuri would break our stalemate with Kroerak. But we are honorable and sworn to protect the people of Zuri. It was given to House Mshindi to provide aid to Zuri and we split from the fleet, knowing that to do so would weaken us both, but also knowing we had no other option.

"When only a single span into our journey, we received the worst possible news," Mshindi Prime continued, her eyes glittering with moisture. "The second Kroerak fleet separated from Zuri and raced to meet us. At the same time the first Kroerak fleet broke through the lines of our defenders and streamed toward the Tamu-Santaloo wormhole transition point.

"Knowing we could not stand as divided against the Kroerak, House Mshindi turned back to the main fleet. By the time we rejoined, our numbers had been cut by over twenty-five percent," she said. "It was in this battle that Perasti Prime and Gundi Prime were both lost. Their loss, while honorable, broke the backbone of our defenses."

"House Mshindi caught up with what remained of our fleet and pinched the Kroerak between our planetary defensive weapons. Our strategy worked, as the mighty Kroerak fleet sustained its greatest losses. Our victory, however, was short, as the second Kroerak fleet arrived at Abasi Prime," Mshindi Prime said, growing quiet as I imagined she was recalling the horrific battle. "Our ships were strong, but our weapons were no match for the Kroerak armor. For over a ten-day we fought, slowing, giving ground, as we were crushed beneath the pincers of the bug warriors."

"And then you gave up?" Moyo asked, her voice holding accusation but with substantially less anger. "How could you run from battle? It is our duty to die if required."

"There is no one in our fleet today that does not wish she had died over our home planet," Mshindi Prime said. "Would that I could exchange my life for my daughter, Zakia's. Many questions haunt me, Moyo, beloved daughter of my friend, Busara. Had we not separated from the fleet to defend Zuri, could we have broken the Kroerak? Would it not be better for us to have died over Abasi Prime? The House of Koman made a decision to send the remaining fleet away from Abasi Prime with a single objective, to await House of the Bold and the Iskstar weapon. I put it to you, Moyo. Will this weapon defeat Kroerak? Was our gamble worth the agony of watching our people die while we fled with tails curled between our legs?"

"Blasters tuned with an Iskstar crystal pierce Kroerak armor as easily as a newborn kit's sharp claws pierce unfurred skin," Moyo answered.

"This must be a lie," Kifeda Prime growled. "I saw the weapon fired. Engineer first says it is nothing more than a blaster."

"It *is* no lie," I said. "We don't know why Iskstar defeats Kroerak armor so easily, but House Perasti and House of the Bold stood against thirty Kroerak and destroyed them all with this weapon. I guess my question is, do we want to stand around peeing on each other's legs, squawking like Strix, and talking about lost honor? Or maybe we could hand out some upgrades and go kick Kroerak ass! What's it going to be, Mzuzi? Whiny bitch or bad-ass bug squisher?"

My last comment earned me a raised eyebrow from Marny. I was contemporizing and wasn't sure if the AI translator would communicate the edge I was looking for. Mzuzi showed his disrespect for humanity each time we met. I'd always fobbed the attitude off as just Mzuzi being pissy about being the only male Prime in a world run by females.

"You have more than one of these weapons?" Mshindi Prime asked. I smiled at her ability to ignore insults. I suspected I'd have to raise my game if I was going to compete with the likes of House Kifeda and Gundi, who seemed to enjoy throwing down barbed challenges as if that were an Olympic sport.

"*Hunting Fog* is equipped with one as well," I said. "The Piscivoru nation has agreed to lend Abasi Iskstar crystals for the purpose of destroying Kroerak."

When we left the Piscivoru back on their home planet of Picis, they had, for the first time in over five hundred standard years, been able to freely venture out onto the planet's surface. Grateful, their elders had offered as many Iskstar crystals as we wanted at no cost. While I appreciated their generous offer, I knew the Piscivoru would need help restarting their civilization. Working together would benefit both Abasi and Piscivoru nations.

"What will that cost?" Mzuzi asked sulkily.

"I've agreed to negotiate with House of Koman in good faith after the Kroerak have been removed from Abasi systems," I said. "I assure you, the Piscivoru offer very reasonable terms."

"You are playing both sides," Mzuzi said. "The human cannot be trusted."

"*Hornblower,* squelch all conversation from Mzuzi until further notice," I said.

"Kifeda Prime, House of the Bold is Abasi. Bold Prime is a member of House of Koman and you owe him the respect given any Prime," Mshindi said.

House of Koman was the peak of the pyramid of the Abasi government. Only the top leaders from the most powerful Abasi houses were allowed a voice within its chambers. The fact that I'd been given a seat within House of Koman was an indication of how dire the Abasi had found their situation. I considered these things as Mshindi Prime apparently listened to Mzuzi's rant, something I no longer needed to do.

"Liam. My friend. It is not necessary to mute Mzuzi. It is the way of male Felio to argue. It is also the reason there are few Felio male heads of house."

"Let's talk about weapon upgrades," I said. "Tabbs, would you transmit specifications so the Abasi can tune their energy weapons? We're willing to provide one crystal to each ship that will participate in combat."

Mshindi looked to her side, as if listening to a question from someone not in view of the video. "How are these utilized?"

"It is a simple replacement of your blaster weapon's tuning crystal. We recommend your longest distance weapon. Size does not seem to be relevant," I said. "Mshindi, I couldn't help but notice your bridge crew appears to be in some distress. While we fit the ships for battle, could we share supplies?"

"Our fleet suffers no more than those whom we abandoned," Mshindi said. "We will take no respite until all Abasi are free."

"Fair enough," I answered. "We'll open *Hornblower's* flight deck. It's only large enough to accommodate a few shuttles at a time, but I'd like to get these crystals handed out. Any ships without a working shuttle can contact me directly and we'll send *Hornblower's* to them."

"It is agreed. Mshindi desists."

"Semper, Tabbs, we're about to have company on the flight deck," I called over comms. "Marny, can you organize the incoming? Semper, I may need you to deliver a few of the crystals."

"Aye, aye, Prime," Semper answered.

"It looks like the Kroerak know we're here," Marny said.

I turned my attention to the holo-projector. Eight hundred twelve was the ship count my AI showed for the Kroerak fleet circling Abasi Prime. I was reminded of the black carrion birds on Zuri that amassed in the same way every time we killed a Kroerak hatchling and left it to rot. Of more significance was the group of one hundred twenty ships that had split off from the main fleet, sailing directly at us.

The details from Abasi Prime were startlingly clear. The Abasi had a mechanism that allowed for long range communication to take place quickly over solar distances. What would ordinarily take fifteen minutes from Abasi Prime was arriving in about a minute. Getting plugged into the network of the Abasi fleet had given us fantastic access.

"*Now* the Kroerak are interested in chasing down the Abasi who broke away? I don't understand why the Kroerak allowed some ships to break off at all," I said. "If they had any idea what we were coming to equip the Abasi with, they'd have skipped Abasi Prime and chased these guys until they put 'em down."

"The desire to plunder a planet is instinctual to Kroerak," Jonathan said. "They will have traveled vast distances to arrive at Abasi Prime. We know they do not travel with large food stores. It is likely they required fuel before chasing down a small fleet that posed little strategic threat."

"I guess we have our answer as to whether Kroerak can communicate over galactic distances," I said.

"What answer is this?" Jonathan asked.

"I'd say they can't. Otherwise, the Kroerak we fought over Picis would have let the fleets entering Tamu know we were coming," I said.

"We see the logic of your argument," Jonathan agreed. "And if the Kroerak were human and had human instincts, we would agree."

"I don't follow. *Every* species wants to survive," I said. "Kroerak would have been better off destroying this small Abasi fleet and not given us a chance to deploy the Iskstar crystals. Can you imagine what the Abasi are going to do to the Kroerak fleet with thirty armed ships? They'll never get close to us with this many battleships and cruisers."

"We believe you will show no mercy, or I believe you would say 'give no quarter,'" Jonathan answered. "The Kroerak do not seek to defeat you. They intend to discover your strength. Imagine the value of this intelligence."

"They should have finished off the Abasi fleet," I repeated. "Leaving this small group of Abasi behind makes no sense."

"Without the Abasi," Jonathan said. "*Hornblower* might have arrived in the Tamu system to a group of Kroerak ships. If this had happened, what would your orders have been?"

"We'd have fired everything we had at them while transitioning back through the wormhole," I said.

"We believe your chance of survival would have been seventy-five percent in that scenario. The Kroerak would have made a similar calculation. Further, the Kroerak are slow to transition. We would have counseled you to stay on the other side of the wormhole and destroy each ship as it transitioned. You would have been successful at destroying as many ships as they would have sent through," he continued. "Only luck would have provided a Kroerak win at this wormhole. Most sentients do not rely on luck. And yes, we are excluding present company."

I smiled. Jonathan was still mystified at how human instinct –

what we often referred to as luck – seemed to be something we successfully relied on. "This fleet they're sending at us, they're sacrificial lambs? The Kroerak want to see how fast our fleet pounds theirs into space dust?"

"Knowing that you have shared Iskstar might change Kroerak strategy in dealing with House of the Bold," Jonathan said. "You refused communication with the Kroerak noble when she wanted to negotiate. Imagine if a species was selling special ordnance that easily killed humans. What would you do?"

"Hate to break it to you," I said. "That pretty well describes just about every weapon out there. Without our fancy ships, we're pretty soft targets."

"The Kroerak have never lived in a universe where this was true," he answered. "For millennia, they have murdered untold hundreds of worlds, simply because they were unstoppable."

"Sure. Tell me something I don't know," I said.

"I think what Jonathan is saying," Nick stepped in, "is that if we're handing out Kroerak death rays, their problem might be bigger than they originally thought."

IT TOOK ONLY an hour for the transfer of Iskstar crystals and the creation of a handful of brackets. Mostly, the crystals we'd handed out fit perfectly. Not surprisingly, Kifeda Prime insisted on installing all crystals slated for House Kifeda onto his battleship *Plays in Tall Grass.* I felt annoyed at his idiocy, but in the end, decided to leave it alone. Abasi houses were all about self-governance.

From their main fleet of eight hundred, the Kroerak had split off a force of two hundred ships to intercept us, including a single, massive battleship. I scanned the rest of the group, looking for one of the unusually-shaped Kroerak ships we'd come against while in the Picis system. We'd seen four of those ships that day and one of them had been carrying the high-ranking Kroerak noble who contacted me during the battle. In the end, we'd been able to destroy one of the odd-looking ships and that, as much as anything, ended the battle. We'd target those ships first, but none were in the attack group.

Even though we ran at each other as knights tilting down the line, we'd get no quick resolution. Abasi Prime was still three days of hard-burn from the Tamu-Santaloo gate. The near thirty hours it would take for us to meet in the middle was mental agony and I spent the entire time sitting or dozing in my captain's chair aboard the bridge.

"All hands, prepare for combat maneuvers." Ada's announcement was a relief when it finally came.

We accepted Mshindi Prime's request to sail with the Abasi fleet and to be a part of their coordinated fleet movements. The four battleships, two of which were House Mshindi, made up the points in a diamond formation. The remaining cruisers flanked the battle-ships, taking cover behind the armored beasts, but also keeping enough separation to have a clear shot on the approaching Kroerak ships.

When we met with the enemy fleet, our instructions were to stay with our assigned battleship, utilizing its heavy armor for cover as we slugged it out. *Hornblower* had been assigned to accompany House Gundi's *Sundrenched Cliff,* which had taken quite a beating and was venting gasses as she chugged along, oblivious to her wounds.

"Anyone feel like a song?" I asked. We'd closed to within five thou-sand kilometers and had circumvolved so we were no longer deceler-ating backwards but were now facing our enemy.

"Seriously, Cap?" Marny asked.

"Have faith, Bold Second," I said. "Play *Another One Bites the Dust* from Queen's Greatest Hits album on public address!"

Steve walks warily down the street

With the brim pulled way down low

...

Another one bites the dust ...

"I have a firing solution," Sendrei called from fire-control. "And crank that music!"

"Fire at will, Gunny!"

If the fleet had been hesitant to engage, *Hornblower* more than pushed them over the tipping point as we let loose arcs of blue, Iskstar-tuned blaster bolts that ripped into the approaching Kroerak fleet. I would love to make the contest sound like a fair fight filled with tense moments, fantastic strategy and hair-raising action, but this wasn't really the case at all. I was reminded of a phrase I'd heard as a child and never fully understood: 'as easy as shooting fish in a barrel.' For me – especially as a kid on a mining colony – fish were an abstract concept. I'd seen vids of fish swimming in vast oceans, but oceans were just as unreachable for me as were the fish. The idea that someone would shoot fish in a barrel didn't make much sense. Although, why shooting them would be easier in a barrel than it would be in an ocean did pass a certain sniff test.

Suddenly, while facing off with the Kroerak halfway between the Tamu-Preish wormhole entrance and Abasi Prime, a picture came to my mind of a chubby, freckle-faced kid looking into a barrel full of fish. I had no doubt that kid, plinking away at those poor fish, had as much luck as we did with the Kroerak who threw themselves at us, presenting fat broadsided targets. I almost felt bad for the Kroerak who'd never had to worry about defensive maneuvers because they thought their armor impenetrable. Equally, the idea of retreat seemed to be just as foreign a concept. Within an hour of meeting the two-hundred strong fleet, our rag-tag Abasi fleet stood alone amidst the debris of ruined Kroerak ships.

"We make for Abasi Prime!" Mshindi uncharacteristically yowled into the comms. "To victory!"

As we turned for Abasi Prime, the remaining Kroerak fleet broke from orbit, their destination clearly set to the Tamu-Mhina wormhole. I ran a quick calculation and discovered, even at our hardest burn rate, we would not be able to intercept them.

"Mshindi, we should send a frigate to chase the Kroerak fleet," I said. "We need to track them."

"You earn your namesake, Bold Prime, for that is a truly bold objective," Mshindi Prima answered. "But due to your actions, the threat of Kroerak has once and forever been eliminated. No, our people need us as they never have before. We can spare no ships."

"We need to strike while they're vulnerable," I argued, frustrated at her apparent inability to see the bigger picture.

Mshindi Prime held my gaze for a minute over the holo projection. "It was the Kroerak that brought you to our galaxy. For this, all Felio will be eternally grateful. You embody the true spirit of a hunter. I pledge to you this: together we will hunt this parasite. But first, we will lick our wounds and bring comfort to those who have suffered for our inadequacies."

Chapter 3

ON TILT

Abasi Prime, a planet very much like Earth in size and composition, is orbited by a single, water-covered moon called Rhema, which is half again larger than Earth's own moon. Before the Kroerak invasion of the prosperous and peaceful Abasi nation, the space between the planet and its moon had been thick with industrial structures and commercial traffic. As we sailed past Rhema, I searched for Chitundu, the massive space station where we'd docked on our first visit. How could that trip seem like yesterday and so long ago all at the same time?

The space where the Chitundu station should have been was filled with a heavy cloud of debris. Thirty hours after the departure of the Kroerak, small vessels flitted about, traveling between the large, disconnected chunks of the once-beautiful station. I experienced the same sense of loss that I'd felt when approaching Earth during the Kroerak invasion. If anything, the loss of Chitundu was more personal, as I had memories of being here.

"Cap, we're receiving multiple distress signals," Marny announced.

"Start prioritizing. We'll need to coordinate with the rest of the fleet," I said.

"Copy that, Cap," she answered. "Ada, change course, bearing twenty degrees starboard, five degrees declination."

My AI, upon hearing my interest in the distress signals, sent a prompt to my HUD and requested permission to display the beacons. Initially, I was overwhelmed by the mass of souls needing help. Thousands of blinking signals appeared in the debris field that surrounded the planet. A ship the size of *Hornblower* was poorly suited to small rescue missions. Our labored movements and mass made us the proverbial bull in a china shop. The need, however, was great and there were few ships in any position to render aid.

"Liam, Mshindi Prime is on comms," Nick announced.

I chinned the virtual acknowledgement indicator on my HUD and a slightly less disheveled Mshindi Prime appeared. "Go ahead, Adahy," I said, not caring about formality.

"Bold, I request that *Hornblower* make way to Abasi Naval repair yard and restore security," Mshindi said.

A section of space in high orbit over Abasi Prime was instantly highlighted on my holo projection. As the ship's sensors focused on the facility and details filled in, it appeared the Naval repair yard had withstood the incursion reasonably well – that is, if having a quarter of the kilometer-wide structure sheared off could be categorized as minimal damage.

"Roger that, Mshindi," I answered. "We're happy to oblige. Ada, please adjust course."

"Liam, we're almost in position for rescue," Ada answered, joining the comm. "We need ten more minutes. There are ten souls trapped and they won't make it much longer without our help."

"Bold, it is imperative that you make all possible haste to Abasi repair yard," Mshindi answered, not addressing Ada directly. "We must secure supplies that will be most difficult to manufacture in the coming long-spans of recovery."

"Understood. Bold out," I said, closing the comms.

"Liam, we can't leave those people," Ada said. "They'll die without our help."

"Tabbs, I need you on the flight deck immediately, and grab a med-bag on the way," I said. "Semper, grab a cut-weld rig and O2 boosters and meet Tabby on the flight deck."

"What's up, Liam?" Tabby asked, having already disappeared from the bridge.

"Wait one," I answered. "Ada, give me your best burn plan to the orbital repair yard."

"Aye, aye, Captain," Ada answered. Slowly, *Hornblower* turned while its massive engines spooled up. Ada's navigation plan would catch the repair station in just under ninety minutes.

"Liam?" Tabby called, still not sure what was going on.

"I need you and Semper to finish our rescue mission and then meet us over at the Abasi Naval yard. We have a priority engagement there," I said.

"Seriously, it couldn't wait ten minutes?" she asked, echoing Ada's concerns.

"Apparently not," I answered, annoyed that I had to explain myself. "Load heavy enough so you can subdue if you need. No telling what shape your group will be in."

"Copy that," she answered. "Semper's here and we're loading. Get Ada to lay off the go-go juice for a minute and we'll take off."

"Cutting engines in five... four...." Ada initiated a count down.

"We're clear," Tabby announced as *Hornblower's* one and only shuttle streaked away at an oblique angle.

"Sensors are picking up hostilities at the Naval yard," Marny announced.

With many of the ship's sensors focused on our destination, previously unseen details were filling in. Traces of small blaster fire registered, although at our current distance it was impossible to tell the source of the fire.

"Seriously? Their planet was just invaded by alien bugs and they're already looting?" I said, disgusted.

Marny huffed. "Happened on Earth, Cap, after the Kroerak left. It happens in virtually every war zone. Whenever there is a vacuum of power, someone always fills it. The first thing they do is collect valuable resources."

"Seems pretty shortsighted," I said. "Abasi will restore order. Attacking them just slows recovery."

"There are many Felio tribes that only participate in the Abasi nation because of their inability to find sufficient power to do otherwise. These tribes are not represented within the House of Koman and yet are forced to abide by its law," Jonathan said. "The Kroerak have potentially changed this balance of power."

"There are Felio who aren't Abasi?" I asked.

"Not publicly," Nick said. "House of Koman declared that all Felio are under the rule of the Abasi nation."

"Seems like that's a recipe for trouble," Ada added.

"Historically, Felio have been a violent people," Jonathan said. "The Abasi nation, under the rule of House of Koman, has brought peace and prosperity for centuries."

"And we have a seat at that table?" I asked. "That's kind of heady stuff. I'm not sure I'm ready to take that kind of responsibility."

"Abasi were desperate when they made this bargain with Loose Nuts," Jonathan said. "They correctly saw the end of their civilization if the Kroerak were not stopped. You must understand, their gambit paid off, as their world was saved."

"Cap, you could probably negotiate for an honorary position within Koman," Marny said.

"Let's hold onto that idea," Nick added. "We just became the proud owners of an entire solar system. We may need the political juice that a seat within House of Koman adds."

"We can't own a solar system," I said.

"We can and we do. That was the agreement. Per Confederation of Planets, Abasi own Mhina system. That ownership was granted to House of the Bold upon Marny accepting a seat at Koman. We'll want to tread lightly and carefully consider the implications of modifying that agreement," he answered.

"We can put that aside for now," I agreed, accepting a small plate of food from Steward Bear, who'd brought a meal up from the officer's mess. With all the excitement, we'd been missing our normal meals in the wardroom, preferring instead to stay on the bridge.

"Cap, we're showing three sloop-class vessels that appear to be attacking the repair station," Marny said. As she spoke, three battered ships appeared next to the station. The ships moved in a well-choreographed dance around a hole in the platform's defenses caused by the missing section.

"Sendrei, three bogies attacking the station. Let's get 'em targeted," I said.

"Aye, aye, Captain. Laying in a firing plan for the seventy-fives," he answered.

"Cap, those are Abasi-flagged ships showing Perasti colors," Marny said.

"Nick, given our lofty position, shouldn't we have codes that would give us control of that station?" I asked.

"Negative, Liam," he answered. " Mshindi probably has them. I'll send a request."

We were still too far out to do anything about the attacking sloops, but I'd started to wonder if the situation was as it had initially presented itself. "Marny, raise those sloops and see whose side they're on."

"*Ripened Forma*, this is *Hornblower*. Come in," Marny called, repeating her message several times before receiving a response.

"*Hornblower,* this is *Ripened Forma*. Please state intent or be fired upon." The Felio voice was tight with excitement.

"House of the Bold is taking command of Abasi Naval repair yard," Marny answered. "You will desist all hostilities."

"Be advised. Taji has infiltrated the Abasi platform and we are attempting to re-take control," the still-disembodied voice answered.

"Who is Taji?" I asked, muting comms.

"A powerful Felio faction that unsuccessfully attempted separation from Abasi on several occasions," Jonathan answered.

"*Ripened Forma,* your ships and the Abasi platform are now under command of House Bold." I had no idea if I could make such a power grab, but in the heat of the moment, I wasn't about to start asking for permission. "You will begin transmitting video."

I wasn't sure if it was the fact that *Hornblower* was only a few thousand kilometers out and we were a mostly undamaged battle cruiser, or if they just decided it was a good idea, but all of a sudden, the three sloops started transmitting. I had no idea what I expected to see, but it wasn't images of three bridges, all crowded with what appeared to be Felio family groups, including juveniles and those of advanced age. The same look we'd seen on Mshindi Prime's face when *Hornblower* had sailed into the system was on every face. The obviously non-military crews looked like they'd been through tremendous trial.

"Who ... what's happened to you?" I asked, my shock at their appearance evident in my voice.

"We are the remaining engineers of Abasi Naval yard." While I recognized the speaker's voice, it took me a minute to locate the female wearing soiled, baggy clothing. "When attacked by Kroerak, we hid aboard these damaged ships. We had planned to return and restore the yard when the Taji ship arrived. They have seized controls."

"Nick. Codes?" I asked.

"I have them, but we're still locked out," Nick said.

"There were Taji working on the station," the engineer added. "They must have installed software that subverted Abasi control."

"What's your status?" I asked.

"We are bruised and battered," she answered. "But we find ourselves alive. We wish to help retake our station."

"Copy that," I answered. "We're going to need you to back off your current position and fall in behind *Hornblower*. Those sloops aren't packing enough armor and you're not wearing vac-suits."

"We will comply," she answered.

"Ada, figure out how to approach the shipyard while causing the least damage to *Hornblower*," I said. "Sendrei, you may need to fire on the station to knock out a few of their weapons. Just remember, if we break it, we're going to have to fix it."

"Aye, aye, Captain." Ada's response sounded more like cap-E-tan and I smiled to myself. We lived for these moments of stress, as much as we wouldn't like to admit it.

"Marny, how many Marines can we field for a boarding party?" I asked.

"Fourteen," she answered.

"Ada, you have the seat," I said. "Marny, you're with me."

"Cap? You shouldn't be leading a boarding party," Marny said. "It's an unnecessary risk. I've got this."

"Couldn't agree more," I acknowledged as she exited the bridge just behind me.

Marny paused at the door to the elevator, confused. "Where are you going then?"

"Just because I'm not leading, doesn't mean I'm not going," I said. "I'll bring a Popeye and Jonathan's remote-presence bot, but I promise to leave the heavy lifting to the pros."

"I'm not sure you're catching on to this whole top of the food chain thing," Marny said, shaking her head as the elevator dropped to Deck Three where the Flight Deck was located. Together we jogged down the passageway. Along the way we were joined by the rugged looking men and women who ordinarily provided ship-wide security or manned fire-control.

"Liam," Jonathan cut in on private comm link. "There is a repair bay which has good access to a conduit that routes secure communication on the platform. We're uploading this objective to you now."

"Thanks, Jonathan," I said. "How much time will you need?"

"If you cut into the conduit and provide a direct link, the Phentera group will perform their own, less visible boarding action," he answered. "Partial control should be achievable within four hundred nano-seconds with full control taking substantially longer, perhaps as long as sixteen hundred milliseconds. Abasi electronic security is quite advanced."

I'd been curious about the Phentera group, comprised of sixty-two sentients who seemed to enjoy a more active role in security, hacking and weapon systems. Within the fourteen hundred thirty-eight sentients that made up Jonathan, we'd never been able to identify individual identities before. The Phentera group, to my thinking, was quite a schism for the exceedingly passive sentient collective, and possibly amounted to wolves in their midst.

"Are you sure we can't do this without Phentera going local?" I asked. "We're not sure what we'll run into. I'd hate to put them at risk."

"We accept the risk presented." An eerily-similar voice to Jonathan's spoke, slightly higher pitched and with a decidedly more mechanical sound.

"Phentera?" I asked.

"That is correct," Phentera answered. "We have transferred to our new vessel and await instruction."

I pinched at the instructions Jonathan had sent us and flicked them to Marny. "This conduit is our objective. Phentera group will accompany us and we'll get them physical access. Once in, they'll transfer control back to Abasi. For now, House of the Bold will take lead on the station and we'll transfer control back once the dust settles."

"Copy that, Cap," Marny answered. "Ada, new instructions. I need to get dangerously close to this location. Sendrei, there are weapons on that side of the station. We'll need to take them out even if they aren't directly firing on us. I don't want some enterprising Taji idiot to figure out where the guns are and start firing at us.

"We'll breach using the 75mm cannons on the position I've marked on tactical. Alpha team, you're first through the door. Bravo and Charlie will be hot on your tail, so don't dawdle. We've started broadcasting an announcement on all channels so any friendlies left behind will know to clear the area. We should have a minimum of twenty seconds before anyone shows their heads. We're to go in hard, but I want enemy casualties minimized since we have no idea how to identify good guys from the bad. I'm hoping once we have station control, we can get some help with that identification. I need all teams to check in. Ada, Sendrei, give me a thirty-second countdown.

Listening to the stream of instructions was exhausting, but I was equally amazed at how prepared the three Marine teams appeared. *Hornblower's* flight deck was small, thirty meters wide and twenty deep, only capable of holding a few shuttles or possibly a single cutter in a pinch. With the armored bay doors retracted, we were only separated from space by an electrically-charged pressure barrier.

A small pang of jealousy for the three groups of Marines stacked up next to the barrier as we pulled alongside the shipyard platform ran through me. Rumbling within the ship alerted us to cannon fire as an exchange between the platform and *Hornblower* erupted. A single, stray blaster bolt sailed through the open bay doors and I jerked in anticipation. In actuality, by the time I'd become aware of the bolt's presence, it had already done whatever damage it was going to do.

I looked around, hoping the Marines hadn't seen me jump. I knew firsthand that a stationary turret could destroy just about anything it struck that wasn't well armored. By design, the flight deck was well armored and even better, had the capacity to absorb the fire, preventing ricochets. Apparently, no one had told this to my nervous system. To compensate, I hurriedly jumped into my well-worn mechanized infantry suit, or Popeye.

On the trip back from Picis, Tabby and I spent many shifts cleaning and replacing a multitude of worn and broken parts on the suits. Having lived in our Popeyes for more than three ten-days while keeping the Kroerak at bay, we had a healthy respect for their value – not to mention how disgusting they could get inside while still working. The fresh smell that greeted me was comforting. Even in the Popeye, I wouldn't be able to take a direct hit from one of the repair yard's cannons, but the tempo of the fight had changed. The rumblings within *Hornblower* had increased and I caught a glimpse of what I was certain were our 250mm cannons.

"Alpha team, go!" Marny ordered, slapping the alpha team leader on the back. I watched in both horror and exhilaration as the team rushed forward and leaned into their arc-jets, sailing through the blaster and cannon fire between *Hornblower* and the platform.

An armored sphere about the size of a pod-ball floated up next to me. My HUD identified the object as Phentera, something I didn't need help figuring out, even though they'd manufactured a different enclosure. With my oversized, mechanical hand, I grabbed the ball and tucked it protectively under my arm.

"Bravo, go! Charlie, go! Cap, bring the package!" Marny continued ordering as she jumped off, leading Bravo team only seconds behind Alpha.

I raced forward, pushing hard against the deck. The Popeye was heavy and its arc-jets had less power-to-weight than the Marines. I knew I had to compensate or I'd be slowly floating through no man's land. I got a good kick off the edge of the deck and watched as my delta-v arcs were drawn on my HUD. The little lines showed I was catching Bravo and Charlie teams and I was moving more quickly than all but Alpha. I laid into the arc-jets and accelerated. In response, Bravo and Charlie both hit their jets even harder and started zeroing out my advantage.

The first team cleared the opening Sendrei had punched out for us and clambered down the hall. To the untrained eye, they looked clumsy. I suppose, in truth, they were as they stumbled and fought for equilibrium. Switching from zero-g to station-oriented .75g was totally a matter of feel and many of these Marines had trained only in simulations aboard *Hornblower*. They were fortunate Marny never missed an opportunity to train crew.

She'd stacked Alpha team with her best. They flooded the hallway, taking advanced positions in their armored vac-suits, with heavy blaster rifles forward. Just about the time Bravo and Charlie hit the hallway, stumbling to gain their footing, a group of Felio in armored vac-suits ducked into the hallway and tossed fist-sized grenades.

Without prompting, a single Marine from Alpha stood and expertly fired an unusual looking weapon. Each round she fired struck a grenade, still in mid-air. With every shot, she manually ejected a large, spent shell by pulling back a slide and pushing it forward. It was a surprised group of Felio that raced into the hallway behind their grenades. Instead of disarray, they were met with a wall of blaster fire that took out three of their team before they were turned away.

I landed in the oversized hallway, wanting nothing more than to race down the deck with Phentera still under my arm and jump into the fire fight as soon as I planted my ball into the goal. The separation between my favorite game and a call to battle had become whisker thin.

"Cap, we've got this. Focus on the mission," Marny said, her voice way more reasonable than I felt necessary for the situation. "Alpha, advance. Bravo, Charlie, on me."

I blew out a hot breath. I tended to get wrapped up in things and Marny's calming voice helped me back the beast off that had been free-ranging on Kroerak far too long. I fell in behind Charlie Team as we ran down the hallway, taking a turn at the end. Standing almost two meters taller than the crouching Marines, I drew fire from a thick group of defenders at the end of the hall.

"Our armor is sufficient, Liam Hoffen," Phentera stated plainly, as if anticipating my next move perfectly.

"Well, shite. Let's do this then. Make way!" I ordered and lifted my right arm with its thick-barreled, albeit relatively short, attached weapon. Blue fire erupted from my weapon as I leapt over Charlie, then Bravo and finally Alpha teams in three quick movements. With Phentera tucked under my arm, I sprayed the forward rank of Taji resistance fighters as their fire bounced off my Popeye's armor.

My HUD blinked, tracing the outline of a heavy, shoulder-mounted weapon I suspected would do considerably more than chip my suit's paint. At almost the same moment, Phentera highlighted a thin section of bulkhead to my right, on a diagonal from the rocket being readied. Without hesitation, I lunged into the bulkhead, bringing my arm up protectively as I smashed through the steel partition. The contrail of the rocket-propelled munition streaked through the open space I'd created and exploded only a few meters past where I'd sheltered, shaking me, but doing no real damage.

"Nice call, Big P," I said, casually grabbing the multipurpose tool from my leg and swinging it through another partition so I could step back into the hallway.

My re-appearance must have surprised the Taji soldiers and I took full advantage of it, throwing my tool into their midst. Three more steps and I was upon them, sweeping my arm across the scrambling group as they tried to flee. Whether dead, knocked unconscious, or no longer willing to fight someone in a Popeye, I soon found myself standing alone.

Sensing a lull, a single Taji fighter lurched up and ran down the passageway. I marveled at her grace and hated the idea of possibly having to kill these Felio. "*Really* sorry about this," I said, as I transferred the armored ball from my left hand to my right and tossed it, hard, down the hallway. As a pod-ball player, my aim had always been dead on, but hitting a Felio on the run was a pretty good trick. To be completely honest, I hadn't planned to hit the wall next to her, but it all worked out anyway. The force of my throw was sufficient that it ricocheted perfectly, knocking her over.

Feeling guilty for using the Phentera vessel as a weapon, I ran forward and quickly retrieved it. Thankfully, I found the Taji soldier alive, but most likely in need of medical attention for broken bones.

"Cap!" Marny exclaimed, catching up with me as her team secured the enemy combatants. "What in the frak! You can't just take off like that in combat. What if they'd had another RPG loaded up?"

"You all good, Phentera?" I asked, inspecting the armored ball. I could see a scratch where hallway paint had transferred on one side and embedded hair on the other.

"Given our hardened shell, no danger was presented. Our analysis is that your maneuver was a tactical, if not slightly unorthodox, mechanism for disabling the Felio," they answered.

"Cap?" Marny pushed, banging on my face shield.

"Sorry, Marny," I said. "I just saw all those squishies firing at me and kind of saw red."

"Cap, I know it feels like you did the right thing, but you need some down-time," she said. "Our Marines had this. We need to work as a team. Do you copy?"

I sighed. I wasn't completely sure why she was so excited, but I trusted her instincts. If she felt I was on tilt, I had to at least listen to her. "I had it," I defended weakly.

"You did, Cap," Marny answered. "That's not really the point. I need to know you can be part of a team and not go solo on me. I won't be able to trust you otherwise."

I nodded, picking up my multitool and extending it into the powerful prybar configuration. We'd reached our objective, a bulkhead next to the conduit Jonathan had identified. I jammed the bar into the wall and peeled off the panel, opening it up wide enough for Phentera to float through. Six seconds later, a new platform status flooded my HUD and the constant thumping of blaster fire ceased.

"We can talk about it," I said. "Some things are hard to unlearn, though, and those instincts kept Tabbs and me alive on Picis."

"Some combat vets never recover from war like you saw on Picis, Cap," Marny said. "Some do. No rhyme or reason to it either. Combat gets in there and messes with your head. You need to be strong, Cap. We all need you. You have to be in control."

With House of the Bold in charge of the station, Marny and her Marines secured the massive structure within a few hours. We offloaded the engineers and their families, allowing them to return home. As we worked, I considered Marny's words. I could see how she might have felt my actions were over enthusiastic and reckless, but I was more than comfortable in my Popeye. I hadn't once questioned if I would be successful at taking down the Taji soldiers. Her point about predictability, though, weighed on my thoughts. It was something we were going to need to work through. The war on Picis *had* changed me, there was no doubt about it. I also knew there would be no going back.

Chapter 4

RAGE FIRES

"You sent me on a rescue mission while you went on a boarding mission?" Tabby asked, pulling up short in the hallway on our way to the wardroom. "Not cool, Hoffen."

I chuckled. Tabby was annoyed but would get over it. In all, the Taji soldiers had been relatively easy to defeat once Phentera gained control of the computer systems. Originally hosting almost nine thousand workers and their families, the Naval repair platform's population had been cut by a third after the Kroerak attack and the takeover by the Taji fighters. Hardest hit, of course, were the Perasti security force, who had been executed during the Taji incursion.

"I needed a fast pilot and someone who could operate independently," I defended. "Seriously, I was in a Popeye. My biggest problem was not getting stuck in the hallways."

"So, what? We just sail around the platform and make sure no bad guys come sniffing?" she asked. "What about your mom?"

I nodded at the hatch that would take us into the wardroom. Marny, Nick, Ada and Sendrei had already gathered inside. "That's what we need to talk about."

Tabby turned and entered the wardroom, but wasn't ready to stop her interrogation. "We haven't heard from York, either. Zuri is supposedly protected by Abasi and since we're Abasi, is that our job too?"

"I picked up a communique from York," Nick said. "They got hit pretty bad."

"How bad?" I asked. "Anything about Mom? What about Hog and Patty and Bish? Did they say anything about Petersburg?" The list of people I was concerned for on Zuri was long. With Petersburg station in geosync orbit over York, we'd become a tight-knit community, even though we were separated by space.

"None of that was in the message," Nick said. "Well, aside from it coming from Hog. They were asking for help. Kroerak took out Zuri's comm satellites so they were lucky to get the message out. Apparently, they're having trouble with roaming bands of Kroerak warriors."

"Frak," I said. "We head there now!"

"That might be difficult," Nick answered. "Same sort of thing we found at the Naval repair yard is happening on Abasi Prime. We may need to help House Mshindi resume control. The Taji resistance is taking advantage of the chaos caused by the Kroerak invasion. Instead of fighting against the bugs, they're attacking Abasi positions."

"That strategy won't work much longer. Taji don't have many resources of their own and I'll bet they were unpleasantly surprised to see the Abasi fleet return," Tabby said. "As for the remaining bugs, they no longer have support from space. It's not as if Abasi Prime doesn't have mechanized infantry. First question I have, though, is why haven't we heard of the Taji before?"

"Second question first," Nick said. "We've known about the Taji, just like we know about Beiki. They're fringe Felio who don't agree with Abasi rule. If you paid attention to the Felio newsfeeds, you'd find references to these groups. I'll let Marny cover what we know about Abasi's mechanized infantry and the response to Kroerak on Abasi Prime."

"Ever get tired of knowing everything?" Tabby asked him, obviously still annoyed.

"You're trying to pick a fight, Tabby," Nick said.

I put my hand on Tabby's arm when she started to respond. Turns out, that was the wrong thing to do. She pulled her arm back and stood up abruptly. "Frak off," she snapped, sending me a glare as she stalked out of the room.

"I'll go," Ada said, standing up and following her out.

"You should stay and hear this," I said. "She's mad at me for leaving her out of the boarding party."

"Rings of Venus, but you're dense, Hoffen," Ada answered, shaking her head as she jogged to catch up with Tabby.

"What did I miss?" I asked.

"If I were to guess, I'd say we're dredging up a lot of bad feelings," Marny said. "Honestly, I don't know how you're keeping it together, Cap. With your Mom missing, you've gotta be a mess right now. Are you getting any sleep at all?"

I sighed. She'd hit pay-dirt. I hadn't heard from Mom for more than thirty days.

"Frak," Nick said, his voice thick with emotion as he gestured in the air, frenetically directing the AI to organize the information on the HUD only he could see. He wasn't generally an overly expressive type, so his concern sent a shock-wave of adrenaline into my stomach.

"What?" I asked, waving away a plate of food brought out by steward Bear.

"I'm sorry, Liam," he said as he flicked a data-stream from his HUD to mine. "This was just sent in by a freighter that passed through the Santaloo-Tamu gate."

I'd stood when Tabby left the wardroom. Now, I sagged back into my chair. Images filled my HUD – floating pieces of Petersburg station. The Kroerak had completely destroyed the asteroid that was home to the station named after my deceased father, Big Pete.

We'd left two ships behind, *Intrepid* and *Fleet Afoot.* I frantically searched the debris for signs of either ship but couldn't find anything. That said, the destruction was so complete it would be difficult to pick out any recognizable pieces.

"When did this happen?" I asked.

"No way to tell," Nick said. "Unless Jonathan has some ideas."

"We're running a number of simulations," Jonathan answered. "Our current, best estimate is that Petersburg Station was destroyed three days after the Kroerak fleet arrived over Zuri. We will continue to refine our data."

"Ada, Tabbs, you need to come back," I called, my AI routing comms so they could hear me.

"What happened, Liam?" Tabby's voice sounded like she'd been crying, something I rarely saw from her. We knew each other well enough that she trusted me to give her space when she needed it. My calling at one of those times communicated urgency.

"We just got a data-stream of Petersburg," I said, trying to hold back my own anguish and keep it professional. I was apparently only moderately successful. A moment later, Tabby re-entered the ward-room and I held my arm out to her after flicking the data-stream across the open space.

"Never again," she said, pulling me close. "If I have to spend my entire life hunting them, I'll kill every Kroerak in existence."

"Liam, we have discovered additional information," Jonathan said. "It will not be pleasant."

"Please, tell me," I said.

My HUD showed a ten-meter strip of armor slowly tumbling through the data-stream. The armor had been caught at long range and could have been anything – that is, until Jonathan further high-lighted part of the surface as it turned over. One side of the armor had been coated in the stealth pattern we'd taken from one of our original ships, *Hotspur.* It was clearly armor we'd placed on *Intrepid.*

"Nick, what is our fuel situation?" I asked.

"Five percent," he answered.

"This station was a fuel depot," Tabby said, her mind skipping to the obvious next step.

"Still is," Nick said. "Along with ordnance. It's why Mshindi Prime wants us to guard it. Its strategic value to Abasi is impossible to underestimate. We can't take *Hornblower* out of here."

I looked at Nick as Tabby grabbed my hand, squeezing it hard in frustration, acknowledging the truth Nick spoke. *Hornblower* was one of a handful of fully operational warships around Abasi Prime. Our presence alone was a stabilizing force. Nick was right.

"Ada ..." I started.

"No. I said never again," she replied, pre-empting me.

"I don't see any other way. I need you."

"Jupiter-piss. This is wrong," Ada complained. But after searching my face, she reluctantly gave in. "Fine."

"Ada will take command of *Hornblower* and finish our mission here in Tamu," I said. "Sendrei, I need you to step up as Number Two."

"Copy that, Captain," he answered.

"Marny, I want you to commandeer two of those three sloops we saw when we arrived. Roby, figure out what we need to do to retrofit them for human operation. Nick, I want Iskstar crystals loaded into each of those sloops."

"What about little Pete?" Tabby asked. "You can't take him into a war zone."

Marny smiled tightly. "Specifically, which war-zone would you have me avoid?"

The two had always gotten along well. Tabby saw Marny as more of a teacher than friend, and the reprimand, while not sharp, caught Tabby's attention. "Right. You've thought this through already. My bad. It just felt like Liam was signing you and Peter up for danger without really thinking about it."

"I appreciate the consideration," Marny said, her voice still carrying an edge. "How about you let me or Nick call uncle first?"

"Consider me sufficiently chastised," Tabby answered.

Marny's face softened. "Look, I don't mean to come on so hard. I've just been getting a lot of advice where Peter is concerned."

Tabby nodded her head and grinned wryly but didn't say anything further. It was about as much apology as either woman could stand and I took it as my responsibility to move the conversation along.

"Good. We'll put Tabby in command of the first sloop with Roby,

Semper, and Jonathan. I'll take command of the second with Marny and Nick. We'll need to get the Popeyes, supplies ..."

Marny held up her hand interrupting me.

"I've got this, Cap," she said. "The sloops are already being refueled and we're taking on O2 and rations. Sorry to say, there hasn't been any fresh food available for at least a ten-day. Semper, I need you to get those Popeyes loaded on the right vessels. Roby, Semper, since you're not wearing grav-suits, make sure you get armored vac-suits checked out. We could run into the shite when we get there. I want to be ready to roll in ninety minutes."

As the group filtered out, Ada stopped and stared me down. "Don't think those glowy blue eyes are getting you off the hook, Hoffen. I said I wasn't getting left behind again and the first thing you do is leave me behind."

"It's important, Ada," I said.

"It always is. You better not make it a habit or we're going to have an adjustment," she said. Her glare was steely. This was no longer the same, timid girl we'd rescued. The memory seemed only months old but, in actuality, was closer to four standard years.

"Message received, Ada," I said, turning to look straight into her eyes. "You're crew, Ada. The only reason I need to leave you behind is because there are only three other people in the entire universe that I trust as much as you. If we're going to put an end to the Kroerak, we need *Hornblower*. I know you'll keep her safe."

"And that's the only reason you're getting by with this," she said. "I'm not blind. I see the need. I just don't like being the B Team."

"If there's anything you're not," I chuckled nervously. "It's B Team material."

"SHE'S SPRITELY," I said. The difference between *Hornblower* and the sloop *Shimmering Leaves* was considerable. Both *Shimmering Leaves* and *Ice Touched Field* had been upgraded with human-inspired gravity and inertial systems. I think, at heart, I'd always been a small ship guy.

"Has claws, too," Nick said. "These are long-range patrol sloops. Abasi apparently don't like being outgunned."

I'd spent the better part of twenty minutes rearranging the virtual displays on the simple vid-screen that sat forward of the single pilot's chair. A blinking light was accompanied by a chime, alerting me of an incoming priority comm.

"*Shimmering Leaves,* Bold Prime, go ahead," I said, not bothering to see who it was.

"Bold Prime, it is unexpected that you leave Abasi Prime," Mshindi Prime's face appeared on the vid-screen. "We struggle to regain control of our populous even as residual Kroerak are hunted."

"Copy that," I answered. My position was to be on par with Mshindi and it was time to figure out just where I stood. "We received disturbing images from Zuri and have set sail."

For a moment, she simply stared at the screen. "Mzuzi will use this to gain advantage upon House of the Bold," she said simply.

"My family is on Zuri," I said. "*Hornblower* remains behind with Bold Tertiary. Ada Chen will make good decisions. You should trust her as you do me."

"Trust not the Pogona," she said. "Now that Abasi are weakened, they will come for Zuri. I ask that you visit my home and ask whomever remains to prepare to return to Abasi Prime."

"Your family will be as my own, Adahy," I said, bringing my clenched fist to just below my solar plexus.

"Keep the breeze in your whiskers and the sun on your shoulders so your quarry smells not your approach and is blinded," she answered, closing comms.

"Easy to forget that her family is on Zuri," Nick said.

"Her duty is to Abasi first," Marny said. "That's a hard choice to make."

"She's had a lot of those, lately," I said.

"House Kifeda will likely try to get us tossed from House of Koman because we're not on Abasi Prime," Nick said.

"Bring it," I said. "I've chewed up and spit out bigger asshats than him."

Marny snorted a laugh, which woke little Pete who lay on her lap. "You make it look so easy, Cap."

"What's that?"

"Leading. How are you always so sure what the right move is?" she asked.

"Mind if I hold him?" I asked, pushing back from the forward bulkhead, allowing *Shimmering Leaves'* AI to take over navigation duties.

"Sure, he might be a little fussy. He's starting to get hungry," she said, handing him to me. I was struck by his warmth as I pulled him in close.

"He smells so good," I said.

"Breast milk," Nick said, as if it were the most natural thing in the universe to blurt out while sailing into the deep dark.

I looked to Marny then to Nick. "Pardon?"

"He smells good because of breast milk," he said. "We can replicate nutritional supplements that are exactly the same, but nothing is as good as milk delivered straight from the breast. It's amazing. Like from the first minute he saw 'em, that's all he wanted. I think the sweet smell is because he's happy."

I opened my eyes wide and shook my head. Someone had stolen my best friend and swapped him out with a crazy person. "For the love of everything I hold dear, can you stop talking about Marny's boobs?"

Nick grinned. "You just said, 'hold dear' and 'Marny's boobs' in the same sentence. Tell me, ever hear of a man named Freud?"

"Nick," Marny giggled in a girly manner I rarely heard from her. "Go easy on him."

"With your name, you've got some big shoes to fill, little man," I said, purposefully changing the subject.

The normally busy run from Abasi Prime to the Tamu-Santaloo wormhole entrance was almost entirely devoid of other ships. The two groups we did run into refused to drop their hard-burn to allow for communications exchange. Arriving in the Santaloo star system, we discovered several shipwrecks within forty thousand kilometers of the gate. According to Jonathan's analysis, the wrecks were the result of ship-to-ship combat with blasters and not directly related to the Kroerak invasion.

It was a five-day trip from the Tamu-Santaloo gate to Zuri. In each of our periodic halts from hard-burn, we'd intercepted small snippets of communication from the planet. The news wasn't good. Much of the planet had devolved into chaos. While the Kroerak had focused on the area near York, the cities that had been left untouched had seen rioting. Terrified citizens had turned first on their local governments and finally on each other as they anticipated invasion.

"We'll drop from hard-burn in ten ... nine ..." I set the countdown on the sloop's bridge address system and prepared for hard maneuvering if it was called for. Our short-range sensors hadn't picked up any nearby ships, but we were coming in next to the debris field that had been Petersburg station and it might be possible for a ship to be lurking nearby, hidden in the junk.

"Holy frak," Tabby's voice floated over comms.

There were so many small chunks of debris deflecting off our ship's armor that it sounded like rain.

Nick's navigation path had dropped us out further from the station than I'd have liked, but I was immediately grateful for his forethought in considering the debris cloud. For unarmored transports, the area around Petersburg station wouldn't be safe for many years to come without a concerted cleanup effort.

From the data-streams we'd already viewed, I thought I'd gained a good feeling for the damage to Petersburg. Breath caught in my throat as I grew overwhelmed at the loss. Virtually no part of Petersburg remained. The damage felt like more than a tactical strike. It felt very personal, like the Kroerak had made a specific point of grinding the station into dust.

When we'd last left, there'd been more than a hundred residents on the station, which was surrounded by extremely heavy defensive weapons. A lightning bolt of anguish coursed through me as I considered that someone would have remained behind to man those weapons. The loss was incomprehensible. For the first time, I understood how the citizens of Earth and those of Abasi Prime felt after discovering they'd survived but had lost so much. Tears streamed down my cheeks and I did nothing to hide my grief.

"Nick, are you picking up anything?" I asked, my voice sounded foreign to my own ears as I took a shuddering breath.

"Nothing, Liam," he answered reverently. "The debris has scattered tens of thousands of kilometers since the event. This isn't even Petersburg's original position, it's just the largest mass of what remains."

Marny handed me a cloth and I wiped at my eyes and blew my nose. I was so overwhelmed I didn't know what to do next. I'd seen enough death and destruction by the Kroerak that my resolve to hunt them down hadn't changed. But today, I desperately needed another objective. Marny wrapped her arms around my shoulders and pulled me to her, holding me close against her chest. The act took me off guard and I cried.

"I'm sorry, Liam," Tabby said over comms. "We'll find her. No matter what. Don't count your mother out. She knew they were coming."

"York," I managed to say. There was nothing left for us in the debris that was once a proud and thriving station. I pushed my feelings down into the rage that burned within my soul. Like many, I hated the Kroerak for what they had taken from me. Like none before me, however, I had the means to carry out judgment. I grabbed that rage and held it close.

"Course laid in," Nick answered. "Are you okay, Liam?"

"Not really. But I've got this."

Wordlessly, I piloted *Shimmering Leaves* into Zuri's atmosphere.

Zuri was a beautiful planet, more arid on average than Earth, but not as much as Mars. There were only a few, moderately-sized oceans and the planet's primary foliage was a dense scrub that rarely grew taller than twenty or thirty meters. From space, the planet was a mixture of red-browns and deep greens. On this approach, however, the planet's beauty was lost on me.

Taking us down toward the small frontier town of York, Tabby stayed close on my wing. We'd flown together in plenty of combat situations and old habits came back quickly.

As we cruised downward, I recalled that it had been the people of York who had originally drawn us to the Dwingeloo galaxy. At the time, we'd been tracking down an abandoned Belirand colony mission. Belirand, an evil intragalactic company, had sent its people – those who would later found York – on a one-way trip to the Mhina system. Only through the kindness of the Abasi had the explorers been allowed to settle on the planet Zuri where they scraped out a life in the wilderness.

"We'll fly over the homestead and Nick's manufactory," I said, adjusting our descent.

We'd arrived in Dwingeloo almost two years previous and the citizens of York, under attack from Kroerak and dealing with failing technology, had received us with open arms. In that time, we'd been able to help fortify and resupply the city. Indeed, it appeared that in the year since I'd been gone, even more had changed. Specifically, Nick's industrial complex had grown to ten-times what I recalled and covered the better part of a square kilometer.

From a few kilometers away, the buildings looked like they hadn't been hit too hard. As we closed the distance, however, we learned that nothing could have been further from the truth. As we slowly passed over, I caught movement from below and my HUD outlined at least ten Kroerak warriors skittering through the ruins of Nick's enterprise.

"Frak, they're still down there," Nick observed, picking up on the Kroerak.

"What would stop them?" Marny asked. "They were abandoned by their fleet. I'm picking up even more in the surrounding scrub."

"What are they doing in your shop?" I asked. "It's not like there's any food in there."

"No idea," Nick said.

We'd yet to get a good look at York, as it was on the other side of Quail Hill. Accelerating, we flew over the hill and looked into the valley where York sat – or at least, used to sit. The devastation of the small city was complete. The twenty-meter-high steel walls that had stood for a century and a half were collapsed outwards and not a building still stood. The terrain had been so trampled as to be unrecognizable. It was as if the wrath of the entire Kroerak army had visited and delivered their judgment.

"*Intrepid!*" Tabby exclaimed. For the second time in its hard life, the once beautiful *Intrepid* lay crash-landed upon Zuri. My eyes searched for damage that would explain the armor we'd seen tumbling in the data-stream. Flying to the other side of the ship we located where an entire section of forward hull had been removed almost surgically. I knew of only one weapon that could do that — the Kroerak's lance wave.

Iskstar-tuned fire erupted from *Ice Touched Field's* forward, lower turret. A group of Kroerak warriors, having heard our approach, had emerged from the scrub near *Intrepid*. The ship's weapon splattered the bugs into the dirt.

"That was a controlled descent!" Nick said, his voice carrying excitement.

"What?" I asked.

"If you were in the forward section it would have been bad, but someone piloted that ship and landed it. Liam, those Kroerak aren't in the warehouse looking for machines," he said. "I think I know where the people of York went."

Chapter 5

I CHOOSE LIFE

"Nick, take the helm," I said, setting the ship on auto. "Marny, Tabbs – Popeyes."

It was one of the joys of working with life-long friends. We didn't require a lot of conversation to communicate big ideas, especially where combat was concerned. Jumping from my chair, I ran from the sloop's bridge and back to the relatively empty cargo hold.

"Right behind you, Cap. I've got to put Peter into his bassinette," Marny said.

"Roby, we're slaving our controls onto *Ice Touched Field*," Nick said. "Take us back to the warehouse."

"Copy that. Tabby explained what we're doing. Do you really think they're alive?" Roby asked, his voice filled with emotion. Everyone he'd known and loved had been in York.

"I'm counting on it!" I said, allowing an ember of hope to grow.

Having spent the better part of the last few months living in my mechanized infantry suit, I wasted little time as I jumped in and fired it up. Marny, a few steps behind for having handed Peter over to Nick, fell even further behind as lack of familiarity slowed her. I breathed deep as I gripped the controls and ran through status, first on my Popeye and then on Marny's.

Satisfied we were good to go, I directed the loading ramp to retract and grabbed *Shimmering Leaves'* frame, peering at the ground as it passed beneath. Sailing in a slow arc over the buildings, Roby and Nick pecked away at any Kroerak that emerged. I grew impatient. Our ship's weapons were more than a match for a Kroerak warrior, even without the Iskstar crystal. The problem here was completely opposite; they were hunting mosquitos with sledge hammers. When they made contact, it was spectacular, but it was slow going.

"On my six," I ordered and jumped from the ship at four hundred meters.

"Cap!" Marny called after me. "Roby, Nick, cease fire, Cap's on the move."

"Copy," Nick answered.

"Waited longer than I thought you would," Tabby said, turning as she fell to look over at me. Popeyes weren't great at providing actual lift, but their arc-jets were designed to safely deliver an operator to the surface of heavy-atmosphere planets.

"I have point," I said, calibrating my sensors on the Kroerak racing through the broken pieces of building. "We'll beachhead here. I'm expecting a decent wave on arrival." I drew a target around our entrance: an opening in the building 's roof.

"Cap, there's likely a nest of them in there," Marny warned.

"Wouldn't be a party, otherwise," I quipped. "Just keep 'em off your back. We had some problems with that on Picis when we'd get overrun. Otherwise, just spray the blue goo on anything that moves."

The Popeye's AI forced my knees into a bend as Tabby, Marny and I landed hard on the floor of the warehouse. Kroerak warriors assailed us from every direction, including dropping on us from above.

I'd started firing before touching down, my instincts so attuned to the movements of bugs that the fight didn't require my full attention. This turned out to be to our advantage as Marny landed hard and stumbled to the side, fighting to maintain balance. A Popeye is designed to protect the operator and catching yourself is harder than you might expect. If the Popeye senses a fall, especially in close quarters with enemies, its AI will harden suit ligatures and go into what we generally called armadillo mode.

Before Marny's Popeye could roll into a useless ball of impenetrable nano-steel, I grabbed her shoulder with my free hand, steadying her. I pushed so she faced away from the dead-space Tabby and I were trying to create between us.

"I'm good, Cap," Marny said, shrugging off my hand. I wasn't sure what the attitude was for, but it didn't matter. We were in the shite and we'd work on feel-goods later.

At this point, the three of us really got to work and started firing into an intense wave of bugs.

"They're not even trying that hard," I yelled over the sound of crashing metal. I'd swung my arm into a doorway, ostensibly to open our field of view.

"Nick's gonna be pissed," Tabby said when a long section of the building collapsed outward, pulling a portion of the roof down with it.

"That wasn't me," I said defensively.

"No, look! That's an armored vehicle," Tabby said.

"Cap, what's the call here?" Marny asked as we backed away from the battered vehicle that had driven through the side of the building.

The armored vehicle ran on tracks, with two weapons mounted into a top turret. The heaviest weapon was roughly the size of a small ship-mounted blaster. In the hands of a skilled operator, the tank could give a Popeye a run for its money.

A group of Kroerak burst through the newly opened corner of the building. Closer to the tank than to us, the swarm hesitated for a moment as if trying to decide which of us to attack first. Raising her weapon, Tabby prepared to take the bugs out.

"Hold on," I said. "Let's see what they've got."

The tank's turret rotated and blaster fire erupted from its main weapon. Receiving fire solidified the Kroerak's decision and they charged the vehicle. The first shot missed, but a follow-up round tagged one of the charging bugs. Not completely taken out, the wounded bug continued to rush forward. A third shot from the tank finished it just as the rest of the group fell onto the tank.

"Put 'em down," I said, marking the tank as a yellow or a questionable target. By denoting the tank in this way, our Popeyes would avoid friendly fire.

The three of us ran toward the tank, which was bouncing and jerking under the swarm. Having made it inside the range of the tank's main weapon, the bugs' only obstacle now was the heavy armor. The occupants wouldn't survive long against the Kroerak's hardened pincers.

For fear of damaging the tank, I retracted my blaster weapon and pulled the multipurpose tool from where it was strapped against my lower leg. Flipping it over in my hand, I gripped the end that would allow me to use the heavier, hammer end as a bludgeoning tool.

"Hold on, Cap," Marny said as I was about to leap into the fray. She'd seen what I'd missed: the meter-long heavy blaster barrel had been retracted into the turret. The small nub that was left rotated and at point-blank range, started clearing itself of bugs that, only moments ago, had a substantial advantage. With proximity no longer a problem, the tank cleared the bugs in short order.

"Isn't that the tank we took from Goboble?" Tabby asked as we scanned the area, looking for more bugs.

"Establish communications with occupants of the tank," I ordered my AI.

As if in response, the turret weapon's barrel extended and a hatch popped open. "Don't shoot!"

Sweaty brown arms rose up through the hatch, followed by the balding head of none other than Roby's dad, who everyone simply called Bish.

"Tabbs, patrol mode," I said. We'd learned a hard lesson on Picis. When standing in the field of battle, especially where enemy had just fallen, distractions could easily get you killed.

"Yup," she answered.

I punched the chest of my Popeye, causing the cavity to open and the face-mask of my heavily armored helmet to lever up. In this open mode, my hips and legs were still engaged with the suit, but I was able to freely use my torso and arms.

"Roby, you copy?" I asked, making eye contact with Bish.

"Go ahead, Captain," Roby answered.

"Never guess who we found down here." I pinched the image of his father, grinning at me from where he sat inside the tank, and flicked it onto Roby's avatar on my HUD.

"Dad!" Roby exclaimed. "I thought you were dead."

When I didn't see any change in Bish's expression, it dawned on me that he must be without tech.

"Looking good there, Bish," I said. I hadn't always loved being around Bish, but our differences were petty and I genuinely felt joy at seeing him alive.

"Oh man, are you a sight for these sore old eyes," he drawled.

"We saw York," I said. "Where'd you come from?"

"My boy?" he asked, ignoring my question.

"Overhead in a sloop," I said. "What's wrong with your comms?"

"Can't be using comms with those bugs around," he said. "They're drawn in by it. Didn't anyone tell you that? And, what's with the blue eyes?"

I raised my eyebrows. The Kroerak ability to hone in on communication signals was something we'd only recently learned. I was surprised to hear the information coming from Bish.

"Where is everyone?"

"Would you get your big butt out of the way?" a voice demanded from inside the tank. Bish looked down into the hole and smiled, shaking his head wryly as a much thinner Hog Hagarson squeezed up beside him.

"Live and breathe, but your mom is going to be happy to see you, son," Hog said, his drawn face turning into a broad smile. For a moment I could see the bigger-than-life mayor of York, instead of the ghost-like man who stood in front of me.

"Mom's alive?" I couldn't help the tear that rolled down my cheek. "How many more?"

"Come and see for yourself," Hog said. "We're on the north side of the building."

"Cap, need to cut the reunion short. We have incoming," Marny said.

WE SPENT the next two hours creating a buffer zone around Nick's building. It was a surprisingly different type of battle than we'd left on Picis. Instead of massive waves of Kroerak, we had to hunt for them in the dense scrub. More than once, I was beset by enterprising warriors that jumped out, tackling me from the side. In the end, we spread out a mesh of sensor disks to provide a warning.

Once the area was relatively secure, Nick and Roby set down next to the warehouse. There had once been manufacturing materials stored there, but the area was now a chaotic mess of debris.

"We'll keep one bird in the sky and one of the mechs rolling round the clock," Marny said, reassuming her role as security chief. "Nick and I will take first shift, unless you'd like to do something different."

There was insecurity in her tone as she spoke. I wasn't exactly sure what to do about it, so I let it go for the moment. "Sounds solid, Marny. Two-hour patrols?" I asked.

"Agreed," she said. "Now go find your family!"

I didn't need further prodding. Tabby and I, still in our Popeyes, led Roby and Semper over to massive steel doors built on top of a granite incline that remained covered by the end of the building. At our approach, Bish and Hog exited the battered tank and gave a friendly wave.

"Those suits of yours are fantastic," Bish said, exuberantly pulling me into a sweaty embrace. "I've never seen bugs so quickly destroyed as with those weapons of yours. Anything to do with your glowing eyes?"

I chuckled. That was Bish; always right to the point. "Iskstar-tuned blaster crystals," I said. "Makes quick work of everything Kroerak."

"Ships too? Is that why their ships left?" he asked.

"Oh hell, Bish, give the man some room already," Hog said, pulling Tabby into a bear hug. "Isn't it enough that they came for us?"

"Nothing's ever free," Bishop said, pulling his son, Roby, in for a hug. "My good night, son, but you're all muscles now. Haven't been missing many meals, have you?"

"Hello, Mr. Bishop," Semper said, demurely. Her standard human speech was quite good and she'd lost the Felio habit of reversing word order.

"Why hello, Semper," he answered, turning his attention to the Felio he'd previously made no attempt to hide his disapproval of. For Bish, it was a simple calculus. Since Roby and Semper were different species and could not have children together, he found no value in their union.

"We're this way," Hog said, approaching the massive door that lay at a thirty-degree angle. With a large hammer sitting off to the side, he banged on the metal surface. The sound of chains moving through block and tackle were heard shortly after and slowly the door slid back.

A wave of sour air exhausted from the entry and several pairs of eyes stared back at us. Seeing Mom, I jumped into the alcove and pulled her into my arms. I might have squeezed a little too tightly, as she coughed but didn't complain.

"You made it," she whispered, holding me fiercely.

"We did," I said, allowing my eyes to look through the grungy group of survivors who crowded in behind her. Like Hog, they were all too thin. Beneath my arms, I realized Mom felt emaciated. I pulled back and stared into her face. Her eyes were sunken and her cheeks hollow.

"Your eyes," she said, touching my face at the temples.

"Long story," I said. "But we're secure up top."

"Liam, the Kroerak are everywhere," she said. "We've already been in the open for too long. Our scent will be on the wind."

" Let them come," I said. "We've established a five-hundred-meter perimeter. Marny's rolling a Popeye and will keep it clear."

"How'd you get past the fleet?" Mom asked. We were being jostled by the crush of curious people and well-wishers. I made eye contact with York's elected sheriff, Mez Rigdon. We'd spent time training her in the Popeyes and it occurred to me that she could help Marny with the patrol.

"Hold on," I said. "Mez, you ready for a turn in the Popeye? We could use another patroller."

"Trust me?" She flashed a smile. Like Mom and everyone else I could see, she was all skin and bone.

"I'll get her checked out on it," Tabby said, lifting Mez from the crowd with her grav-suit.

"Let's go to the meeting area," Hog prompted. "I'm sure everyone would like to hear what young Hoffen has to say.

I followed the growing group through a tunnel hewn from the rock. The only obvious technology being utilized were the bright lights strung from the ceiling. I flashed back to the Piscivoru caves and was grateful for high ceilings and wider spaces.

"Where did this come from? Was this part of Nick's plant?" I asked.

"Nope," Hog answered. "It was yer Mom's idea. We used Mr. James' replicator hive to dig into the hillside. Barely had enough time before those bugs arrived. Lost a lot of good people."

I knew better than to ask how many, even though the question was on the tip of my tongue.

"Liam Hoffen." The child-like voice of Jester Ripples peeled through the crowd. The meter tall, amphibious alien raced toward me and jumped into my arms, his tri-fingered hands and feet gripping my body in excitement. I rubbed my fingers on the red fur over his eyes, something Norigans enjoy immensely, and he purred with contentment.

"Hey, buddy," I said, trying to calm him. "I'm glad Jester Ripples is alive."

The cave opened up as we walked through the crowd of people.

The space they'd created was little better than a tomb. It was large enough for the people to hide in and even had provisions for waste, but there was little personal space and even fewer remaining supplies.

"Has the Abasi fleet come to save us?" a voice asked from within the mass behind me.

"Yeah, how'd you break through the blockade?" a second voice prodded.

"The Kroerak fleets have been driven back," I said. "There is no fleet over Zuri."

"You mean except for Abasi," a woman whose face I recognized, corrected.

"No," I answered. "There are no ships over Zuri other than possibly some trade ships that we didn't see."

"What about the Abasi? Why did they abandon us?" The tone of the questions was turning negative quickly.

"A lot of things have changed," I said. "It's up to us to focus on the survival of York."

"York is gone," another anonymous voice declared.

"So are many other cities on Zuri as well as Abasi Prime," I said. "The Kroerak attacked with a combined force of more than a thousand warships and twice that number of troop carriers. I won't lie. The Abasi nation is struggling. We're going to have to rely on ourselves for survival."

"That's new," an angry, sarcastic voice said next to me.

"What about the bugs? Did they go with the fleet?"

I appreciated an actual useful question. I understood why people were complaining and bitter, but the emotion wasn't helpful.

"Good question. No," I answered. "That said, we have some technology that is pretty devastating to the Kroerak."

"What's wrong with your eyes?" a child piped up.

"When can we go back home?" a woman asked, not waiting for me to answer.

I looked to Hog. His ashen face told me everything I needed to know. The citizens of York had no idea that they had no home to go back to. I opened my mouth to respond and was cut off by Hog.

"York is gone," he said, stepping up next to me. "The bugs wiped it out completely."

"What do you mean? When were you going to tell us?" The woman looked like she might be eighty stan years old, but I suspected was much younger. Life in this makeshift hideaway, with limited food, had been very hard on them.

"Betty, you know as well as I do that not a one of us in here knew if we were going to live to see tomorrow," Hog said. "I wasn't about to pull the rug out from under us when things looked so bad."

"Well, we can't live here. According to my grandparents, it took almost thirty long spans before the bugs were cut down enough that crops could be grown and people were able to live," Betty retorted.

"No reason you can't," I said. "We can make York a bug-free zone. Same thing that makes our eyes glow blue can tune a blaster so it disintegrates everything Kroerak. If you want to rebuild here, we'll help you get going. But you need to know something. We believe that Abasi are going to pull out of Zuri entirely. Our next stop is the Mshindi compound."

"If they do, the Pogona will take over," Bish said, joining the dissenting voices. "No good will come of that."

"What is it, Liam?" Mom asked. She'd been studying my face and I'd no doubt given away that I had something up my sleeve. I'd never once been able to keep a secret from her.

"How can Abasi abandon us? I thought they were our friends!" Betty demanded. An angry wave of grumbling rolled across the group. "I guess now we know the truth!"

"Betty is it?" I asked, looking at the older woman.

"It is. And I ain't afraid of you," she said, clenching her teeth defiantly.

"You should be," I said, getting tired of her attitude. "The only thing between those bugs out there and you, is me and my crew. And do you want to know something else? We only have room for people looking to be a part of the solution. Right now, you're getting people upset and making them distrustful of the only frakking thing that's going to keep them alive."

"Well! I *never*," she said and turned away from me.

Inside, I might have snapped a little. I'd been pushed by angry, petty tyrants for much of my life and it took everything I had not to strangle her. I won't say I'm proud of what I did next, but I can't say that I completely regret it either. As the woman turned her back and started to bad-mouth me, I grabbed her arm and spun her around to face me.

"Perhaps I'm not being clear," I said. "I am here representing the Abasi. I am Prime of House of the Bold and I'm here to offer assistance. I guess I'd like your answer right now. Betty, are you rejecting our help?"

"Liam!" Mom said, grabbing my arm in horror, trying to separate me from the woman.

"Don't, Mom," I said, not looking at her. "I am frakking dead serious here, Betty. I'm going to need your answer."

The woman's eyes had gone from narrow beads to wide saucers and I felt a shudder as she attempted to breathe. The problem was, I'd seen too much death. Betty's fear didn't bother me, but her negative attitude was a virus that would infect the very people who needed saving. There would be a lot of hardships in front of us and I needed to establish a pecking order.

"I... I..." Betty stuttered.

Somewhere the part of me that was still a decent human felt like a first-class heel. I was committed, however, and unrelenting as I stared at her.

"I don't know what to say."

"Tell me you want to live, Betty," I said. "Tell me you'll do what it takes to keep your friends and neighbors alive."

"I do. I will," she said and broke into sobs.

I allowed Mom to push my arm away from the bitter old woman and comfort her. No doubt I would be hearing about my treatment of Betty later if the daggers from Mom's eyes were any indication.

"Uhh, we're going to take a bit of a break here, folks," Hog said, stepping up next to me. "We're going to need some volunteers to help us go out into the forest and get fresh water and supplies. I'd ask anyone interested to meet us by the door in a few minutes."

For a moment, the crowd that I believed represented the entirety of York quieted. The room where we'd gathered was too small for all of them, but the adjacent hallways were filled to capacity. Even so, the only sound that could be heard was the dripping of water.

"I want to live," a tall man offered quietly, standing from where he'd been leaning against the wall. As he stood, I could see that his broad shoulders were slumped forward as if he carried the weight of the world on them. "I'll go."

"I want to live," a young woman offered, nodding and stepping forward.

"Me too," an older woman in soiled clothing added, joining her.

What followed was like a dam breaking. The room was soon filled with the murmurs of people stating their desire to live. I'd like to say it was what I had in mind when I'd threatened the old woman, but it wasn't. However, I wasn't about to admit that to Mom or anyone else in the near future.

Chapter 6

PHOENIX

"Walk with me," Mom said, catching me from behind and pushing her hand past the bend of my elbow so our arms interlocked.

Gaining control of the land around our homestead on Zuri had been our first priority. While we'd rebuffed a few roving bands of Kroerak in the process, we were relatively secure. Although, I might not have been the best judge given my experience on the planet Picis, where a few dozen Kroerak warriors was considered light duty.

"Look, I'll apologize to Betty," I said defensively. I'd been feeling bad about how I treated the old lady and had no doubt Mom was ready to give me a good dressing down.

"What? Oh, do *not* apologize. That crazy old lady had it coming," she said. "Trust me, you don't want to get locked in a cave with her."

I chuckled and extracted my arm so I could pull her close, grateful she'd survived the Kroerak invasion of Zuri.

"Did Katherine stay behind?" I'd wondered how *Intrepid* had ended up on Zuri with only minor damage to its forward compartments. The only answer I could come up with was that someone had provided cover from Petersburg station so *Intrepid* could make a break for Zuri. Katherine LeGrande had once been a captain for Belirand Corporation. Our paths crossed when *Hotspur* found her ship abandoned in the deep dark by a corporation that cared more for its reputation than the lives of hundreds of its employees. She shared that dubious distinction with the colonists who had settled York.

"She wouldn't come with us," Mom said, her voice carrying grief.

"Brave woman," I agreed. "What about Munay?"

Gregory Munay was a commander in Mars Protectorate Navy and had followed us to the Dwingeloo galaxy. Making no bones about the fact that he still served Mars, Munay had also been willing to follow my lead as it concerned the Kroerak. I'd never liked the man. I wasn't sure if my dislike was because of his interest in Mom or because I generally didn't trust someone who had ulterior motives.

"He and a group of ten of his most loyal took *Fleet Afoot,*" she said.

"To do what?" I asked, immediately annoyed. The tiny sloop-classed vessel hardly had a place in the fleet-based combat the Kroerak had brought.

"You know Greg. Operational security," Mom said. "He wouldn't tell me."

"And you let him go?"

"We didn't have a choice," Mom said. "By the time I knew what was occurring, my only choice was to shoot him down."

I nodded. We both knew that was something she wouldn't have done.

When Mom had caught up with me, I'd been on my way to the original shop where Nick had started his manufacturing company. While he'd long since abandoned the small area in favor of the plant he'd built across the road, it had one distinct advantage; it had been built into the side of Quail Hill. Our hope was that a replicator we'd salvaged a long time ago was still operational.

The whir of a mechanical infantry suit caught my attention just as we stepped onto the gravel road twenty meters from our destination. Instinctively, I turned, checking my HUD for identification. The Popeye operator was York's sheriff, Mez Rigdon.

"I think she's looking for a salute," Mom said under her breath.

Indeed, Sheriff Rigdon had her gloved fist held at mid-section and was standing still. It was an odd thing that had been happening more and more, as people became aware of my new status as Prime of House of the Bold. For me, there had been no change. I'd always seen myself as the one in charge of Loose Nuts, along with Nick, Marny, Ada and Tabby, that is. I hastily returned the salute.

"What are you finding, Mez?" I asked, establishing comms.

"We've secured twenty square kilometers," she said. "We're not a hundred percent locked down, but we have sensor pucks in enough places that we can react to wandering Kroerak within a few minutes."

"Any word from Mshindi compound?" I asked. The edge of the territory controlled by House Mshindi was a hundred kilometers east of our position.

"Not yet."

Our plan was to secure the citizens of York and then split off and help Mshindi. I wasn't thrilled to separate our forces but saw no alternative.

"Copy that," I answered. "I'll let you get back to patrol."

"Thanks, Prime," Rigdon answered and jogged off along her patrol route, obviously looking to make up for lost time.

"Prime? Do we need to have that talk about egos again?" Mom asked. She was only half joking.

"Probably," I answered as the two of us hustled across the road and up to the shop.

Even before entering, I heard the make-shift replicator we'd pieced together so many months before. Though we'd replaced just about every part, the machine had never sounded right. In that the Abasi sloops didn't have replicator technology aboard and the Kroerak had ruined the manufactory, the dilapidated replicator was the only one we had ready access to.

"That can't be good," Mom said, hearing the noise as we approached.

I chuckled. "You'd think," I agreed, placing my palm onto the security panel. I caught Nick's eye as we approached. He and Roby had been working on the replicator and I was gratified to see a substantial pile of water filters, meal-bars and med-patches. "Looks good!" I shouted over the noise.

"We're going to have to run some new parts for it once we get access to a real replicator," Roby answered. "It was never designed to make meal-bars and med-patches, but Jester Ripples can make just about anything work."

At the mention of his name or possibly the sound of my voice, Jester Ripples' comically-proportioned frog-head popped up above a stack of supply crates and he grinned widely at me. I braced myself for impact as he propelled himself across the shop floor and jumped up into my arms. He'd been clingier than normal.

"You must promise to never leave me behind again, Liam Hoffen. I do not care that you are powerful and important."

"I left Jester Ripples behind because I wanted him to stay safe," I said.

"Your plan was unsuccessful," Jester Ripples said, placing a warm finger on my eyebrow. I'd explained to him that rubbing eyebrows wasn't something humans found particularly enjoyable, but he'd ignored me.

"Nick, any word on *Intrepid?"* I asked. We'd prioritized the replicator, but he and Jonathan had been looking through the data-streams to assess damage.

"She could sail right now," Nick said. "She's just not space-worthy with the damage to her forward hull. I'm sorry, Mrs. H. That must have been a bad ride."

Mom smiled tightly in acknowledgement. In what seemed like an entirely other lifetime, Mom had been our secondary school teacher on Colony-40 and Nick had never gotten past her nickname.

"We were lucky," Mom answered. "We had ninety souls aboard and we only lost five."

"I watched the data-streams, it was more than luck, Mrs. H.," Nick said. "You turned *Intrepid* at just the right angle to minimize damage. You could have lost the ship."

"Hard to feel good about losing those people," she said.

"Understandable," Nick agreed. The muted cry of a baby caught Mom's attention and she looked around, almost startled.

"You have a baby in this combat zone?" Mom asked. "He should be on the ship."

"Safer here, Mrs. H.," Nick said, opening the armor-glass panel that made up the top of the crib. The crying sounds grew louder as the always-squirming Peter emerged from the safety of his armored cocoon. Nick turned and handed him to Mom. It wasn't lost on me that she was instantly mollified by the baby's presence. "Want to feed him?"

The proffered pouch of milk hung for only a moment in the air as Mom grabbed it from Nick and set to work. I grinned knowingly at Nick's sleight of hand and changed the subject.

"Raaawwr!" An orange streak of fur jumped on top of the table next to me and then onto my chest. Pulling my arms up, I held onto the overly-thin housecat we'd rescued so long ago. A pang of guilt surged through me as I stroked the upset kitty.

"You might ask Nicholas how much effort a baby takes, Liam," Mom cooed, her attention almost completely focused on the baby. "I suspect Filbert might appreciate a little more of it."

"I was thinking that Tabbs and I could take a run over to Mshindi's compound. Bish offered to take the tank and we could bring one of the Popeyes along. If we left both of the sloops behind, I think York would be secure enough," I said, opening a food bar and spreading it out for a very hungry Filbert.

"In *Intrepid?*" Nick asked. "She's not exactly a puddle jumper, you know."

"She'd provide a lot of cover," I countered.

"She was also shut down hard," Mom said. "We had to kill the power. The Kroerak were tracking us and I wanted them to believe we'd crashed."

"I saw where you landed," I said. "You convinced me."

"It's just a flesh wound," Mom quipped, in her baby-cooing voice.

"Do you need anything from us?" Nick asked.

"I came over to grab Jester Ripples. Once we secure *Intrepid*, we'll need help getting systems up and running. Jonathan's Phentera are already on their way," I said.

"Yes!" Jester Ripples agreed enthusiastically, pulling closer to me.

"Phentera has been spending a lot of time separated from the main collective," Nick said. "Think we have anything to worry about?"

"No idea," I said.

Our conversation was cut short as I heard the approach of a Popeye. When I checked my HUD, I also discovered the sloop, *Shimmering Leaves,* had taken a position a thousand meters above the shop.

"Cap, we're ready to roll out," Marny called over comms. Tabby, Jester Ripples and I, along with Marny in her Popeye, would accompany the Abasi sloop over to *Intrepid*. The two sloops had added *Intrepid's* location to their patrol routes and had been reporting on Kroerak movements, as well as plinking away at any bugs caught out in the open.

"Copy that," I said. "You good here, Mom?"

"Someone's got to take care of this baby," she said, jealously pulling Pete to herself.

"I think Nick and Marny have been doing a pretty good job," I said.

"Not really. It's stressful because he needs a lot of attention," Nick answered. "Mrs. H. if you want to help out, I could really use it."

"Of course, Nicholas," she said. "After all that we've seen, I can think of nowhere I'd rather be."

I plucked a handful of meal bars from the table and stuffed them into the pocket of my grav-suit and made for the door. "Talk later," I said as I locked the door behind me, still carrying Jester Ripples.

"Let's go, Hoffen," Tabby said, holding an Iskstar-tipped staff she'd brought back from Picis.

"Be safer if you flew with me," I said, glancing back at Marny, who was alertly scanning the area for danger.

"For Kroerak!" Tabby said with a wild look, just before she sprinted up the road that led to York.

"Fifteen meters elevation, Cap," Marny said, as she jogged after Tabby.

Using the grav-suit's repulsors, I easily lifted into the air. Jester Ripples only weighed twenty-five kilograms and the grav-suit would lift anything I could carry, especially this close to a massive object like the planet Zuri.

I felt a certain awe at the near-complete destruction of York that came into view as I cleared Quail Hill. Kroerak generally focused more on life forms than they did structures. There was no doubt in my mind the additional damage was an expression of Kroerak rage, just as the total ruination of Petersburg station had been.

Even with near constant patrols and our ship hovering overhead, a few unlucky Kroerak warriors waited as Marny and Tabby approached *Intrepid*. Apparently, danger wasn't something the Kroerak communicated well amongst each other. Every bug we ran into had the same one-track mindset bent on killing anything that moved. I understood the need to eat, but there had to be safer meals than Tabby, wielding an Iskstar-tipped staff, and Marny in a Popeye.

As expected, the armored ball holding Jonathan's Phentera group joined us as we approached the ship. I'd learned that Phentera wasn't overly interested in conversation, so I honored this by acknowledging their presence with a simple nod. Additionally, Bish arrived, having given Semper a ride over in York's tank.

"I'll hold this position," Marny said, jumping up ten meters onto the damaged portion of *Intrepid's* hull. Enterprising Kroerak warriors could have gained access to *Intrepid,* but they wouldn't have found anything to eat and would have had no reason to believe we'd return. Our danger would more likely come from a bug following us in, rather than one hiding aboard.

"Let me do a quick sweep before you bring Jester Ripples aboard," Tabby said, dropping down and grabbing Semper from where she'd exited the tank. After setting Semper next to Marny, Tabby disappeared into the inky blackness of the lifeless *Intrepid*. Zipping past, Phentera chased after Tabby.

Landing next to Marny and Semper, I helped Jester Ripples onto the torn deck. Without power, the gravity generators weren't working and it required effort to hold ourselves in place. With Jester Ripples no longer in my arms, I pulled out two Iskstar-tuned blaster pistols and handed one to Semper.

"Will this be difficult to repair?" Semper asked, inspecting the damage caused by the Kroerak lance.

"Looks like I could get this sealed off in about an hour," I said. "Wouldn't be pretty, but the patch would hold. We'll need to put in a lot more work to get her back to ship-shape."

Even though she was talking, I was pleased that Semper remained alert and continued to scan the opening into the ship. The once immature Felio had grown up and I felt a certain pride at my contribution.

"Nothing so far," Tabby announced a couple minutes later. I checked her progress. She'd started on the forward, lower deck, just below where we'd entered and worked her way back into the ship. "Engine room is clear."

"That's my cue." I lifted from the slanted deck and floated aft with my pistol held defensively in front of me. In my other hand was a very nervous Jester Ripples.

While Tabby hadn't checked the main level entirely, I could see her progress. She had just checked out the starboard passageway and was headed in our direction. Swinging port first, I made sure the area was clear and pulled Jester Ripples around the corner to the starboard. While I might not admit it to Tabby, I was relieved when I saw the lights on her facemask coming in our direction.

"So impatient," she said, acknowledging that she'd seen us. "You know I haven't checked that section yet."

"Marny's just around the corner. We've also made enough noise that any bug hiding in here would have already come out and gotten us," I said. My statement might not hold up to deep analysis, but I was confident I could handle myself, if necessary.

"It is enjoyable to be aboard our home once again," Jester Ripples observed. I nodded, but felt it an odd thing for him to say. He had always preferred the wet environment of a swamp over that of a clean spaceship.

"I'm not getting movement," Tabby said, as she passed us. "You're probably safe to go back to the engine room."

I nodded. We both knew Kroerak were capable of hunkering down and jumping out at inopportune times. I preferred not to live my life like a bad horror vid and, therefore, kept my pistol ready as I brought Jester Ripples aft.

"You know, for as many times as *Intrepid*'s been brought back from the ashes, we should have called her *Phoenix,"* I observed as we approached the engine room.

"A fiery bird," Jester Ripples said as imagery apparently filled his HUD.

"Seems appropriate. So what do you think?" I asked as soon as Jester Ripples had scanned the control surfaces for the ship's electronic and mechanical systems. I walked back to close the door to the engine room and lock it mechanically. A Kroerak warrior would be able to get through it after a few minutes, but the steel hatch would provide warning.

"A ship such as *Intrepid* is not designed to be without power," Jester Ripples said. "There are quite a number of systems that must be inspected and repaired. I am happy that planet Zuri is temperate and crystallization of water did not occur."

"Can you turn her back on?" I asked.

"Oh yes," Jester Ripples answered. "I thought perhaps Liam Hoffen desired to do so?"

I chuckled and checked my HUD. My AI displayed the correct sequence of actions that would power up *Intrepid's* various systems. I started the sequence and was almost instantly rewarded with a gravity field that pulled us to ninety degrees with the deck, instead of forcing us to stand in line with Zuri's gravity and the slope of the ship, twenty degrees askance.

"What? Ooph." It was Marny's voice. Hastily, I swiped at a vid-screen in front of me, changing its view so I could see the forward area where Marny stood sentry. For a moment, my heart raced as I looked for her, only to find that she'd toppled over and was pulling against the ragged deck, looking to gain her feet.

"You okay, Marny?" I asked.

"Might warn a girl about a sudden shift in gravity."

"Oops, sorry."

Having grown up on Earth, Marny wasn't overly comfortable in a changing-gravity environment. Even so, it was considered polite to let people know when such a change would occur. In my defense, I felt it was an obvious next step.

"I'm good. What's it look like back there?" Marny asked.

Distracted by the video screens as they booted up, I didn't immediately reply. I watched as Tabby walked past on one image, dragging an oversized Kroerak warrior behind her. She must have been aware of the vid sensor and suspected I was paying attention because she gave me a sidelong glance as she dumped the dead husk off the edge of the deck.

"I think we got lucky. Only red statuses are related to the forward damage," I said. Several of the systems were showing yellow, signifying that they required attention, but we could operate without them. "*Shimmering Leaves,* return to patrol status," I ordered. "We're operational."

"Okay, will do," Steve Basto replied. He hailed from York and had limited experience piloting a ship, which made him more qualified than ninety percent of the rest of the population.

With a few swipes, I shot a message to Phentera, asking them to begin an internal security sweep.

"Tabbs, meet me on the bridge," I said.

"Copy," she answered.

I pulled the door to the engine room shut behind me as I exited, making sure to lock it. Jester Ripples wouldn't last even a few seconds if there was another Kroerak aboard.

There's a smell that develops on a ship when it sits unoccupied. I'm not exactly sure what it is, but it's unpleasant. As the air handlers began to circulate the odor, a chill went down my spine. I sat in the captain's chair and pulled up the familiar holo projection.

"Marny, you okay for lift-off?" I asked.

"Copy that, Cap. I'm locked in and ready for a hard insertion at Mshindi's compound," she said.

"PG-rated, Master Chief," Tabby cackled into the comms as she took control of *Intrepid's* lower turrets.

I lifted us and leveled out the ship's orientation.

"What?" Marny asked.

Tabby ignored her, discovering instead a number of Kroerak targets in the scrub surrounding *Intrepid* as we rose. Judiciously, she used the smallest weapons we had and cleared the bugs. All of our weapons were capable of killing a warrior. It was the ships they tended to travel in that gave us so many problems.

"Oh, seems like maybe you and Nick need a little *you* time. Feels like you're making some Freudian slips," Tabby answered after taking care of the threats.

I closed my eyes and shook my head. I knew Tabby was just messing with Marny and that Marny had no idea what Tabby was implying.

"What in the world are you on about?" Marny asked. After twenty seconds, which she apparently used to rewind the conversation, she came back with, "Oh. No! I was ... you're so naughty, Tabitha Masters."

"Are you turning down date night? We're offering free babysitting," Tabby said.

"Seems like a distant dream," Marny said.

"Eyes on the prize, ladies," I said. It hadn't taken long to sail the hundred kilometers and we'd already passed the edge of Mshindi territory. "I'm hailing Mshindi compound now."

"Take it slow, Liam," Tabby instructed, firing *Intrepid's* turrets. "This place is crawling with bugs."

Chapter 7

NEEMA

Our earliest introduction to House Mshindi had been when Loose Nuts was invited to visit Mshindi Prime aboard the aptly named battleship, *Thunder Awakes.* My first impression of Mshindi leaders and their ship had been one of state-of-the-art sophistication. It was with some difficulty that I reconciled that image with the desecrated scene unfolding beneath *Intrepid.*

"We should have brought a second Popeye." Tabby interrupted my thoughts. "It's hard to line up on these bugs with ship's weapons and we're causing a lot of damage."

Mshindi's home was a hundred kilometers on a side or ten thousand square kilometers. The first fifty kilometers had been densely-packed forest and Marny hadn't wanted us to drop down near the surface until we saw the first signs of civilization past the broad fields of a crop closely equivalent to wheat. The few structures we could see were made of wood timbers and natural materials and could have been built in just about any century.

I winced as Tabby fired on a group of bugs running through an open field. She was right. *Intrepid's* turrets tore up giant chunks of ground as they eradicated the bugs. We hadn't yet seen any sign of the Felio, but the damage this short war had already wrought on the landscape was disheartening. The Kroerak hadn't been quite as enthusiastic in their destruction of the Mshindi farmsteads as they had been at York, but they hadn't pulled their punches either. I'd yet to pass over a building that didn't show signs of significant damage.

"I'm not seeing any Felio corpses," Marny said, still standing in the jagged opening at *Intrepid's* bow and peering down from her cat-bird's perch. Our destination was the center of the property where I hoped we'd find a clue as to the whereabouts of the several hundred Felio of House Mshindi.

"That's positive, at least," I said, nervously.

"Now that's impressive," Tabby said as we finally reached the main buildings. Nestled against a rocky slope sat what could best be described as a multi-level hunting lodge, made of massive timbers and stone. I felt a certain loss as our data-streams showed where Kroerak had torn into the structure, no doubt looking for inhabitants.

"I'm off," Marny announced, releasing her grip from *Intrepid* and freefalling into the center of a large group of buildings. There was no obvious spot to land *Intrepid's* one-hundred-thirty-meter-long bulk and still be able to provide cover for Marny.

With anticipation, I kept my eyes glued to the high-resolution vid-screens that made up the forward bulkhead of *Intrepid's* bridge. As soon as Marny touched down, several groups of warriors rushed her from where they'd found cover inside the buildings. While not as precise as we might have liked, Tabby chewed up the bugs at the periphery and left the others for Marny to deal with.

"Damn, Cap, never get tired of these Iskstar tuned blasters," Marny gloated over tactical comms.

I had no desire to tamp down her fun, but Tabby and I had taken down thousands, if not tens of thousands, while on Picis. I was tired of shooting the mindless killing machines.

"Ten more, at ninety degrees left," Tabby warned. "I don't have a great shot on their lead, so you'll get at least three."

"Copy that," Marny answered, turning serious as she focused on the group. Tabby was carefully picking them off to keep the splash of the heavy weapons from impacting Marny.

Kroerak warriors were drawn to the sounds of battle. In the wild, like we were, it was a good idea to remain vigilant for quite a while after initial contact. As expected, more and more Kroerak rushed out of the surrounding terrain as they became aware of our presence. Joining this fight was proving to be a bad plan for them, however. Kroerak were used to dominating every species they ran into and the instinct to run toward combat had worked for who knows how long. The Iskstar weapons changed the fight and I felt no remorse at the destruction we brought.

"Liam, I think there's Felio on the mountain," Tabby said, highlighting a wooded area on the tall hills behind Mshindi's cabin. In real-time, whatever she'd seen had just as quickly disappeared, but my AI was smart enough to superimpose a window on the screen and roll back to the movement Tabby had caught. A lone Felio wearing nothing and holding only a sword had poked out of the tree-line and looked over at *Intrepid.*

"She's naked," Tabby observed. "And look at that war-paint." The AI highlighted dark brown smudges that had been drawn on her fur.

"Marny, I'm going to need you and Phentera to secure *Intrepid,"* I said. "Tabby and I are going on a walkabout."

"You sure, Cap? Wouldn't it be safer if I did the walkabout in the Popeye?"

"I am," I answered. "We've got Felio on the mountain behind the main buildings. I need to go talk to 'em."

"Copy that, Cap," Marny answered. She followed *Intrepid* as I moved over about a kilometer and set down on a roadway. It wasn't a perfect fit and I was surely crushing crops on both sides of the road, but we were doing less damage than what had already been done by the Kroerak.

"So," Tabby said, her voice edged with sarcasm. "You want to talk to the naked Felio."

"Perks of the job," I said, then flinched as she slugged me in the arm.

"Semper, please meet us in the aft cargo bay," I continued, rubbing my arm and giving Tabby a wicked grin. "Phentera, please coordinate with Marny. We'll need you to watch the data-streams and alert her if Kroerak approach. Jester Ripples can you hang out on the bridge, just in case we need you to lift off?"

Even though Phentera Group was interested in all things related to combat, they were just as pacifistic as the rest of the Jonathan collective and would not fire weapons. That said, you couldn't find better analysis of sensor data and they'd give Marny plenty of advanced warning if an attack were imminent.

"Good choice on the armor," Tabby said.

Semper outfitted herself in an armored vac-suit. She also had a heavy blaster rifle strapped to her back and the pistol I'd handed her was prominently displayed in a holster on her leg.

She nodded and looked nervously at the airlock we'd be using to exit the ship. She had no grav-suit and would be tied to the ground, fodder for Kroerak. What she hadn't experienced, however, was just how effective the Iskstar-tuned blaster could be.

"We're clear outside, Cap," Marny called.

A familiar twinge of anticipation rushed through me as I palmed open the outer airlock. We were squishies entering a field of battle better suited to mechanized infantry, tanks and anything else with at least half an inch of nano-crystalized armor. Tabby and I both wore grav-suits and could sail up out of harm's way, but we were all vulnerable.

"Any advice, Semper?" I asked as Tabby and I helped the armored Felio to ground level.

"The female you saw in the trees is called Penda," Semper said.

I mentally kicked myself for not engaging Semper earlier. She'd taken a not-speak-unless-spoken-to approach around Tabby and me and while I found the restraint admirable, this was once her home and she'd have valuable insight.

"Not Neema?" I asked.

"That is our familial name," Semper said. "It is used like Hoffen, but in reverse. Penda is Neema First. She is responsible for everything before us. Her mother was sister to Mshindi Prime's mother who is credited with building the wealth of Mshindi."

"Which is it?" Tabby asked. "Mshindi or Neema?"

"Neema is appropriate," Semper asked. "Mshindi is always Neema, but only the select become Mshindi. We should go this way. Please follow."

"Did you live here?" Tabby asked as Semper ducked behind a building and climbed onto well-worn rocks that were too steep for walking. Even in the armored vac-suit, Semper exhibited the grace I'd come to associate with Felio as she clambered up the path.

"This was my home. I am Penda's seventh daughter," she answered. "My heart was lightened to see her today. She will most likely not speak to me. I left our home and live as an outcast."

"You are no outcast, Semper," I said. "You are of House of the Bold and I am proud to have you as part of my crew."

"You're cheating, Hoffen," Tabby admonished, breaking the awkward silence that followed. "You could use a little exercise, you know. You don't always have to use your grav-suit."

"I like to think of it as tactical preparedness. If there are Kroerak at the top, I'll be ready for them," I said.

"Like I won't," Tabby grunted.

"So why was your mom running around naked in the woods?" I asked.

"She has called Atieno," Semper said. "The people return to the woods in the dark of night and hunt. Penda believes that Zuri will provide for the needs of the people and that technology weakens the spirit."

"I thought this was the farm-team," Tabby said.

"Yes. My mother, sisters and all of Neema work the farms," Semper said, reaching the top of the forty-meter climb. I'd already scanned the area and found neither Kroerak nor Felio.

I chuckled, catching the farm-team reference that Semper hadn't. "I think Tabby and I were under the impression that to be Neema meant you were not chosen to be a warrior."

"It is true, only the best warriors are chosen to be Mshindi," Semper said. "It is Neema that train these warriors when they are young. Please be still, Penda has arrived."

We'd stopped only a few meters into the forest and my sensors showed nothing at all. Surprisingly, Semper pulled her long blaster rifle from her back and laid it on the ground. She followed by pulling off her helmet and then continued to disrobe until she was stripped down to nothing but fur.

"Eyes front and center, Hoffen," Tabby said. While I wouldn't say I was gawking, I'll admit she was difficult to ignore.

"Penda, protector of Neema, honored mother. I present Hoffen Liam, Prime of House Bold and his mate, Masters Tabitha, fourth of Bold. Mshindi Prime, Adahy, has sent us to offer respite in your time of Atieno," Semper called into the trees around us.

Tabby turned a moment before I caught the slight movement in the trees. A dark-gray figure swung easily through the branches and fell seven meters to the ground. She landed gracefully in a three-point stance, bending her knees and swinging the sword she held out to the side. A moment later a second figure dropped to the ground: the red-brown Felio we'd seen from the ship.

"Who are you to speak of Atieno, Semper, who left to work for Golenti?" the dark-gray female asked, stepping in front of the one I believed to be Penda. I looked back to Semper who, instead of responding, simply stared at the ground.

"Hali, your sister honors us all," Penda spoke, bending at the waist and setting her sword on the ground. She ran gracefully to Semper and pulled her into an embrace. "I have joy at your return, Semper, my daughter."

While Felio don't cry, they do have clues about their emotions in their posture. Semper's tail twitched wildly as she embraced her mother.

"Mother, you stand before a Prime," Hali hissed, tail twitching for a completely different reason as she glared at the embracing women. Her words had their intended impact and Penda pushed away from Semper, holding her at arm's length for a moment before she turned to me.

She straightened, her demeaner shifting from mother to leader in an instant. "Please, Bold Prime. I apologize for my break in etiquette. My breast overflowed with joy at the return of my daughter."

Diplomacy was a skill I'd never been particularly good at. For me, honest and plain speech served where fancy words were unavailable. "Standing naked in this forest, wearing only your sword, you demonstrate the clarity of purpose that only war brings. Between us on this day, let there be no pretense. Semper is an honored member of House of the Bold and it brings me joy to see her reunited with family who we feared dead."

"She is Neema and not strong enough to be Mshindi," Hali growled.

Penda held up her hand to silence her daughter. "Is this true, Semper? Are you Bold?"

"I am, Mother." I wouldn't have been surprised if Semper had lowered her head when she made the admission, but instead, she straightened and looked at Hali with fierce determination. "I am not the child who left to sit in Goboble's shack for pittance. I am not great with House of the Bold, but I have found my place."

"Then today I am glad twice," Penda answered.

The sound of blaster fire interrupted our conversation. I switched focus to my HUD and abruptly sailed up through the trees. Marny had engaged another band of roving Kroerak. Seeing that things were under control, I returned to ground only to find the group of Felio had increased by a score. I wasn't sure what I found more disconcerting, the fact that I hadn't been aware of their presence or that I was now surrounded by so many naked Felio.

"Semper, hand me your blaster rifle and pistol and put your suit back on," I ordered.

"Yes, Prime," she answered. It wasn't lost on me that she used my Abasi designation rather than the ship's, which was Captain.

I'd learned a lot about the construction of blasters and knew that the tuning crystal I'd placed in the pistol could switch to the rifle without much effort. As Semper dressed, I swapped out the crystals and continued the conversation with Penda.

"How many have you lost?" I asked.

"We were six hundred forty and are now four hundred twelve," Penda answered.

"How many Kroerak have you defeated?" I asked.

Penda straightened with pride. "Thirty-two."

"Three have been attributed to me," Hali added. "There is no need for Semper's help."

"That's impressive," I said. "I have only killed a single warrior with a blade. I was lucky and had it not been distracted, I would be dead. But technology will win this war, not skill with a sword. Penda, Adahy is recalling House of Mshindi to Abasi Prime. She asked that I deliver this message and facilitate in any way possible."

"A Felio's greatest weapon is her sword," Hali challenged, interrupting me for a second time.

Annoyance flicked through Penda's whiskers as Hali again spoke out of turn. She started to reprimand her daughter when I stopped her.

"If I may address the fiery Hali, honored Penda," I said.

There wasn't much Penda could do to stop me. As a visiting Prime, I had quite a bit of latitude.

"Of course, Bold Prime," she answered, clearly embarrassed.

"Hali, you are plainspoken and focused as only one with a warrior's heart can be. I respect that," I said. "Today, your focus has not served you well. You see in me a hairless male, someone you could very likely best in hand-to-hand combat. You have missed important details that I haven't shared out of a desire not to embarrass you."

"You cannot embarrass me," Hali chuffed. "I have proven my strength in battle and even you acknowledge that I am superior."

"Right. Possibly superior in hand-to-hand. And let's be clear, I said maybe. I'm not just a pretty face under this svelte grav-suit," I said.

"You also said you would have been killed by the warrior," she said. "I have killed a Kroerak with my sword with no distractions. You have killed one."

"With a sword," I corrected. "By our own hands, my mate and I killed over eleven thousand Kroerak in the field of battle."

I pushed the Iskstar-tuned blaster rifle into Semper's hands.

"How can this be?" Penda asked.

"Long story, but there is a crystal inside this weapon. It is part of the Iskstar, the same thing that turned my eyes blue," I said.

A trio of Felio bounded into the small clearing where we stood surrounded. At least most of the Felio faced out, obviously guarding their leader.

"One moment, please," Penda gestured to the group. A single orange-striped female approached. "Report, daughter of Adahy."

"An operator in a powered suit guards the ship we saw," the Felio answered, attention fixed on Penda. "We believe the operator to be the powerful Bertrand Marny. At her feet lie the husks of fourteen Kroerak. We counted an additional sixty-two Kroerak that lay in plain sight. The one in the powered suit has secured our home."

"Did you observe combat?" Penda asked.

"The powered suit fires a blue energy weapon. It is effective," she said simply.

"It will be as you say, Bold Prime," Penda said, turning back to me. "We will return to our home and establish communication with our Prime."

"I will leave Semper behind to provide support," I said. "Her weapon is as powerful as the one used by Marny James-Bertrand."

"Left behind, Captain?" Semper asked, her tail twitching.

"Temporary assignment, Semper," I added hastily.

"Volunteer assignment," Tabby said, stepping between us. "Say the word and I'll take the assignment. I think Liam wants to give you some time with your family and isn't communicating very well."

"You will not leave me?" Semper asked, clarifying further.

"My promise," Tabby answered, pulling a closed fist to her solar plexus.

"I would stay," Semper answered, her tail twitching in excitement.

"Ada, do you copy?" I called from *Intrepid's* bridge. The quantum comm I'd used to talk to Mom on Petersburg station had been left on *Intrepid* when it crashed. Its twin sat aboard *Hornblower,* which we'd left at the repair station over Abasi Prime. While rare, the quantum devices allowed communication over vast distances, with one half of a perfectly cut crystal inside each.

"Liam, finally. I've been waiting for your call," she said.

"Everything okay?" I asked.

"Looks like Abasi are making good progress in regaining control of the surface," she said. "Kroerak left a lot of destruction behind, but the Iskstar weapons are a big hit."

"What do you mean?"

"Mshindi Prime is using the Iskstar in a propaganda campaign. She's been broadcasting vids showing how they defeated the Kroerak fleet. At the same time, she's quelling the Taji rebellion by having Abasi troops show up with Iskstar weapons to eradicate the Kroerak armies. The Taji are no different than any other group of people. With Kroerak in the equation, they now want peace and they're willing to live under Abasi to have it," she said. "Mshindi Prime is scary good at this. I'm pretty sure you never want to cross her."

"Never crossed my mind. So what's the situation? Can you get out of there?" I asked.

"What's up? Are you guys safe?" Ada asked. "What about my girl, *Intrepid?*"

"We're good. I assume you saw what happened to Petersburg Station and York from the messages we sent," I said.

"That's hard, Liam. I'm sorry," she said.

"Thanks," I acknowledged, never really knowing how to handle emotional conversations.

"Your message said something about giving the York folks an option to go to Mhina with us. Any word on that?" she asked.

"That's why I'm calling," I said. "There's a big vote in a few days. Either way, we're outta here after that."

"Where are we going?"

"Bug hunting."

Chapter 8

BACK IN CHILI

"We are going to eventually go after the bugs, right?" Tabby jabbed her fork into a pile of steaming noodles. She'd been staring at the food, unwilling to look up.

While more circumspect with my angst, I felt the same pressure. Running the Kroerak off from the Santaloo and Tamu star systems was a worthy objective, but we all knew it wasn't permanent. Like the Selich root poisoning, the Kroerak would eventually find a defense against Iskstar and they'd be back to finish what they'd started.

"That's not fair." Unexpectedly, it was Ada who came to my rescue. "Those bugs left behind a giant mess. Abasi almost got overthrown by Taji because of the power vacuum created by battle. York and Petersburg were destroyed."

Having arrived with *Hornblower* only a few hours previous, Ada joined the large group I considered my leadership team to discuss our next steps. In Tabby's defense, the entire conversation had centered on talk of rebuilding York and securing Zuri.

"I get it. Doesn't change anything," Tabby said. "We need to deal with the bugs right now while we have an advantage. This isn't the time to let off the pressure."

Blood rushed in my ears as my stress elevated. The Kroerak fleet had at least two ten-days head start and without a fleet behind us, we couldn't possibly afford to chase them. In our best simulations, *Hornblower* and *Intrepid* could expect to stand against no more than forty ships. Even worse, Abasi intelligence had only tracked the retreating Kroerak fleet for a few jumps before they'd been discovered and forced to flee.

"And what? Leave citizens of York behind to die of starvation?" Bish asked, angrily. "Maybe you haven't noticed, Missy, but we just got kicked back to the stone-age around here. Sure, we're holding back the bugs for now, but it took generations to build York to what it was when you arrived. And don't forget, we accepted you with open arms."

"Enough, Bish," I said, recognizing the familiar pattern of the older man getting himself fired up. "Nobody is abandoning York."

"Speaking of power vacuums. I heard a rumor that Abasi are pulling out of Zuri," Hog Hagarson added. The once heavyset man was hard to recognize due to a starvation-enforced diet. "Those mech-suits of yours do a good job against bugs and I suspect they'd make quite an impression on the bandits that are likely to follow. The fact is if Abasi leave Zuri, the Pogona will move in."

I turned to Hog and nodded thoughtfully. I appreciated his level tone in the tense conversation. He was a reasonable man and wore the mantle of leadership naturally. "House Mshindi will be relocating all its holdings to Abasi Prime," I said. "Mshindi Prime won't admit it publicly but her house took extremely heavy losses. She's consolidating her resources and power. The fact is, Abasi don't have the capacity to stand against the Pogona that are coming."

"Are Abasi worried about a Pogona invasion of Abasi Prime?" Bish asked.

"We are," I said.

"You keep saying *we* when you talk about Abasi," Bish said, his voice challenging. "You know they'll always consider you an outsider. You're a means to an end. Nothing more."

"You're an ass-hat," Tabby spat, slamming her hand onto the table and standing. "You wouldn't be alive without Liam, and all you bring is this petty crap."

"How easy it is for you when the shoe's on the other foot," Bish said. "Remember, *we* saved you when Strix took your ship and left you creditless."

"I don't need this crap," Tabby turned and stormed toward the door. Ada stood to chase her but I held my hand up, freezing Ada in place.

"Bish, probably best if you headed back to camp," I said. "Things are a bit too raw for you still and I need more level-headed advisors."

"Who do you think you are?" Bish stood and pointed a finger at me, allowing the anger he'd been barely holding at bay to surface again. "You're nothing here. Barely more than a kid. I don't take orders from you."

Wordlessly, Marny stood and straightened her vac-suit. "Mr. Bishop, I'll remind you that you are aboard House of the Bold's vessel, *Hornblower.* Liam Hoffen is not only Prime of this Abasi house, but he is also the captain of this ship. You were invited as a guest and remain aboard at his pleasure. You will be escorted from this ship and I strongly suggest you do not provide resistance."

I watched the confusion in Bish's face as he realized just how serious Marny was when she grabbed his arm firmly. I felt for the man. He'd seen his friends and neighbors die from bugs and starvation, and was struggling to rectify how much his universe had shifted.

"Hog? Are you going to just sit there?" he asked, his anger turning to pain.

"Could I walk him out?" Hog implored, gently placing a hand on Bish's other arm. Marny nodded, releasing him.

"We'll break for ten." I appreciated having a moment where I might be allowed to take care of my own hothead.

"Thank you," Hog said.

I had to use my HUD to track Tabby down, but I found her in a darkened hallway, one deck below where we'd been meeting, with back against the wall and knees up. She looked away and wiped at her cheeks, too proud to admit she was crying. I placed my back against the wall and slid down next to her, wrapping a protective arm over her shoulders while I pulled her to me. We were past the point of words. We'd been through so much together that she had a permanent pass from me on things like storming out of a meeting. I was only concerned about how she was feeling.

She buried her face against my shoulder and I stroked her head as the dam of tears broke. "We'll get 'em, Tabbs," I said, comfortingly. "We've gotta help these people first, but we'll get 'em if it's the last thing we do."

"He's such a jackass," Tabby said.

"Kind of reminds me of your Dad." It was a true statement. Tabby's dad and Bishop had a lot in common as both were bright men who tended to say what was on their mind, not caring how it impacted those around them. This elicited a chuckle, even as she continued to cry.

"I'm not going back in there," Tabby said, finally. "I can't pretend to care about all this. Nobody gets it, Liam. York doesn't matter. Abasi Prime doesn't matter. Those bugs have killed tens of billions. How many have they slaughtered while we've been having our little pity party here?"

"Are you having more dreams?"

After my encounter with the Iskstar crystal, I had dreams of civilizations that had been destroyed by Kroerak. I had no way to verify the veracity of the dreams, but like Tabby, I believed they were sent by Iskstar to show us the extent of Kroerak atrocities. Since arriving back in the Santaloo and Tamu star systems, my dreams had stopped, but Tabby still thrashed around in the night. When questioned, she denied the dreams, but I wasn't convinced.

She nodded her head, which still rested on my shoulder. "It's just so horrible," she said, fumbling with something at her waist before pulling out a sliver of blue-glowing Iskstar crystal. I felt the pull of the crystal and reached for it. Unlike Tabby, I'd decided to no longer keep a crystal on my person. She'd talked about doing the same, but somehow always reverted.

"I might know where a smaller fleet is," Tabby said.

"Kroerak?" I asked.

"Yes. I'd like to take a ship and check it out."

"By yourself?" I asked.

"I was thinking of taking *Intrepid* and a small crew. It's just ... you're so busy with helping all these people. I get it. But I have to know if my dreams are real or not," she said.

"What if I put Ada in charge of the mission and let her pick a crew?"

"You don't trust me," she said, stiffening.

"Not really." I never wanted to lie to Tabby. Even if it caused short-term problems for us, I knew Tabby needed the bald truth. "When you see bug, you think smash. I need you to come back, and Ada will make that happen."

I didn't realize I was holding my breath until I found Tabby's lips on my own. Her kiss conveyed a desperate urgency. It twisted my gut, as I realized just how broken the two of us were at this moment. I wondered if we'd ever feel normal again.

"Come with me," Tabby said, standing. "I want you. Now."

"People are waiting for me," I said.

"Fine," she said, pushing on a hatch in the darkened hallway and pulling me into a small room. The strong smell of cleanser gave me a clue to the room's function as Tabby disrobed in the dim light.

"Now?" I asked, already knowing the answer as my mind shifted focus to Tabby's naked form. My eyes traced the slim and familiar curves of her athletic form. My question became irrelevant as I reached for her.

"Doesn't look like it's going to be a problem," she answered, pulling at my suit.

"CAP, YOU JOINING US?" Marny called over comms.

"I'm here," I answered, stepping through the hatch into the large conference room, grateful she'd waited a few minutes longer than I'd originally requested.

"Liam, on behalf of York, I apologize for Bish's attitude. He's had a rough run of things. We all have," Hog said, giving me his best earnest look.

"No apology necessary," I said. "We've all seen things, done things, and endured things that no person should have to. Best answer is to let those who can, continue. We have issues that need addressing and we'll push on."

"Well said," Hog answered.

"Liam, what are your plans?" Mom asked. "The people from Petersburg are worried, just like those of York."

"Let's clear up a couple of things," I said. "I've had some of this conversation with different people, but I don't think I've had it with everyone. The Mars corporation Loose Nuts was dissolved and replaced by a new Abasi entity, House of the Bold. I am the leader, with Marny as number two, Ada as tertiary, and so on. Further, House of the Bold has been given the responsibility for the entire Mhina star system. This means we have the authority to collect taxes and must provide protection to those who reside there."

"Isn't that system cut off from Confederation of Planets by a blockade?" Hog asked.

"The blockade was in place to stop the Kroerak from returning," I said. "It has been dismantled. As long as we keep our system clear of Kroerak, the blockade will remain defunct. The fact is, there are currently few ships that could man the blockade."

"I'd heard this, but really? Abasi gave you an entire solar system?" Hog pushed again.

"It's not a gift," I said. "House of the Bold is Abasi and there are two types of ownership for a house such as ours. The first is total, permanent ownership like the land Mshindi has only a hundred kilometers from here. The second is much more like responsibility. We collect taxes, enforce laws and provide protection for the remainder of it. To be honest, it's a daunting task."

"For an entire solar system," Hog repeated.

"Which has exactly one inhabitable moon – Dorf – in orbit around a gas planet," I said.

"Two," Nick corrected.

"Not really," I answered. "J-F99214-E-07 has a breathable atmosphere, but its average annual temperature is two degrees. Almost nothing grows there."

"We've already received inquiry from the Musi," Nick said.

"About oh-seven?" I asked, remembering that we'd seen a couple of towns on the arctic moon when we'd first arrived in Dwingeloo. They had resembled rat's nests found on space stations and didn't seem like any place sentients might want to live. We hadn't found anything alive there, just great piles of bones. Turned out, the inhabitants had been a burrowing, meter-tall, mouse-faced species called Musi. All who had failed to escape had become a Kroerak food source almost two hundred stans before we'd been there.

"The Musi live on the fringe of society," Nick said. "Most sentients don't trust them."

"For good reason," Hog said. "Musi don't honor their contracts unless forced to do so."

"They have no place to live," Nick said. "And the planet has little mineral value."

"They don't honor contracts. Why would we get involved with them?" I asked.

"Because they're already there," he answered.

"What do you mean, already there? On whose authority?" I asked.

"No one's," Nick answered. "But Musi have been migrating to Oh-Seven ever since the Kroerak cleared out eighteen days ago."

I rubbed my temples. "Fantastic."

"We'd be better off with a treaty than trying to figure out how to remove them," Nick said.

"Doesn't sound like there's much we can do at this moment," I replied with an annoyed shake of my head. "Let's work on things we can. Ada, I need you to run a mission."

"You're doing it again, Liam," she said.

"True, but you'll like this one," I said, trying to win her with a smile. "Tabby believes she has a lead on a Kroerak infestation. I need you to take *Intrepid* and check it out."

"Crew?" she asked.

"You pick," I said, flipping a quantum comm crystal to her. "Roby should have her sealed up and ready for flight by 0400."

"What are my mission parameters?"

"We don't know if Tabby's intel is good. If we did, we'd take *Hornblower*. But for right now, *Hornblower* is too important here. You'll be loaded up with a couple of *Iskstar* tuned turrets, but this is intel gathering. I need cool heads on this, which is why you're in charge," I said.

"Tabby's okay with this?"

"She is," I said. "Don't mistake me, though. Tabby is raw. She'll push you toward combat."

"Targets of opportunity?"

"You're in command, Ada," I said. "I trust your judgement."

"Jonathan, Sendrei, Roby, Semper ..." She continued to rattle off a crew of twenty. I smiled as she did. She'd anticipated the possibility and was ready for me.

"Godspeed," I said, mimicking something I'd heard both Sendrei and Marny say in the past.

Ada nodded, her eyes twinkling with mischief as she stood. "I request my leave in that case, Prime. I've a ship to get ready."

"You're dismissed, Captain Chen." I embraced her as she walked toward the door to leave. "Keep my girls safe, okay?" I whispered in her ear.

"You counting me in that?" Ada asked, waggling her eyebrows.

"What? Of course," I replied, not thinking it through completely. I quickly realized she might have been referring to the 'my girls' part instead of the 'staying safe' piece. "You're a wicked woman, Ada Chen."

"Glad you finally see that." She gave my bottom a pinch – which caused me no end of confusion. Fortunately, she left the conference room before I could dwell on it further.

"What are you proposing? That we move York to the Mhina system?" Hog asked.

"There's not much to move," Mez Rigdon, York's sheriff, added.

"Most of the homesteads on the other side of Quail Hill are completely ransacked."

"There are twelve hundred citizens," Hog said. "We have more than you'd think. *Hornblower* is plenty big, but she can't get it all."

"Not in one trip," I agreed. "It's up to you all. If you come to Dorf, you'll be under Abasi rule – specifically House of the Bold rule. That might be hard for some folks to take."

"The moon you're calling Dorf, is named Kito," Nick said. "The planet is Elea, unless you plan to rename them."

"Can we do that?" I asked.

Nick rolled his eyes. He knew me so well. "No. Call it Kito, please."

"Let me get this straight," Hog said, ignoring Nick and me. "You're saying you'll give us a ride to this Kito moon and you become what? Our king?"

"It's not a fair comparison," Nick said. "He'd no more be your king than Mshindi Prime is your queen now. You'll owe House of Bold taxes, just like you do House Mshindi. We'll be responsible for providing protection, just like Mshindi does."

"Mshindi's protection hasn't been very good," Mez Rigdon spoke up. "I'm not just talking about the invasion. We've mostly been on our own."

"When we visited Kito," I started. "We found four cities evenly spaced around a large lake. Around each of the cities we saw farms with equipment that had been stored neatly away. I have no idea what shape any of this is in because we didn't stop long enough to inspect anything. My guess is that after two centuries, it's in bad shape."

"Might not be as bad as you think," Nick interjected. "Felio building materials should last well past a couple of centuries. With replicators, we should be able to replace whatever rot has destroyed. Hog, I don't even see what the counterargument is. An ancient city with no bugs is worth a lot more than anything you've got here."

"I hear you clucking, big chicken," Hog answered. "One of the things we liked about living here was that Mshindi mostly left us alone. Aside from the taxes, that is. I understand what Mez was saying about security. Fact is, for almost two centuries, Mshindi hasn't allowed anyone to build next to us. That's been good security. It'll be hard for us to give up our independence."

"Then don't," I said. "You pick a city and your town council manages it. Only things we want a say in are taxes, law making, and real estate purchases."

"Hold on, I've looked at York's charter," Nick said. "They basically follow Mars Protectorate law with a few modifications. We should agree to what is on your books right now."

"You'd do that?" Hog asked. "Give us a town and let us manage it?"

"It's not a gift and we'll reserve one percent of it for House of the Bold," Nick said. "You get to manage it as long as you pay taxes and keep the peace."

"No real estate ownership for our people?" Hog asked.

Once again, I was glad to have Nick at the table, negotiating for us.

"I've thought about this some. My ideas aren't fully thought out, but here's where I'm at," Nick said. "What if you claim up to four times the space you had in York? These claims would be temporary for the first five years. After that, they become permanent ownership but will be subject to taxes."

"Curtis Long would love that," Mez Rigdon said, bringing up the name of a farmer who controlled a significant portion of land. I could see the inequity of allowing him to claim four times that much space within the city.

"Farmers. Right," Nick said. "Like I said, I haven't thought it through entirely. I'd say it becomes a problem for the town council. You could get everyone to submit their requests and then review them all next to each other. If you find inequity, you fix it then. For example, maybe you require the land be of similar use. I've done preliminary calculations. Each of the cities on Kito is at least fifty times the land-mass of York. There will be a lot of vacant space, even if each of you take four times what you had before."

"Shouldn't real estate taxes typically go back to the city?" Hog asked.

"Ninety percent," Nick said. "House of the Bold will take ten percent. Bold will collect a value-added tax. City will get ten percent, Bold will get ninety. We'll keep the tax-rate down to encourage people to report correctly."

"No one will have any credits," Mom said. "Can't pay taxes with money we don't have."

"Says the woman who is going to represent House of the Bold in all this," I said.

"I'm asking for the people of York," she said, which earned her an appreciative grunt from Hog.

"Look, Bish is right. York took us in when we needed it most," I said. "Shoe is on the other foot now. York needs us and we're going to make this work."

Nick looked at me and raised an eyebrow, cutting me off. "To make this work, York has to be self-sufficient. While we have impressive credits for a small company, we could burn that up in a single project. We're looking for partners, not employees."

"Bish doesn't believe you'll stick around long enough to make this work," Hog said. "Way he sees it; the last time you ran off, Kroerak invaded and killed half our town."

"That's an ad hominem attack. Kroerak were coming regardless of our actions," Nick said. "Besides, you won't be negotiating with either me or Liam."

"Who then?"

"I'm hoping Mrs. H. will do it," Nick said, looking to Mom. She'd successfully run Petersburg station and I was certain she was up to the task.

"At what point did I become your go-to administrator?" Mom asked.

"Will you do it?" Nick asked.

She raised her eyebrows. "I assume you'll stay involved, just like you did with Petersburg?"

"Of course, Mrs. H," he answered.

"Let me work out details with Hog. We should also get Bish back into the process," she said. "Let me guess, you want to lift off tomorrow."

"Seems premature. York hasn't agreed to any of this," I said.

"I'm not sure you understand your leverage here, son," Hog said. "We have little choice in the matter. I'm just trying to figure out what you want from us."

I gave him a grin. "Hog, that's easy. Help us create an environment where Patty can be back in the restaurant business."

"She does make some damn fine chili," he said, chuckling.

"I think Cap's been hoping for more of those cinnamon rolls," Marny added.

"That hurts just to think about," I said.

"I'll talk to Bish and the council tonight," he said. "If you wouldn't mind sending over the maps for those four cities. I suspect there'll be quite a lot of interest in your offer."

"Done."

Chapter 9

IN THE REARVIEW

"This is sloppy," Ada snapped, clinging to the side of *Intrepid's* hull and inspecting the damage caused by a Kroerak lance wave. "I want stealth armor over the top of all of this."

"She'll hold atmo," Roby defended. "And we can't do much more than a stealth skin. Even that would take two hours with the replicator hive. I don't know if we're allowed to re-task the machines or if we even have materials. Besides, Kroerak see right through our stealth."

"Mr. Bishop, I picked you for this crew because I believe in your ability to think creatively," Ada answered. "You have fourteen hours to complete this task. If you are not up to it, please let me know."

"If I may," Jonathan offered over the comm channel Ada reserved for her own command crew. "In reviewing data-streams from the sortie into the Mshindi compound, we believe a large supply of the necessary raw material is available. I have been in contact with the Mshindi inventory console. They have recently lowered the price of their material – we believe, in preparation for departure."

Ada raised her eyebrows and didn't have to wait long for Roby's response.

"Captain, I need you to authorize a re-task of the replicator hive," Roby said.

"Authorized." As third in House of the Bold, Ada had theoretical boundaries to her power that she was ready to test. "I want this mess of a hull patch taken out and cleaned up. Last I saw, Jester Ripples was hanging on Liam's leg. I suspect he'd appreciate it if we gave our little frog friend something to occupy his mind."

"Aye, aye, Captain," Roby answered somberly.

"Is there a problem, Mr. Bishop?"

"You were a lot more fun when you weren't Captain."

"Roby, you're an amazing natural engineer. You took shortcuts here because you're only considering Kroerak. What you failed to grasp is that this part of the universe just became a lot more dangerous."

"Nothing's more dangerous than a Kroerak invasion," Roby pushed back, crossing his arms defiantly and settling in for a debate.

"Excel at the tasks given to you, Mr. Bishop," Ada answered. "When you come to an understanding of why your sloppy approach put us in danger, please set aside time so we can discuss it."

"How was I supposed to know you wanted this to look perfect?"

"Add that to the list for us to talk about," she said coolly, releasing her hold on *Intrepid*. With her grav-suit, Ada gracefully glided around to the main airlock, fifteen meters above the ground.

Intrepid was primarily a single-deck ship with its heavily-armored bridge set just aft of center. Located forward were crew bunks for up to sixty souls, a large galley, mess hall, exercise gymnasium and what used to be an observation deck atop a large cargo hold.

Turning forward toward the gym, Ada marveled at the damage caused by the Kroerak lance wave. Having watched a replay using the combat data-streams, she'd seen Silver Hoffen, Liam's mom, turn *Intrepid* into the wave, sacrificing the one part of *Intrepid* that had the least impact on survivability for the majority of her crew. It was a maneuver Ada knew she was physically capable of, but one she was terrified she wouldn't consider when her time came.

"You are a sexy beast in that pirate getup," Tabby said, slapping

Ada on the butt as she caught her from behind. "We need to get you back into a man-rich environment so someone other than Liam can appreciate all of this." Tabby waved her hands together, outlining an imaginary hour-glass, while waggling her eyebrows suggestively.

Initially annoyed at Tabby's lack of decorum, Ada's irritation immediately dissipated at her best friend's perhaps too-close-for-comfort observation. Early on, Ada had developed a crush on Liam when he'd taken her in. While she had no illusions that Tabby and Liam would ever separate, she still felt something for the man.

"I don't know, maybe you've got it wrong. Maybe it's Liam who should be worried. Maybe you're all the man I need," Ada said, huskily. "You're so sweaty. So strong."

"Point to Chen," Tabby laughed. They had a long-running competition of saying inappropriate things to each other and Ada had definitely won this one. A moment later, a flutter of discomfort ran through her and she looked back at the smaller woman. "You are joking. Right?"

"I'm going to count that as two points," Ada answered, turning serious. "How much more workout time do you have? I wanted to talk to you about the mission. I can jog with you. I'm surprised you're not outside, hunting bugs and all."

Tabby set off at a pace most would consider a hard run and Ada followed, directing her AI to pace the grav-suit a meter back. "Too many of them," she said. "I'd spend all my time in combat and my legs are aching for a workout."

"How many kilos are you adding?" Ada asked. Tabby's synthetic muscles were too strong for her to gain meaningful exercise by simply running unencumbered.

"Grav suit is only adding forty kilograms. Seriously, I'm in horrible shape," she said.

"Look pretty good from back here," Ada quipped, mischievously.

"Man, you really are a horn dog," Tabby said.

"What do you know about the system we're headed to?" Ada asked. While she enjoyed the playful banter, she had issues that needed to be worked through.

"Four jumps from Mhina," Tabby said.

"There's another wormhole in Mhina?" Ada asked.

"That's the good news. If my dreams are real, the wormhole will be there. Otherwise it's a short trip."

"Are the systems in between occupied?"

"Not clear."

"What about the system we're headed to? What's their level of technology? How are they standing up against the Kroerak?"

"I saw a lot of firepower and heavily entrenched positions. But they're fighting each other more than Kroerak," Tabby said. "I didn't see many Kroerak: twenty ships maybe."

"What's that about?"

"I guess we'll find out," Tabby answered.

Ada slowed as they passed the entrance to the bridge and allowed Tabby to continue without her. Her friend didn't have much information and there was a lot of work left to do. "I'll catch up with you at breakfast."

"Copy that," Tabby called back.

"Captain on the bridge," Sendrei announced as Ada entered.

"As you were," Ada answered. "Gunny, how are we for ordnance?"

"We've replicated an Iskstar harness for three of our blasters and I'm pulling four missiles from *Hornblower* to top off our load. We've transferred fuel and forty thousand credits in precious minerals for trade," he answered. "I've also started drilling the fire-control team. Thanks for bringing Clingman and Brockette along. Nice to have a couple of vets in the mix."

"Marny might not love me for it, but we can't afford to make this a training cruise," Ada answered. "Jonathan, how are primary systems?"

She sat in the elevated captain's chair toward the aft of the bridge and pulled up the holo-display in front of her.

"We're looking into a number of small system failures most likely caused by the abrupt landing on Zuri. With functional replicators and transit time, we believe each of these items to be addressable," Jonathan answered. "We will require manual assistance for many of the repairs and request two hours of down-time in zero-g to resolve the repair on your starboard panel." Ada turned her attention to a wire-framed animation of a repair to the armor just beneath a grav-repulsor plate.

"Sendrei, please coordinate with Jonathan on personnel," Ada said.

"Roger that, Captain," Sendrei answered.

"READY FOR SOME BREAKFAST, SLEEPING BEAUTY?" Tabby asked, nudging Ada awake from where she sat, still in the captain's chair.

"What?" Ada's eyes flew open and she tried to straighten, but instead brought a hand to her back, wincing in pain. "What time is it?"

"0600," Tabby answered. "Everyone else was afraid to wake you up. Did you know Garcia was such a good cook? Is that why you brought him along?"

"Garcia? Jose?" Ada asked, her mind still spinning on the details of repairs and last-minute decisions. Her sleep had been anything but restful. "The other pilot?"

"Did you bring a bunch of Garcias aboard?" Tabby asked.

"Stop already," Ada admonished. "My brain hurts."

Tabby handed Ada a mouth-fresh strip and a cup of tea as she helped her from the chair. Setting the cup aside for a moment, Ada leaned forward to stretch her back and pull the dreadlocks from her eyes.

"What's that smell?" Ada asked, as Tabby turned her toward the front of the ship instead of aft, toward the wardroom.

"Seriously, the man has mad cooking skills," Tabby said. "Apparently he had a whole chicken thing going in York and traded for enough eggs to get us going."

"That's not eggs I'm smelling," Ada said.

"Bacon. The livestock was scattered, but the Kroerak didn't kill 'em. They've rounded up most of the escapees and Jose twisted some arms so we could have fresh meat for our trip."

"Meat?" Ada wrinkled her nose.

"It's bacon. Trust me," Tabby said.

Having skipped dinner the night before, Ada's stomach demanded attention.

"Attenshun!" Sendrei announced as Ada entered the crew mess hall. Ada had assembled twenty-eight crewmembers for their mission and while she didn't know them all personally, she'd selected each person carefully.

"As you were," she said, returning the salute she was still uncomfortable with.

The external repairs had been delayed by her insistence on fixing the stealth armor, but she was pleased to discover that Roby had pushed through and completed his work. He'd even asked Jonathan to review the repairs. Catching Roby's eye, Ada thought he looked as tired as she felt. She gave him a nod of approval and mouthed 'thank you' across the busy room.

"My friends, today we're sailing into the unknown in our continuing push to rid the galaxy of Kroerak. I appreciate the effort required to get us to this point. Since Mr. Garcia has gone to all the trouble of making a fantastic meal for us, I won't bore you all with a long speech. To *Intrepid*!" She raised her tea cup into the air and was rewarded with a return salute from the crew.

"Captain." A man with dark hair approached, holding a plate with a small biscuit, scrambled eggs and a single strip of red-brown meat.

"Mr. Garcia, thank you for a great send-off. I didn't realize you were a cook as well as a pilot," Ada answered.

"My flight skills have mostly been deliveries to and from Petersburg," he answered. "I hope my skills have not been overstated. I do not consider myself capable of sailing a ship such as this."

Ada accepted the plate and gestured to the end of the table, inviting the man to sit with her. "Do you believe you could get us to orbit just like you did with your freight runs?"

"Aye, I would not expect that to be overly difficult," Garcia answered. "I have been reviewing combat data-streams. I would be most concerned to be in that situation."

"Good," Ada answered. "Honest assessment is critical for advancement. I placed the standard Mars Protectorate curriculum on ship handling into your message queue. Get started with that and consider me your mentor. If you have a question, ask. Be prepared. If I feel you're being lazy, I'll go hard on you."

"I am anything but lazy," Garcia replied stiffly.

"And you know how to stand up to power," Ada said. "You'll make an excellent pilot, Jose."

I THUMBED my ring as I watched *Intrepid* lift skyward. The small, matching quantum crystal chip that my engagement ring shared with Tabby's was too often the only link between us. I smiled when my ring throbbed momentarily as she returned my message. I regretted splitting the team, but knew it was the right answer. I had to get the citizens of York to a safe place and we couldn't afford to ignore leads on Kroerak activity.

"They're good together," Marny said, clapping me on the shoulder, pulling me closer. "Ada and Tabby make each other better."

I brought my hand up and rested it on Marny's back. "Like you and Nick make me better," I said. "I just wish I didn't have to watch them sail away without us."

"Cap, I had to watch you and Tabby sail away just one time to understand that it wasn't acceptable," she said. "Tabby's different. If you ask me, I'd say the only way you keep her is to make sure she has room to fly free."

"I can't argue with that," I said. "She'd resent me if I tried to keep her back."

"Been looking for you two." Hog Hagarson's voice boomed through the courtyard in front of Nick's warehouse where *Intrepid* had just been sitting next to *Hornblower*. Even though the battle cruiser outmassed the frigate by ten times, the courtyard felt empty.

I turned to find Hog, Bish and Mom all walking quickly toward us.

"You're all up early," I said, pushing *Intrepid's* departure from my mind.

"Burning daylight," Bishop said.

"Can I assume York and Petersburg came to a decision last night?" I asked.

I'd decided to stay away from the giant bonfire they'd hosted. Instead, I'd taken a shift helping Roby manufacture and install armor on *Intrepid* so he could meet Ada's deadline. I appreciated having gotten the chance to talk with him. Ada had injured his pride and he needed help understanding where he'd gotten off track.

"We have some modifications we'd like to discuss," Bish said.

"But it doesn't change anything," Hog added quickly. "The decision was unanimous and that includes old Bish here. Don't let his surly disposition bury the lead."

"I hate it when you do that, Hog," Bish said, turning on his friend. "We'll never be in a better position to negotiate than we are right now, but you've gone and given it away."

"Is it something we can work out once we get there?" I asked, looking at Mom. I was exhausted from working on *Intrepid* the night before and wasn't up for a negotiation.

"We can," she answered, with some exasperation in her voice. "Like I tried to explain last night, Bish, this won't be the end of the items we need to work out. House of the Bold wants to create an environment where the people of York will thrive on Kito."

"Not much we can do now," Bish said sourly, glaring at Hog.

"That's the spirit," Hog answered, clapping him on the back.

"Like I was saying before," Nick said. "We've plenty of room for everyone. We'll have limits on items that can be moved on the first trip. We'll spread folks out across the lower four decks. We'll need to keep livestock on Deck Six, though."

"Livestock?" I asked, recalling a particularly nasty delivery that had left our sloop, *Hotspur,* completely soiled.

"What do you think thirteen-hundred people eat?" Bish asked, still annoyed.

I tugged a mealbar from a pouch and waved it at him. "Spent most of my life eating nothing but these. Turns out, they're quite a lot cleaner than your livestock."

"Deck Six is mostly open and we can construct partitions easily," Nick said. "As it is, we're seven days travel to the Santaloo-Tamu wormhole entrance. Add another day to get to the Tamu-Mhina wormhole and three more past that. We'll only be sailing for a total of two-hundred eighty hours."

"Forget about food, that's a lot of O2 and water," I said, thinking about providing for thirteen hundred people and their livestock.

"*Hornblower* has a water splitter," Nick said. "We've been using O2 crystals because of power usage, but with enough fuel, the splitter can easily keep up with atmo demands."

"I assume you've already done the calculations," I said.

"I have," Nick said. "Our biggest burn will be escaping Zuri since we'll be fully loaded. We should have between fifteen and twenty percent reserve."

"Didn't we take on fuel at the Abasi ship yard?" I asked.

"We did," Nick answered. "*Hornblower* isn't really designed for atmospheric entry. The fuel usage is considerable, especially over-loaded like we'll be."

"What's the quickest we can get underway?" I asked.

"Two ten-days," Bish answered, before Nick could.

"You have ninety-six hours," I answered, hotly.

"You can't ..." Bish objected.

Hog put one hand up, interrupting the irascible old man. "We'll get started on it right away."

"NICK, WE NEED MORE," I urged.

Hornblower's massive engines were generating an enormous amount of power, all of which was being directed into the gravity repulsors. So far, we were making quite a racket, shaking a lot and generating a giant cloud of dust and debris. What we weren't doing was gaining elevation.

"Hang on, Liam," Nick answered. "Gravity systems take a while to reach peak."

My eyes were glued to a virtual gauge that showed an altimeter. "That's it," I said, breathing tightly as the gauge suddenly shifted from twelve hundred thirty-two meters to twelve hundred thirty-three. A warning light showed as *Hornblower* listed to port and slid twenty meters over, crashing into Zuri's thick undergrowth. A screeching sound reverberated through the ship as metal scraped against heavy vegetation. Slowly, I adjusted starboard, migrating a small amount of power portside. I'd had plenty of experience moving heavy loads and knew that fast adjustments brought problems of their own.

"Armor is holding, Cap," Marny reported, calmly.

"We're at one-hundred two percent," Nick said. "I've only got a little left."

"I'm going to need it," I answered.

Hornblower's port slide slowed and we started moving back. We didn't have a great deal of room before we'd start hitting the hill behind us, but I held steady, not ready to make adjustments.

"Do it," I hissed under my breath as suddenly we gained two, then three, then five and then twenty meters. "Go, baby!" I urged.

Hornblower responded and continued to rise, accelerating upward at a rate I'd hardly be willing to brag about – but it was progress.

"Nick, how are we doing for fuel?" I asked.

"We're having a yard-sale," he answered, adopting a term often used to describe when a miner decided to call it quits and leave, selling everything he had at ridiculous discounts. "But we're good."

"All hands, this is Captain Hoffen," I called over public address once we'd reached fifty thousand meters. "We'll be switching from gravity systems to main engines in five minutes. I'll ask everyone to have a seat, the transition can be a bit abrupt."

I sat back in the pilot's chair I'd commandeered for lift-off and allowed my shoulders to relax. The responsibility for so many people weighed heavily on me and I looked forward to the relative safety of space flight.

"Almost there, Cap," Marny offered from her workstation.

"Copy that," I agreed.

A few minutes later I accepted my AI's offer to provide a shipwide P.A. system countdown from ten. As the count hit zero, I dialed down the engine power, causing an uneasy feeling in the pit of my stomach as we lurched downward. As we fell, I maneuvered the controls so we rotated, bringing the powerful engines beneath us. With a light touch, I powered up, watching as the acceleration vectors relative to Zuri shifted from a bright red – which indicated falling – back through lighter shades until they turned blue and finally green.

"That's my girl," I said, patting the forward bulkhead lovingly.

"Cap, we have a fleet of Pogona-flagged ships at forty thousand kilometers," Marny warned.

"Head down to fire-control," I instructed. "Stolzman, you're needed on the bridge."

"Aye, aye, Cap," Marny answered.

"Reporting for duty."

Ken Stolzman was the only remaining pilot from Munay's crew. While low on actual flight-hours, he was technically qualified for the helm and had chosen to stay behind when Munay had absconded with *Fleet Afoot* to chase the Kroerak. His voice surprised me as I hadn't realized he was on the bridge, although I had been pretty focused.

"Take number-two spot," I ordered.

"Aye, aye," he answered, slipping into the second pilot's chair.

"Helm is yours, Mr. Stolzman," I said.

"Helm is mine," he repeated.

While against my instincts, I knew I could hardly command *Hornblower* if I was also piloting her. I walked calmly back to the Captain's chair. While I might have hoped to escape Zuri without conflict, in the back of my mind, I knew better.

Chapter 10

NOT IN KANSAS ANYMORE

MHINA SYSTEM, INTREPID

"Captain Chen, we have two freighters on our heading at forty thousand kilometers," Jonathan announced. "There are also seven smaller vessels operating within a radius of thirty-five thousand kilometers."

Twenty hours previous, *Intrepid* entered the Tamu star system from the Santaloo-Tamu wormhole and had been on hard-burn to the Tamu-Mhina wormhole end-point where the Confederation of Planets' blockade had once been. At forty thousand kilometers, Ada knew they were in no immediate danger and she awaited sensor updates on the holographic displays to her left.

"There's quite a bit of debris from the battle," Tabby said. "I'm taking manual control."

"Copy that, Tabby," Ada answered, allowing her eyes to trace the fantastic amount of rubble left behind months ago during the battle between the Confederation of Planets' fleet and the invading Kroerak. Even after all that time, arcing electrical circuits and small gas leaks were detectable in the broken husks.

"Frak, this was bad," Tabby said, her chest constricting as she nudged *Intrepid* onto a course recommended by the ship's collision avoidance system. "Do you think there are people still alive in there?"

“You doing okay?” Ada asked, cognizant of Tabby’s own close call when the Mars Protectorate battle cruiser she’d been on had been destroyed, leaving her near dead among the wreckage.

“You mean, am I going to turn into a freak because of some crazy flashback?” Tabby asked with an edge to her voice.

“Well, not to put too fine a point on it, but yes,” Ada answered. The two women had a kinship that only those who’d been through traumatic events and survived could share. Tabby grunted a chuckle at Ada’s bald-faced admission.

“Point to Chen,” Tabby answered. “Suppose they’re finding anyone?”

“In fact, they are,” Jonathan answered. “To date, the Confederation rescue mission has recovered over nineteen hundred of its citizens, including six species and nine governments. Most, as you might expect, have been Felio.”

"Those two freighters just passed through the wormhole," Ada said. "I doubt they're part of any rescue mission. What in Saturn could they be doing? There's no one in Mhina to trade with."

"The wormhole has been unguarded for two ten-days," Sendrei answered. "And therefore, so have been the cities on Kito. I believe Liam suggested the cities were mothballed when the Abasi left. There would be significant capital value in the material left behind."

"Looters?" Ada asked.

"Yes and they've a considerable lead on us," Sendrei said.

"Well, frak," Tabby answered, "those freighters aren't going to outrun *Intrepid.*"

"If the wormhole has been unguarded for two ten-days, there's been enough time," Sendrei said. "In my experience as a Naval officer, looters are by far the most efficient at taking advantage. It is particularly disheartening to see their disregard for what has been hard-earned by others."

"Ada, we need to at least check it out," Tabby said.

"If our understanding of orbital trajectories is correct from our previous, brief visit," Jonathan said, "such a redirection would potentially add seven days to our journey."

"Can you imagine how much those freighters could haul?" Tabby asked.

"I'm with you on this, Tabby," Ada answered. "When we clear the wormhole, we'll make way for Kito directly. If I recall, there were a number of fuel dumps on the moon's surface. We can make up time by using a Schedule-A burn rate and refuel there."

"Now you're talking," Tabby said and accelerated *Intrepid* through the debris field toward the Tamu-Mhina wormhole.

"There is risk that the fuel left behind has been a primary target of the looters," Jonathan uncharacteristically argued. "The remainder of the mission will be in jeopardy if this is the case."

"Understood," Ada answered. "We have thirteen hundred souls depending on us for survival. I'm not about to let scallywags and cutthroats steal their future."

As captain, Ada had the last word. They sailed in uneasy quiet as Tabby picked her way through to the wormhole.

"Roby, we're approaching the wormhole. Can you give me status on the transition engines?" Tabby asked when they crossed the invisible boundary where transition was possible.

"I copy," Roby answered. "Wormhole drives are all green. We'll transition on captain's mark."

"Sendrei, is fire-control ready? Could have Kroerak or just about anything on the other side," Ada said.

"Fire-control is standing by," Sendrei answered.

"Roby, I want you ready to bring us back to Tamu if we run into a trap. Do you copy?" Ada asked.

He responded snappily. "Aye, aye, Captain. I'll be ready."

"Ms. Masters, I want combat burn on transition."

"Roger that, Captain," Tabby answered.

"Transition at your leisure, Mr. Bishop," Ada announced.

Ada blinked away the queasy feeling associated with transition through the wormhole. She nodded with satisfaction as she was pushed back into her chair, the baritone-throated hum of *Intrepid's* massive engines momentarily overcoming her suit's sound cancellation waves.

"We're taking fire," Tabby announced a moment before the ping of blaster fire on the hull became recognizable.

"Return fire?" Sendrei asked.

Ada could see the firing solution Sendrei had planned on the two ships. Between transition and combat burn, the sensors were having difficulty dialing in details and were currently only showing the mass of each ship. She had to make a split-second decision to jump back or stay in system. The vessels were close to that of *Intrepid,* which could mean they were only outnumbered two-to-one if they were frigates, but Ada didn't believe that was the case.

"Hold," she answered, more interested in the fact that *Intrepid* had received no injury from the exchange. So far, the attacking vessels closely matched the two freighters they'd followed through the wormhole.

"Seriously?" Tabby asked, annoyed, unpredictably pushing *Intrepid* hard to starboard.

"Give me sixty clicks separation," Ada answered.

"Copy," Tabby grunted.

Not unexpectedly, the distance between *Intrepid* and the two vessels rapidly increased, and even though *Intrepid* continued to take fire, her armor sluffed off the bolts.

"Tabby, keep separation but back off the combat burn," Ada ordered.

"Aye, aye."

"*Intrepid,* hail those ships," Ada ordered. "Unidentified ships. You're firing on an Abasi warship in Abasi territory. You will desist and submit to turret lockdown."

Dropping from combat-burn, the sensors quickly resolved. The two vessels firing on them were indeed the freighters they'd seen in the Tamu system. Each ship had a small turret that had little chance of damaging *Intrepid.*

"What in the frak were they thinking?" Tabby asked.

"*Intrepid*, this is *Slefid.* I am Captain Grossmek. Our weapons system is not responding. Please do not kill us."

Intrepid's vivid forward screens showed a high-resolution, wide-angled view of a rat-faced sentient nervously rubbing at long whiskers with narrow fingers. Behind the worried figure stood three more crew, glancing furtively at the vid-sensor amid a filthy, cluttered bridge.

"Captain, the freighters *Slefid* and *Carisfid* are sailing under a Strix flag," Jonathan said, muting comms. "Captain Grossmek and crew are Musi. I suggest asking their destination."

"He could be bluffing about his weapons," Tabby said. "I don't trust them."

"With the Musi, distrust is advised," Jonathan answered, "but his weapons are inoperable because we have made them so."

"You hacked their weapons from sixty kilometers?" Tabby asked.

"Little effort was required," Jonathan answered. "Musi are of well-below-average intelligence and incapable of independent star-flight. Their systems are unprotected and easily accessed."

"Unmute," Ada answered, not sure what she'd stepped into. "Why did you fire on *Intrepid?*"

The rat-faced captain squealed in horror as he reached for and successfully shut off the communication link between his freighter and *Intrepid.*

"They're powering up," Tabby said. "I think they're making a run for it."

"What heading?"

"Directly away from us," Tabby answered what Ada's AI projected on her holo. Indeed, the Musi were slowly accelerating away from *Intrepid.*

"Captain, if you would like I can shut down their engines," Jonathan said.

"Do it," she answered. "Can you get him back on comms too?"

"With little difficulty," Jonathan answered.

The forward vid-screens blinked back to life, this time showing the ships in the background with a superimposed picture of Grossmek chittering wildly at the crew behind him. If it hadn't been so pathetic, Ada would have laughed at the surprised jump by

Grossmek when one of his own pointed at the screen and he realized they were being observed.

"We are very sorry," Grossmek said. "It was my horrible crew that fired upon the great and powerful ship, *Intrepid.* Please. I beg you. Do not destroy us. There are children aboard."

"Stop groveling," Ada demanded, not willing to see if the terrified Musi would continue. "Grossmek, what is your destination?"

"We sail to the moon Querid where our ancestors once lived," he answered.

"Querid?" Ada asked, looking over to Jonathan.

"The second and only other generally inhabitable celestial object within the Mhina system. Better known as Faraji, it is the seventh moon of the gas giant Kobe and in the fifth planetary orbital position," Jonathan rattled off. "If the captain will recall, when we first observed this moon upon entering Dwingeloo so many stans previous, we discovered ruined Musi cities on the moon's surface."

"They were shite-holes," Tabby said. "Like that bridge they're sitting in."

"It is well-established that Musi are actually very sanitary in their practices," Jonathan said. "In that they prefer to be surrounded by what most species consider clutter, they have developed an undeserved reputation of being dirty."

"Please let us go. We meant no harm," Grossmek begged again.

"You shot at us," Ada answered. "Jonathan, any way to figure out if they were headed to Faraji or Kito?"

"They were indeed headed to Kito and not Faraji as Captain Grossmek has indicated."

"Nooo ..." Grossmek screamed and clawed at a control surface that was out of the vid-sensor's range. "Why won't it turn off?"

Unsuccessful at stopping the transmission, the rat-faced captain turned and raced to the bridge's exit, a rooster tail of garbage flying up behind him. Frantically, he pounded on the security controls as he reached the door. The captain looked around in panic as he realized it would not open.

"Grossmek, calm down. Answer my question. I don't plan to shoot you today," Ada said.

It took a bit more convincing, but Grossmek finally returned to the sensor.

"When ships chase, they kill Musi," he answered. "We just want to go home."

"You're lying," Ada said. "You were not headed to Querid. You were headed for another moon, where Abasi once lived."

"We have nothing," Grossmek admitted. "Felio have everything. We were only going to take what we needed for our children to grow. Please do not make us die in the cold of Querid."

"Why would you come all the way out here if you couldn't survive? How'd you get that ship?" Tabby asked. "It's worth a lot more than supplies."

"We have performed an inventory of the freighters," Jonathan said. "Indeed, they will struggle to survive on Faraji without additional supplies. They do, however, have enough for many ten-days and perhaps as long as an orbital cycle." Ada's HUD showed that planet Kobe's orbital cycle was one-point-four standard years. "Longer if they are able to learn to harvest what Faraji has to offer like their predecessors before them."

"Can you reprogram their nav-computer to only allow them to go to Faraji or back to the worm-hole and Tamu for half a stan?" Ada asked.

"Perhaps we could simply disallow navigation to the moon Kito or the planet Elea which Kito orbits," Jonathan suggested.

"That would work," Ada answered. "Captain Grossmek, I assume you understand what I've requested from my crew. Neither *Slefid* nor *Carisfid* will be capable of navigating to the planet Elea. I assure you, if you do figure out how to visit, you will discover that you are neither welcome nor safe. I will utilize *Intrepid* in a most unpleasant way. Do you understand?"

"You are most gracious, Captain Ada Chen of the Bold," he answered, bobbing his head up and down solicitously, his beady black eyes focused on her.

"Show up on Kito and you'll discover just how welcoming I am not," she snapped, cutting comms.

"Captain Chen?" Jonathan asked.

"Yes, Jonathan?"

"We propose that you do not divert to the moon Kito," he said. "Liam has successfully lifted from Zuri and *Hornblower* will reach Kito only seven days after *Intrepid*. If you were to reach out to him and explain your concern, he could direct the Abasi sloops *Shimmering Leaves* and *Ice Touched Field* to make all haste. Their arrival at maximum acceleration would only be forty-eight hours behind *Intrepid's*."

"That is a reasonable idea," Ada answered. "Tabby, what do you think?"

"If Kroerak are attacking the planet from my visions, every minute we delay means death for thousands," she answered. "I hate that Kito might be picked clean by looters, but I don't think they're equal considerations."

"Good point," Ada answered. "Set a course for where you think that wormhole is. It's time to go exploring."

"Copy that," Tabby answered.

"I'll be in my quarters." Ada stood and walked from the bridge, turning aft. Even with a crew of twenty, *Intrepid* felt unusually empty to her. Walking past her quarters to the galley, she grabbed a fresh pouch of hot water and turned back. She palmed her way into the oversized captain's quarters, sat at the ornate, wooden desk and took a moment to pour steaming water over some of her quickly dwindling supply of tea leaves.

"This is *Hornblower*." A voice she didn't recognize answered the quantum comm set. Unlike *Intrepid*, Liam had installed the comm crystals onto *Hornblower's* bridge. "You have Stolzman. Go ahead."

Ada recognized the name if not the voice. The man was one of the pilots in training she'd been teaching to sail large ships. "Ken, this is Ada on *Intrepid*. It's urgent I speak with Captain Hoffen."

"I copy, Bold Tertiary. Will comply," he answered. "The old man just went down two hours ago, but prioritized any comms from *Intrepid.* I'll wake him."

Ada winced, hating to wake Liam. Two minutes later, she heard rustling and then Liam's tired voice. "And here I was thinking to get a good night's sleep without all you around."

"How did lift-off go? Any problems with the load?" Ada asked. In her estimation, *Hornblower* wasn't well suited to the task of ferrying so much weight in and out of the atmosphere.

"We're hauling livestock," Liam answered, dryly. "You'll need to define problems. Turns out poultry have an adverse reaction to space flight. Three crew were wounded by terrified chickens. Also, that whole thing where livestock void bowels when transitioning to and from fold-space?"

Ada chuckled. "Yeah? *Hornblower* doesn't even have fold-space engines."

"Well, turns out these same chickens have that reaction to gravity transitions, like when you switch from repulsors to hard-burn," he said.

"Every time?"

"So far. Yes."

"It feels like livestock and space travel probably aren't compatible," Ada answered, doing her best not to laugh out loud.

"And yet, we keep doing it."

"I take it you're underway then."

"Copy, that, we're currently thirty-two hours from the Santaloo-Tamu wormhole," Liam said. "I suspect that's not why you pinged the bat-phone."

"Bats?" Ada asked.

"Never mind. What's up?"

"We ran into trouble coming through to Mhina," Ada started. "A couple of freighters loaded with Musi fired on us. They said they were headed to the old Musi city on Faraji, but Jonathan did some snooping on their systems and discovered they were first headed to Kito. We believe they were planning to load up on supplies and fuel before making the trip out to Faraji."

"They fired on you?" Liam asked, obviously concerned. "Did you put them down?"

"Their blasters were barely bigger than rifles," she exaggerated. "*Intrepid* took no damage. I've gotta say, they're pathetic little buggers. I decided not to return fire. Jonathan reprogrammed their systems so they can't go to Kito, but we believe there are probably other ships already there, looting. I'd planned to head over and take care of them, but Jonathan talked me out of it."

"How?" Liam asked. "We're depending on those supplies."

"He says if you send the Abasi sloops at max burn, they'll get there almost as fast as *Intrepid* could. If Kroerak really are attacking another planet, that means people are dying. I don't feel like we should make that trade," she answered.

"Yeah, I see what you're saying," Liam answered. "Appreciate your thinking on that. I'd have been blinded by the looting."

"Wasn't my idea," Ada answered. "It was actually Tabby's."

"You must be rubbing off on her. It's not like her to walk away from a fight," he said.

"These Musi were pathetic, Liam. There's no fight where they're concerned. Jonathan had to lock the bridge doors on their ship. The captain was so scared, he kept trying to run off the bridge during our conversation."

He heaved an audible sigh. "That's just great. Really looking forward to dealing with these guys. Go ahead and stay on mission. We'll send the sloops. Everything else good?"

"I think Tabby misses you. She's been hitting the gym equipment hard. Make sure you give her a call after you get up," Ada said.

"Copy that," Liam answered. "*Hornblower* out."

"JONATHAN, ARE YOU PICKING ANYTHING UP?" Ada asked, starting to believe that Tabby's dream of an undiscovered wormhole out of the Mhina system was just that – a dream.

"We can say with ninety-percent confidence that there are no cosmic anomalies resembling those we associate with wormhole travel within four-hundred thousand kilometers of our position," he answered.

"A simple no would suffice," Tabby grumbled.

Intrepid had sailed to three different locations at Tabby's direction and each time they discovered nothing more than the vast emptiness of the deep dark. At the outset she'd felt such confidence, but now she felt like a fool. She'd taken to holding the Iskstar crystal in her hand as she slept, hoping for another dream that would clear things up.

"And yet it would be inaccurate," Jonathan answered.

"Can it," Tabby snapped. "I'm gonna go work out. Let me know when you're done scanning or whatever you do."

Irritated by both her friend's attitude and the situation they found themselves in, Ada considered challenging her. Technically, Tabby was under her command and needed to ask permission to leave the bridge. She also knew that enforcement would be impossible.

"I believe you misunderstand our statement," Jonathan said. "We do not seek to be pedantic. While it is significant that no anomalies are present, we failed to communicate that we have picked up on fuel residue from a significant passing of Kroerak vessels."

"The Kroerak fleet came this way?" Ada asked.

"It is the only reasonable explanation," he answered.

Tabby sat back in her chair and looked out into space, trying to see what wasn't visible. "What are the odds of us coming across the Kroerak fleet's path this far from the Mhina-Tamu wormhole?"

"While an interesting arithmetic problem from the perspective of working with extremely small numbers, most of us believe the actual answer is insignificant beyond that it is not possible," Jonathan answered. "You seek to verify the veracity of the information delivered by the Iskstar. This incident confirms what most of us already believe. Iskstar is a sentient and communicates via the Iskstar crystal."

"Nice to know I'm not crazy," Tabby said, her body relaxing. She'd been holding onto a great deal of stress that she hadn't wanted to admit to.

"Can we trace the fuel trail?" Ada asked.

"Our sensors are not well tuned to this," Jonathan answered. "If permitted, we could manufacture a sensor strip that would allow for better tracking."

She nodded. "I'm not sure I see an alternative."

"We propose that you set *Intrepid's* heading as we've transmitted. It is possible the sensor is unnecessary, although we've directed the replicator to commence construction of one presumptively."

Ada felt *Intrepid* accelerate. Once again, she felt irked by Tabby's unwillingness to follow chain of command. Practically, there was no reason to question Jonathan's direction, but it was not the role of pilot to make that decision.

"Um, guys, are you seeing this?" Tabby asked.

"Seeing what?" Ada asked, her voice more peevish than she'd like to admit.

"It's blurry, like there's something in front of us," she said.

Ada peered at *Intrepid's* super-high-resolution screen but found nothing unusual. "I'm not seeing anything." Disorientation occurred as a familiar sensation hit her stomach.

"Tabby, what's going on?" Ada asked, through clenched teeth.

"I don't think we're in Mhina anymore."

Chapter 11

FULL OF CRAP

TAMU SYSTEM, HORNBLOWER

"We really lucked out when you decided to do a full install on those septic fields at refit," Nick said. "Laterals two and three are completely down and four is under quite a bit of pressure. We're also bleeding O2 almost as fast as we can manufacture it. We've started venting hydrogen and methane as we're out of storage for both. I think we're going to need to shut down the waste drains from the livestock. If we blow the last two fields, the final few days of this voyage are going to stink."

The trip from Zuri to Kito was dragging on much longer than I thought possible. There seemed to be a competition between the livestock and the thousand-plus passengers to clog *Hornblower's* brand new septic. It was true most of these people had never been on a ship and I really should have anticipated problems, but I couldn't imagine how I had missed making clear that trash and bio-waste were completely different ideas.

"What do you expect when you take a half tonne animal and fling it into space?" Curtis Long drawled.

We'd gathered the command crew and community leaders into our largest conference room and were working to hash out issues.

Mostly, I was trying not to get worked up about the treatment of my ship.

Long continued, "Yer lucky all they did was crap buckets. We've got half of 'em sick of some new thing we've never seen and there've been two bovine miscarriages. If you shut down the drains, we're gonna be knee deep if it keeps up like it has."

"From what I saw, I'd guess they're probably empty by now, wouldn't you think?" Hog asked, grinning widely.

"No," Long answered, annoyed.

"We're shutting down the drains," I said. "Curtis, you'll need to deal with the crap best you can. If you need more labor, let us know, we can get some folks to help."

"There's a positive to all this," Nick said.

Hog looked at Nick with eyebrows raised in surprise. "Just how in tarnation do you get anything good from piling hog crap in the bottom of a ship?"

"There's the matter of restarting a new waste treatment plant for York's new home," Nick said. "That requires live bacteria. Seems like we've a good head start on that."

"We'll see if you still feel that way in six days," Long answered.

"As annoying as slogging through poop is, it sounds like septic is managed and O2 is holding," I said. "Let's change topics. We need your final choice for the city of York."

The four cities on Kito were arranged like points of a compass around the lake which had a name that translated simply as Clear Lake. The northernmost city sat nestled against a mountain range to the northeast, the westernmost by a broad forest, and the eastern and southern cities both opened to broad plains. My expectation was one of the latter two would be chosen. While less scenic, both the eastern and southern locations had more ready access to tillable soil.

Clear Lake had been naturally formed and fed from snow-pack on the mountain range to the northeast. A roughly egg-shaped basin, the lake was thirty kilometers across east-to-west and fifty kilometers north-to-south. According to Jonathan, the climate of Kito was such that the lake's edges would only freeze during a short part of the winter period. It was a romantic notion to look forward to a time when the four cities would be thriving and tied together by trade across the lake. I'd been holding onto that idyllic picture for the times when I panicked, thinking about all the things that could go wrong.

"We have," Hog answered. "We choose the western city."

"Isn't that a bit short on farming ground?" Mom asked, having done the same analysis Nick and I had.

"There are only ten who expect to start farms," Bish answered. "The value of the lumber generated from virgin forests looks to be considerable. The industry would jumpstart our economy, providing Mrs. Hoffen would consider granting logging permits."

"It's not something I'm familiar with," Mom answered. "If we harvest responsibly, I don't see why an agreement couldn't be reached."

"I was thinking the same thing," Bish said. "I've pulled resources from our old data-stores. The North Americans had a good model. Did you know that trees are more productive if thinned? And fires are critical for some forests to repopulate?"

She looked straight at him. "I was a secondary school teacher."

"Western city it is," I said. "The area isn't one I flew over directly, but you already know that from the quality of the data-streams. I'm glad you're concentrating on how to generate capital from natural resources."

"What of Loose Nuts Mining and Manufacturing?" Merrie asked. "I'm not sure what's become of the entity, now that all of our equipment is lost."

Merrie and her blacksmith husband, Amon, were an ambitious couple we met on planet Ophir. Like York, the citizens of Yishuv had been stranded by the Belirand Corporation when their mission hadn't met the corporation's objectives. Perhaps the thing I most appreciated about Merrie was her desire to own something. Her admission about being set back to zero, while a shared experience with many of York, hit me particularly hard. She'd followed Mom to Zuri on Petersburg station out of loyalty and a sense of adventure. That decision had cost her significantly.

"What would you like the company to be?" Nick asked.

"Cash assets were roughly a hundred twenty thousand credits in the Abasi banking network," Merrie said, "While sailing through Tamu, I attempted to access these funds. The banking network is closed and there's talk of revaluation of credits. I doubt that we can count on those funds. As it is, we have no equipment. We also don't have right of land ownership under the arrangement with York since we all lived on Petersburg."

I glanced at Mom. She was aware of the issue and wanted us to get it out on the table.

"You didn't say what you wanted," I said.

"I want things to be back to where they were before the Kroerak came. We had so much demand, we were fighting off customers, but I know that can't happen," she said. "Instead, I want to salvage the broken Abasi ships that were used to transport and defend Felio when the Kroerak attacked two centuries ago."

That confused me. "What would you do with those? There are more than enough raw resources planetside."

Nick nodded and put his hand out. "Hold on, let her finish."

Merrie pulled at something in her vision. Our new home, the giant gas planet Elea, appeared on the holo projector in the center of the conference room table. The image showed the half-Earth-sized moon, Kito, in orbit. The camera pulled back and turned out toward space. At two million kilometers from the planet, a rendering showed the broken personnel transport that had been destroyed when Kroerak attacked.

"That's capital," Merrie said, with finality. "We capture that and bring it into synchronous orbit with Kito around Elea and we have an instant space station."

"What about all of the dead?" Mom asked, even while Merrie pulled at the transport and placed it in orbit. "There were over thirty thousand souls on those transports. Abasi will never go for that."

Ignoring Mom, Merrie pushed the video's viewport so they were looking down on the resting place of the remainder of the broken fleet. Any ships that could be made operational had already been removed a few stans back. What remained were mostly just scattered pieces left behind to commemorate a long-ago battle.

"The dead have all been removed," Merrie said. "There should be no remaining personal attachment. We also know the ruined personnel transport was never important enough to recover. To Silver's question, I propose we offer to return any remaining Felio corpses we find to Kito's surface."

"That's ridiculous. You'll never pull that off," Bish said, skeptically. "There's more than enough resource on Kito for everyone. We need engineers. I'm sure York can find housing for you. Right, Silver?"

"How would you capture the transport?" Nick asked, ignoring Bishop.

"The transport wouldn't be our first target. That would be," Merrie answered, turning to Bish and lifting her eyebrows as she pointed to the holographic image of an old Abasi battleship that had been sheared off just forward of midship. I'd seen Merrie underestimated often enough that I was anticipating whatever was coming, even though I had no idea what she had up her sleeve.

Bish picked up the bait and ran with it. "Abasi reclaimed all the ships they could. That thing isn't going anywhere."

"It would take a lot of fuel," Nick said.

"Nineteen tonnes, give or take," Merrie answered.

"That's worth two million credits," Bish spluttered.

"We'll supply the fuel, a Class-C replicator and transportation. In return we get thirty percent of your company," Nick said.

"I'll give up thirty-five, but my list is bigger," Merrie shot back.

"You can't seriously be considering this?" Bish continued to interrupt the conversation. "How are you sailing a ship that doesn't work? Where will you get all that fuel?"

"Kito," Merrie and Nick answered simultaneously.

"The cities we sailed over had piles of fuel left behind by the Felio," I explained. "The Abasi left behind ships that were broken beyond repair, but there are plenty of working engines in that boneyard. Merrie doesn't need to sail it back to the Tamu system. She just needs those big engines to bring the transport back."

"That'll take years." Bish once again stated the obvious.

"You'd be right if Elea wasn't orbiting Mhina's star," Merrie said. "We cut off half the trip if we can get the transport to this position in two-hundred days." The view shifted from broken ships to a top-down planetary orbital map.

"We're in. Make your plans, Merrie. We'll back your play as much as we can," I said. "But we might have a problem with the fuel."

Nick furiously typed and gestured at a virtual keyboard and display only he could see. "I know."

"What problem?" Merrie asked.

"We received a report from *Intrepid.* They intercepted a Musi freighter that was headed to Kito. Ada thinks it's likely there's been looting. That's why we sent the sloops ahead," I said.

Merrie sat back in her chair, her excitement deflating. "Looters? The wormhole hasn't been open for more than a few tendays."

"We don't know if it's a real problem," I said. "The sloops will arrive at Kito just before we transition to Mhina in twelve hours."

"Including *Intrepid* and excluding the Kroerak fleet, seventeen ships have transitioned through the Tamu-Mhina wormhole," Nick said. "I'm looking. Seven freighters sizeable enough to cause trouble. Oh, that's interesting. If all those ships were empty, we're talking significant theft."

"No one can enter a strong man's house," Hog said. "We need to prioritize defense because we'll have to fight off more than Musi once word gets out."

"We'll leave the sloops behind under Silver's command," Marny said. "The cities will no doubt have a defensive apparatus, but we shouldn't fool ourselves, they'll need repair. I agree with your priority, Hog, as long as getting Patty back in the restaurant business is still high on the list."

Marny's comment earned her a chuckle around the table and broke some of the tension that had been building.

"Nick, how are you finding this information?" I asked.

"House of the Bold is Abasi," Nick answered. "As such we have access to sensors in this part of the system. All I did was download their data-streams."

"You said something was interesting, what?" Marny asked. "I didn't like the sound of that."

"*Fleet Afoot* was the first non-Kroerak vessel through the wormhole," Nick answered. "It was only an hour behind the main fleet."

"We knew Munay had taken off to chase the Kroerak," I said. "That sure is ballsy. I wish I could have given him an Iskstar crystal."

"He'd never last against those odds," Nick said. "And neither will we. Kroerak are surely using the data they gathered from our two encounters and are coming up with some way to counter the Iskstar."

"I know. I guess I was hoping once we figured out where they are, we could get Abasi or someone else from the Confederation of Planets interested," I said.

"Wishing something doesn't make it real," Bish grumbled.

"I think Steward Bear has a meal ready for us," I said, working to avoid rolling my eyes at Bish's surly attitude. "Unless there's more business, this meeting is adjourned."

"I'VE NEVER FELT claustrophobic while sailing before," Ada admitted. "It feels like the walls are closing in around us."

"An unusual perspective," Jonathan said. "Indeed, the opposite is very much the case. *Intrepid* is surrounded by the complete absence of material. Do you believe it is that we have sailed for over thirty days without any visual references beyond the distant galaxies?"

"We've jumped through three invisible wormholes. Even the endpoints have no substance to them, not even stray light or magnetic waves. Nothing," she said. "It's like we haven't even moved once we go through them."

"We have most definitely changed positions at quite a dramatic scale. *Intrepid* is four orders of magnitude further from the planet Zuri than Zuri is from your own Mars."

"I hate to burst your bubble, but there's something headed right at us at twenty meters per second," Tabby interrupted. "Looks like a big old asteroid. Maybe eighteen hundred tonnes."

"Where did that come from?" Ada asked.

"There's a line of them." With her finger, Tabby traced the distance between the first rock she'd spotted and the next, which was two kilometers away, ten percent smaller, and moving just a little faster. The AI, recognizing her pattern, located and connected forty additional asteroids of varying sizes, all moving in roughly the same direction and at the same speed.

"They're coming from that wormhole transition," Ada said. "It's like someone's throwing rocks at the transition point from the other side."

"It's not an overly sophisticated attack," Sendrei observed. "But if you get plugged by one of those, you'll know it."

"Check out that wormhole," Tabby said. "Vid sensors can actually pick it up. It's not invisible."

"Do you think the Kroerak are trying to cover their trail by throwing asteroids?" Ada asked, leaving Tabby's observation alone for the moment.

"While in contact with the Kroerak noble, we discussed a number of Kroerak offensive strategies," Jonathan answered. "There is a particular species of semi-sentient, giant arachnids that mine asteroid belts. We discussed how these arachnids were forced to bombard a hostile moon for twenty days, bringing destruction upon a particularly recalcitrant species."

Tabby rolled her eyes at Jonathan. "Great. Rock throwing spiders?"

"Anything in your conversations suggest how Kroerak learned of these wormholes?" Ada asked. "It just doesn't seem like Kroerak are that sophisticated."

"I'll tell you," Tabby interjected. "Just like they learned everything else. They stole the information from some other species and then beat their civilizations to a pulp."

"That's right," Sendrei added, lounging in a chair that swiveled to allow him immediate control of *Intrepid's* weapons system. "Kroerak don't have an original bone in their bodies. And before you correct me, Jonathan, I know they don't have bones. It's an idiom."

"The noble would not discuss space travel, although she was interested in fold-space. However, I would say we find Sendrei's description accurate." Jonathan gave a slight smile and raised his eyebrows. "A bone inside a Kroerak would either have been recently eaten or would very much be a new concept – and therefore original."

"See the humor I had to live with on that ship?" Sendrei complained. "That is what *Jonathan* finds funny."

"Sorry to break up the chat, but we're closing on the transition point," Tabby said. Her announcement caused the team to straighten in their chairs and start a flurry of small tasks. "Anyone want to guess why this wormhole is all pretty?"

Instead of the invisible transition points they'd been jumping through for so many ten-days, this endpoint was a swirl of colored lights caused by gasses interacting with the magnetic fields. Just as they closed to five thousand meters, the general distance considered safe for entering a wormhole, a new asteroid blooped through.

"If we're going, we should do it now," Tabby said. "We have about fifteen minutes before the next rock pops through."

"All hands, we're approaching transition," Ada finally announced. "As you know, we're likely chasing unicorns, but this next jump could place us into a hostile environment. The time to look sharp is now. Team leads, complete your scans of comm devices and report back when complete. We're going to be sailing quiet. Even though we have Iskstar weapons, *Intrepid* is in no position for the kind of combat we know Kroerak are capable of."

Sendrei sat up and swiveled his chair so he had access to fire-control. He'd drilled his crew for hours each day, providing structure and discipline, but his gunners were still rookies. They would require a lot more training before they could be trusted to independently assess and prioritize remote targets during battle.

"Fire-control is secure and weapons are hot," he added on tactical comms.

"Engineering is secure," Roby answered. "All systems are at one-hundred percent."

Ada waited until each of her leads reported in before sitting up straight in her chair and pulling her lap-belt firmly across her legs. "Engineering, engage low emissions mode. And helm, take us in."

"Transition in ten ... nine ..." Tabby started the countdown, her heart pounding in her chest in anticipation. Only through sheer force of will was she able to relax her grip as the countdown reached zero and she was beset with familiar wormhole sensations.

The disorientation cleared almost as soon as transition was complete. Recovery hadn't always been that quick, even after the surgical modifications and enhancements she'd received following the Battle for Colony-40. Tabby wondered if the difference was due to Iskstar. A red-warning light was her first indication of a problem and without hesitation, she veered *Intrepid* to port at ten degrees declination, dodging away from a massive, fifteen-hundred tonne object.

"It's a frakking rock! Moon-humping, rock-hucking spiders!" Tabby exclaimed, pushing *Intrepid* further into a spiral. "Why did you have to tell me about the spiders? I hate *spiders!*"

"Captain, I'm picking up planetary signatures and a twin star," Jonathan said.

Ada was more concerned about near space, but tore her focus from Tabby's viewscreen. She found it difficult to relinquish the pilot's chair. Tabby could handle it and she needed to focus on what would come next.

"Clear of the asteroid," Tabby said. "We seem to have come out in a belt. I bet those buggers saw us coming and sent a surprise our way. That asteroid was way too close and not on the same frequency as the previous twenty or so."

Ada's holo projector finished filling in near-space details. As the planets and stars resolved on the sensors, the unique characteristics of this particular wormhole became obvious. Within the circum-stellar disc around the dual stars were millions and millions of aster-oids. Noticeably, just beyond the wormhole, a completely clear swath of space stood out. Rock, dust and debris simply disappeared as the wormhole sent them through, starting them on an intergalactic voyage.

"I'm picking up no enemy ships," Sendrei said.

"There is a considerable amount of electromagnetic radiation being emitted from the fourth planet," Jonathan said.

"EM? Are they talking to us?" Ada asked.

"The source of the radiation is not consistent with communication," Jonathan said. "The band is too wide."

"What about the other planets?" Ada asked.

"There is one other celestial object suitable for sentient development," Jonathan said. "It is the moon of the fifth planet and is the origin of a weak and repetitive signal."

"Fourth planet is right," Tabby said. "My dream showed two warring nations on continents divided by oceans. Are you sure there aren't attacking Kroerak warships?"

"We're too far for our sensors," Jonathan said. "Initial indications suggest no life. Sentients would create considerably more EM range variation."

"I thought you said you were getting a signal from that moon," Tabby pushed back.

"You are correct," Jonathan said. "Its origin is most definitely sentient, although it is repetitious, at a period of eighty-minute intervals."

"Eighty minutes?" Ada asked. "We've only been in system for eight."

"The highly complex signal is transmitting on a multitude of frequencies. While we're not able to translate, the mechanism for reconstruction of the message is obvious," he answered.

"Tabby, what exactly did you see in your dream? Where were the Kroerak attacking from? Were they invading? Space battle? What?" Ada asked.

"I had the dream on several occasions," Tabby said. "I saw enough details that I was able to record the locations of each of those transition points we came through. The two nations on the fourth planet were different. Sometimes I saw what was happening from one side's view, sometimes from the other. These two nations were the same species, but they hated each other at their core. If the Kroerak hadn't shown up to take them out, they were ready to do the job themselves. I definitely got the feeling the conflicts were happening right now, though."

"The radiation from the fourth planet is consistent with nuclear weaponry as was popular with humanity in the twentieth and twenty-first centuries," Jonathan added.

"I thought you couldn't tell what it was," Tabby said, annoyed.

"We are receiving data in real time," Jonathan added. "We believe there is less than a five percent chance that sentient life continues on this planet."

"So this entire trip is for nothing," Tabby said.

"We have learned much on this trip already, Tabitha Masters," Jonathan said. "The discovery of a new type of wormhole is significant and has wide implications. Also, we have been discussing internally that it appears the sentient we refer to as Iskstar might not be temporally registered in the same way as other sentients we have found."

"Registered by what?" Tabby asked

"*Temporally* registered," Jonathan corrected. "Bound by time, in the same way as we are."

"You think they're time travelers?" Ada asked

"There is no evidence of this. Consider the following. My species operates typically in a silica media. Our speed – of what is generally and loosely referred to as thinking, or less flattering, computing – is on the order of a thousand to ten thousand times faster than human, Felio, or most warm blooded, carbon-based life. Within our conclave, we've held thousands of conversations in the space of this conversation I'm having with you just now. What if Iskstar thought was hundreds of times slower than humanity?" Jonathan asked.

"On Earth those are called sloths," Sendrei said. "It's hard to believe such a creature would be a worthy opponent of Kroerak."

"Your perception is modified by your own experience. Humans

live one hundred standard years. Felio live closer to eighty standard years. In this amount of time, you are right. Iskstar would have difficulty reaching the level of sophisticated thought that would be equivalent to humanity."

"You're asking, what if Iskstar lived for centuries?" Sendrei's eyes grew wide as comprehension set in.

"Or thousands of millennia," Jonathan answered.

Chapter 12

FOWL STENCH

MHINA SYSTEM, HORNBLOWER

The massive gas planet, Elea, occupied the fourth orbital position around Mhina's star and it grew in *Hornblower's* armored glass as we approached. Even from a hundred thousand kilometers, the planet's giant size was evident and I strained to locate the moon, Kito, that had just appeared from the planet's back side.

"What a sight," Marny said, her voice holding the same awe I felt as she took in the view.

"Captain, I have four ships on sensors," Stolzman reported from the helm. "It's *Leaves* and *ITF.* They're chasing those two freighters. *Leaves* looks like it's venting gas pretty badly."

We'd taken to shortening the sloop names, *Shimmering Leaves* and *Ice Touched Fields,* as they didn't exactly roll off our tongues.

"Add *Leaves* and *ITF* to tactical comms," I said. We were just about to come out of hard-burn and would have comms back up in four minutes. The interference from the engines made communication and full sensor resolution nearly impossible, especially from a hundred thousand kilometers. As a result, the four ships jerked across my holo-field as positions were slowly updated and details filled in.

"Nick, any read on why they've taken such a beating?" I asked.

"Not much data yet," he said. "*ITF* has a hole behind its number one engine. Must have gotten hit by something big. I'm surprised Lathrop is keeping up as well as he is."

We were only a hundred twenty seconds from exiting hard-burn and there was no doubt our presence was known by the four ships engaged in the furball. I found it ironic, when approaching a dogfight, that it never really looked like much was happening. Sure, as usual, blaster bolts were exchanged and the ships worked on positioning themselves, but it seemed to be happening very slowly. I knew for a fact, when actively engaged in combat, nothing felt slow.

"*ITF* is going down," Nick said. "She's hit hard. That little freighter is tossing missiles."

Never in my imagination would I have believed that a pair of heavily armored Abasi sloops would have difficulty with a pair of freighters.

"That's nuts. Those freighters *have* to know we're almost on them. It's suicide. Stolzman, as soon as we break hard-burn, jump to combat configuration. We need to give our boys some cover," I ordered.

"Aye, aye, Captain," he answered, drawing a proposed navigation plan that would effectively shield *Ice Touched Fields* from further attack, but would leave *Shimmering Leaves* open.

My stomach flip-flopped as *Hornblower* transitioned from hard-burn to combat-burn. The main difference between the two modes was that in combat-burn, the pilot was given considerable control over steerage. The gravity and inertial dampeners would also respond to force-vectors in all directions. At its essence, combat was significantly less efficient, but it also generally didn't last as long.

"*ITF* is tumbling on an intercept with Kito," Nick announced. "I can't raise Lathrop, but someone is trying to fight for control."

"Marny, focus on those freighters," I said, ignoring Nick for the moment. I'd seen *ITF's* plight and knew that Lathrop was in trouble. The fact was, there was nothing we could do for the crew. The only chance they had was to get their engines back online. "I want those ships captured and crew alive. Captured is highest priority."

"Copy. Fire-control, fire package six. Weapons are free. I repeat fire package six and weapons are free."

"Six?" I asked.

"The 75mm cannons only and targeting preference for ship disabling," she answered. "Prepared strategy groups was something I learned from Gunnery Sergeant Raul Martinez, rest his soul. He had a total of eighteen packages and drilled the team daily. I'm just picking up the playbook he wrote. Very efficient."

"Are eighteen packages enough for all the variation?" I asked.

"No. Gunny Simons will be down there coaching them to be aggressive. Package six could be used to slow a ship you couldn't afford to destroy. We're taking the gloves off. It's an easy modification," she answered.

"Where'd you get Simons from and why isn't she called gunnery sergeant?" I asked. I'd thought I had a handle on the terminology and was sure I'd been told not to refer to Martinez as gunny.

"She's Navy. Originally a Brit, too. Marines are gunnery sergeants. Navy's gunny," she answered.

"Jupiter," I said. "Can't we just come up with one thing and stick with it?"

"Give me the word, Cap, I'll make it happen," she said.

During our conversation, Stolzman positioned *Hornblower* to provide *Shimmering Leaves* cover. At the moment we came into range of the first freighter, a brilliant golden line of fire stitched out across my holo field, looking for a home on the larger of the two freighters. In that our presence was a complete game changer, the battle switched rapidly from full-on furball, to get-the-frak-out-of-Dodge.

"Sandoval, sit-rep," I ordered, addressing the captain of *Shimmering Leaves*.

"*ITF* is hit bad, sir," he answered. "She's not going to make it. We're all up here. Those bastards jumped us. Started launching missiles. Lathrop didn't have a chance."

"Copy," I answered.

"You gotta let me go after that smaller freighter," he said. "She's going to get away."

I'd been watching the displays and Sandoval's assessment was right. We'd hit the big freighter first and the smaller one had run around behind, using the larger vessel's position to partially guard its flank. If I'd been aboard *Intrepid,* I'd certainly have run it down. I understood his concern.

"Negative, Andy," I said, using Sandoval's first name. "She might have more missiles."

"Jupiter piss. If she had any more missiles she'd have used them by now," he retorted.

"Watch your tone, pilot," Marny snapped.

"I need you to follow *ITF* in," I said. "Lathrop might be able to pull out and you may need to provide assistance if he makes it down."

"Apologies. Will comply," he answered sullenly, his face anything but conciliatory.

That said, I wasn't about to hold utterances in the heat of battle against him. From the corner of my eye I could see that Marny was about to further correct but I shook my head slightly, deflecting her ire.

"Simons, any firing solutions on that smaller ship?" I asked.

Gunny Simons and crew had quickly disabled the larger of the two freighters and peeled off the single turret it sported. It was definitely the softer of the two targets, but I was happy to accept the win.

"Negative, Captain." I hadn't talked to the woman very often, but her slight accent was memorable. "Mr. Stolzman gave us his best vector and the freighter is just out of range, even for golden bullets."

"Golden bullets?"

"Aye, Captain, lucky shots, perfectly aligned and all that. The freighter will simply move out of the way if we fire. There's too much distance."

"Nick, what's your read on the big freighter?" I asked. This ship did not show up in the Abasi database of known vessels. It was also, conveniently, not transmitting a transponder signal.

"Procyon manufacture," he answered.

"Where's that?" I asked.

In response, my AI overlaid the holo field with a two-dimensional, rectangular map of the Aeratroas region of the galaxy — essentially what we knew as the Confederation of Planets. The Procyon species came from a system east of Mhina and eight wormhole jumps away. Of course, just about everything on the map was east of Mhina, as it was the western-most system of Aeratroas. The Procyon lived in the center of the eastern third of the map and down about two thirds of the way toward the bottom boundary.

"Doesn't mean there are Procyon aboard," he quickly added. "They just manufactured it."

"Hail, Procyon freighter," I ordered.

"They're not responding," Stolzman said, as we slowly circled the disabled ship.

"Looks like we're going to have a good, old-fashioned boarding party," I said. "XO, put together a team. I'll meet you on the flight deck."

"Cap, you shouldn't be boarding. We talked about this," she said.

"I'll let your Marines handle it," I said, "unless there are Kroerak aboard and then there's some possibility I'll strap on my angry."

"Promise?" she asked.

I nodded. I might be captain of the ship and prime of our house, but there were several people who could reach beyond rank or position. Marny was probably second only behind Tabby in her ability to override my decisions, especially when they were tactical in nature.

"I'm carrying a weapon and wearing armor, but I'm happy to be last through the door," I said.

"Then we're burning daylight," she answered, stepping in front of me as I made my way to the bridge hatch.

"Stolzman, you're Officer of the Deck," I said.

"Copy, I have the deck," he answered, glancing furtively at Nick.

Our flight deck was a thirty-meter-wide opening in the side of the hull about a fifth of the way back on *Hornblower's* port side. Twenty meters tall, it occupied two decks and stretched across the entire width of the ship. Originally designed to be open on both sides, the bay had been closed off and the armor reinforced on the starboard side. We were using the deck as an easy access hold and as a docking bay for shuttles, not in its original configuration as a fighter bay.

Thoughtfully, Marny had located the ship's main armory just aft of the flight deck and when we arrived, five Marines were already pulling on bulky armored vac-suits and grabbing blaster rifles, grenade strips, flash-bang-discs, and everything required for a hostile infiltration.

I kept my kit simple, pulling my favorite slug-throwing 1911 from the rack and strapping it onto my hip. I didn't need armor, as my grav-suit had as much armor quality as the suits our Marines were donning. I also didn't expect to be breaching or cutting, so I left behind grenade strips and the torch I almost always carried.

"By the numbers, boys and girls," Marny instructed.

We entered the blacked-out flight deck through an airlock. Ordinarily, a translucent barrier would have kept the flight deck pressurized, but Marny didn't want the freighter's occupants to see the glow and know where we were coming from. It wasn't until we were poised at the edge of the bay that I saw the virtual numbers projected onto the freighter's hull. Marny had assigned each Marine a specific number that corresponded to their job and position on the infiltration team.

"Cap, I'll have you join us once we're through."

I blinked acknowledgement on my HUD, not wanting to distract her from the mission with unnecessary chatter.

She slapped the back of the Marine in position one. In close formation, they all kicked off and floated across the eight hundred meters that separated *Hornblower* from the enemy vessel.

One after another the Marines landed lightly on the hull and I found it anticlimactic when the breaching charges puffed a small amount of smoke which dissipated almost instantly. Of course, sound doesn't travel through vacuum so ultimately it was a tiny, intense flash followed by a stream of leathernecks.

Watching through Number One's video sensors, I saw a flash only a moment after he did. A small, but intense firefight ended twenty seconds later with three Procyon slumped in the hallway. With the entry clear of fighting, I pushed off and fell in behind the boarding party.

"Are they alive?" I asked as I looked ahead at the three, meter-tall aliens who had their arms and legs bound and were being dragged back down the hallway. To my eyes, the species resembled tall, thin racoons from Earth, complete with long narrow noses; short, thin fingers; dark fur; and pointy ears. In vac-suits, it was difficult to tell if they had fluffy tails, but it wouldn't have surprised me.

"Two up. One down," Number One answered.

"You're early, Cap," Marny chastised.

"Copy," I agreed.

"Six, restore pressure," she ordered. I suspected she'd want to have yet another conversation with me about roles and responsibilities.

If there was an all important rule about breaching a ship, it was that speed and intensity mattered. The longer a ship's crew was given to mount a defense, the more dug in they could become. Now that the airlock had been breached, hallway secured, and everyone inside, Number Six erected a temporary partition behind us to hold atmo. We'd lose access to much of the ship as long as the main hallway was open to space. In an emergency evacuation we would still be able to run through it if we had to.

"Ready," she said, just as the partition sealed itself in place.

"Move out," Marny ordered.

The freighter's design was simple. The airlock led into a hallway that T'd off. To the aft was access to the large holds. Forward would be sleeping areas and the bridge. Even though the freighter was five times the size of our old sloop *Hotspur,* its crew space wasn't much larger. I estimated perhaps a max of ten crew, three of whom were bound and lying on the deck behind us.

As we approached each hatch, Marny's team shared three responsibilities: cover the hallway, cover the doorway, and weld the door shut with a portable plasma cut/weld rig. With a few centimeters of weld, a hatch would resist most forces designed to open it. Similarly, when the time came to clear the rooms, the door could be freed with a single cut. The only problem with this plan was if someone inside the room had a cutter and the means to put up a solid offense. With only six hatches in the hallway, it took us less than five minutes to secure them and make our way to the bridge.

"Cap, down," Marny urged.

I sighed and hunched down so as to provide a smaller target. I couldn't fathom any fire making it past the knot of Marines ahead of me, but Marny had tactical command and it was more expedient to accept her call.

"Go!" Marny's one-word command set into action a series of events that were over quickly. Fire-wire was applied to the bridge door and when ignited, it burned through in milliseconds. Not waiting for a reaction, the door was kicked inward and FBDs (flash-bang discs) were sent through the door as the Marines flooded in behind.

"Clear," Number One announced and green ready-checks appeared next to the avatars of each member of the team.

I stood and walked through the cloudy haze. I couldn't have been more surprised when I discovered, seated in the captain's chair with three Procyon standing behind, a Strix. And not just any Strix, but Quering, a particularly nasty Strix we'd met when first arriving in this galaxy so many stans ago. It had been Quering who tried to kill my cat, Filbert, because he didn't recognize the species. It had also been Quering who seized our comm crystals.

"I thought I recognized your stench," Quering spat as we locked eyes.

"Foul stench," I corrected.

"What are you blathering about? It is as I have always said. Humanity should never have been identified as sentient," he spat.

"Bind him, especially his beak," I ordered.

"You can't," he said. "I'm protected by diplomacy. You are breaking treaties. You must release me and my ship at once."

Number One looked at me for approval and I nodded for him to continue.

"Nick, we've secured the bridge," I called over tactical. "We found that Strix named Quering in charge."

"I saw that," Nick answered. "He's probably right. There's a treaty between Strix and Abasi."

"They'll need to work that out in a different way," I said. "Attacking our ships and looting our cities isn't going to work for me."

"Do you know they've been looting?" Nick asked.

"Not yet, but we'll check out the holds and interview the crew. I can't imagine why else there'd be a freighter this size taking off from Kito."

Quering attempted unsuccessfully to talk around the edge of his gag. I shook my head.

"Cap, stay here this time. We're going to clear aft," Marny said.

"Copy that," I said, sitting at one of the two bridge consoles. The system was still logged in, so I navigated the menus and found the internal vid sensors. I piped the feed to the team as they worked aft.

"We're clear," Marny finally announced twenty minutes later. "They're loaded with fuel, some machinery and a hefty stockpile of minerals, mostly precious."

"Nick, can you run a calc? Do we have room to bring this all aboard?" I asked.

"That and more," he answered. "We burned a lot of fuel taking off from Zuri. I'll get a crew organized. What are you doing with Quering?"

"Watch." I stood up from the console and turned back to Quering. I wasn't exactly sure where the rest of the bridge crew had been taken, but I mostly didn't care. Looking into the feathered, owlish face, I pulled the binding from around his beak. As a reward, he snapped and caught the fleshy part of my hand, just between my thumb and forefinger.

"You are as slow as you are dull-witted," Quering cackled.

I shook my hand, trying to stop the pain. I inspected my hand and discovered he'd taken a small chunk of flesh.

"And you're about to be space debris," I said.

"Why? You have been the aggressor here," he said. "You attacked us during a lawful flight plan. We have no affiliation with the ship that attacked one of your own."

"You've been looting Kito," I said.

"A lie, you pasty casing of bovine refuse. The material aboard this ship is property of Strix," he answered. "We were on a diplomatic mission of trade when your delirious sloop crews attempted intercept of a ship that intended to do Strix harm."

"Marny scan the material. Is it from Kito?" I ordered.

"Your scan is of no use," Quering replied. "We waited for you who have suckled at the emaciated teat of Mshindi since your arrival."

"You waited on Kito?" I asked. "You mean, you loaded material from Kito so you could steal it."

"The material was unloaded onto Kito surface and then loaded back into our hold. It will show the residue of that which has originated on Kito," he answered.

"Save it," I said. "We're taking our material back and you can stay on your ship."

"It is not yours to do so. What has caused your brain to be so addled that you so easily misunderstand the obvious?"

"You might want to make a call to your buddies who left you here," I said. "We'll be on Kito if you decide you still need our help."

"We will never need the help of a human," Quering answered.

"Works for me," I said, walking from the bridge.

"Wait. Will you not release me from my bonds, you puss-filled vessel of rotted meat?"

"I believe you've proven your beak is sharp enough," I said. "I'm sure you can nibble through your bindings over time."

"Cap, I don't think he can," Marny said over private comms. "Our bindings are very strong."

"I know," I said. "Once we have the hold unloaded, we can release him and the rest of the crew."

"Liam, we have new issues," Nick said as I sailed across the gap between ships.

"What's that?" I asked, feeling a little off after dealing with Quering. The Strix's constant berating was annoying, but I took no enjoyment from setting the little ass-hat adrift.

"*Ice Touched Fields* crash landed in a gravel pit. Sandoval says Chief Petty Officer Lathrop and crew were all killed on impact."

"Frak, darn it," I said. I hadn't gotten to know the man very well, but I hated that he'd died on a mission I sent him on. It was a tough universe and we were getting chewed up by it. We desperately needed to find equilibrium, which could only be gained from a position of power.

"That's not the only thing," Nick said.

Someone had turned the lights back on in the flight deck and the glow indicated the pressure barrier was once again up. Nick was standing a couple of meters inside, waiting for my arrival.

"What's that?" I asked, setting down in front of him.

"Our sensors picked up an inbound ship. It's coming from the same direction from which *Intrepid* left the system," he said.

"A Kroerak ship?" I asked, my heart firing in my chest. While I hadn't been overly concerned about breaching the Procyon freighter, the thought of an imminent battle with Kroerak definitely got my attention.

"You'll never believe it. It's *Fleet Afoot*," Nick said. "Munay's back and he's moving at top speed."

Chapter 13

ALWAYS SPIDERS

MENDARI SYSTEM, INTREPID

"Tabby, put in a course for the moon of that fifth planet. Someone is trying to talk to us," Ada said.

"Fourth planet is what I saw," Tabby answered. "We should go there first."

Ada bit off her first response before saying something that would be difficult to walk back. There'd been a subtle battle of wills on the bridge for most of the trip. She had to decide if this moment was the time to address it.

"First things first," Ada answered. "The most compelling feature in the system right now is the comm signal from that moon. After we figure out what's happening there, we'll check out the planet. You've seen the sensor analysis. No species could live through the radiation we're picking up, not for very long anyway."

"You're the captain," Tabby responded, annoyed.

Ada quietly checked off agreement to the navigation plan Tabby entered. "Schedule-C burn plan, on your mark," Ada answered. They'd been conserving fuel for most of the trip as they had no idea where they'd end up. With a target in sight, she was willing to upgrade from the slower, fuel-conservative schedule they'd been executing.

"Let's do this," Tabby said. "All hands, prepare for hard-burn in ten ... nine ..."

"Thank you, Tabby," Ada said.

"Are you going to be on the bridge for a while?" Tabby asked, turning so she faced Ada.

"Sure. What's up?"

"Mind if I go work out? Doesn't look like we've got much going on."

Ada nodded. "Of course. I've got this."

"Captain, there is a possibility you might consider. We could reply to the communication signal on this moon," Jonathan said.

"Silent running, Jonathan," Ada answered. "I'm not about to give anyone a ten-day to prepare for our arrival - friend or foe."

"CAPTAIN, the moon has a light atmosphere, breathable with assistance from standard vac-suits," Jonathan said moments after exiting hard-burn only thirty-thousand kilometers from the moon. "We are detecting a complex series of structures at this location."

A red X flashed on the surface map on Ada's holo projection. As was common, the vid showed the moon and planet together with their current relationship to *Intrepid.* Recognizing Ada's focus, the AI magnified the location of the red X. The planet disappeared from view and the terrain of the moon grew more distinguishable, clouded by significant pockets of vapor. The AI identified the material as mostly water, but with toxic levels of chlorine and sulfur.

Ada saw nothing but rocks at first, but as the thick clouds moved through, she could just make out the unnatural square edges of a heavily-rusted building. "How many buildings?"

"It is difficult to count as it appears the structures are interconnected and built into the surrounding landmass," Jonathan answered. "If we make a few assumptions, that one third is visible and that the species responsible for their construction to be roughly human sized, we estimate the structures would support a population between eight hundred and four thousand."

"That's quite a range," Sendrei said. "Are you sure you can't dial that in a bit?"

Ada smiled to herself. One of the things she'd most enjoyed about this mission was getting to know the crew. Sendrei, though generally quiet, wasn't without humor and seemed to enjoy needling Jonathan about statements that appeared to be guesses. Even more interesting was that Jonathan understood the interaction and seemed to enjoy it.

"Variation is appropriate, even after we eliminated many life forms who would not conform to the structures below. Certainly, you must admit that not every species is willing to shed its clothing and live in a tunnel structure. Species such as the North American gray wolf need a much larger territory. They will defend several hundred kilometers for an average pack size of eight to ten. At the other end of the spectrum, a colony of red ants contains millions and occupies less than a square kilometer," Jonathan defended.

"Mr. Garcia, would you call Ms. Masters to the bridge?" Ada asked. She felt a twinge of guilt at pushing the young pilot from the helm. If *Intrepid* were to run into trouble, she needed Tabby's experience at the helm.

"I'm here. Sorry I'm late," Tabby said, entering the bridge before Garcia made the call.

"Just in time," Ada answered, more cheerily than she felt. Tabby had been pushing her buttons, but she didn't want it to show.

"What's the play?" Tabby asked.

"Jonathan, have you made further progress in deciphering the signal that's being transmitted?" Ada asked.

"We are not sure that it is progress, but the precision of the message is such that it appears to be completely machine generated," he answered.

"And the destination of the message?"

"We are eighty-five percent confident it is intended for the entrance to the wormhole," he said. "As we have sailed directly toward its source, it is possible the message is more broadly aimed, but our best analysis suggests the tighter focus."

"Machine generated, focused at the wormhole, and repeating for who knows how long," Ada said. "That's not a lot of information."

"If Jonathan can't break the code, we're talking about a high level of sophistication," Sendrei said. "We're dealing with something fairly advanced. I think that's as important as anything."

"Jonathan, attempt to hail the inhabitants of the moon," Ada said. "Keep it tight to the source of the transmission, though. We don't need to overly broadcast our location."

"Aye, aye, Captain." Jonathan barely paused before turning back to Ada. "We've made some sort of contact. The message has changed. It appears to be some sort of security prompt."

"I'm getting power readings on the surface," Tabby said. "Something's awake down there."

"*Intrepid* is being painted by a target-locking computer," Sendrei said.

"Moving to orthogonal orientation," Tabby said, swinging *Intrepid's* aft over so the bow pointed directly at the threat coming from the moon's surface. In that *Intrepid* was long and thin, Tabby's movement would provide the smallest target and guarantee the greatest benefit from its stealth armor.

"Good," Ada answered. "Although I had to look up orthogonal."

"That did it. Their locks didn't hold, but they're still searching for us," Sendrei said. "Five land-based cannons have emerged from the structure below. We could be in trouble if they lock on. I'm not sure what those things are firing, but they sure are big."

"Easier to dodge," Tabby answered. "Maybe we should go in fast and close."

"Not yet. Jonathan, what's all that communication?" Ada asked.

Still indecipherable, the transmissions from the moon's surface had exploded in volume.

"I believe that was exactly what we needed," Jonathan answered. "Previously, we lacked sufficient sampling to decipher the alien communications. The message is clear. We are to present security credentials or we will be fired upon."

"If we wanted to, could you form a response in their language?" Ada asked.

"Yes, but that may not be necessary. There is a flaw in their security protocols," Jonathan said. "We requested permission to reply with manufactured credentials."

"Tabby, prepare to make a break for it," Ada said. "If this fails, they're going to have a good lock on our location."

"Up or down? We could probably strafe those cannons. I bet they're nowhere near as fast as we are," Tabby said.

"Let's keep confrontation at the bottom of our list," Ada said. "There'll be plenty of time for that if we're unsuccessful."

"Copy that. Up it is," Tabby answered.

"Send those credentials, Jonathan," Ada said.

"Message is sent," he answered.

The response was nearly instantaneous. The aggressive targeting computers and more than half of the communication signals from the surface immediately ceased. In their place, a single message appeared. Jonathan's new translation algorithm presented an invitation to land.

"Sendrei, Tabby, this could get dicey," Ada said. "If we're attacked, you're to respond aggressively, but measured. Primary goal is survival of this ship."

"Aye, aye, Captain," Sendrei answered.

"Finally off the leash," Tabby said. "Roger that. We're headed in."

Under Tabby's direction, *Intrepid* lunged forward into the light atmosphere.

"Jonathan's communique appears to be working," Sendrei said. "Cannons are retracting."

"Tabby, what can you tell us about this species?" Ada asked.

"The people I saw in the Iskstar vision were humanoid," Tabby answered. "Very heavy brows, kind of had a Neanderthal look to them. They were at war. Everyone I saw was wearing some sort of a uniform, like they were all part of an army. Two different sides were fighting each other. I didn't see much past when the Kroerak showed up. Neither side would stop fighting the other, even as the invasion started."

"Jonathan, is this consistent with what you're finding?" Ada asked.

"There is little to go by in the communications," Jonathan answered. "The style of the buildings and the hostile response to our appearance do line up with Tabitha's description."

"They barely had space travel," Tabby continued as she pushed *Intrepid* toward the structure indicated by the message. "All of their space assets were used to shoot down other space assets. They didn't have any sort of fleet to meet the Kroerak. It was a slaughter."

"So, you don't think this civilization is the one you saw?" Ada wasn't as convinced as Tabby was about the accuracy of the dreams.

"No idea," Tabby answered. "Technologically, the humanoids in my dream were pretty advanced. I saw drone, electronic, robotic, conventional and every other type of warfare you could think of. If you're asking if I think they were advanced enough to send someone to this moon? Yes."

"A civilization bent on the conquest of its neighbors would have difficulty colonizing orbital space. The environment would be too fragile and open to attack," Jonathan said. "This moon, however, might have provided a sufficient platform for one of the warring nations to survive. It would hold little strategic advantage, however."

"Only so much we can guess," Ada said as Tabby slowly sailed over the thick, steel structures that had suffered greatly in the moon's caustic atmosphere.

"Want me to set her down?" Tabby asked.

"Yes. Tabby, Sendrei, Jonathan, you're with me. We're going to have a look around. Jose, you have the helm," Ada ordered.

"Aye, Captain, I have the helm," Garcia answered sharply.

"Request permission to bring Clingman and Brockette," Sendrei said. "If this group is all fight, I'd like to have my boys along. I'd feel better if you'd let us go in first."

"Decision is yours. You have tactical command while on the ground," Ada said.

"Understood," Sendrei answered. It was the strategy they'd discussed, and he appreciated her willingness to abide by it. "Tabby, I want you on the old lady. We'll keep Jonathan with us."

"Copy," Tabby answered, accepting a heavy blaster rifle from Sendrei as he pulled equipment from the armory.

"Old lady?" Ada asked. "I'm younger than the both of you."

"Term of endearment," Tabby chuckled and slapped Ada on the butt, handing her a rarely-worn helmet that went with the grav-suits they both wore.

"Careful," Ada warned, not appreciating the overtly familiar gesture in front of the crew.

"Almost never," Tabby answered with a defiant glint in her eyes. She turned aft and made for the cargo bay that would give quick access to the moon's surface.

"Give us a ten count, then follow." Sendrei palmed the security panel that opened the cargo bay door. The atmospheric pressure of the moon varied considerably from that of the ship, so the pressure barrier automatically deployed.

"Looking sharp, boys," Tabby said, taking in the trio who were all wearing the tight, but bulky armored vac-suits that left little to the imagination. Sendrei and the two Marines were heavily muscled and all business as they waited for the hatch to clear.

"Move out." Sendrei was the first to jump from the lip of the cargo bay, followed closely by Jonathan's armored egg and the Marines. The three men were in free fall for ten meters before lighting their AGBs (arc-jet gloves and boots) and landing in the low gravity, rocky environment.

A cold wind carrying ice crystals blew across Ada's faceplate as she followed Tabby, who'd jumped only a few seconds behind Sendrei's group. She couldn't help but respond irrationally to the wintry scene, and dialed up her grav-suit's heater, knowing full well that the suit maintained a consistent temperature without her intervention. With Tabby only slightly in the lead, the two jogged across to the heavily-pitted, red-orange face of the steel building that loomed ahead.

"Go!" Sendrei urged. The three men surged through the doorway, leap-frogging around each other as they momentarily held defensive positions, then sprinted ahead, leaving only one on the move at any given moment.

"So chivalrous," Tabby quipped as they passed through a doorway three meters tall and two meters wide. "I sure hope this entry was built for show and that our hosts aren't actually this big."

The thirty-meter-long hallway they entered ran across the front of the building. The last of Sendrei's team was just disappearing around the corner.

"Ada, we're secure, but you're going to want to see this," Sendrei called before she and Tabby reached the end of the hallway.

"Sounds like something got interesting," Tabby said, picking up the pace enough that Ada had to lift and propel with her grav-suit.

They found Sendrei, Clingman, and Brockette standing equidistant apart facing outward with guns half-raised, surrounding a large computer console.

Even without looking up, Ada sensed that the room soared above her. In front of the console, in the middle of the three, Jonathan hovered, no longer projecting its human visage.

"That's about as creepy as it gets," Tabby said, lifting her gun so it pointed up at forty-five degrees. Like the others, she didn't shoulder the weapon.

Everyone was staring past the console where the room stretched back farther than she could see. A sense of dread filled Ada as she realized the walls were lined with rectangular steel boxes, roughly the dimensions of a large person. What looked like rows of dim lights was actually the glow from small windows near the top of each box. Backlit in each frosted green glass window was a head-shaped outline. Turning to take it all in, Ada realized that every wall was entirely lined with the boxes and the room continued deep into the earth, soaring above them for at least forty meters.

A repeating series of five long whistles pealed through the room. Thin beams of green light formed a grid on the floor, a meter long and the width of the floor. The grid swept forward at high speed and as it encountered *Intrepid's* crew, it split off and inspected each person in turn. When the lights reached Tabby, the grid paused on her face plate, slowing scanning her eye sockets. The whistles changed to a klaxon.

"Frak, that's not good," Tabby said, turning slowly, catching movement in her peripheral vision.

Ada followed Tabby's gaze and discovered a bank of boxes that numbered in the low hundreds. They were a different size from the others, measuring three meters on each side. Three of the cubes now had blinking lights atop them, strobing in sequence with the klaxon alarm.

"Ada, we might want to clear out," Sendrei said nervously. "I don't like the look of this."

"Jonathan, are you getting anything on that console? Can you stop whatever's happening here?" Ada asked.

"We have limited control over the console. Apparently, Tabby's presence triggered a security algorithm. We are attempting to gain access and shut it down. Also, we've discovered lessor secured data stores and are transferring them," he said.

"How long do you need?" Ada asked.

"The systems are antiquated," he answered. "The transfer speed is limited."

"Have you found anything useful?" she asked.

"Are you serious?" Tabby asked. "Maybe we could have this conversation on *Intrepid?* From the looks of things, we're about to have company."

"There is much history here," Jonathan said. "We have discovered a reference to Iskstar."

Ada watched in awe as steel panels fell away from the blinking cubes and clattered to the floor so loudly her AI had to cut off the external feed and deaden sound with a cancelling wave.

"Ada? Seriously, I think it's time to go," Tabby said, uncharacteristically backing up as the contents of the cubical crates became exposed. Inside each box, a heavily armored spider, complete with eight metallic legs, fidgeted as if discovering a long-forgotten freedom. Atop the spider's body, a man's torso had been inelegantly joined.

"Jonathan?" Ada called, her heart pounding in her chest so much that her voice quavered. "We're running out of time."

"A retreat is critical," Jonathan said. "Please exit with all haste."

The next sound they heard was twenty-four metal claws hitting the ground all at the same time as the spider-men jumped from their positions on the wall.

"Smeglofy!" the deep voice of one of the creatures bellowed. As if in response to his exclamation, the lights of the remaining hundred or so cubes blinked in response. While Ada nor the rest of the crew had any idea what was actually said, the being's intent was quite clear.

"Ada, get out of here! Move it!" Tabby said, pushing her friend back toward the hall. "Get that ship ready to fly. This is about to suck."

Tabby turned back just in time to see a spider leap across the open floor and stab a long, thin leg through Clingman's body, pinning him to the floor as if he wore no armor at all. Sendrei and Tabby opened fire with their heavy blaster rifles, cutting the man's body off the spider.

In her peripheral vision, Tabby caught the advance of another creature and turned to meet it with her rifle. Moving more quickly than she expected, the man-spider got under the gun, forcing her to swing around and deflect a steel leg. If not for her preternatural speed, Tabby would have ended up just as Clingman had. With eight legs, however, the spider-man was already attacking with the others. Tabby found herself in a fight for her life as she spun, twisted, and jabbed her nano-crystalized, steel-reinforced hand into the armored skin, deflecting as quickly as she was attacked.

The sound of steel on steel alerted Tabby to Sendrei's battle, but she couldn't allow herself to be distracted. Pulling the Iskstar-crystal blade from her waist, she twisted up between thrashing claws and drove the blade into the bare chest cavity of the hybrid humanoid. The Iskstar blade, while no more effective than a sharp knife, penetrated the skin and brought the beast to the ground.

Something steel clattered to the ground and Tabby surged forward, lifting away from the hybrid to take stock of the situation. Sendrei remained intact, but the fight would end soon. He was barely holding his own, even with twin swords, trying desperately to keep the relentless spider from skewering him. With a flick, she threw the Iskstar blade, imbedding it between the creature's shoulders.

Not needing to be told, Sendrei bolted for the hallway. Tabby retrieved her blade and flew out of the room at high speed in her grav-suit. The sound of hundreds of metallic legs clicking on the floor was all she needed to hear. She swooped down and lifted Sendrei off his feet.

"Grav boots," she urged as they sank. Their weight was too much for the grav-suit to have superior speed. "More thrust, I'll control us."

Sendrei lit his arc-jets and Tabby struggled to keep them from careening into the walls as he straightened his legs.

"Ada, we're coming in hot. Go!" Sendrei warned as they were twenty meters from the craft.

"What about Clingman?" she called.

"He's gone, Ada," Tabby answered. "And we will be too if you don't get out of here."

Intrepid lurched forward as Tabby and Sendrei exited, ricocheted off the front door, and squirted toward the open loading bay. With a final push, Tabby guided Sendrei inside. Unfortunately, her angle was high and they skidded across the ceiling before falling to the deck a moment later. Even as they fell, they were tossed into the aft bulkhead as Ada entered an in-atmosphere combat burn.

"Jupiter piss, but that's going to leave a mark," Tabby said, slumping to the deck atop Sendrei as gravity dampers and inertial systems took over. "And *why* did it have to be spiders?"

Chapter 14

OVERLOAD

MHINA SYSTEM, HORNBLOWER

"Can you contact Munay?" I asked, reviewing the data-stream showing *Fleet Afoot's* rapid approach. With concern, I focused on the fact that the ship had already crossed the mid-point between where we believed he entered the Mhina star system and Kito. "Frak, he's moving way too fast."

I projected his current navigation path, attempting to discern where he might otherwise be headed. *Fleet Afoot* would just miss the massive gas planet Elea and its moon Kito by eighty-thousand kilometers. From where he'd started his burn, that distance was barely a rounding error. If he missed Kito, his current path would take him out into the deep dark.

"*Fleet Afoot* entered the system well after *Hornblower*," Nick said. "*Hornblower* isn't exactly stealthy. Munay should have been able to detect our presence."

"Something's wrong," I said. "Sandoval, you copy?" I waited for *Hornblower's* transmission to make a round trip from our position to Kito. At one hundred thousand kilometers from the moon, there was only a slight delay.

"Go ahead, *Hornblower,*" Sandoval answered.

"What's your fuel and consumable situation?" I asked.

"Running thirty percent on fuel, fifty days of consumables for current crew," he answered.

"Wait one," I answered, then spoke to my AI. "Calculate intercept of *Fleet Afoot* by *Shimmering Leaves*. Assume *Fleet Afoot* has zero fuel and is badly damaged. What materials do we need to bring both ships back with a significant safety margin?"

I pushed my HUD's view aside and stepped onto the elevator. My AI would calculate the trip in micro-seconds, but I was having trouble walking and interpreting all the data being presented. Fortunately, my AI recognized my limitations and switched to audible.

"*Shimmering Leaves will need an additional eight hundred kilograms of fuel. Further recommendations include replenishing atmospheric crystals, water and the following medical ...*"

"Stop, please," I ordered, causing the AI to cease its litany. Entering *Hornblower's* bridge, I slid into my chair, flicked my HUD display onto the holo projection and organized my AI's recommended loadout.

"What's the plan for *Fleet Afoot,* Cap?" Marny asked, entering the bridge a few moments behind Nick and me.

"Munay doesn't appear to be in control of the ship," I answered. "I'm sending Sandoval and *Shimmering Leaves* on a recovery mission. How soon will we be done offloading the freighter?"

"Forty minutes," she answered.

"Sandoval, please rendezvous with *Hornblower* at your earliest convenience," I said. "We're going to have you take on supplies and intercept *Fleet Afoot.* We're still working out the details and will give you a full mission brief on arrival."

"Copy that, Captain," he answered. "We're on our way. *Shimmering Leaves* out."

"*Fleet Afoot* could be having mechanical or system problems. I'd like to send Jester Ripples along," Marny said. "We could sweeten the pot by sending Semper to keep him out of trouble. Mind if I take this one over?"

The little blue-green alien, Jester Ripples, was more of a friend than crew and Marny and I were both sensitive to treating him like family. He was a soft-hearted alien who enjoyed being part of a group and I knew he'd do whatever we asked. By sending Semper along, he'd have both a protector and companion. While I loved the little bugger, he could be a bit cloying, especially now that Tabby was gone. He'd decided my bed was available to be shared. I'll admit to feeling relief at the notion of a break from him.

"Figured you'd be busy with the freighter," I said. "It's not like we don't have an enemy ship sitting next to us."

"I believe that's well under control," Marny said, pinching at her HUD and flicking an exterior view from just behind the number one 400mm cannon. The cannon was pointed directly at the Strix freighter's bridge. Poignantly, someone had programmed a series of lights that ran the length of the barrel so they turned on and off in a sequence, indicating the imminent launch toward the freighter.

"Subtle," I said.

"Wasn't what I was going for," Marny answered, raising an eyebrow. "Change of subject?"

"Sure."

"I'd have thought Ada and Tabby would have passed *Fleet Afoot,*" Marny said. "They didn't report seeing anything?"

"According to Tabby, they've been sailing through the deep dark," I answered. "They haven't seen as much as a rock, much less *Fleet Afoot.*"

"I saw that the wormhole transitions weren't showing up on their scans, but I didn't realize that area was so empty," Marny said. "Hard to imagine they missed Munay."

"They wouldn't have," Nick said. "No way would *Intrepid* miss that ship. Her sensor package is top-of-the-line."

"I guess we'll know more when we recover *Fleet Afoot,*" I said. "Mission is all yours, Marny."

"Aye, aye, Cap," she answered, sweeping her hand through my holo projection, taking my current plans with her.

I sat back in my chair, disappointed by the loss of a concrete task. As a leader, I rarely got to see tasks through to completion. Marny had explained that delegation was important, not only in building new leaders, but in freeing my mind to focus on bigger, more important things. When described like that, the concept was reasonable. However, it generally meant I never got to finish anything.

It turns out, there's a well-known problem for pilots called cognitive overload. Simply put, there are thousands of critical data-points that a pilot can focus on. Each of these data-points by themselves are important and a pilot has to get good at prioritizing them. For example, knowing that you're venting atmo is almost always critical information. That issue should receive immediate attention unless you're being fired on, are about to crash into something else, or dodging missiles, etc. In calm moments, it's always easy to identify top priorities. In the thick of things, not so much.

The problem I was running into, however, was that there were too many open problems, none of which were being resolved. I had a ship full of people who relied on me to deliver them to a city that hadn't been functioning for almost two hundred stans. Strix ships were attacking my people and *Intrepid* was off on a mission that had taken them to either another galaxy or possibly the empty space between galaxies. Abasi were under attack from within by Taji and no doubt would soon be under attack from Pogona. The problems seemed endless and I was at a loss as to what to do next.

"You doing okay over there, Cap?" Marny asked, breaking me from my reverie. She was at her station a few meters from where I sat on the bridge. She was busy dispatching orders about the supplies being loaded and was relaying commands to *Shimmering Leaves.*

I looked over to her but found that I couldn't form much of a response. "I think so."

She stood and walked back over to me, placing a hand on my shoulder. I felt the warmth of her body and the connection of her hand seemed to ground me. "I need you to get in the moment, Cap," she said. "If it isn't a priority in the next twenty-four hours, you need to let it go."

"There's so much," I responded, looking into her eyes.

"Not today, there's not," she said. "In fifteen minutes, you're going to land this old girl on Kito and we're going to focus on getting York settled. Kroerak will wait. Munay will wait. Strix will wait and, frankly, so will Abasi. You have twelve-hundred people who are depending on you to stay on target. Anything that distracts you from that plan is out of bounds. You copy?"

I nodded my head in agreement as the issues fogging my brain dissipated and I focused on settling the new town of York.

"Mom, Bish, Merrie, Hog, Nick, please report to the main conference room," I called. "Steward Bear, we're going to need a fresh pot of coffee."

"Aye, aye, Captain," Bear answered immediately.

"There you go, Cap. I'll get Sandoval and Jester Ripples on their way and join you," she said.

"HELM IS YOURS, CAPTAIN," pilot Ken Stolzman said, transferring control as I jumped into the empty pilot's chair. *Hornblower* had just touched the outer atmosphere and while I would have preferred to give the controls to Ada, she wasn't here.

"Sorry, son," Mom said, tapping Stolzman on the shoulder. "I'm going to need that chair."

I smiled, looking over to Mom as she relieved Stolzman from the starboard chair. Having served in the North American Marine Corps as a drop-ship pilot, Mom had hundreds of combat flight hours. She might be rusty, but I trusted her instincts and welcomed her presence.

"Aye, aye, ma'am," Stolzman answered, recognizing he really had no other choice.

"Our mass to lift is tight," Mom said, dialing through the various displays. "Are you sure we don't want to drop some weight in orbit before we go planet-side?"

"We'll be okay," I said. "Landing has to be easier than lifting off from Zuri. We're looking at .65g not .89g."

"Frak, right," she said. "Surprised my AI didn't catch that. We're still going to blow a lot of go-go juice."

I switched my calculations to use the .89g and saw what she'd seen. *Hornblower* would have landed, but we'd have likely made quite an impression when we did.

"That what you jarheads called it?"

"Damn straight," she said.

"Not a lot to be done about the 'go juice'," I said, drawing air quotes. I knew that would annoy her. "Livestock is stressed. We need to get this done."

A vibration rolled through *Hornblower* as we hit the upper atmosphere. I pulled back on the sticks, slowly orienting the battle cruiser so its massive engines pointed against the pull of the moon's gravity. From this point forward, I'd be limiting our fall much more than I'd be sailing. For atmospheric entry, I much preferred smaller ships like *Hotspur* and *Intrepid*, both of which had gravity repulsors powerful enough for controlled flight. The thought of our lost ship, *Hotspur*, gave me a pang of wistfulness. The small sloop would be vastly outclassed given the problems we currently faced, but the joy of sailing the nimble little gal brought back good memories.

"Silver finger for your thoughts," Mom said.

I couldn't afford to look over to her as I carefully watched the myriad gauges, adjusting control surfaces in turn to keep us in perfect line.

"Kind of hoping to keep us from going splat at this point," I said.

"No, that's not it," she said. "You were smiling."

"Thinking about simpler times," I said as we started jiggling even harder. "Nick, can you do something about that?"

"Got it, Liam," Nick answered and the jiggling dropped off considerably.

"Whoever says old ships aren't like old lovers has never sailed," she answered.

"Mom! No! Eww," I said.

"Focus," she said, chuckling and pointing out a potential problem I'd already seen but hadn't reacted to yet. "And don't be naïve. Pete was the love of my life, but he was hardly the only man I knew. And I seem to remember a few girls back on Colony-40 that took quite a shine to you."

I rolled my eyes. I knew her well enough to know that if I kept responding, she'd keep pushing. I had pretend-dated when I was younger, but had only really ever had eyes for Tabby. And I certainly hadn't felt about those girls anything like I had *Hotspur* or even *Sterra's Gift.*

"Nick, spool up those gravity systems. I'm going to cut over in twenty seconds," I said.

The process of landing the ship was straightforward, although I'd never personally executed the maneuver. Engineering, or in this case Nick, would bring up our gravity repulsors when we were at roughly three thousand meters. It would be my job to feather out our engines while at the same time, powering up and then down the other systems. According to Ada, the most likely error was overcompensation on the repulsors, which would cause us to bounce upward.

"Looking good, Liam. Nice and steady," Mom encouraged.

I suspected the twelve hundred people aboard were focused on the details of their new home, which they'd decided to call York. I could imagine them trying to locate homes they'd eventually have to draw lots for. For Mom, Nick and me, however, there was a three-hundred-meter-diameter landing pad that had our full and undivided attention.

"Drifting aft," Nick said.

I glanced at our inertia and discovered he was right. I'd been fighting a weird port slide and had momentarily been distracted.

"Got it," I said. "What's with the clouds? I've lost visibility."

From twenty thousand meters, we'd been given a great view of the region below. Clear Lake was a brilliant, sparkling, cerulean blue. The image fought with my recollection. I suspected the confusion was caused by the white blanket of snow coating the entire land mass.

"*Hornblower* is kicking up snow," Nick said. "You'll have to rely on instruments."

The visual data, while reassuring, was mostly unnecessary. The only issue would be if the snow was covering a significant change from the survey Sandoval and Lathrop had done when they'd first arrived a few days previous.

I took a deep breath. "All hands, prepare for touch-down in ten ... nine ..."

Someone opened the ship's public address so all twelve hundred ninety-two people could hear and join in as the AI finished the countdown.

I'd like to report that I landed perfectly without a bounce or a bump. The fact was I did both. In my defense, landing *Hornblower* as weighed down as she was, was like landing on a water balloon. I almost had a perfect touchdown at the point where the downward force became completely arrested and the repulsors only held the mass of the ship. This was exactly what Ada had warned about, but I thought I had it handled. We only bounced up about three meters. Of course, I did what any self-respecting pilot would do in that case, I over-corrected in the opposite direction.

Joyful cheers at a safe and soft landing were abruptly cut off as we swung up again and people realized things weren't exactly going as planned. When we landed hard, there were complaints, but the cheering soon returned and I took that to mean there was no harm done. Turned out I did disable a few. Really, my maneuver only dislocated one shoulder, tore a few tendons, and broke three fingers. I never did get a good accounting about how the particular injuries occurred.

I sighed and pushed back from the controls. "Any landing you can walk away from?" I asked, looking to Mom for reassurance.

"Battle cruisers aren't exactly designed for atmospheric operation," she said. "That was a first-rate piece of sailing, Liam. Same to you, Nicholas. Very impressed with the both of you."

"Pretty sure Ada didn't bounce," I said.

"She wasn't carrying twelve hundred ninety-two souls and twice that in livestock," Mom argued back. "Someday you'll look back on this and understand just how important that landing really was. The people of York owe you everything and you're worried about a little bump."

"I bet they're chomping at the bit to get out," Marny said, rescuing me from the conversation.

I'd always been uncomfortable with praise, but it felt good. I knew Mom wasn't the type to pull her punches. I also wished Tabby had been there to enjoy the moment, so I thumbed my ring to let her know I was thinking of her. Almost immediately my own ring pulsed in response.

I couldn't help the smile that crept to my lips. "Let's go."

IT SHOULD GO without saying that unloading twelve hundred people, four hundred twenty chickens, three hundred cows, two hundred nineteen pigs and the accompanying crap tonnes of feed – both pre and post processing – into the frigid cold required significant effort and was accompanied by quite a lot of complaining.

From my perspective, however, the move was executed flawlessly. What was now the new town of York had roughly been home to around sixty thousand. Its new residents were doing a pretty good job of figuring out how to make the best use of what the area had to offer.

"Might have been nice if we'd picked a warmer season," Curtis Long said, holding up a cup of synth coffee, nodding at me. It was as close to a compliment as the man was capable of and I raised my own cup in his direction.

"Sounds like you've had good luck hunting?" I answered, looking down at the bowl of steaming chili in front of me. Eating real meat was taking some getting used to, but that was one of the virtues of the highly-seasoned stew Patty cooked. Really, it almost always tasted the same, whether with real meat or otherwise.

Hog's wife, Patty, had wasted no time in taking over one of York's existing restaurants. While much of the equipment required repair, she insisted the level of tech wasn't considerably different from that of Zuri, only now she had a captive audience. It hadn't taken us a lot to get the restaurant operational as it had been one of the municipal priorities, behind energy and water.

"Wildlife is starting to smarten up," Curtis Long piped in from across the restaurant. "Won't always be this easy."

I smiled, looking back at those gathered at my table.

"Man would complain about ice water in the desert," Hog chortled.

"I understand coffee plants don't like cold weather," Patty said. "What are you doing about those plants you brought along?"

"I'm paying the Begorian boys to bring soil up to the third floor of the Bold building," I said.

On the opposite corner from Patty's restaurant, House of the Bold had claimed a five-story office building that sported a curved glass façade overlooking the slushy Clear Lake a hundred meters farther east. I'd personally claimed a conference room, several adjoining offices and an area to lay out planting beds and artificial lights for my coffee. As far as I knew, there was only one other coffee plant in the entire galaxy aside from the plants left behind to grow wild on Zuri. I just knew I was sitting on a gold-mine. Of course, I'd have to up my production from twelve plants, but I was willing to be patient. "I told those boys I'd cut 'em in on sales going forward if they helped with production."

"Good luck with that," Bish scoffed. "Those boys been a pain in my side for as long as I can remember."

"Mez, any more trouble?" I asked, ignoring Bish.

Mez Rigdon was York's sheriff on Zuri and had volunteered to stay in the job. There'd been some initial friction concerning people's housing choices. Some of the units had turned out to be less than desirable and there had been bad feelings. Fortunately, Mez intervened, keeping peace long enough for York's council to step in and find a long-term solution.

"We're going to need to move the Springfields," she said. "If I'd seen they were moving in next to Grubs, I'd have stopped it. They just don't get along that well."

"Are they okay moving?" Hog asked.

"No. They think Grubs should move. It's simple math, though. If Grubs move, it's five households. Springfields only have two," Mez said. "Neither family wants to give in."

"Give 'em ten percent extra allotment," Hog said. "That should ease tensions. You okay with that, Silver?"

"Will ten percent do it?" she asked.

"If they get to rub it in Grub's face, it will," Mez answered.

I felt a presence over my shoulder and looked up to find Curtis Long looming.

"Need something, Curtis?" I asked, uncomfortably.

"What are you doing with those grounded freighters?" he asked. "Anyone make a claim on em?"

"They belong to the Musi," Marny answered.

With all the activity, I'd almost forgotten about the four Musi crews running loose. Before we arrived, Sandoval and Lathrop had discovered four different crews looting the cities, filling miserable little freighters with anything that wasn't tied down, including substantial piles of fuel.

"They're criminals," Long said. "We should hunt 'em down."

"And do what? Kill 'em?" Marny asked. "They're just trying to survive. Did you know the Musi have no homeworld? Strix and Musi came from the same place and the Musi are only allowed on that world if they're in an ownership contract with the Strix."

I sighed. I'd heard the story before. Some Musi voluntarily enslaved themselves to the Strix for a place to live. I couldn't imagine how low you'd have to feel to voluntarily live with Strix.

"Look, I wanted to stop the looting until we could figure out what was going on. Now that we're here, we have enough fuel. Was it wrong for the Musi to try and take material the Abasi worked so hard for? Yes. The fact that we have permission doesn't exactly mean we worked any harder for those materials," I said.

"What are you saying, Cap?" Marny asked.

"Make contact with the Musi," I said. "We'll repair their ships and give them enough food and fuel to get them home. If they want to live on Faraji, we can work out a treaty."

"You're giving them the only other inhabitable planetary object in the system?" Bish asked incredulously.

"I've been there," I said. "I guarantee you don't want to go. Once they get going, we can collect taxes or something."

"I'll take care of it," Marny said, standing.

"You don't want to see Munay?" I asked.

We'd received word that Sandoval had recovered *Fleet Afoot* and was expected in York in less than thirty minutes.

"Is he conscious yet?" Marny asked.

Munay had been discovered alone and unconscious on *Fleet Afoot*, which had taken a significant beating. Whoever he'd found, they had very nearly done him in. I looked to Nick.

"Medical AI says it'll take a night in the tank," he said.

"Do we know what happened to the navigation data?" I asked. "How is it possible to lose it all? I didn't think it was even possible with smart fabrics and all the systems we had in there."

"*Fleet Afoot* isn't human manufacture," Nick said. "I'm hoping we can find some piece of equipment where the information got uploaded. Sandoval's team didn't find anything yet."

"Jester Ripples couldn't find it?"

"No," Nick said, crushing what I considered our biggest hope. "*Shimmering Leaves* is down. Sandoval is moving Munay over to *Hornblower* now."

"Let's go," I said, standing.

"What about our meeting?" Bish asked, annoyed by the sudden change.

"Keep having it," I said. "In our absence, Mom has authority to make decisions for House of the Bold."

"And you're going to run off and take our only protection with you?" he pushed back.

"I've been down this road before, Bish," I said. "*Hornblower* doesn't belong to York. We'll do our best by you, but we have our own priorities."

"That's crap," he argued.

"That's reality," I said and leaned in to give Mom a quick hug. "Come over when you're done. I'm sure Greg would like to see you."

"I will," she said.

Nick and I exited into bright sunshine which reflected off the quickly melting snow. Where Zuri had been hot and muggy, its cool season barely reaching five degrees at night, Kito had an entire half a dozen ten-day periods where the average low temperature was below zero. I thought I'd find the cold annoying, but our suits did a fine job of keeping us warm, so the iciness just added variation.

"You going to try to wake him?" Nick asked as we flew through the pressure barrier and onto the flight deck.

"If Flaer says its safe," I answered, sailing through the hallways at speed to the medical bay. Flaer, of course, was our resident doctor and the significant other of our primary gunner, Sendrei.

"If Flaer says what's safe?" Flaer asked, uncannily picking up the conversation I'd thought was too far away for her to hear.

"I want to talk to Munay," I said. "Can you wake him?"

"I'd rather give him a night in the tank first, but I don't think it'll cause too much trouble," she said. "I was just prepping him. You can help."

I wasn't about to argue with her, so I helped peel back Munay's charred vac-suit. His AI had done a good job of keeping him alive, but it was clear he'd run into something bad. Sections of his leg were badly burned and the control circuits of his suit broke as we pulled it off. I'd held out some hope that his suit held the information we so desperately needed, but it looked to be a complete loss.

For several minutes we worked in quiet as Nick and I helped Flaer apply patches and swabbed at things best left undescribed.

"Man, he's really been through the wringer," I said.

"He's responding nicely, though," Flaer said. "This one has the heart of a fighter."

I chuckled. I'd found Munay rather annoying on multiple occasions. There was no doubt in my mind that he had a fighter's heart.

"Can he hear us?" I asked.

"Hoffen?" His voice was so quiet that if he hadn't been elevated on a table in front of me, I wouldn't have heard him. The sensors Flaer had placed on him showed increased stress and I could sense he was trying to sit up.

I placed my hands on his shoulder and gently pushed him back. "I'm here, Greg. You're safe. I can hear you."

"I got 'em," he whispered and reached around with his burned arm, trying to get to his mouth.

"Easy Greg," I said, my heart starting to race as I gently resisted his attempt to move. "Got who?"

"Frakking bugs," he said, coughing violently and jerking his hand away with more strength than I'd have expected. "I found their home."

"I'm sedating him," Flaer said. "He's hurting himself."

"No!" he coughed again and spat blood onto his bare chest, then relaxed as the medicine calmed him.

I swabbed at the goop he'd coughed up and tossed it into a nearby reclaimer port when I heard a clank against the metallic wall inside the small cavity.

"Stop reclaimer!" I ordered, hoping my AI was fast enough.

"What is it?" Nick asked.

"He had something in his mouth," I said, reaching into the goo and trying not to think about what I was doing. My hand closed around a small object and I extracted it, using a fresh swab to wipe it off. It was shaped like a tooth, but I could tell it was much more.

Chapter 15

GOOD COP, DEMON COP

MENDARI SYSTEM, INTREPID

"Clingman never stood a chance," Sendrei groaned, slowly getting to his feet after having been thrown against the bulkhead. "And what kind of bull-shite civilization attacks with no provocation?"

"They call themselves Mendari," Jonathan answered. "At least that is a reasonable translation."

"They're spider people and I thought I'd seen everything," Tabby said, making her way forward, not bothering to remove the pistol at her waist before entering *Intrepid's* bridge.

"That would be a poor classification," Jonathan said. "The sentries which attacked were a fusion of biological and mechanical. The biological entities are rather mundane by our current standards."

"They looked like spiders," Tabby answered hotly.

"What happened to Clingman?" Ada asked.

"We were attacked by three of those man-spider hybrids," Sendrei answered. "After we dispatched the first, they were upon us. Clingman's armored vac-suit was pierced by a mechanical limb."

"How many were there? It looked like we woke the entire station,"

Tabby said, tuning *Intrepid's* forward screen to replay the data-stream of their hasty exit from the rusted building.

With rapt attention, she watched as Brockette hustled Ada toward the ship, followed a few moments later by Sendrei and Tabby rocketing out, unstable in their dual grav-suit and arc-jet-fueled flight. At first, only a pair of man-spider creatures emerged, giving chase, but as video continued, the entire entrance to the rusted ruin boiled, disgorging one after another. Tabby froze the scene and rolled it back, freezing on the forward pair as they leapt toward *Intrepid.*

"Sendrei, are you seeing this?" Tabby asked. "This thing's not over."

"Scan ship's skin," Sendrei ordered, bolting back up from his station. "They're trying to get around to the cargo-hold. It's still open."

At about the same moment the external vid sensor discovered two hybrid warriors clinging to *Intrepid,* Warning klaxons sounded on the bridge, alerting the crew of a potential breach.

"Seriously with the alarm timing?" Tabby said sarcastically as she followed Sendrei from the bridge.

"All hands, emergency combat burn," Ada announced and spun *Intrepid* over hard.

With virtually no warning, those on the ship who weren't strapped in, were flung into the nearest bulkhead. As if to add insult to injury, Ada spun *Intrepid* once again in the opposite direction, tossing the same crew in the opposite direction.

"What the frak, Chen!" Tabby complained, peeling herself from the bulkhead.

Tabby's complaint was overridden by Ada's whoop of exultation over tactical comms. "I got one!" Her celebration was cut short a moment later when she recognized a new problem. "Frak. There's one in the hold. It's got Brockette!"

Using her grav-suit, Tabby squirted around Sendrei, who was still finding it difficult to identify up and down. Before she cleared the hallway, Tabby heard heavy gunfire followed by a short-lived scream. The scene she came upon in the hold was grisly. The body of Brockette, having been torn in two by the invader, lay on the floor.

"Tabitha, if you could keep the invader alive, it would be of benefit," Jonathan said over comms.

Tabby grunted in response, "Find another one."

The man-spider whirled, sensing Tabby's presence as she entered the bay. Standing three and a half meters high, the sentry was roughly man-shaped on top. It had no hair on its gray, bumpy skull, pock-marked and unhealthy-looking skin sagged down the torso where it met machine, and heavily-muscled arms ended in four-fingered hands, which grasped thin, metallic arms leading into the spidery body. Where skin met machine, the humanoid body was inflamed, its skin attempting to reject the joining.

Tabby lunged forward, taking advantage of her ability to float above the deck. At the last moment, the man-spider jumped nimbly up to meet her. Subconsciously, Tabby picked up on something she wouldn't have been able to easily put into words. Having left the ground, her attacker had no further mobility and was clearly looking for a grapple.

"Demon!" it shouted as they met in midair.

In the back of her mind, Tabby questioned the translation Jonathan had put together. Pushing the unproductive thought away, she slapped at the nearest leg as it bent and twisted unnaturally toward her.

Instead of dodging the next attacking leg, Tabby grabbed the metal, encircling the shaft with both hands. Pushing with her grav-suit, she surged into the torso, sending the two hurtling toward the deck. Just before impact, the metal legs snapped outward, swiveled and caught them both, cushioning their landing. Tabby smiled, having expected the move. With her hands grasping the leg, she swung a foot up to brace against its base and pulled with her considerable strength. For a moment, nothing happened, although the torso of the man-spider turned, its face looking down at her with rage-filled eyes.

The feel of metal giving way fueled Tabby's efforts and she brought her other leg up beneath her. A great scream filled the room as she and the leg came free. Trails of green fluid and long wires followed behind the severed metal.

"Port side!" Sendrei yelled.

Without hesitation, Tabby dropped the leg and turned, just as a second spider leg caught her mid-abdomen, piercing her side and sticking her to the floor. She screamed in pain but had the presence of mind to roll into the leg as yet another sought to finish her off.

The sound of Sendrei's gunfire drew the man-spider's attention and Tabby felt the metal slide out of her flesh. For ordinary humans, the trauma would have been enough to keep them down, with continued life expectancy low. Since most of Tabby's abdomen had been manufactured on Mars in a military hospital, her pain was very real, but she was far from disabled.

Taking advantage of Sendrei's distraction, she pushed up from the deck and grabbed the very leg that had pinned her. Unaware of the trouble she was about to cause, the man-spider charged at Sendrei, flattening two of its metallic legs as a shield in front of the human torso.

"Not sure how many of these you need," Tabby grunted, vital fluids leaking from her stomach as her grav-suit sought to staunch the bleeding.

Tabby knew she couldn't continue long but didn't dare allow the advantage to pass. Having a feel for the pressure required, she planted both feet and ripped out the leg, even as the beast sprinted toward Sendrei. With only two legs left on its left side, the spider was forced to drop its shield to maintain balance, just as additional crew joined Sendrei at the door.

Faced with multiple blasters, the man-spider sprang to jump, but instead spun out of control, unable to adjust to the asymmetric pressure caused by an uneven number of legs. With dripping leg in hand, Tabby hurled herself at the flailing creature and drove the metal through its chest, pinning it into the forward bulkhead. Tabby allowed herself to sink to the floor, carefully watching the thrashing beast in its death throes.

"Oh, frak, does that hurt," Tabby said, throwing an arm over Sendrei's shoulder as he lifted and carried her from the hold.

"How are you even talking?" he asked, half-running down the ramp that led to the smaller Deck Two which held the brig and medical bay, just behind crew country sleeping quarters at the ship's bow.

"Decided not to go with factory originals," she answered, lightly tapping her stomach. She winced in pain.

"Rings of Saturn, you're a complete mess," Ada exclaimed, having arrived in the medical bay before them.

Tabby groaned, but turned on her friend. "Frak, Ada, who's sailing the ship?"

"Garcia has the helm," Ada answered. "Sendrei can you get back to the bridge? Jonathan wants us to capture one of those bugs alive and we've got one pinned down."

"Capture, how?" Sendrei asked.

"Same as you did when you were a kid," Tabby grunted. "Pull out its legs."

"I never..." Sendrei started. "Never mind, we'll figure it out."

Ada pushed her back onto the table. "Frak, Tabby, you're hurt. Sit back and stop talking."

"Maybe it was just Liam who pulled out spider's legs." Tabby chuckled as numbing medicine brought sweet relief and drug-induced bliss. "I was gonna pull out all that sucker's legs and let him spin like a top. You're so pretty, Ada." She reached up to push Ada's dreads out of her face.

"Might have overdone the pain meds," Ada muttered and pushed Tabby's hand back to the table.

"I don't know what I'd do without you," Tabby continued. "You're like the sister I never had. You know I used to be jealous because Liam has a crush on you."

"We are sisters." Ada chuckled as she peeled back Tabby's suit and started working on her wound. "And, Liam has a crush on a lot of women. I've always been impressed at how you don't let that bother you."

"He can't help it. He's a horny little toad, but he's faithful and he knows I'd remove his little toad if he wasn't. Is everyone okay?" Tabby asked, her mind drifting. "Are we safe?"

"Brockette didn't make it," Ada answered, "but we're safe because of you. Now go to sleep. You'll feel better in the morning.

"Yeah, he got messed up bad. I hope he didn't suffer," Tabby said, finally giving over to the drugs.

Ada continued to strip her friend down and then moved her to the medical tank, filling it after securing a mask onto Tabby's face.

"Captain," Jonathan's voice called over comms as Ada dropped the bloodied tools into a cleaner.

"Go ahead, Jonathan." She instructed the room to self-clean and stepped out, carrying Tabby's soiled grav-suit. The suit would eventually repair itself, but she could speed the process by placing it into a special bath Jonathan had constructed for the specific purpose.

"Sendrei has captured the Mendari sentry," he said. "We are bringing it to the aft hold now."

"I'm on my way," Ada said, running up the ramp leading to Deck One and the aft hold. Instead of heading there directly, she diverted to her quarters and dropped Tabby's grav-suit into the repair solution. Checking herself in the mirror, she wiped away a dab of blood that had somehow transferred to her face. She sighed, cleaning the spot. There was always a price to be paid for their missions and some days it bothered her more than others. Tabby would be cavalier about the attack she'd survived, however, had the claw been five-centimeters up and to the left, her friend would be dead.

With resolve Ada entered the aft hold and took in the blood-soaked deck. The badly wounded man-spider sat quietly, several of its mechanical legs lying on the deck, victims of some massive trauma. The other legs were bound in a bright, green gooey substance. The alien locked its eyes onto her as she approached.

"Your pistol, Sendrei," she said.

"Ada?" he asked.

"Captain," she corrected. "Your pistol."

Sendrei nodded and handed his pistol to her.

"Why have you attacked my people?" Ada asked, approaching so that she stood next to the goo-covered legs. She returned the alien's gaze looking for signs of intelligence.

"You are blasphemy," he said. "Iskstar must be destroyed."

"Jonathan, are you sure the translation is right? How could they know of Iskstar?" Ada asked, not turning away as she spoke. "Is this why Kroerak let them live?"

The alien narrowed its eyes. "Iskstar is of devil. Kroerak bugs are plague from god. You are demons," he said, spitting into Ada's face.

Ada accepted a towel from Sendrei and wiped her face.

"Much of the Mendari social structure is entwined with deep religious beliefs," he said. "We are using familiar human constructs for the translation of gods and demons. Also, we have sufficient evidence in the recovered data stores to have confidence translating both Iskstar and Kroerak."

"You attacked us because of Iskstar?" Ada asked.

"The demon my compatriot banished carried Iskstar, and the one whose eyes glowed has the demonic possession," it answered.

"You know of Kroerak," she said. "We came because we believed your homeworld was under attack by the bugs. We came to help, but you attacked us. Why? We're not demons. Our common enemy is Kroerak."

"The Kroerak are no longer our enemy," it answered. "They were easily stopped."

"How?" Ada asked.

"By fire," he responded, smiling. "Only the faithful survived the great cleansing and now you have awakened us. We killed our devil, but now we know that more Iskstar live. We will hunt it as we did before. We will cleanse those that stand in our way."

"You burned the Kroerak? That couldn't possibly work," Ada said. "They don't burn."

"No, but our world did," he answered.

A chill ran through Ada's body and goose flesh raised on her arms. "You burned your world to get rid of Kroerak? What about your people?"

"The faithful were brought to slumber upon this moon," he said. "The sheep were sacrificed to the fire. How can you not understand this simple tactic? The bugs require food. We forced them to leave by removing their food source. Our home has not yet recovered but we know of others. Now that we are again awake, we will begin our civilization again. Only this time, we will start as faithful."

The alien strained against the goo and plopped a single leg free, whipping it around toward Ada. Had she remained in place, the leg would have pierced her, as one had Tabby. She'd been expecting the attempt and shot from the floor before the leg was completely free.

Instead of flying back, however, she moved up next to the bound alien and pushed Sendrei's pistol against its head. "You're not going anywhere, champ," she said, struggling not to pull the trigger.

"Send me to my maker, demon," he said, eyes wide as he pushed his head into the pistol's barrel. "I will die a hero at the hands of the devil's own."

"Not today, bug man," Ada said, pulling away with sheer force of will and handing Sendrei's pistol back to him. "Roby, report to the cargo hold."

"Aye, aye, Captain," Roby responded a bit too quickly. Ada grinned darkly as she realized he'd likely watched the entire sequence.

With the engineering bay only a few meters from the aft hold, Roby showed up a couple of moments later. "Oh, frak. What's that smell?" he asked. "I think I'm going to be sick."

"Knock it off, Roby," Ada said.

"I can't there's, ugh, stuff everywhere," he said, staggering away toward the hatch where he'd entered.

"Raise your face plate," Sendrei offered.

Roby did as Sendrei suggested and straightened, his eyes darting between Ada and the alien. "Um, what do you need?"

"We're taking this Mendari prisoner," she said. "I need you to figure out how to remove its legs without killing it."

"How?" Roby asked.

"Tabby just pulled them out," she answered. "I was hoping as an engineer you could be a bit more elegant. Sendrei, maybe you should stay and help. This guy's going to be a handful."

"Aye, aye, Captain," Sendrei answered. "And, if you don't mind my saying, not pulling that trigger was the right thing to do."

"I'm not sure of that," she answered over her shoulder as she walked out.

"RISE AND SHINE, SLEEPYHEAD," Ada said gently into the comms that linked her to Tabby in the medical tank. The AI had already started waking Tabby and Ada knew a friendly voice would put her at ease.

An old pro in a medical tank, Tabby placed a hand on the mask that covered her mouth and nose. Tracing its features, she located the strap that held it around the back of her neck and pulled it free. The tank's monitor, recognizing the danger of an unmasked, submerged patient, executed an emergency dump of the suspension fluid. By the time the mask was off, the liquid was rolling away from her body.

"You know it's customary to give the patient shorts and a bra-top," Tabby said. "You know, for privacy."

"Since I'm the only one who's been here and the one to take off your clothing, I think your point is moot," Ada answered. "And you definitely have nothing to be ashamed of."

Tabby rolled her eyes. The two had made a game of uncomfortable innuendo and she was sure someday one of them would take it too far. She also wasn't about to let Ada win by admitting her fears either.

Tabby stepped from the tank and accepted a towel from Ada, pushing the translucent blue gel from her body. When she got to her abdomen, she inspected the scar left behind by the mechanical leg. "Wow, that sucker really got me," she said. "Liam is going to be pissed."

"He's not the only one. You nearly died, Tabby," Ada said. "You need to be more careful. There are a lot of people who care about you."

"I thought I had it," she said. "Something's off. I've slowed down and I'm losing strength."

"Looked plenty strong when you pulled that thing's legs out," Ada said.

"Pretty great, right?" Tabby grinned, shimmying into the suit liner Ada offered. "But the loss is measurable in the gym. I've lost at least thirty percent of my strength. I'd guess speed is roughly the same."

"That's not good. When we get back, we'll have to get you checked out," Ada said.

"Back where?" Tabby asked.

"Good point," Ada said, with a quick rise of her eyebrows. "Change of subject. The aliens are officially nuttier than a hundred-stan fruit cake."

"Why would fruit cake have nuts?" Tabby asked.

"Not sure, but it's something my dad used to say. They claim the Iskstar is the devil and they attacked us because your eyes glowed. It called you a demon," Ada said.

"That's nutty all right. Although, I do get these dreams," she said, shrugging.

"There's more. There were originally two warring nations on the planet you wanted us to visit," she said.

"Already told you that," Tabby said, raising an eyebrow.

"Right. But according to what Jonathan found, that war was fought millennia ago," Ada said.

"Could have been a different war. My visions have been dead-on so far." Tabby leaned against the medical table and crossed her arms, feeling uncomfortable with the direction the conversation was taking.

"If I may, Tabitha," Jonathan interjected, startling her. Jonathan wasn't in the medical bay and she hadn't realize he was monitoring the conversation.

"Frak, a little warning would be nice," Tabby answered.

"My apologies," Jonathan said. "It is our assertion that your visions have been validated with the information we've discovered. If you accept that the Iskstar species has a life-span in the tens of thousands of standard human years, your vision perfectly aligns with the independent datum we've gathered."

"You're doing that thing again," Tabby said.

"Thing?" Jonathan asked.

"If you want the short kids to have cookies, you need to put 'em on a lower shelf," she said.

"An amusing idiom," Jonathan said. "We are certain you recognize the validity of the Iskstar species having long life."

"I just wanted to talk about cookies," Tabby said, earning her a raised eyebrow from Ada. "No, seriously, I'm starving. And, wait! How would Mendari know enough about Iskstar to decide it's evil?"

"We have several theories," Jonathan answered. "We attempted discussion with the Mendari prisoner, but he has been unwilling to participate in conversation."

"Oooh. You played good cop." Tabby nodded with a glint of mischief. "Maybe I could get those cookies to go."

"Go?" Jonathan asked. "We feel you are mixing metaphors. Where are you going?"

"Why, I'm going to go play bad cop."

Ada pulled Tabby's Iskstar-tipped dagger from beneath a towel on a nearby table and handed it to her. "Go get 'em."

"We assume you've lost interest in cookies," Jonathan said dryly, as Tabby turned to walk out of the medical bay.

"Sendrei said you had a sense of humor," Tabby answered, over her shoulder, as Jonathan turned to follow. "I didn't believe him, but there you go."

"Humor does present a significant challenge," Jonathan answered.

Tabby palmed her way past the brig's security panel only two doors forward of the medical bay. "Don't get a big head."

Initially, she was shocked to look on the prisoner. With mechanical legs removed, it sat immobile in the middle of the cell, its bulbous thorax nestled in a hastily assembled nest.

"I speak not with demons," the Mendari sentry said before she could speak.

"Do you know how people become Iskstar demons?" Tabby asked.

"I do not care," he answered.

"Sure you do. Your enemies were once like you, before they became Iskstar," she said, taking an educated guess.

"We destroyed them along with the seed that spawned them," he answered, watching her carefully as she opened his cell and stepped in close, daring him to grab at her.

"So, you do know." Tabby grinned and pulled her Iskstar dagger from beneath her grav-suit. "Have you ever seen the devil's seed in person? Or was it just rumors you whispered to each other while locked in your cages."

Intently, Tabby watched for a reaction. She wasn't disappointed. As soon as she'd drawn the weapon, the Mendari's eyes locked on it, unblinking.

"Where did you get that? The Iskstar was destroyed," he whispered, his bluish lips forming a frown.

Tabby brought the dagger up to her face and licked the side of the blade, inadvertently catching the side of her tongue on its sharp edge. In that it added to the fiction she was building, she smiled at the pain and rolled her eyes lustfully, not sure if facial expressions translated, but selling it all the same. "You didn't tell me if you knew how your friends became polluted with Iskstar." She touched a finger to her tongue and held it so she could inspect the blood.

"I am not afraid."

Tabby reached forward with her bloodied finger and smiled when the Mendari batted her hand away, clearly worried about transfer.

"Blood doesn't do it," Tabby said, switching hands so quickly that a normal person couldn't have followed. Her Iskstar blade was suddenly thrust into his face. "This, on the other hand..."

"Stop," he interrupted, lunging away and falling out of the basket that held him upright.

Tabby pressed her lead and followed him to the ground leaping onto his body and keeping the blade next to his face.

"You'll tell me everything I want or I'll turn you into Iskstar," Tabby growled. "Tell me, sentry, what's it going to be? Want to have some fancy glowing eyes?"

"Please. Do not make me a demon," the sentry begged.

Tabby straightened and slid the Iskstar dagger back into its slit in her grav-suit. The sentry flinched as she grabbed his hand and pulled him upright. "I'm going to leave now," she said. "I strongly recommend talking freely with the next person through that door, because next time I visit, it won't be for a chat."

Chapter 16

TOO MANY SECRETS

MHINA SYSTEM, KITO MOON OVER PLANET ELEA, HORNBLOWER

"Cap, Mez Rigdon rounded up those Musi over by Plymouth," Marny reported, handing her infant son, Little Pete, to a young woman who'd offered to help nanny the child. "Do you want to say anything to them before we send them away?"

I raised an eyebrow at the mention of the city's name. A group of York citizens had requested permission to assign names to local features, but I hadn't realized Mom had agreed to it so quickly. In fact, my HUD showed otherwise; the four cities that surrounded Clear Lake like points on a compass were all renamed: York to the west, Plymouth to the east, Vancouver to the north and Rio de Kito to the south. The latter, whose name translated to 'River of Kito' in Spanish appropriately sat next to the wide river that flowed from the lake.

"Did we give the Musi enough supplies to survive their trip to Faraji?" I asked.

"There were dozens of them," Marny said. "But we gave them the fuel you specified and enough meal bars and water to last three ten-days."

"Did they seem okay with that?" I asked. "Are their ships in good enough repair to make it?"

The trip to Faraji, the cold moon of the second gas planet in the system, Kobe, was estimated at two ten-days. That generous span took into account the current location of the planets in the solar system, the poor design of the Musi ships and the disrepair of their systems. Even though the Musi had come to Kito to steal whatever material they could find, I still felt responsible to not send them to their deaths.

"They grovel too much to tell," Marny answered. "Rigdon thinks they still believe we're going to shoot 'em down."

"Probably not," I said. "We have exactly two ships, three if you count *Fleet Afoot*, to patrol an entire solar system. No. Double the rations we gave 'em and have Mez send 'em off."

"We have an update on ships," Marny said. "Good news for once."

I narrowed my eyes. I'd been paying close attention to repairs on each of our ships and couldn't imagine Marny had more up-to-date information than I did. "What's that?"

"Well, you know when the Felio left Mhina, they didn't have room for machinery, right? They packed it all up so it wouldn't get ruined."

"I just reran the data-streams from our first visit a couple years ago," I said. "I was surprised at how little degradation there had been in the machinery."

"Well, the Walton boys were out running an exploratory mission for Silver and found a municipal warehouse down by the docks," Marny said.

"That's something." I was suddenly very interested. "What'd they find?"

"No spaceships, but that shouldn't be much of a surprise. They found patrol vehicles, both marine and air-based," she said. "They need work, but initial scans show they're not in horrible shape. Rigdon is already asking about them."

"She's tired of running around in a Popeye?" I asked, grinning.

The Popeyes were great for extended fighting, but were a complete pain in the butt if you needed to climb in and out very often. Moreover, if Mez intended to patrol more than just the York area, the Popeye's speed was simply too slow – ditto for the tank and Stryker vehicles.

"Anything I need to do about that?" I asked.

"No, just letting you know. Silver has it under control. Fixing them comes down to prioritizing time on the replicators we have access to," Marny said. "There's a lot of infrastructure available, but it's in pretty bad shape. Since we have access to the Abasi knowledge base, we have all the information we need to repair everything. It's just going to take time."

"Not sure what I'd do if Mom wasn't here," I said. "This stuff drives me nuts."

"We'd find someone else who was good at organization," Marny said. "The value Silver brings is that she has a tie to you, so you don't have to worry she's not considering House of the Bold."

"Feel like she might give the store away," I said. "She's overly compassionate sometimes."

"Apple doesn't fall far from the tree, Cap," Marny answered. "You're more generous than a lot of people in your position would be. Don't forget. This isn't Mars Protectorate. If we need to walk back decisions she makes later, we can do that. This isn't a representational democracy, even though you and your mother are setting up the local government that way."

"Seems like a goal though, doesn't it?"

"Democracy for Mhina system?" Marny asked.

"Yeah. I love Mshindi and all that, but the way Abasi governs doesn't feel right to me," I said.

"Pick your battles, Cap," Marny said. "I'm not sure the people of York are ready for anything much beyond survival."

"You're right, and I'm not ready to battle the likes of Bish daily, either." I had some experience seeding small communities of refugees. More often than not, there was one person I clashed with on an epic scale and it gave me a bad taste in my mouth just thinking about it.

"So, you ready to go wake up Munay?" she asked.

"That seems fast," I said. "He was pretty messed up. I'd like to know how he got that ship back here in the shape it was in."

"Agreed," Marny said.

We'd been talking in my personal office, the first room off *Hornblower's* bridge and part of the captain's suite. With Tabby gone, I slept on the couch, not interested in using the empty bedroom without her.

As if hearing my thoughts, Marny continued. "What do you hear from Tabby and Ada?"

"Not much more than is in the report I sent out," I said. "Notably, she is feeling some weakness. She says her strength and reflexes are off from her peak and she isn't sure what's going on with that."

"It's easy to get lost in the forest of urgency," Marny said sagely as we stepped onto the lift that would take us to Deck Two where the medical bay was. "How far off?"

"Thirty percent. She's still way beyond everyone else, but it bothers her," I said. "*Intrepid's* medical AI couldn't find anything specifically wrong but did verify tissue degradation."

"What if it's Iskstar causing this?" Marny jumped on the subject. "Have you gotten scanned? Cap, this could be a big deal."

"You think Iskstar is harming her?" I asked.

"I have no idea," Marny said.

"What's harming who?" Nick asked, joining us as we entered the medical bay.

Marny ignored the question and pointed to the outline of human feet on the ground. "Clothes off, Cap," she ordered.

I raised my eyebrows, catching Nick's eyes. "But ... your husband is here," I said, grinning.

"I'm with Liam on this," Nick said, joining in. "You're entirely too quick to get his clothing off. What? Now that we're married, you're losing interest and going after low hanging fruit?"

"I'll thank you not to talk about my fruit," I quipped back.

"Are you boys about done?" Marny asked, pursing her lips, not even remotely amused. "Liam left out of his report that Tabby is experiencing tissue degradation. It's affecting her strength and reflexes. You both know she nearly died to that man-spider that attacked. What if it's Iskstar? I'm not messing around here."

"A man can hope," I said, sighing dramatically as I pulled off my grav-suit and suit-liner, stepping onto the scanner pad.

Flaer, who had been standing next to the medical tank where the unconscious Munay still rested, stepped over, recognizing the change in focus. "Have you been feeling run-down or tired lately?" she asked, as the scanner's bright-green lights danced across my skin. She pulled a glass tablet from a pocket on the wall and swiped a finger across the surface.

"We good here?" I asked, accepting my suit-liner from Marny. I'd long since lost whatever need for privacy I once had, although I kept my body turned to keep things rated PG.

"There is degradation," Flaer said, flicking the results to me. "Twelve percent from your last scan. Some of this is explained by a recent dip in exercise, although the AI suggests that should account for one percent at most."

"You're not exercising?" Marny asked, raising her eyebrow.

"Haven't really felt up to it lately," I said.

"Still don't think it's Iskstar related?" Marny asked.

"Is there evidence of that?" I asked sincerely, looking to Flaer.

"Nothing direct," she said. "It is beyond our technology to identify the source of the degradation. There appears to be no active agent; no disease or parasite."

I looked back to Marny quizzically and she answered my question. "Tabby carries the Iskstar crystal with her everywhere she goes. You don't. You need to tell her to stop carrying it."

"That's quite a leap," I said, defensively.

"Cap, we don't know what Iskstar is doing, but clearly you're still infected. Just because our AI can't see the parasite, we know it's there. Your eyes glow blue. We need to get that out of your body," she said.

"The Piscivoru have lived with Iskstar for generations," I said. "It isn't fatal to them. Marny, as you're so fond of saying, we have bigger fish to fry."

"I don't like it, Cap," she said.

"Trust me, neither do I," I answered. "I'll tell Tabby to stop carrying the crystal, but right now I think we need to wake Munay."

Grudgingly, Marny nodded, accepting my words. "You're right. One last thing. Just because Iskstar wasn't harmful to Piscivoru doesn't mean it isn't to humans."

"Flaer, can we wake Greg?" I asked.

"The fluid has drained." The petite, red-haired woman proceeded to pull straps from the grav-board Munay rested on, securing them across his chest, waist and legs.

"What's that about?" I asked, before she could finish.

"His sleep pattern while in the tank has been very active. The medical AI suggests he might awake violently. The straps are to keep him from harm."

The sounds that issued from Munay's mouth as he woke up were as horrifying as they were pitiful. For fully two minutes he howled at maximum volume, gasping raggedly to draw more breath, only to howl again.

"Greg, you're safe." I tried to comfort him, but he withdrew at my touch as if my hands burned. "It's Liam. You're with friends."

The mention of my name seemed to get his attention and he snapped his head around, staring at me intently. His eyes, however, darted wildly about, unable to focus. "You are warned. Do not seek us. Only death awaits," he hissed.

I'll be honest. I absolutely hate horror vids. The occult, creepy dolls, ghosts, ghouls and – frak! – even zombies just aren't my thing. Tabby loved it all and at the beginning of our relationship, I tried watching a couple of vids with her. Sure, I liked when she got scared and snuggled into me, but the fact was, I found I couldn't sleep afterwards. Spooky evil is my kryptonite, kind of like spiders are for Tabby. I only bring this up because what happened next is a little embarrassing.

I startled, involuntarily jumping back so forcefully that I bounced off Marny and sent us both to the ground in a tangle.

"Greg, who aren't we supposed to seek?" Nick asked, ignoring my inability to keep calm.

"The Empire," he hissed. "You will stop hunting us or you will die."

"Are you talking for the Kroerak?" Nick asked.

"I am Kroerak! And I control this weak flesh bag's mind. You will not be warned again," Munay hissed.

By this time, I'd found my feet again and stepped forward to look into Munay's face. Tears streamed from his eyes and the look on his face was one of absolute terror. "What have they done to you, Greg?"

He whimpered at the sound of my voice. "Commander Greg Munay. Mars Protectorate Navy. Serial number 0229233A5D0. Compromised." The rest of his words were almost impossible to understand. Whatever he was trying to say took him great effort and he finally dissolved once again into a howl of pain.

"Sedate him, Flaer," I said.

She responded immediately.

"No," he said, cutting off his howl in midstream. "Kill me, please ... "

The sedation cut off his plea and he fell back against the table, no longer straining at the straps holding him down.

"What the frak was that?" I asked. "He wasn't like that when he came in. Do you really think he was being mind-controlled by Kroerak?"

"We've seen that nobles can communicate to their own over long distances," Nick said. "Munay did say he was compromised."

"What have we learned from the data device we got from his tooth?" I asked.

"Without Jonathan here, we're having trouble," Nick said. "Mars Protectorate military-grade encryption is theoretically impossible to break."

"What do you need to access it?" Marny asked.

"Munay would have an access code that only he and Mars Protectorate would know," Nick said. "We can contact Mars Protectorate; we have a crystal. Maybe they'd give the code to us if we explained what was going on."

"Let's not talk here," Marny said. "If Kroerak are in control of Greg, it's possible they can hear us even when he's unconscious."

"What will we do with Mr. Munay?" Flaer asked.

"For now, we need him to remain unconscious," I said. "Perhaps over time we can help him recover."

The three of us walked from the sick bay and climbed into the lift to the bridge. "I saw that look on your face, Marny," I said. "You're thinking something."

"That wasn't Munay's serial number," she said. "It's not the right number of digits and there was an alpha-numeric."

"Every wrong combination we try locks us out by a geometrically increasing amount of time," Nick said. "I've already reached out to Mars Protectorate and tried the four security codes Belcose could come up with. But you need to know, they don't have any record of a secure data storage device associated with Munay."

"How long are you locked out for now?" I asked.

"It's currently not locked," he said. "But, if we blow our next attempt, the lockout goes to sixty-four hours. And you don't want to know what happens after that one."

"Had me at geometric," I said. "Crazy as it seems, I think this all fits together. Munay found the Kroerak. I've been mind-controlled by a noble, so I know that's possible. What if there's Kroerak one step, or even two or three steps above a noble? It's not that crazy to think a more powerful bug would be able to control a person from a long distance. That's why all the smart fabrics were ruined. This ultra-noble forced Munay to destroy everything that could provide a record of his trip and then sent him back here to warn us."

"And he somehow neglected to tell the noble about his tooth spy storage?" Marny asked. "That's a lot of ifs."

"Not for me," I said. "I was able to resist the noble in my head, but I had to be tricky. Munay is an extremely disciplined individual. If anyone could hide something while under duress, it's him."

"Are you telling your mom about this?" Nick asked.

There had been a time when Munay and Mom seemed to be getting closer than mere acquaintances. The situation had changed and things cooled, but she wasn't the type to turn off her feelings like a light switch.

"She should know what's going on," I said. "She'd want to be in charge of organizing his care."

"Are we going to try this code or not?" Marny asked, impatiently. "You guys act like this isn't the biggest secret in the universe right now."

"Mr. Stolzman, clear the bridge, would you?" I asked, sitting in my chair and bringing up the holo projector.

"Aye, Captain," he answered. "I'll head to the galley for an early lunch."

I smiled and nodded as he walked from the otherwise empty bridge. He wasn't an overly talkative man but seemed to genuinely appreciate being given the chance to grow into the pilot's chair on *Hornblower.* Idly, I wondered if he understood the danger we were about to place him in if Munay's data store showed what I hoped it would.

"I've got it connected," Nick said, once Stolzman cleared the door. "I'm attaching a remote access scanning harness and recorder, just in case we only get one shot at this. You ready?"

"Drama queen," I said, smiling at Marny as I sat back into my chair. The comment couldn't be further from the truth. Nick ordinarily didn't show a lot of emotion or seek to be in the center of anything.

"We'll have to work on that," Marny answered, returning my smile.

"You see the man naked and now you're ganging up on me," Nick complained.

I was about to respond when Greg Munay's face appeared on the holo-projection in front of me.

"This is Commander Greg Munay, Mars Protectorate. The Kroerak fleet looks to be breaking up," he whispered. *"I've stolen a ship, Fleet Afoot, from Loose Nuts. If you are listening to this, my guess is I'm dead, so suck it up. I did the right thing here. My plan is to follow these guys home. I've stripped all the comm gear and everything I can put my hands on that might generate a signal. So far, so good. Either they don't care about my presence or they can't see me. I'm hoping the latter, because for this to work, I need to*

get out alive, or at least a recording does. Here's hoping I have another recording."

Replacing his bust, a menu of recordings popped up. Twenty in total. The last was less than a ten-day ago. A chill ran down my spine and goose-flesh skittered along my arms. I selected the next in the series.

"*Three days later and still alive,*" he chuckled, his face darker with beard growth. "*We're not headed toward any gate I'm familiar with. Coordinate stream is attached. Look at that bizarre looking gate. Like nothing we've seen before.*"

My holo projector showed the Santaloo star system and the projected navigation from Zuri to the location Greg gave. *Fleet Afoot* had indeed ventured well away from the beaten path. We'd seen the approach vectors the Kroerak used when starting the invasion, and this trajectory was completely different. The recording ended, and I started the next.

"*Well, frak. We just jumped out of Dwingeloo. Pretty standard retreat, though. We just keep matching their navigation so we're headed in the same direction,*" he said. "*I'm pretty sure Kroerak know we're here. Not sure why they're not doing anything about it. I'm hoping it's because one ship doesn't present a threat. Feels like wishful thinking, but since we're doing this on our own and this recording isn't likely to see the light of day, you'll just have to grant me that.*"

"Brass balls," I said. "He knows they're on to him, but he's not stopping."

"Munay knows what he's doing. The intel isn't useful until he finds the Kroerak home planet," Marny said.

"*Looks like we're not alone,*" he whispered, on the third to last update. To this point, the updates had been mundane. In some cases, he talked about things in his life that he wished he'd done differently. In others, he talked about goals he had for the future like finding a wife and settling down. The tone of his speech was completely different, much more like when he'd first started following the fleet.

"*We just joined up with another large fleet,*" he said. "*I can't tell if it's the same group that attacked Abasi Prime or not. It's a reasonable guess, but I destroyed all of Fleet Afoot's data stores, including the scans that could help me identify those Kroerak vessels."*

The next update was marked only a day after.

"This might be it," he said, his voice conveying excitement. *"We've joined with eight more fleets and are about to jump through another gate. My god, but the scale of the Kroerak empire is terrifying. I must be sailing with over four thousand ships. Some of them would give Bukunawa a run for her money.*

"And if you thought you had to be at a complete stop to go through a wormhole end-point, you're wrong. We've been hitting these things at ten thousand meters per second. Kroerak can clear an entire fleet in a few seconds. That said, they appear to have gate sickness for an extended period. Up to thirty seconds or longer. I've seen some pretty remarkable wrecks because of it.

"Here we go ... Oh, rings of Saturn, this is it. I'm going to try to turn around and get out of here. We just entered the system maybe two-hundred thousand kilometers from a huge, orange planet. There might be as many as twenty thousand ships in orbit. It's impossible to tell. They look like fleas on a dog ..."

Uncharacteristically, Greg looked to the side, as if someone was on the bridge out of view of the vid-sensor. *"Is someone there?"* he asked. His hands flew up to the side of his head and he closed his eyes and screamed. *"Get out of my head!!"*

It was the last of the recordings.

"Twenty thousand ships?" I asked. "Even at ten-to-one odds with Iskstar, we'd need two thousand ships. There's no way."

"We need to get this information out to Mshindi and Mars Protectorate," Marny said. "We can't hold on to this secret or Munay's sacrifice will have been for nothing."

I pulled the quantum crystals from the secure compartment where they sat next to my chair. "Nick, can you arrange a conference call? It's time to call in some favors."

Chapter 17

LONELY AT THE TOP

MENDARI SYSTEM, UNNAMED MOON OVER FIFTH PLANET, INTREPID

"You seem to have loosened his tongue," Ada observed. She and Tabby sat in the open cell across from Jonathan and their Mendari prisoner. For them, the armor glass of the cell appeared transparent, but on the prisoner side, it was fully opaque. "The whole lick-the-blade-like-a-crazy-person thing was very convincing. That *was* an act, right?"

Tabby waggled her eyebrows. "Are you asking if I'm actually a demon?"

The women's exchange was cut short as Jonathan pulled out a chair and sat across from the legless man-spider.

"Think the Mendari would feel better if they knew Jonathan was a thousand sentients and that chair was just an illusion?" Tabby asked as Jonathan started to speak.

"I apologize for the poor treatment you have received," Jonathan started. "May I offer nutrition or refreshment?"

"Or a bucket of grease?" Tabby snickered.

"You have removed my legs," the Mendari answered. "I would have them returned."

"That is possible," Jonathan answered. "The technology to do so is well within our capacity. There are several questions to which we require answers before such a procedure may be accomplished."

"I will not betray my brethren," he answered, stiffening.

"That is acceptable," Jonathan answered. "What precipitated your sleep on this moon?"

"After the war, our planet was no longer capable of sustaining life," he answered.

"The war with Kroerak or with the other people of your planet?"

"We waged war with the Iskstar that had taken over our neighbors. Believe me, killing friends because they have been possessed is difficult, but it is the only way. You have Iskstar amongst you, brother. You must destroy the vessel that holds it, or you will lose your souls. I beg of you. Act before it is too late," the Mendari said.

"You speak as if you were part of this war," Jonathan answered. "How long have you been asleep?"

"For me, the war was yesterday," he answered.

"Ask why they attacked us," Tabby urged.

"We will later confirm that this was because they detected the Iskstar within you," Jonathan answered, via message.

"During this war, did you also fight with Kroerak?" Jonathan asked.

"At first the Kroerak invaded our lands," he answered. "The demons quickly thwarted the Kroerak vessels and troops. Our own Kethacho made armistice with Kroerak and we joined forces to destroy Iskstar."

"And that's why Kroerak did not destroy you?" Jonathan asked.

"To destroy Iskstar, we attacked our very own planet," he answered. "Few of us remained. The Kroerak could have easily finished us, but instead they honored the treaty with Kethacho. We were allowed to flee to the moon and put ourselves to sleep. You speak of time. Tell me, how much has passed since we were put to our rest?"

"It is common for species to measure time in the cycle of their own planet as it orbits the central star of a system," Jonathan said. "Your system has two stars, which is relatively unique, but the same principal applies. With this as measurement, you have slept for four-hundred-thirty-two of these cycles."

"That long." The Mendari looked down, dejected.

"You are upset?" Jonathan asked.

"Some were required to stay awake. They were to watch over us. They must no longer live," he answered. "Did you discover any people when you entered our rest chambers?"

"We will get to that," Jonathan answered.

"Do you intend to give me my legs and allow me to rejoin my people?"

"We will assess the truthfulness of your answers," Jonathan said. "How did you destroy Iskstar?"

"That was a neatly-deceptive non-answer," Tabby chortled. "Seriously, though, find out if they know where the Kroerak came from."

"In time, Tabitha," Jonathan responded.

"The inhabited are weak," he answered. "It is as if Iskstar wants them dead."

"Then why would you attack them? If your people were weakened, why would you not help them?" Jonathan asked.

"They were not our people. To provide aid to demons is to act against our gods," the Mendari said, puffing out his chest. "Destruction is the only justice."

"Why is that?"

"Look at your companion," he answered. "The seed already works to transform her. It will turn her body to crystal over time and then the devil will possess you all."

"From where did the Kroerak come?" Jonathan asked.

"It is unknown," the Mendari answered. "As we waged war, the Kroerak appeared. Our great leader, Kethacho, met with great leaders of Kroerak and exposed our final plans to destroy Iskstar. It was then armistice with Kroerak was reached."

"What part were Kroerak to play in this armistice?" Jonathan asked.

"We simply needed them to stop attacking our people so that we could finish Iskstar. The Kroerak were displeased that so many would need to die. But Kethacho and the Kroerak agreed that destruction of the planet was a small price to rid us of Iskstar. Our people would sleep for a thousand cycles, then our planet would be restored and we could start once again."

"You used a weapon to destroy your planet?"

The Mendari smiled. "God was delivered to Fashaka, our home. A mighty bomb was dropped upon the Iskstar devil itself and the wave of its power was felt in all corners. Our people were delivered to the heavens. The devil was brought low. It is indeed unhappy news that Iskstar yet lives and has come back to our home. We will once again prepare for war."

"Oh, that's just great," Tabby spat. "At least they don't have spaceships."

"This is not the case," Jonathan answered. *"There is evidence of a fleet of vessels in the records we have accessed."*

"Fleet?" Tabby asked. "Talk about burying the lead. We should find those ships."

"We have no justification for seizing their vessels," Jonathan messaged.

"Might beg to differ with you there," Tabby answered.

"We believe that inspection of the planet is critical," Jonathan answered. *"If Iskstar is as dangerous as Mendari believe, we must discover what happened on the planet."*

"Seriously?" Tabby asked, annoyed. "We're here to stop Kroerak, not Iskstar. The only reason we're alive is Iskstar. We have to take down Kroerak, no matter the cost."

"And if Iskstar is hurting you?" Ada asked.

"What is one person for all Kroerak has done?" Tabby asked.

"Understanding Iskstar is key to defeating Kroerak, Tabitha," Jonathan answered. *"Do you not believe Iskstar brought us here? The battle is four hundred years past. The Mendari are zealots against Iskstar. We see no logic in exposing us to this truth. If Iskstar is an intelligent species, they must have a deeper objective than sending us to their most outspoken enemies."*

Tabby harrumphed, no longer certain why she was annoyed. She'd been keyed up for a fight. Discovering that Kroerak hadn't been in the system for centuries seemed outrageous. "Fine. Let's dump this guy and check out the planet. I still say we should find their fleet and commandeer it."

"We would continue our conversation with the prisoner," Jonathan messaged. *"It is reasonable to ask Roby to join us so the Mendari's legs can be reattached."*

"I'm not letting that thing loose in our ship!" Tabby said, jumping up from her seat.

"Roby, we're going to release the Mendari. I will not allow its legs to be functional until the alien is no longer aboard." Ada added Roby to their comm channel. "Can you accomplish this safely?"

"Easy as potato pie," he answered. "We'll interrupt the primary pathways from the biological host to the machine's electrical systems. It's a pretty sophisticated setup, but it looks like the designers put in a shut-off switch. Probably for maintenance."

"That'd be great," Ada said. "I want three guards, fully armed, while Roby is working on him."

"Just let me do it," Tabby said, irritation in her voice.

"You can stand outside as backup. We don't need to make this any harder than it already is," Ada answered.

Tabby shook her head and stalked from the room, heading forward toward the gymnasium, which thankfully hadn't been ruined by the Kroerak attack. Lying on a bench, she grabbed barbells and pushed them up. Her arms ached as the gravity plates within the bars engaged and pulled downward.

"Too much," she complained, tears of frustration squeezing from closed eyes. The load lightened, and she pushed through the pain. After ten minutes, however, she was completely spent and moved to the heavy bag.

"I thought I'd find you here," Ada said. "Is there anything I can do to help?"

Tabby ignored her friend for a moment, striking at the bag. Never before had her hands hurt so badly when she boxed. She continued jabbing, trying to work through the pain.

"Tabby, stop! You're hurting yourself," Ada finally said after watching for a few minutes.

Tabby pulled back in surprise when Ada slid in front of the bag.

Ada grabbed Tabby's wrists, absorbing a blow in the process, and was knocked to the ground.

"Ada, no. Why would you step in like that?" she asked, suddenly brought back to reality.

"It's okay. I'm fine," Ada said, fighting back tears.

"I didn't mean to ... why?"

"Your hands, Tabby," Ada said, pushing up the wrist she still held so Tabby was forced to look at it. A trickle of blood dripped from beneath the wrap on Tabby's hand. "You're bleeding."

Tabby pulled her hand from Ada's grasp. "I'm fine."

"You're not fine, Tabby," she said, eyes locking onto the blue crystal that sat in the band of Tabby's workout clothing. "What if Mendari are right? What if Iskstar is hurting you?"

"You think I'm a demon?" Tabby scoffed.

"You know better than that." Ada took a more conciliatory tone. "I'm your friend, Tabby. I'm worried for you."

"We need to see this through, Ada," Tabby said, stiffly. "I meant what I said. I'll do anything to stop Kroerak."

"I will too," Ada answered with hushed tones. "But I need to know our sacrifice is worth it."

Tabby nodded tersely.

Ada continued. "Roby is starting the procedure to reattach the Mendari's legs. Once we drop him on the moon's surface, not far from where we grabbed him, we'll be on our way to the planet."

"Don't give up on me," Tabby finally managed through gritted teeth.

Ada held Tabby's gaze and nodded, finally pulling the woman into a hug. "Why would you ever think that was possible? I'm with you to the end, Tabitha Masters."

"Sorry to wake you, Captain, but we've established high orbit," Nikulinsky announced, pulling Ada from a fitful sleep. Ordinarily, she preferred to be on the bridge for major events, but with Tabby's degradation she'd taken more shifts and was fighting for sleep.

"Thank you, Andrei. What are you seeing, Jonathan?" Ada asked groggily, sitting up and trying to clear her head.

"The conditions on the planet's surface are consistent with what was reported by our prisoner," he answered.

One of the benefits of a stable, high orbit was the capacity for detailed scans that weren't possible while the ship was underway. Ada sighed. They'd learned as much when on the moon and she feared they were simply wasting time, as Tabby suggested. "No life at all?" she asked.

"Oh, no, Captain Chen," Jonathan answered. "There is much life on the planet, including small vertebrate animals that learned to adapt. It is however, quite inhospitable. We believe the Mendari's estimate of a thousand solar cycles to be inadequate for renewed habitation."

"Not our problem," Tabby growled into the comms.

Ada sighed. Tabby's mood had not improved substantially in the last few days, even after they'd heard from Liam. Apparently, *Fleet Afoot* had been located and he had sent a ship out to retrieve it. She stopped in the galley and poured hot water over her tea, waiting for a moment while the leaves gave up their flavor.

"Captain, there is a feature on the surface of the planet we believe to be of critical importance," Jonathan reported as she pushed open the bridge hatch, balancing her teacup atop a meal bar with one hand.

"On primary view screen," Ada ordered, setting breakfast onto a platform next to the captain's chair. Glancing at Tabby, she saw exhaustion in the darkening circles below Tabby's eyes.

"Looks like a crater." Tabby was first to speak.

"A reasonable observation," Jonathan said. "There is sufficient evidence to support a conclusion that this was the main target of the Mendari weapon that brought destruction to this planet."

"Just a single weapon?" Ada asked. "Why not hundreds or thousands?"

"They were attacking the Iskstar," Tabby answered. "I can feel it. We need to go down there."

"You heard Jonathan," Ada answered patiently. "It's not safe."

"I need to get down there," Tabby answered. "I saw it."

"Saw what?"

"It's why we're here," Tabby said. "Look, I can't explain what I saw because that's not how the dreams work. It's like we've had this conversation before, and I just know we need to go down there."

"Because Iskstar wants us to," Ada added.

"No!" Tabby exclaimed. "Because I want us to. Is that so hard? For frak's sake! We've sailed a million kilometers to get here. Why wouldn't we at least go take a look?"

"Because I'm concerned for you," Ada answered. "You're not exactly acting rationally."

Tabby pursed her lips and blew out a breath. "The other day in the gym, you wanted to know if I was okay. I didn't want to answer, because I'm not. I'm whatever *not okay* looks like when it's having a really bad day."

Tabby lifted her arm and held her hand so it hung in the space between them. With her other hand, she painfully removed her grav-suit's glove. Ada's breath froze as she saw the changes. The tips of Tabby's fingers had turned a bright blue, transforming from tissue to glowing blue Iskstar crystal.

"Oh Tabby," Ada gasped, tears suffusing her eyes.

"Don't, Ada," Tabby said, her blue eyes locking onto Ada's. "This is important. We have to go to the planet's surface. It's dying."

"The planet?" Ada asked.

"No. The Iskstar," Tabby answered. "We have to help it."

"What Iskstar? We need to get you to the medical bay. Andrei, plot a course for immediate return to Abasi Prime." Ada's voice quavered as she spat out orders.

"Stop. The medical scanners can't see anything. We have nothing to fear from Iskstar," Tabby said, placing her gloved hand on Ada's arm. "They just want the same thing everyone wants. They want to live free without being hunted or attacked."

"Course is set," Nikulinsky answered.

"You've been talking with them? Are they controlling your thoughts too?" Ada asked. "Go, Andrei, maximum possible speed."

"Please. Ada. Don't do this. It's not like that," Tabby said. "It's more like feelings. It's still me."

"But they're hurting you," Ada protested. "What species hurts another to help itself? I'll tell you what. A predatory parasite, that's what. You can't even see what they're doing to you. Tabby, you're dying!"

"This is more important than me, Ada," Tabby said. "The Iskstar are ancient. They live in harmony with other species."

"Chicken crap!" Ada exclaimed. "They're killing you."

"Ada, I gave my permission," Tabby said. "And before you say anything else, I'm stronger than you think. I can take it. I've allowed them to prepare my body."

"Prepare for what? I thought you weren't talking to them!" Ada shot back.

"I'm not," she answered. "This hand, this arm, my legs, they're not even mine. They're synthetic replicas of what I once had. Ada, there are over a million sentients on the planet and they won't survive much longer. Especially now that the Mendari are awake."

Ada found herself panting with frustration. "How long have you known?"

"I didn't really know until right now," Tabby answered. "Iskstar doesn't really talk. It's all just feelings and dreams. They've been showing me their history. The Kroerak have all but obliterated them. The Iskstar are peaceful. They feel joy and sadness. In my dreams, I've seen entire civilizations grow from small villages using primitive tools to space explorers centuries later. Do you know the overwhelming feeling I get from the Iskstar when they show me these things?"

"I don't even know what to say," Ada answered.

"They feel pride, Ada," Tabby said. "It's like they're grandparents watching their favorite grandchildren learn to fly a transport for the first time or graduate after citizenship exams. This is a noble species. They're worth saving."

"What about Kroerak? If they're so peaceful, why do they attack Kroerak with such ferocity?" Ada asked.

"Why does Jonathan help us in our fight against Kroerak?" Tabby asked. "Do you know a more noble species than Jonathan? Would you not give your life to save them?"

"Of course, but we know Jonathan. They're one of us," Ada answered. "Sendrei, Jonathan, do you have anything to add to this? Am I wrong?"

"We find it difficult to speak," Jonathan answered. "The conversation has taken an unusual turn and we find a certain incapacity to process."

"Why? Because I said you're one of us?" Ada asked.

"We should turn back to the planet and let this play out," Sendrei answered before Jonathan could. "Either Tabby is right or she is not. She has committed to this course and I believe, with the threat of Kroerak and Greg Munay's return to Mhina system, we will come to regret not exploring every avenue."

"Am I the only one who sees that she's dying?" Ada asked, exasperated.

"It is precisely because she understands the risk that I believe this," Sendrei answered. "Tabby has survived the fire of combat. She understands the price of her actions."

"Jonathan? The Mendari were so terrified of Iskstar that they burned their own planet. Tell me Sendrei and Tabby are wrong."

"A true measure of a people is not their enemies, but their actions," Jonathan answered. "The danger to Tabitha is a compelling argument against aiding Iskstar. Her knowledge and acceptance of this suggests permission having been requested and is therefore positive. If this were all we had observed, a response would be difficult. But that is not all that we understand. The Iskstar have positively coexisted with the Piscivoru. Further they allowed portions of their crystal to be used to defeat Kroerak. We are in agreement with Sendrei Buhari."

"Thanks for the vote of confidence, Jonathan," Tabby said ironically. "I'm glad it was Sendrei's argument that swayed you."

Ada slumped in acquiescence. "Fine. Where do we go?"

"You won't regret it," Tabby said, closing her eyes and slowly bowing her head. "This morning, the Iskstar showed me the bomb that destroyed the Mendari people. At the bottom of the crater, there is a broken mother crystal. Millions of Iskstar were killed, but even so, over a million still live."

"Ma'am?" pilot Nikulinsky asked, not having not received a formal order.

"Take us back, Andrei," Ada said and turned back to Tabby. "No one told me how lonely leadership would feel. Tabby, Liam will never forgive any of us if you die and I won't blame him."

Ada sank back into the chair and watched nervously as Nikulinsky turned *Intrepid* around and proceeded to enter the planet's turbulent atmosphere.

"It's just as I dreamed," Tabby said as they finally approached the bottom of the rocky crater. Dust swirled around the ship as *Intrepid* settled into a wide valley, devoid of life.

"What will you do?" Ada asked.

"I feel the crystal," Tabby said. "I must go to it."

Chapter 18

WEAPON OF CHOICE

MHINA SYSTEM, HORNBLOWER

"Liam, you're going to want to talk to Tabby before we get into this," Nick said.

I looked at him expectantly, still holding the quantum communication crystals that would link us to Mshindi Prime and Mars Protectorate. It was true that Ada had taken many of our critical crew off on a mission that seemed to be a bust, but there was no question in my mind what our next move should be. We had an advantage over the Kroerak and knew right where to find them. It was time to act. The numbers were overwhelming, but I had no doubt we could overcome the odds.

"*Intrepid* would have some value in the fight we're headed into, but honestly, we're going to need big iron for this fight," I said. Mid-conversation, I recognized his 'you're not getting it' face. I pushed on regardless. "She'd be fighting way above her weight class. What?"

"Take the crystal to your office and call her. While you're out, I'll see about raising M-Pro and Mshindi," he said, holding up the comm crystal that linked to *Intrepid*. The crystal looked out of place in his hand. He had to have entered my quarters to retrieve it and it was unusual that he'd done so without my knowledge.

My pulse quickened. I chatted with Tabby nearly every night.

Something was up, but when pressed, she only said she'd been feeling tired. I assumed she was talking about burn-out. I felt it too. We'd been on the run for months, our lives constantly shifting between battle and recovery. The pace was taking a toll, but we both knew what was on the line and there was nothing either of us wouldn't do to put an end to the Kroerak menace. I'd privately worried that something more was up with her and Nick's actions set those alarm bells off.

"How bad?" I asked, accepting the crystal from him.

"I'm not sure," he answered. "Ada is worried, though."

If I'd needed any further prompting, his words were more than enough to push me along. I accepted the crystal and half-jogged, half-walked from the bridge, palming my way into my quarters. I was only partially surprised to find that Marny entered a moment later, carrying a sleepy Little Pete in her arms.

"Nick said something's up with Tabby. I don't have to stay if you want privacy," Marny said.

"It's okay," I said, sliding the quantum crystal into its socket. "*Intrepid* this is *Hornblower* over," I called.

It took only a minute before Ada answered, "Liam, this is Ada, go ahead."

"I just talked to Nick," I said. "He said something's up with Tabby. I thought she recovered from the Mendari attack."

"It's not the Mendari. It's Iskstar. I think Iskstar is hurting her," Ada said. "Are you having any symptoms?"

"Symptoms, like what?" I asked.

"Loss of function. Tired. Bleeding at extremities," Ada said.

"Frak, Ada, no. Let me talk to her."

"She's not on the ship, Liam."

"What do you mean she's not on the ship? Where the frak is she?" I felt a bead of sweat roll down my cheek.

"We've landed on the fourth planet," Ada answered.

"I thought that planet was a rock," I said. "What are you doing there?"

"You and Tabby haven't talked about it?" Ada asked. "Rings of Saturn, Liam, I thought she was working this out with you."

"Working what out?" I was so far behind in this conversation and the world was spinning out of control around me.

"Iskstar, Liam!" Ada said, her voice sharp enough to get my attention. "She said the Iskstar was calling to her and that she had to make a sacrifice for the greater good."

"Sacrifice? What did she mean by greater good?" I could barely form coherent sentences. My thoughts were overrun with worry.

"Her fingers are blue, Liam. And I don't mean she's not getting enough oxygen. It looks like there's crystallization and she's lost control of her right arm."

"And you let her leave the ship?"

"Without sedating her, she wasn't going to be stopped," Ada said. "She said there's an Iskstar mother crystal on this planet that the Mendari didn't completely destroy and millions of Iskstar would die if we didn't do something."

I started to speak but felt Marny's strong hand on my shoulder. "Ada, does Jonathan believe she's in communication with Iskstar?"

"We do, Marny," Jonathan answered. "We believe the dreams given to Tabby were specifically targeted to bring her to this place."

"What is her medical condition?" Marny asked.

"On last scan, Tabitha had lost forty-percent of the function of her limbs and her internal organs are under considerable pressure," Jonathan said.

"Why?" I asked. "Why would Iskstar attack her?"

"We can only speculate based on Tabitha's own admissions," Jonathan answered. "She invited Iskstar to utilize her body as a host. We believe this is due to media failure of the crystalline host. In short, we believe she is allowing her body to be transformed as a life-raft for Iskstar."

I blew out a breath. I knew it was the panicked state of my mind, but I was having difficulty tracking. *Intrepid* had been sent on a mission to help Mendari defend against an imminent Kroerak invasion. As far as I could tell, no part of that remained true. The only attack was against the only woman I'd ever loved and to make matters worse, she was helping them do it.

"Liam, you have to trust her," Marny said, sensing my thoughts. "Tabby is going through something right now that's hard to understand, but *she* made the call."

I shook her off, confusion and fury battling for control. "You're all nuts. Iskstar has twisted her mind."

"Cap, are you saying you're not fit for command?" Marny asked.

"Of course not. But I'm not the one letting an alien take over ..." I blinked, trying to comprehend her question. "Frak, Marny, I'm fine. Are you seriously questioning me?"

"You've set a high standard, Cap," Marny answered. "You take big risks and they pay off. You put your life on the line repeatedly and people have been saved because of it. You can't question it when Tabby does the same thing. Let her call the play. Do you really believe Ada, Sendrei, and Jonathan don't have the same concerns you have right now? They're there. Trust them."

"Frak, that's a big ask," I said. "She's my world, Ada."

"I know, Liam," Ada answered, her voice quiet and filled with emotion.

I had difficulty swallowing around the lump in my throat, but Marny was right and I knew what had to be done. "Ada, last night we discovered that Greg Munay had information on the location of the Kroerak homeworld. Later this morning, we'll be talking with Mars Protectorate, Mshindi Prime, and hopefully a representative from the Confederation of Planets. I'm going to push for an all-out assault."

"When will you set sail?" she asked.

"That'll require some coordination, but I'd expect soon. What's your fuel situation?"

"It's not good. The best case is a schedule-C burn which will take us thirty-four days minimum," she said. "What's the nav-plan to the Kroerak homeworld look like? Maybe we could intercept *Hornblower* and refuel on the way."

"No good," I answered. "The only common jump is the exit from

Mhina. I just don't think we'll be able to wait long enough for *Intrepid* to arrive. Maybe, though. It's a developing situation."

"Copy that," Ada answered. "Keep us updated. I'll do the same and I'm sorry for not telling you about Tabby."

"I do trust you, Ada," I said. "So does Tabby. I need you to look out for her even when she doesn't want it."

"We'll be lifting off in no more than two hours," Ada said. "Even if I have to tranq her."

"I'd pay to see that," I said, chuckling mirthlessly. "Hoffen out."

I looked over to Marny who was rocking back and forth with Little Pete as she stared at me. "You're doing the right thing," she said, sympathetically.

"Doesn't feel like it. I feel like we're marionettes and the Iskstar are pulling our strings."

"It's possible," Marny answered, "but you're forgetting one big thing. Without Iskstar, we'd all be dead. That's a pretty big show of good faith."

"But Tabby."

"But nothing," Marny answered. "I'm serious about the fit for duty conversation. Either you're under control of Iskstar or you're fit for command. You can't argue both sides. Don't make that mistake with Tabby. She's either in control of her mind or not and she believes there are a million Iskstar at risk. Tell me, Cap, how many Piscivoru would you put your life on the line for?"

"These aren't Piscivoru," I said, fondly remembering the small reptilian people who had taken us in and treated us like family.

Marny raised an eyebrow at my weak response. I didn't like where we were at, but her point was made. I needed to move past it, at least for now.

"ADMIRAL STERRA, Admiral Alderson, thank you for agreeing to talk with us," I said, sitting forward in the conference room chair and staring intently at the communication box. We hadn't been able to facilitate a simultaneous connection with Mshindi Prime, so rather than wait, we had decided to push forward with Mars Protectorate.

"Anino says you've a line on the Kroerak homeworld." Admiral 'Buckshot' Alderson was a force of nature and I wasn't a bit surprised that he was ready to take charge of the conversation. "What do you want for that information?"

"Not a negotiation, Alderson," I said. "We're transmitting it now."

"I know you, Hoffen. You want something or we wouldn't be having this conversation," he said.

"And I know you, Admiral," I answered. "You're trying to manipulate me into doing something you want, but something you *don't* think I want. For as smart as you are, you've totally missed the mark on who *we* are."

"So, you don't want anything and we can just hang up now? I can't fathom any reason for us to talk further now that you've given us the enemy's location," he said pompously.

I grinned, even as I gritted my teeth. I dearly wanted to punch that man in the face – because he was right. There was an epic ask in the offing and he knew it. Just how he'd gotten me to suggest otherwise was beyond me.

"I believe we've sent data-streams of the combat effectiveness of Iskstar-tuned weapons against Kroerak vessels and troops," I said, trying not to directly answer his jabs.

"Mr. Anino was kind enough to pass them along. We assume they've arrived with limited editing," he answered.

"They were unedited," Thomas Anino's boyish voice added. I hadn't realized he'd been included in the conversation. The ridiculously wealthy inventor of the TransLoc system of interstellar travel had been both benefactor and a friend in previous adventures. I'd learned to be careful of his involvement, as things were rarely simple when he was around.

"I understand you've been given an entire solar system for your discovery of this Iskstar weapon. So perhaps not the humanitarian you'd have us believe," Alderson said.

"Right," I said, not looking to mince words with him.

"Admiral, let's skip the posturing," Admiral Sterra said. It had been a long time since I'd heard LaVonne Sterra's voice and I smiled, despite the annoyance I was tamping down. She'd given us our first break so many years ago when she'd accepted our application to becoming privateers.

"You give these Loose Nuts boys too much credit, LaVonne. You always have," Alderson said. "They're wolves in sheep clothing and I'm wise to it."

"Do you ever make yourself tired with all this, Admiral?" I asked, finally having enough. "The deal is as simple as it always is. You're the one who makes this hard every single time. We've shown you where the Kroerak homeworld is and have evidence they're gathering their ships and bringing them home. We have a weapon that destroys them. This is simple. We just need a fleet to go take them on."

"You want to oversee said fleet, no doubt?" Alderson shot back.

I held back the sigh I wanted to release. "No. We just want to come along. I need to make sure Kroerak get dealt with once and for all."

"How many Iskstar crystals do you have available?" Sterra asked.

"I think a better question is, are the estimates from Munay correct? Are there really twenty thousand Kroerak vessels? I don't care what kind of weapon you have, at some point quantity has a quality of its own," Alderson harrumphed.

"Do you recall the range of the Kroerak lance weapons as compared to your longest-range laser or blaster weapons?" I asked, answering neither question.

"It varies," he answered.

"We've developed a new class of weapon with the data gathered from Piscivoru. We can put a beam out about ten thousand kilometers. It's low power, but I believe it'll work," Anino said. "You need to know that Alderson is playing hard to get because you've already given him what he wants."

"Which is?" I asked.

"The location of the Kroerak homeworld," Anino answered. "Right now, Alderson has a team headed to Picis. His people will visit the

Iskstar grotto – or whatever you call it – and collect their own Iskstar crystals."

"I could have you tried for treason, Anino," Alderson growled. "You're giving away state secrets. The fact of the matter is, we don't need you, Hoffen."

"You do know that Iskstar doesn't accept everyone," Liam said. "Connecting with this species is dangerous."

"Sounds like someone trying to protect their territory," Alderson answered. "The fact is, we have a lot to offer the Piscivoru. I think they'll be more than open to a trade."

"Iskstar and Piscivoru are different species," I corrected.

"I think we can figure it out," he said. "We've sent our best xeno-biologists, along with the translation matrix provided by Mr. Anino and his pet, Jonathan."

I turned to Nick and shook my head. "I'd love to see this guy negotiate with Strix. Talk about peas in a pod."

"Do you think we'll have trouble negotiating with the Iskstar, Liam?" Sterra asked.

"Anino, did you give Admiral Sterra Jonathan's analysis on Iskstar and how they view time?"

"We've all read it, Liam," Anino answered. "But I don't see why one of the biologists wouldn't be able to establish the same rapport as your team did."

"Because they don't need you. I believe the only reason the Iskstar communicated with us was to get rid of Kroerak over Picis," I said. "It's likely you'll be ignored, and if you try to take crystals by force, your crystals will be dead."

"As in blackened, or dead as in clear but not glowing blue?" Anino asked.

His question was a dead giveaway. There were a million ways a crystal could appear dead. Blackened was exactly what happened to a crystal when it was detached and the Iskstar no longer inhabited it.

"How many people do you have on Picis right now?" Nick asked. "And by the way, you better be treating them right or you'll risk an incident with the Confederation of Planets."

"You pompous little ..." Alderson started.

"We've been there for three weeks," Sterra interrupted. "We're in negotiations with the Piscivoru and are currently not welcome on the planet."

"You tried to force them," I said, catching up.

"We'll do whatever it takes to eliminate the Kroerak, Hoffen," Alderson answered. "I'd swallow a live cobra if I thought it would finish the job."

"Very graphic," I quipped. "Time to open wide in that case."

"At least you understand your role," he answered.

"How many ships can you field?" I asked.

"Enough," he answered. "How many crystals do you have?"

"We have two hundred ships, Liam," Sterra cut in. "Only twenty of them are capable of carrying the weapon Mr. Anino has alluded to. We need four hundred fifty crystals, give or take. Do you have that many?"

"We do. Are you ready to negotiate now?" I asked. "I'm sure I'm not as bad as a live cobra."

"What do you need, Liam?" Sterra asked.

"We want access to fold-space again," I said. "You've either turned it back on or you've made something new."

I raised my eyebrows at Nick and he nodded appreciatively.

"Why you little shite," Alderson spat.

"And you'll invite Abasi and Confederation of Planets to be part of the battle group," I said. "Kroerak are as much their problem as they are yours. They deserve to share in the victory."

"Feels like you're counting chickens well in advance of hatching," Anino said. "Kroerak Empire hasn't survived this long without a few challengers."

"Anything else?" Alderson asked.

"When this is over, you return all of the Iskstar crystals to the Piscivoru," I said. "Might be the grand gesture you need to establish a good relationship."

"If we take out Kroerak, we won't need to be friends with the

Piscivoru," Alderson said. "For frak's sake, there are only a few hundred of them."

"I've always heard you were a master negotiator, Alderson," I said. "Are you sure your dislike for me and mine hasn't pushed you to make bad decisions? We have the technology needed to rid humanity of its premiere threat. We're willing to share it and the price is more than fair. We're just asking you to restore what we've lost. The cost to you is negligible."

"Hoffen, I learned a long time ago in training that there's always a guy like you around. For me, it was a guy named Pete Bargan. Good guy. Likeable. Smart. Talented even at a number of things. Never had to work for it either and that was the problem," Alderson said. "Because he was able to get what he wanted without working for it, he never put any effort into anything. He was lazy. He took shortcuts. You know the problem with lazy people? I'll tell you. They get other people killed. You know how many good men and women got killed over Cradle? How about the Kroerak invasion of Earth? Cat got your tongue? What about Kroerak invasion of Abasi Prime? Or Zuri?" He spluttered.

"You can't lay all that crap at *his* feet," Marny barked back, having remained quiet up until now. "Belirand had free reign under *your* watch, Alderson. You could have stopped them. Instead of blaming Liam, how about you look inside and figure out just what you were doing when Belirand was feeding humanity to the Kroerak. I was there. Don't try to bull-shite me."

I sucked in air, trying to catch my breath. In my darker moments, when I unpacked the list of sins I saved for special times, I knew exactly who was responsible for the timing of the Kroerak invasion of Earth. Sure, you could sugarcoat it any way you wanted, but we'd poked the bear. It was a demon I would never be able to put back in the bottle and I would do anything to end the pain I'd caused.

"Hit a nerve, didn't I?" Alderson said. "I've made plenty of mistakes, but you're *that* guy, Hoffen. Worst of all, you don't realize that you're worse than any live cobra. You get people killed and you don't even know it."

"This isn't productive," Sterra said. "Admiral, why don't you take a break. Liam, your terms are acceptable. We'll initiate communication with the Confederation of Planets and keep you apprised. I am surprised, however. I would have expected you to persist in your demand to come along with the battle group."

"Haven't you heard?" I asked, the wind having been successfully knocked from my sails. "I'm Bold Prime, head of House of the Bold. If you're bringing Abasi, I'll be part of that fleet."

I reached over and turned off the comms. It had been a long time since I felt this low. Between Tabby's plight and Alderson's attacks, there was nothing left.

"You can't let him get to you," Marny said. "He's using emotion as a weapon. He's exploiting your feelings of guilt."

"I am guilty," I said. "There's nothing to exploit. I'm exactly who he says I am."

Chapter 19

HUNGER

GALAXY UNKNOWN, MENDARI SYSTEM, INTREPID

"At least take Sendrei with you," Ada argued, standing between the airlock and her beleaguered friend.

"There's no need," Tabby said. "I'm not an invalid yet. If I'm not back in two hours, come looking for me. I'll drop tracker dots as I go."

"Have you told Liam?" Ada asked.

Tabby locked eyes with Ada and considered shading the truth just to get her friend off her back. In the end, it didn't matter. Her course had been chosen and no amount of talking would stop her.

"No," she answered. "Liam and I talk about important things — like what he had for dinner and how bad Little Pete's poop smells."

Ada smiled in spite of the circumstances. For both women, Marny and Nick's baby was a favorite conversation and there was no detail too small. "I won't withhold it from him," Ada said.

"I know," Tabby said. "He's going to be mad, but I'm okay with that. I just wanted normal to last as long as possible."

"What part of *this* is normal?" Ada asked, spreading her hands widely in the space between them.

"I need to go, Ada," Tabby said, using her grav-suit's buoyancy to propel herself forward.

"Don't make me regret this, Tabby." Ada forestalled her friend, pulled her into a hug, and kissed her lightly on the cheek. "You're important to all of us. Remember that."

Tears welled in Tabby's eyes as she pushed away, avoiding eye contact with Ada. She turned, partly to hide the pain caused by their physical contact. She raised her face shield and entered the readied airlock. Tabby could still feel the spot on her cheek where Ada had kissed her. The small act of love, given freely, spurred her onward.

Once outside the ship, Tabby first looked up. According to Jonathan, the crater *Intrepid* sat in had been created by a powerful weapon setting off a chain reaction. The residual radiation of that weapon still burned hot. If not for the nanites in her blood and the grav-suit's exceptional shielding, she wouldn't have survived even a few seconds in this environment. As it was, she'd be required to apply a course of med-patches daily for at least ten days to replace the protective little workers who dealt with the toxicities. The dangers were common to anyone who'd grown up on a mining colony, however.

Intrepid had settled at the bottom of the crater, not far from the point Jonathan identified as ground-zero. Shards of shiny black glass glittered everywhere around her, poking up from sand of the same material. Their edges were worn smooth by half a millennium of winds, unhindered by vegetation or structures beyond the crater's tall walls.

The Mendari's bomb had missed the mark, if only by a small margin. With that instinctive knowledge came the understanding that a direct hit would have indeed wiped the Iskstar from the now-barren planet.

The bomb's crater was uneven; the end result of the powerful explosion affected by the composition of rock where it had been dropped. As a result, the shape varied considerably in its width, from only a kilometer across where dense rock had directed the energy up, to several kilometers where less dense rock had been either vaporized or blown outward.

It was as she struggled across the barren landscape that Tabby began to understand the depth of her communication with Iskstar.

Until recently, she and Liam had discussed at length each of the dreams they'd experienced. They'd continued to search the dreams for hidden meanings and context, often frustrated by the sheer obscurity of what they'd observed.

Perhaps it was the physical changes to her body, as non-critical tissues transformed to crystal, that caused her to become more attuned to Iskstar. Tabby now realized the communication she and Liam were receiving was much less about the physical events depicted. They had been focusing entirely too much on what they'd seen and not enough on what they had felt during the dreams.

Tabby smiled as she recalled the juvenile Piscivoru, Boerisk – or perhaps it had been Baelisk? – who'd tried to explain Iskstar to them. It had been easy to dismiss the child's wisdom. Now she recognized the truth of his words when he'd explained how the Iskstar spoke in whispers. At first it had been impossible to recognize the messages as anything but her own active mind proposing explanations. Tabby now realized that creating visual images to share with her and Liam through dreams had been equally difficult for the Iskstar.

"I know," she said, mostly to herself, but also to the sense of urgency she felt toward a fissure in the ground almost a kilometer from her position.

"Come back?" Ada answered immediately. "I didn't catch that last."

"Sorry, talking to myself," she answered, gliding across the surface.

"Where are you going, Tabby? Jonathan says we're right on top of ground-zero."

Tabby glanced at the menu on her HUD and pulled down the communication controls. She muted all incoming feeds and visual prompts. It was a mode sometimes described as 'going native.' It was also something few people ever chose to experience.

As she approached, the fissure became more prominent: a jagged, lightning-shaped hole stretching out from the crater floor like a spoke on an ancient, rotating space-station. The crack was too narrow to enter, but it ran for well over a kilometer. Soon there was enough room and Tabby floated beneath the lip of the fissure, descending even deeper. At some point, Tabby's AI popped on her suit's external illumination. She paused to switch it off, her Iskstar-enhanced vision now perfectly suited to the darkness.

Listening to the urgings of the quiet voice, she navigated through a network of subterranean tunnels. Tabby paused as a cloud of mist marked a group of thick stalactites that had broken free and crashed to the tunnel floor. Worry entered her mind and she wondered what force had caused the solid structure to break apart. She pushed aside the insistent urging of the Iskstar and turned her electronics back on.

Tabby remembered her promise to Ada. She'd neglected to drop the repeaters that would allow her signal to escape the cavern.

She mentally shrugged. If there were issues topside, Ada, Sendrei and Jonathan were more than capable of dealing with them. A sense of calm filled her as she resumed her forward progress, turning one final corner to enter a small chamber. A faint blue glow drew her forward and she settled to the ground, preferring to walk the final meters. Similar to the surface of the crater above, the material she walked on crunched underfoot, a sound like walking on tiny shards of glass.

Tabby paused as a thought eluded her. Something was off, and she chased the problem. There was no way the bomb's blast had penetrated so deeply into the ground, yet the fused and blackened glass looked nearly identical to what had been above in the crater. A great sense of sadness washed over her and she fell to her hands and knees, the magnitude of what she was seeing finally reaching her conscious mind. The glittering shards that littered the surface of the crater were not clumps of sand turned to glass by the heat of the explosion. They were the remains of not millions, but billions of Iskstar.

Tabby let out a great wail and rolled onto her side in agony, experiencing deep, uncompromising grief. Curled into a ball, she lay sobbing as she mourned for a people she'd never known.

Time passed. Had it not been for being struck by a dislodged chunk of the ceiling, Tabby might not have found the strength to move again. Barely thinking and her motions mostly on autopilot, she worked to free her trapped legs from the pile of shattered, dead crystal. There was no compelling reason to stand, so Tabby sat on the scree and closed her eyes. A cool sensation fluttered on her cheek, right where Ada had kissed her. Tabby could have sworn Ada was beside her, kissing her cheek once again. She cried new tears as the love of that single, innocent gesture filled her being.

Slowly, Tabby opened her eyes and was met with a throbbing blue glow coming from beneath a great pile of broken crystal. Holding onto a sense of hope, she fought against despair and clawed at the crystal chips, shoveling material to the side. Even though her hands felt like they were on fire, she continued, pushing down into the pile as a child would do to sand on a beach.

More time passed, but Tabby felt nothing beyond her need to reach the faint blue glow. Finally, she saw the tip of the remaining live crystal. She was incapable of holding back, reaching for the crystal and running her gloved hand along the exposed surface. The contact was not enough, so she fumbled with pained fingers to remove her gloves, gasping in the poisonous air as she opened her suit's helmet so she could use teeth to peel back to the material. She gagged and would have vomited from what she'd pulled into her lungs, but she hadn't been eating and only managed a few dry heaves. Her suit's AI took over and closed her mask, recognizing imminent peril.

Her efforts had been enough. She tossed the gloves from ruined hands to the side, flicking them off with a painful shake of her arms. Flopping to the ground, Tabby wrapped her hands around the top of the buried crystal, having no idea just how deep it might go. Recognition, gratitude, and finally joy filled her being, pushing out the feelings of despair. She cried, this time for the salvation of the remnant of Iskstar.

It was no simple matter to extract the crystal from its grave, but Tabby labored tirelessly, finally extracting the narrow, three-meter-long crystal. In the process, she'd discovered a break in the shard's substrate. In that moment, she realized the purpose of her body's transformation. With only a touch, hundreds of thousands of Iskstar sentients transferred to the crystalline structure that had replaced most of her left side.

"TABBY, CAN YOU HEAR ME?"

Tabby's eyes fluttered open. The man who was looking at her was familiar; she recognized his close-cut, curly hair and resonant voice. The latter carried a tone of concern.

"Sendrei," she said, trying to reach out and touch him. Her arm didn't answer her call and she just smiled. "You found us."

Sendrei looked around. "Us?"

Tabby looked around. She was sitting atop the large Iskstar crystal on the lip of the fissure within the bomb's crater. She recalled laboring to reach that point because she knew Ada would find her.

"Tabby, it's been five days. We've been looking everywhere for you," Sendrei said. "How did you survive? You had no supplies and your hands – they're blue."

"I am thirsty, now that you mention it," Tabby said. The pain in her limbs had long passed. Sendrei pulled a water pouch from his pack and held it out to her. Unfortunately, she found she was unable or more possibly, unwilling to move her arms. "Maybe a little help?" With her eyes she instructed her AI to provide a hydration straw to her lips and she watched as a very concerned Sendrei squeezed the contents of the pouch into her suit's reservoir.

"Ada, I have Tabby," Sendrei called over comms. "Coming in hot. I'll get her into the bay."

"That is ridiculously delightful," Tabby said, her mind wandering as she enjoyed the refreshment. Sendrei's anxiety felt mismatched and she focused on his words. "Why hot?"

"Mendari have ships," Sendrei said. "They've been harassing us. I'm here to rescue you, but we have to be quick. Can you move?"

"Probably," Tabby said, dopily shaking her head up and down as if she'd solved one of the world's greatest problems.

"Never mind," he said. "I'll get you in, but we're going to have to go fast. Mendari ships are swift and we won't have much time."

"Iskstar too," Tabby said, leaning over and falling onto the crystal she'd worked so hard to unearth. "Don't forget them or we'll really be sorry."

Tabby's voice was sing-songie and Sendrei looked between her and the perfect, blue crystal that she lay on. She was obviously delirious, and he wasn't certain he could save both her and the crystal.

"Twenty seconds." Ada's voice pierced Tabby's consciousness as comms started making sense.

"You got anything to eat?" Tabby asked sleepily. "Maybe something with berries. They're the best." She chuckled drunkenly.

Sendrei scooped Tabby from the crystal as a great cloud of sand covered them ahead of *Intrepid's* rapid approach. He leapt up, using arc-jets to boost his speed, surprised to see Jonathan jump from the open cargo hold to the planet's surface.

"Jonathan, what are you doing? We have to move, now!" Sendrei words were punctuated by blaster fire that stitched into the crater wall.

"Help with Iskstar," Jonathan said, his robotic body unable to lift off with the burden of the crystal.

Sendrei carefully set Tabby down and looked around the hold frantically, finally finding what he was searching for. He grabbed the end of an old winch line and flipped the lever so the spool free-wheeled as he jumped to the planet's surface.

"Attach this to the end," Sendrei ordered, hearing *Intrepid's* turrets returning fire. For days, *Intrepid* had been on the run from the relentless Mendari hunters. He knew full well that to be caught on the ground put them at a huge disadvantage, but he wasn't willing to lose Jonathan.

"We gotta move!" Ada said into the comms.

"Buy us thirty seconds," Sendrei called back.

"The sling won't bind," Jonathan calmly intoned. "The crystal's surface does not have sufficient friction. Wrap it around me."

"What?" Sendrei watched as Jonathan lay face down on the large crystal, wrapping one arm around the back side and holding the sling at the end of the winch cable out to Sendrei with the other.

"Trust," was Jonathan's simple response.

Sendrei worked frantically as blaster fire erupted near them, ricocheting off *Intrepid.* He'd barely affixed the sling when *Intrepid* lurched to the side, skidding a few meters under a barrage of fire. The cable jerked, sending Jonathan and the crystal flying. The force clipped off the sentient's lower half and it fell away, cartwheeling behind the crystal as it was jerked from the ground.

"Going up!" Tabby said drunkenly over comms, "First floor, cosmetics."

Sendrei lay into his arc-jets and directed himself into *Intrepid's* open bay. Pushing Tabby out of the way, he steadied himself in front of the winch controls and reeled in the crystal and Jonathan's upper half.

"Jonathan, are you okay?" Sendrei asked, not releasing the winch.

"We are without harm. Ada Chen, please apply all haste to evasive maneuvers," he added.

"Am I going to get anything to eat?" Tabby asked, oblivious to the fact that she was skidding across the cargo hold deck as Ada engaged *Intrepid's* powerful engines.

Sendrei punched the controls to close the cargo bay and raced after Tabby, concerned she no longer had the sense to protect herself.

SLOWLY, Tabby opened her eyes. An itch on the side of her nose prompted her to reach up, only her arm refused to move. Panic filled her and for a moment, she flashed back to a time when she'd been grievously injured and confined to a grav-chair, only having the use of her right arm.

"Tabby, calm. I'm here." Ada's cool hand slipped into Tabby's and gave a reassuring squeeze.

"What ... where are we?" Tabby asked.

"We're still in the Mendari system," Ada answered. "We're being pursued by a fleet of Mendari warships."

"Mendari? I don't know..." Tabby found the name familiar but couldn't quite put her thoughts together. She recognized the room she was in as the officer's quarters on *Intrepid,* but she wasn't sure how she'd gotten there.

"Man-spiders," Ada answered.

"Oh. *Those* I remember," Tabby said. "They have ships?"

"Not too many," Ada said. "And they're nowhere near as fast as *Intrepid.* That is, if we had a full tank of go-go."

"My arm." Tabby tried to sit up and with Ada's help, she was successful. She reached across her chest and felt for the arm she was sure was missing, only it was there. The feeling confused her. She continued to probe for her legs, which were also there. "I don't understand."

Instead of answering, Ada walked around to the other side of Tabby's bed and lifted the blanket away from her arm. Instead of skin, the arm had been completely transformed into a beautiful blue crystal. A feeling of gratitude filled her, and Tabby immediately understood that the feeling was not her own.

"Sendrei found you like this on the planet," Ada said. "You were lying on a cylindrical crystal, roughly the size of one of *Intrepid's* missiles. Jonathan said you were severely dehydrated."

"The mother crystal ... we have to go back for it," Tabby said.

"No need. We got it," Ada said. "Almost got blown up because of it too."

"How did you know?"

"What? That we needed to grab it?"

"Yes."

"Not because of your excellent communication skills," Ada said, with mild reproof in her voice. "Actually, it was Jonathan. I was trying to get us out of the crater and would have left it behind, but Jonathan just jumped out of the cargo hold and attached himself to the stupid thing. You'll have to watch the video. I'm not sure my description would do it justice. Let's just say that you and Jonathan now have more than a few things in common."

"Right. We have about nothing in common," Tabby said.

"We estimate the crystalline structure that has taken over the synthetic fibers within your body hosts in excess of two hundred thousand distinct Iskstar," Jonathan said, his egg-shaped vessel levitating up into view. "While it is true you are now a collective, we believe Ada is referring to our recent loss of the lower portion of our corporeal body as further commonality."

"Thank you, Jonathan, you saved us," Tabby looked a little confused, but lifted her hand as if to touch the egg. "Thank you all."

"Is that Tabby talking or Iskstar?" Ada asked.

"Yes. We are ... together. Please, you must put me back into my grav-suit. Where is the mother?"

"The big crystal?" Ada asked.

"Your choice of words is interesting," Jonathan said. "You've used it consistently. Why do you call it the mother crystal?"

"The Iskstar was born from what is inside the crystal," Tabby said. "Without the mother, there is no life."

"The Iskstar are separate from the crystal?" Jonathan asked, unable to resist learning more.

"Yes. My grav-suit, please," Tabby said.

"You need to talk to Liam, Tabby," Ada said. "He's worried about you."

"They're moving on Kroerak," Tabby said, the information more of a feeling than specific knowledge. "The people of two galaxies will fail. The Kroerak will spread as a virus."

"That's kind of creepy, Tabbs," Ada said, peeling back Tabby's covers to expose the bright crystals that had taken over her legs. "Maybe come up with a few more details when you talk to Liam, okay?"

"When Kroerak and Iskstar were children, they lived in harmony. But a hunger festered inside the Kroerak," Tabby relayed, seemingly oblivious to Ada's work at pulling on her grav-suit. "It was a visitor who showed both species that there was life beyond their own world. Iskstar sought peaceful coexistence throughout the galaxies. Kroerak, however, consumed all they touched and were lost to their hunger."

"How long ago?" Jonathan asked.

"Time is hard. There isn't a reference," Tabby said. "Others don't really experience time the same way Iskstar does. I'm sorry."

"Apology unnecessary," Jonathan said. "You've already provided much information."

"Comms are set up in my quarters," Ada said. "I'd like to listen in. I know it's a big ask."

Tabby lifted from the bed and oriented vertically using the grav-suit. "You're family, Ada. We have nothing to hide from you."

"You know ... you're ... kind of talking weird, right?" Ada said as they entered the captain's quarters.

Tabby allowed a small grin. "There's a lot going on in here." She tapped on her temple. "I don't think Jonathan gets enough credit for not sounding like a lunatic."

Ada chuckled and opened the comm set. "*Hornblower,* this is *Intrepid.* Come in, please."

It took a few minutes for a response. "*Intrepid,* you have Liam and Marny, go ahead." The voice belonged to Liam.

"You sound like a warm bed on a lazy morning," Tabby said.

"Say again? Tabby? Is that you?" Liam asked. "Are you okay?"

"That was Tabby," Ada answered. "We've got a lot going on over here, but we're mostly calling to let you know we found her and she's mostly fine."

"What's this about a bed?" Liam asked.

"You are in danger, Love," Tabby said. "Tell the children of Earth, the brave children of Abasi, and the many who sail with you that your path leads only to death."

"What's going on, Tabby?" Liam said. "You don't sound right. Ada, are you sure she's okay?"

"Listen to me, beautiful child," Tabby said. "The Kroerak hunger will consume all."

"Sorry, Liam, she's not exactly in full control of her body," Ada said.

"What do you mean? *Not in control of her body*?"

"The synthetic portion of Tabitha's body has been transformed into crystal," Jonathan said, having followed the procession into Ada's quarters. "She is host to many Iskstar. We believe the warnings originate from Iskstar and should not be taken lightly."

"They took over her body?" Liam asked.

"It was her choice," Ada said. "I assume your mission is underway."

"We're preparing," Liam answered.

"Understood. I think we're going to be late to the party," Ada said. "We're just now making our way out of Mendari system."

"Do you still have that Mendari fleet after you?" Liam asked.

"Yes, but they're falling back too far to be of any concern," Ada said. "I'm glad we had speed on our side, because they pack some serious punch."

"How did we miss an entire fleet?" Liam asked.

"Everything was asleep when we first arrived," Ada said. "Problem for another day, though."

"Tabby, are you still with me?" Liam asked, thumbing the ring on his finger. He was rewarded with a return pulse a moment later.

"Liam, you have to listen. Kroerak have experienced hundreds of civilizations. All who've attacked, have failed," Tabby said. "It's the only reason the Iskstar allowed themselves to be used as weapons. But they want only to defend us."

"Don't you see? That's why we have to try," Liam said. "The Kroerak must be stopped. We have a new weapon. It will be enough."

"The Kroerak do not need weapons to win," Tabby answered. "It will not be enough."

"How can you know?" Liam asked.

"It's just a feeling," she answered. "But the Iskstar are ancient, I think you should listen to them."

"It's too late for that, Tabby," Liam said. "Entire fleets are in motion. I couldn't stop this thing if I wanted to."

Chapter 20

THE QUIET BEFORE

MHINA SYSTEM, MOON KITO OVER ELEA, HORNBLOWER

One of the things I most despised about leadership was that more often than not, what I wanted to do often conflicted with what I knew needed to be done. Tabby's condition was critical and according to Jonathan, her body was slowly rejecting what the Iskstar had done to her. Our best hope was to attempt an extremely risky surgery to remove the infected portions of her body – something she'd rejected out of hand when it had been brought up.

According to Tabby, the surgery would result in the death of hundreds of thousands of Iskstar sentients that lived in the crystalline masses that had taken over her legs, a portion of her back, and her left arm. It wasn't lost on me that those exact areas of her body were the ones taken by pirates and replaced by synthetics so long ago.

I'd run myself ragged. We were preparing York to defend itself in the absence of *Hornblower* while simultaneously preparing *Hornblower* to once again engage with the Kroerak. While my time talking with Tabby had been limited, it had also become increasingly difficult to find something to say. She'd resigned herself to what she thought was her fate: dying for the cause of many. The concept was something I understood at a high level, but not when it applied to my best friend and life-mate.

"When will the Confederation fleet arrive?" Tabby asked, changing the subject.

Intrepid had left the Mendari system and had been sailing toward Kito for fifteen days, with at least twenty more before they would arrive. Apparently, combat maneuvers used to evade the Mendari fleet had further drained their fuel supplies and they were limping home. I was glad that *Intrepid* wouldn't take part in the great battle that was to come. While Ada was a fantastic captain in her own right and *Intrepid* was both fast and now deadly with an Iskstar-tuned weapon, a small voice in the back of my head agreed with Tabby's assessment that our attack on the Kroerak homeworld wouldn't be successful.

"Forty warships entered the Mhina system late yesterday," I said. "They'll send two fuel tenders to Kito but the majority of the fleet is headed directly to the wormhole that leads to the Kroerak."

"You're going to be leaving soon then?" Tabby asked.

We'd agreed to stop talking about the larger events around us and simply enjoy the time we had left. Even so, the conversation was strained and I had a persistent lump in my throat.

"We're lifting off in a few minutes. Tabby, I feel like I'm never going to see you again," I said, breaking our agreement.

Tabby thumbed her ring, communicating more than she could say. "I know," she answered.

A knock at the door to my quarters interrupted our conversation and I wiped a tear from my cheek.

"I gotta go, Tabbs. I love you," I said.

"I know," she answered, turning off the comms. Despite the heavy moment, I smiled at the inside joke.

"Cap?" Marny's voice barely penetrated the entry hatch.

I stood, straightened my vac-suit and grabbed a med-patch from a stack on my desk. I wasn't about to let the crew see me as mopey or defeated when we were headed into battle. I placed two thin strips beneath my eyes. After waiting a moment for them to clear my face, I blew out a hot breath, removed the patches and palmed open the door.

"We ready?" I asked, forcing my voice to sound positive as I looked into Marny's face. I was surprised to see a similar strip hanging beneath her eye as if she'd torn one of the patches as she'd removed it. "Uh, hold on a sec." I reached over and peeled the remnant away.

"Appreciated, Cap," she answered, just a little too snappily.

"Little Pete doing okay with Mom and Flaer?" I asked.

While Marny had insisted on bringing Little Pete with her to rescue us from Picis, she would not bring him on this trip. I saw her logic, the Mhina system would be safe from Kroerak, something she couldn't have guaranteed when she'd left Zuri so many months ago. On the other hand, our next journey would be perilous indeed, Iskstar-tuned weapons or not.

"Your mom's great," Marny said. "She didn't even bat an eye and says she'll raise him as her own if anything happens."

"That's a little morbid, right?"

Marny shook her head. "Not really. She knows what we're up against. Peter's safety is my highest priority now. It's a big relief to know he's got family."

"What a pair we are," I said, turning toward the bridge. "How have you done this all these years? Why would you come back to it after getting out of the Marines?"

"That's a question every combat soldier asks," she said. "Hardest years of my life were on Baru Manush as a civilian. Running security for a space station isn't like being in the shite. The pull of combat isn't really something you can turn off. You haven't experienced it."

"I've seen plenty of battle," I said defensively. I was surprised she would say such a thing. I was positive I'd seen more combat that most soldiers.

"Aye Cap, that you have," she answered. "Ever wonder why we always end up back in the crapper?"

"You can't believe that's my doing?"

"You want it straight up or a lie?"

"You think I'm looking for fights?" I asked, incredulous. The implications were huge if that was the case. That would make me responsible for Tabby's current condition and I found such an idea hard to accept.

We'd stopped in front of the entry to the bridge and Ken Stolzman stood at the opposite end of the passageway, having just exited the lift. I chuckled, recognizing he didn't want to get into the middle of a conversation between Marny and me.

"Come on through, Ken," I said, waving him over. "You know, I never had a chance to ask. Do you have family back on Earth?"

"Roger that, Captain," Stolzman answered. "That's why I signed up for the mission to come to Dwingeloo and look for Kroerak."

"You didn't know, Cap?" Marny asked. "The Marine who saved us on the first Kroerak invasion was Ken's dad."

I recalled floating through space in our Popeyes, in the middle of doing a high orbit insertion, when our guide – apparently Stolzman's dad – had been killed.

"Your dad was very brave," I said, placing a hand on his shoulder. "Without his sacrifice, Earth might have been lost."

"Good of you to say, sir," Stolzman answered. "I hope I can live up to the name."

"Walking onto that bridge today takes a lot of courage," I said. "XO and I will finish up and be there in a minute."

"Aye, aye, Captain," he said.

"XO?" Marny asked after the door closed.

"You have more titles than the North American Library of Congress," I said. "Seems like we should pick one that's actually appropriate."

"Okay," Marny laughed. "Back to our conversation. You're not looking for fights, Cap. You're just not willing to look the other way when something needs doing. What I'm saying is, when you finally try to let go of all this fighting, you're going to wrestle with it."

"Good thing we don't have to worry about that today." I opened the door to the bridge and raised my voice. "Because I'm ready to go kick some bug ass."

"Oorah!" Marny grunted.

"All hands, this is your captain," I said, allowing the AI a moment to open ship-wide communications. "Today we set sail on possibly the most important mission of mankind. No matter the outcome, I could not be prouder of your willingness to stand forward and put yourselves on the line. I won't mince words and I won't sugarcoat it. We're up against an enemy that has, to this day, obliterated all challengers. This enemy has taken what is not theirs, has murdered our families and countless billions of peoples across multiple galaxies. But today, this ends. Today, we will take decisive action ... we will take *bold* action ... and we will put an end to the blight so many cower from, so that all civilizations might live in peace. Today, most of all, we bring judgment to the Kroerak."

Marny returned my smile as we enjoyed the exuberant cries from the crew.

"All hands, report system statuses and prepare for liftoff," she said. "Captain, I assume you'll want the number one spot?"

I nodded at the pilot who sat in the portside pilot's chair. With a smile, she stood at attention as I approached. "At ease," I said. "I'll give her back once we're in orbit."

"Aye, aye, Captain," she answered enthusiastically.

Taking the lead pilot's chair, it was my responsibility to run the pre-sail checklist. Stolzman, seated to my right, was already working his way through it. I scooped off the lower half of the work and tossed it onto the crisp vid-screen on the forward bulkhead.

"I can do that, Captain," Stolzman said.

"Negative," I answered. "I want the seat, I take the work. It's only fair."

"Did you know my dad very well?" Stolzman asked, as we worked on validating the systems.

"I'll be honest," I said. "I was a little afraid of him."

Stolzman laughed. "I guess you did, then. You weren't the only one."

"Once we get under way, I'll clip out my personal data-streams of him," I said.

"I'd like that. I wasn't able to get back for the memorial," he answered. "And don't hold back his last moments. I owe him that much."

"Can do."

I continued working through the checklist. We were heavy with fuel and munitions, but it was nothing compared to a belly full of York townspeople and their livestock. Once I'd completed my checklist, I switched to view statuses for the other sections of the ship. As expected, engineering was the last to complete their work as they had by far the most critical systems.

"Captain, I'm showing green," Marny announced a moment after the last status updated. *Hornblower* wasn't at one hundred percent, but the dings and scrapes we'd received were both well-earned and not critical. I felt they gave the old girl personality.

"Open channel with York municipal and all-ship," I said.

"This is York," Mom answered.

"This is *Hornblower*, requesting permission for liftoff."

"Permission granted, *Hornblower,*" Mom answered. "Godspeed. Come back safely. There are a lot of people here who love you."

"Copy that. Oh, and one more thing," I said.

"What's that?" Mom asked.

"Cue Big Head Todd and John Lee Hooker's, *Boom Boom Boom*," I said.

I heard a slight groan as an ancient electric guitar started playing and a raspy-voiced musician sang. I'd previously instructed the AI to cut right to the chorus because it was exactly what I was after.

Boom boom boom boom ...

Bang bang bang bang ...

I didn't wait for what I knew would be a chorus of groans and slowly pushed forward on the left stick. *Hornblower's* powerful engines shuddered to life sending a great cloud of dust billowing out around the big ship. At the same time, I flicked a virtual lever with my right hand, switching the right stick to grav-repulsor controls. With almost no warning, *Hornblower* lurched forward as it came free of the ground.

"Hold on there, girl," I said sliding two fingers up the stick and nudging more power into the forward grav lifters. It was tricky business that I was glad the AI was helping with. After sliding down a hill ten meters, I regained control, only after dragging the aft keel along the hard surface of the overly-small landing strip we'd been perched on.

"You good, Captain?" Stolzman asked, his voice calm.

"Copy," I answered, unable to talk much given my current focus. "Watch that starboard clearance, would you?" We weren't overly close to the tall trees that lined the city, but I didn't want to get tangled in them.

"You have eighty meters, zero delta-v and will clear in five seconds," he answered immediately. His response made me believe he'd already been paying attention to them. I appreciated his composure.

Escaping the ground was by far the most difficult task for *Hornblower.* Understandably, she enjoyed her time nestled against Kito's wild surface. She did grudgingly give way, apparently knowing once I got our main engines beneath us, the battle would be over. I pushed the gravity systems to maximum, surprised at how hard I had to go to accomplish the task but was soon rewarded. The song – still playing – muted as a cheer from the crew erupted. I turned the bow skyward and *Hornblower's* massive engine's propelled us into the light clouds and blue sky.

"Nick, set a course to intercept with the Confederation fleet," I ordered once we finally broke free from the atmosphere and were once again surrounded by the inky black of space I'd always considered home.

"Course plotted," Nick answered.

"Mr. Stolzman, the helm is yours," I said.

"Helm is mine, Captain," he answered, grabbing the sticks on his own chair.

"And, thank you for the use of your chair ..." I said, looking back to the pilot I'd displaced and reading the name plate my AI projected. "Ms. Shults."

The woman nodded and slipped back into the chair. It occurred to me that I probably should have taken Stolzman's chair as Shults was his senior with substantially more experience. I also appreciated that she was completely nonplussed by the event.

A LIGHT BEEPING sound woke me from where I slept on the couch in my quarters. I was awake enough to realize it wasn't my alarm, but an internal comm request from the bridge watch.

"This is Hoffen. Go ahead, bridge," I said.

"Captain, we're being hailed by *Thunder Awakes*."

"I'll take it in here," I said.

"Copy that, Captain."

"Go ahead, *Thunder Awakes,*" I said, pushing sleep from my eyes. I hadn't been sleeping very well and the anticipation of joining up with the Confederation of Planets fleet had me on edge. I pulled at an indicator in my peripheral and tossed a view from *Hornblower's* external data sensors onto the smaller vid-screen on my desk.

"Bold Prime, you are welcomed to Fleet of the Confederation," Mshindi Prime said, a three-dimensional bust of her showing in the lower right corner of my screen.

"Thank you, Mshindi Prime," I said. My display showed we were still an hour from overtaking the forty Confederation warships.

I'd been surprised to discover that only eight of the Confederation fleet were Abasi, not including *Hornblower.* I'd voiced my concern to Mshindi in a previous communication exchange about the small showing. Her answer had been direct, as I'd learned to expect from her. With the capability to defend Abasi Prime within their grasp, she would not leave her citizens open to a counterattack by Kroerak. To say I was disappointed was an understatement. We needed a full-court press on the Kroerak if we were to destroy them. It was not the time for defense.

"I have dispatched a patrol from Abasi Prime to travel to the moon Kito," she said. "They will provide protection in your absence."

I felt a flash of anger at her presumption. Kito was mine to defend and we'd left a sloop and several recovered atmo fliers for protection. Further, *Intrepid* would arrive in twelve days. "What in the frak, Adahy? Are you aware of a specific threat? We have defenses." I said, trying to tamp down my irritation.

"We have entered a time of extreme danger within Tamu. We have desisted all travel off-planet due to presence of large numbers of enemy ships," she answered. "We have intercepted communiques specifically targeting Mhina system. I apologize for my presumption."

I sighed. She was doing me a solid. The least I could do was to be grateful. "No, sorry about that. I'm just feeling edgy. Thank you for your assistance. How can I be of assistance to you?

"My Engineer First has worked with the Confederation fleet to identify our needs for Iskstar," she said. "I would transmit so that you would have time to prepare."

"Understood," I said. "Send the list and we can raft up before we hit the wormhole for transfer."

"That is acceptable. Mshindi desists."

"Nick, are you up?" I asked.

"Yup," he answered, sounding refreshed. "Amazing how much sleep you can get when there's no baby in the room."

I chuckled despite my mood. "Might have to get me one of those. I can't seem to sleep."

"Not sure it works that way. What's up?" He was slightly out of breath as he spoke.

"Where are you?"

"Quarters, we were just getting ready to head over to the bridge."

"Oh. *Oh...*" I said, understanding coming to me all at once.

"Hi, Cap." Marny's voice came over Nick's comm. "Just getting in some exercise."

"Stop," Nick whispered.

"Uh, Mshindi sent an inventory of Iskstar crystals for the Confederation. When you get a chance, could you work on getting that organized for raft-up?" I asked.

"Sure. I've got it," he answered.

I smiled as I closed the comm. I was glad Nick and Marny had each other. I thumbed my ring as I often did throughout the day. Tabby answered a moment later. It wasn't much, but the simple connection meant a lot.

What the fleet lacked for in numbers, it worked hard to make up for with sheer firepower. Each of the different species-based nations had sent what looked to be their very best ships, from the spherical behemoth battleships of the turtle-looking Chelonii, to the sleek but equally large battlecruiser-classed ships of the rat-faced Abelineian. My hopes buoyed, and I felt both pride and relief at the eclectic, yet powerful collection of ships. I was a little surprised at my reaction and realized I still very much had things to prove to the enigmatic Admiral Alderson.

"LIAM? ARE YOU AWAKE?" Tabby asked.

I startled. "Yeah, sorry, I must have dozed off."

"*Intrepid* just transitioned into Mhina," she said. "The Iskstar like what we're doing on Kito. It's like they're proud of us for recovering the moon and making a place for families."

I just nodded. Tabby and I shared something important with the Iskstar: an innate sense of what was worthwhile in this world. "Any further thought about that surgery?" I asked. "Things are going to start heating up on my side. I don't know how much time we'll have to talk."

"When will you meet up with Alderson and Sterra?" she asked, ignoring my question. She would give her life for the Iskstar and there was nothing I could do about it.

"Forty hours and then we're only two jumps to the system adjacent to the Kroerak homeworld," I said.

"I wish you had convinced them to turn away," she said. "The Iskstar believe you can't win."

"Not exactly an inspiring talk," I said, equally uninterested in her attempts to get me to turn away.

"I know. I'm sorry," she said. "Do you ever feel like we don't have as much control of our lives as we think?"

"Lately, I can't think of anything else."

Chapter 21

FOR ALL THE MARBLES

"Any minute now." Nick answered the unasked question of when the combined ships from human space would join us. Not only were we expecting ships from Earth and Mars, but we'd learned that at the last minute, humanity's Bethe Peierls and Tipperary systems had joined with twenty additional heavy warships.

"There, Cap." Marny pointed at the forward armor glass that moments ago looked over an empty, darkened starfield. This location of space was technically not associated with any known galaxy. In the vast emptiness, the glittering light that appeared could have been a previously unseen star, but soon that single point was accompanied by dozens, then hundreds of similar points of light. Even at this distance, Admiral Alderson's massive dreadnaught *Bakunawa* wasn't hard to pick out, as it was twice the size of even Earth's largest battleships.

"Confederation fleet is moving out," Nick announced. "Navigation instructions have been transmitted."

I pulled the plan onto the holo display. As expected, it showed Mshindi Prime moving the fleet to meet up with Alderson's much larger group.

"Accept plan. Engage on my mark, Mr. Stolzman," I said.

We'd subjugated *Hornblower* to Mshindi Prime's command for the sake of keeping an organized fleet. Humanity's battlegroup had been set to arrive four hours in advance of the Confederation fleet, but with the aid of quantum comm crystals, Mshindi and I had negotiated with Alderson and Sterra throughout the transit about our general strategies and assignments.

"Cap, we're being hailed by battleship *Iowa,*" Marny said. "It's marked as private."

I rolled my eyes at what seemed like unnecessary operational security. If you were on *Hornblower's* bridge at this point, your very existence depended on us getting the next seventy-two hours right. I sighed and tapped the earwig that sat comfortably along my upper jaw bone.

"This is Hoffen. Go ahead, *Iowa,*" I said.

"Greetings, Captain Hoffen." Admiral Sterra's face appeared in a virtual window on my HUD. She'd aged since our last face-to-face, but then I suppose I had as well. It had been a long four years.

"Greetings, Admiral," I answered. "I have to say I'm glad to see you guys made it. Even with Iskstar, I'm not sure our Confederation fleet would be up to the horde we're about to face."

"Our simulations tend to agree with your analysis," she answered. "Apologies for the privacy requirement, but I don't have to tell you what's on the line."

"What can I do for you?" I asked.

LaVonne Sterra was one of my favorite people in the universe, but I was done with pleasant conversation. Me and mine had paid a big price – and were about to again – to do what we knew was right. I was ready to get on with things.

If my abruptness bothered her, she didn't show it. She gave me a crisp nod. "I'm dispatching fifteen fleet tenders to intercept. We're asking you drop out of hard-burn, away from the Confederation fleet, and allow for offloading of the Iskstar weapons."

"You're changing the plan?" I asked. "Confederation fleet will be to you in four hours."

"It is a small adjustment. We want to equip the Iskstar as quickly as possible," she answered, her face impassive. I sensed her discomfort.

"Liam, we're showing a small group of ships headed our way. They're accelerating hard," Nick cut in.

I muted. "Tell Mshindi they're coming to grab the Iskstar crystals."

"Copy," Nick answered.

"Cap, what's going on?" Marny asked.

"Not sure," I answered, unmuting the private comm with Sterra. I could think of only one reason they'd be accelerating the timeline. We'd chosen our meet-up location because it put us three days from Kroerak space. Timing had been planned down to the minute. Everything was perfectly choreographed for Alderson's fleet to jump around the wormhole's endpoint only moments before the Confederation fleet transitioned. We'd worked out the details all the way down to the amount of time it would take to ferry the crystals from *Hornblower* to the various ships. Sterra's modification, however, gave the engineers a bit of breathing room. It was reasonable.

"Is there a problem, Captain Hoffen?" Sterra's demeaner was once again settled, further confirming my belief that she was under stress about the conversation.

"No, we're just updating Confederation with the new plans," I said. In the short span of the conversation, Mshindi had updated *Hornblower's* navigation plan and requested contact once I was off with Sterra. "Do you mind if I ask you something?"

"Please do," she said.

"Tabby says Iskstar doesn't believe we'll survive contact," I said. I'd passed the information on in a previous briefing only to be dismissed by Alderson. He'd suggested that our inexperience in battle and Tabby's feelings for me were getting in the way of reason.

"We've talked about this," Sterra reminded me.

"No. I told Alderson about a legitimate threat and he diminished it," I said. "If we lose to Kroerak, there's nothing that will stop them from rolling humanity or the dozens of species in the Confederation of Planets."

"Perhaps you have taken my reticence in accepting everything Admiral Alderson has said as a weakness in our command," she said. "While I do not appreciate his mechanism for delivering information, his analysis mirrors my own. You should not be engaged in this battle. You are emotionally compromised."

"That's rich," I said. "We wouldn't have this chance without my emotional involvement. Clearly, I'm good at tamping that down. Or have you forgotten the last four stans?"

Sterra's face softened. "Every commander feels doubt before battle, Liam. Perhaps Iskstar does have some piece of knowledge and the Kroerak will bring an end to us. Without specifics, can you really ask us to turn away? We have a chance to take the worst threat to humanity off the board completely. We have to at least try."

And there it was. I finally figured out why the conversation between us had felt off. I half-smiled at the revelation and felt saddened by it all at the same time. "If the battle turns against us, you're jumping away, aren't you?"

Surprise registered on her face. "Did Iskstar tell you this?"

"We're not exactly on speaking terms, contrary to the fact that my eyes still glow," I said. "I'm right, though. You know if you jump away, the Confederation fleet won't prevail. They'll slaughter us."

"One of the tenders that is coming to you now carries TransLoc engines that can be inset into your wormhole engines," she said. "Thomas Anino insisted we deliver them. He said you'd know how to use them best."

I felt physically repulsed at the suggestion and held back a gag. "And leave Mshindi behind? You've got to be kidding? How in the world did someone get Alderson to buy off on that?"

"Mr. Anino can be very convincing. That's why the change of plans. We need extra time to install the TransLoc engine insets," she said. "Can you now see why we needed a private conversation?"

"You think Mshindi hasn't guessed that you'll bug out if things get too hairy?" I asked.

"Sometimes the hardest thing to do is to keep living," Sterra said. "Death is easy. Life is the real challenge. Sterra out."

I was dazed by the conversation. The thought that part of the plan for Alderson's fleet was to see how things were going and then run if the odds were too bad was horrific to me. I knew for a fact that no Abasi would do the same. Before I'd met the Abasi, I'd believed honor was something reserved for the best of humanity. I now knew better. Part of me also understood Alderson's cold calculus. Returning home with a way to defend against Kroerak might lack honor, but it would save a lot of lives, albeit at the cost of many other lives.

MY ALARM WOKE me as a med-patch shot nanites into my blood stream to remove the melatonin added to help me sleep. The pit in my stomach instantly refilled as I recalled what we were up against. I'd told myself that I'd take a shower before heading to the bridge, but four semi-urgent comms were already in my queue. I ran water in the sink and splashed it on my face, running a sani-wipe through my unruly hair that apparently had chosen this moment to need to be cut. Ignoring all that, I palmed myself through to the bridge.

"Captain on the bridge." I didn't bother to even look for the speaker before I allowed everyone to return to their duties.

Marny met me at my chair and handed me a bar. "Go time, Cap. I got your favorite."

"Strawberry?" I asked, thumbing my ring. I received a weak response from Tabby, but it was enough. She was still with me, but I could feel her slipping away.

"Last one," Marny quipped, handing me a cup of coffee and turning straight to business. "*Thunder Awakes'* long range sensors have picked up what looks like a welcoming committee at the wormhole entrance to the Kroerak homeworld."

"How many?" I asked.

"Two hundred," she said. "Nothing we can't handle."

"I can't figure these Kroerak," I said. "They must have some way to communicate to the main force and don't mind losing two hundred ships just to learn of our arrival. Why not sacrifice just one ship?"

"Caution," she said. "Kroerak have no idea how many we're bringing. If we only brought a handful of ships, they'd knock us out before we made it through the wormhole."

"Anything else shaking?" I asked. "Have we heard from Alderson's fleet?"

"We're set to rendezvous in T-minus three hours twelve minutes. As long as we're not delayed by this group, we'll be right on schedule," Marny said. "Cap, do you mind a question?"

"What's up?" I asked.

"It took a lot of guts to tell Mshindi about the TransLoc engine inserts," she said. "I believed you when you said you had no intention of using them, but Alderson isn't wrong. If it goes badly enough, retreat might be the best answer."

I studied Marny's face. This was a woman I trusted with every fiber of my being and I resisted the urge to scream at her. My anger was at the situation and because I had a bad feeling again that I was missing something. The small voice inside me that went against all reason was telling me we couldn't possibly defeat the Kroerak by force. I finally relented and nodded slightly. "If it gets to that, but not a second before."

"Copy that, Cap," she answered. "Not a second before."

"I'm activating fleet comms," Nick said. "Our bridges are linked. Remember, if you want to address the entire fleet, prefix with *fleet*."

Along with reestablishing comms, I noticed that several Confederation ships jumped slightly, repositioning as better data was transmitted over the full data-streams that had become available.

If trying to sleep before battle was hard, it was nothing compared to the two-hour-long deceleration to the Kroerak wormhole where we were outnumbered four-to-one. If the Kroerak had a secret weapon, now would be the time we'd find out. I'd wracked my brain, trying to come up with a game changer, but if the Kroerak were anything, they were consistent – ridiculously so, even. Their goal at the gate was to soften us, hoping to win a slow battle of attrition.

"BETA WING, you are cleared to engage," Mshindi Prime ordered. She'd actually said something entirely different, but I'd programed the AI to translate certain expected combat phrases clearly. *Hornblower* was the lead ship in a wing of six battlecruisers: two were Abasi, one was a spherical Chelonii, and two were sleek Abelineian. We had the honor of leading the charge to the gate. Shortly behind us the other nine wings would follow with Mshindi Prime coordinating the battle space.

"Boggus-12, keep tight," I warned. The turtle-like Chelonii were often slow to respond to directives and I wasn't going to lose them because they strayed from the protective formation we'd created. Unlike every other species, Chelonii traveled in water-filled spherical vessels. Their ship engines were substantially more powerful than every other ship here to make up for the difference in mass.

"Compliance is acceptable," came the reply.

Our lane of engagement was tight and our goal was simple. We were going to make a fast pass through the upper third of the spread-out Kroerak fleet and attempt to split their forces. The maneuver was from Mshindi who'd suggested that to cull a herd of prey, it was most effective if they weren't allowed the safety of the large group. The problem with her statement, of course, was that our prey could shoot waves of lances with devastating impact.

"Increase acceleration to forty," I instructed, pleased that the spherical ship had pulled back into position.

"We're in firing range," Marny announced a moment later as we passed the outer edge of the Kroerak fleet.

The blasters had a relatively slow recharge with the new, longer-range enhancements we'd added. Our first pass would be our most dangerous as we'd come too close to several of the enemy. "Assign targets, Marny. Save our shots for any ships that can get a target on us."

"Aye, Cap." I heard disappointment in her voice as we passed several targets of opportunity. We had the capability to reach them with our weapons, but Marny would keep us on the safer choices I'd made.

"Lance waves," Nick announced, highlighting a confusing array of waves fired from long range. I realized almost too late that the Kroerak had indeed formed a new plan. They would fill the battle-space with lance waves, regardless of how many of their own they impaled.

"Pull up. All ships, evasive actions. I repeat, evasive actions," I ordered. "Marny, targets of opportunity."

"Aye, aye, Cap," she said, excitement thick in her voice. I had to grin as I heard her. Like me, she found waiting for battle impossible. Once in the middle of it, she came alive.

"Liam, Chelonii are having trouble adjusting," Nick said. "They're gonna get splattered."

And just like that, first blood in the mighty battle was spilled. Four hundred generally kind-spirited, noble beings were exterminated as they ran across the line of lances they should have been able to avoid. Upon contact with the vacuum of space, the water crystalized as it spewed from the great ship, much of it vaporizing as it rapidly boiled due to the low pressure.

The thrum of *Hornblower's* main turrets firing and recharging caught my attention a moment later. The sounds were shortly followed by the staccato of our medium, shorter-range blasters. The Kroerak had anticipated our attack and positioned ships almost perfectly, herding us into a kill box. I'd heard the phrase *the hunter becomes the hunted* and it fit the situation very well.

"*Chudlo*, pick up your assigned target. They're boxing us in!" Marny ordered.

The Abelineian ship, *Chudlo*, had taken the opportunity to fire at and destroy a long-range target, missing Marny's assignment.

"Bravo wing, they're trying to distract us," I said. "Keep your targets, I don't care how tempting the low-hanging fruit is."

"I can't avoid it," Stolzman said, banking *Hornblower* as hard as he could. The fact was, a ship the size of *Hornblower* didn't turn all that quickly and he was right, there was no avoiding the wave emanating from the ship *Chudlo* had missed.

"Turn into it," Nick snapped. "Take it across the bow."

"But we'll lose the forward turret," Stolzman argued. To his credit, however, he was already maneuvering back.

"All hands, prepare for collision," Marny announced. "Evacuate forward sections immediately. This is not a drill."

Hornblower shuddered as a wave of weapons crashed across our bow. From my vantage point, the damage didn't look too bad, although three crew were immediately marked as missing. *Hornblower's* aft, medium blaster turret barked and drilled the attacking Kroerak ship that had sacrificed itself to injure us.

I updated the wing's orders and called the remaining ships to form up. We hadn't given the Kroerak enough credit. What had appeared a loose grouping of ships was instead a thoughtfully organized placement. Fleet-wide, they had reduced our numbers by ten percent and damaged even more.

"Stay sharp!" I ordered. If the fleet of two hundred Kroerak were the end, my confidence would have been higher, but suddenly I realized we were in for a long battle. "We take our time, we keep our distance."

I set our path back through the battle space. We'd lost six ships on contact with the enemy and had taken out more than twice that number, plus we'd split the Kroerak forces. *Hornblower* had sustained damage, but it was more an inconvenience than a real hindrance, that is, as long as we didn't need to land on a planet anytime soon.

On our next pass, things turned out substantially better. The Kroerak weren't the type to run, and without time to set up clever traps, we plunked away at them from a distance, far beyond their ability to return fire.

"We've got this, Cap," Marny announced on our third pass. *Hornblower* had delivered eight kill shots and four assists. Beta wing had cleared the targets in our space and joined with the remainder of the fleet that was mopping up just as easily.

"The math won't work," Nick said glumly. "If Munay's numbers were right, we need to be hitting twenty to one. We barely hit five to one here."

"First contact," Marny said, firmly. "We adjust ... and I don't need to hear the numbers anymore."

"Cut the chatter, guys," I said. "We're still on fleet comms."

After saying it, I realized that Nick had muted our conversation while he and Marny had been talking. Still, it was good discipline.

"Captain Hoffen, that was an impressively executed maneuver," Mshindi Prime said, surprising me with her praise.

"We lost the Chelonii," I said. "The Kroerak outmaneuvered us."

"Yet we adjusted. Your quick thinking showed us the trap before it was sufficiently set. Many more could have been lost," Mshindi said. "Now, we must make haste to the wormhole. I will leave Epsilon Wing behind to finish the survivors and then they can join us."

"Copy that," I answered. If we survived, there would be plenty of time for me to tell Mshindi how poorly conceived her flock-separating tactic had worked against Kroerak.

"We should take it slower," Marny said. "We're not sprinting here. We should clean up first and then go through as a group."

"Negative, Bold Second," Mshindi answered. "The Sol fleet has promised to meet us, and the appointed time will pass without our haste. The battle awaits."

I hit the mute. "Her call, Marny," I said, not at all surprised Mshindi had placed *Hornblower* behind her group of battleships. I didn't like going through second but recognized the value of a single voice of command.

"Roger that, Cap," Marny answered.

Per agreement with Tabby, I was to let her know with two taps on my ring when we made it through the first battle. I did that and laid in a navigation plan that would send my wing through on the heels of Mshindi's.

The trip through the broken hulks on our way to the wormhole was disquieting. Combat in space was not typically a long, drawn-out affair. Powerful weapons had a tendency of making quick work between forces bent on destruction. Even a run-and-gun ended quickly. Either you could outrun or outmaneuver a stronger foe or you couldn't. There was rarely any middle ground.

For some reason, the victory felt hollow even as Tabby's rapid, happy tapping on the ring reminded me of why I fought.

Chapter 22

TO THE END

"Hard starboard, twenty degrees," I roared. Before Iskstar, I'd been one of the slowest when it came to recovering from wormhole transition. Now, I was always the first to become aware of our surroundings.

Stolzman, no doubt still blind, slammed his stick to the right, allowing *Hornblower* to narrowly avoid collision with debris that was strewn about in front of the wormhole terminus. With senses reactivated due to a healthy dose of adrenaline, he adjusted to the floating chunk of rock in our path.

Through Munay's eyes, we'd seen the Kroerak taking the wormhole at a slow but manageable speed instead of being at full stop relative to the wormhole's position. Further, they'd transitioned many ships simultaneously. As a captain, I'd embraced the idea of moving a bunch of ships through all at the same time, while maintaining some speed with respect to the wormhole.

I bit down hard as it dawned on me that the Kroerak might have counted on us seeing that data-stream. They had filled the area with every chuck of debris they could find and drag over.

Like a worm, the idea that we were following a Kroerak playbook ate at my brain as I took in a scene of complete carnage. The once-great Abasi fleet, the few ships that had survived, were damaged almost beyond recovery. My heart sank as I found the wreckage of *Thunder Awakes*, broken in two at the front of the line.

I watched helplessly as the second wave of our fleet appeared through the wormhole. Many of the newcomers were unable to miss colliding with the broken hulks sitting in their path. I tasted blood as I bit down on my tongue. Without firing a single shot, the Kroerak had cut the Confederation fleet in half.

"Regroup on me!" I ordered. A swarm of hundreds if not thousands of Kroerak sailed in our direction. They were coming from everywhere all at once and we had only minutes to find a new plan or we'd be trapped.

"If you're going to jump, now would be the time," Nick said flatly, not bothering to mute.

"No," I said firmly, "We fight. Where the frak is Alderson?"

"Not sure," he answered tightly.

"I've got a hole," I said, having searched local space for breathing room. A gap widened between the groups of inbound Kroerak ships. If we cut over tightly, we might have enough room. "Marny, widen that gap! Fleet, I'm taking command. If you want to live, get on me!"

I didn't bother to watch which ships chose to join us and which chose to go it on their own. In the end, there were eighteen of us, mostly battlecruisers. We were maneuverable enough to avoid the static weapons that had been laced across the wormhole's entrance. So far, the Kroerak had guessed our every move. They'd used every bit of data we had against us. Worse yet, I had no idea where Alderson had gone. A part of me wondered if he'd taken his entire fleet and run off, taking their Iskstar crystals back home.

"I found them," Nick said. "Alderson's fleet is at the fourth planet. They jumped straight to the Kroerak homeworld."

We had more than we could deal with, so I had to let that sit for a minute. My small fleet was doing better than we had any reason to hope for. Judicious use of the longer-range weapons was having the intended effect and a corridor formed, giving us just enough room to maneuver. I quickly adjusted our formation so the most heavily armored were in fore and aft, ordering the fleet to take a slow bend around. Shortly, the final wing of Abasi ships would come through the wormhole and I hoped our timing would be sufficient to catch them.

As if sensing our intent, the Kroerak pushed against my path. Even though we were a small group, we had range and superior firepower. We *were* making progress. If only we could survive the next two or three hours, we might have a chance, especially if Alderson was having better luck than we were. For the first time, hope buoyed. Alderson was ten times the tactician I was. I might not appreciate him using us as bait, but we were after the same thing and we all knew the consequences of losing. If we needed to be a tasty morsel so he could put down the Kroerak command structure, I was all in and my friends and the whole crew stood with me.

As if to feed my optimism, the final wing of six Abasi ships exited the wormhole just as we crossed in front of their position. Blasting positional data on the debris and navigational updates, we successfully saved all but one of the ships, further strengthening our numbers to twenty-three.

"They're not moving," Nick said.

No matter what he was seeing, I was positive he was wrong. There were at least ten thousand ships moving at any given time within a hundred thousand kilometers of *Hornblower's* position. If we continued to chew through them at our current rate, we'd clear the system in twenty-five days, give or take. We certainly didn't have the energy reserves to do that, but we also had two hundred or so angry Martians ready to join in. I was pretty sure we had more than a fighting chance.

"Who's not moving?" I asked.

"Alderson's fleet."

"What do you mean?" I asked. "How are they not moving? Maybe they're negotiating? Get him on quantum."

I turned back to the battle. The Kroerak were taking losses at an extreme rate, although they were still able to fill in where each ship was destroyed. Fortunately, the debris and confusion caused their fleet to thin out as we stretched the battle space, moving further and further away from the wormhole entrance.

We'd achieved a small amount of breathing room, so I took a moment to push us back toward our pursuers. I enjoyed watching the enemy ships crash onto the wave of blue-hued lasers as we fired and jumped away, stringing them along as we opened up a path toward the fourth planet.

"I can't raise Sterra," Nick said. "She's not responding."

"That doesn't make any sense," I said. "We need them. We're never going to make this without them."

"Toss me the crystal for Tabby," he said. I wondered what he was thinking, but I didn't hesitate, pulling it from my waist and throwing it to him. I hated the idea of losing the only contact I had with her, but I trusted him and needed to keep my mind on other things.

"Cap, are you sure this is all our doing?" Marny asked, as I continued providing instructions, taking what the Kroerak would give and making them pay dearly for it.

"Not following," I was pleased to see the number of destroyed Kroerak ships growing with each maneuver.

"What's our chance of survival if Alderson's fleet doesn't respond?" she asked.

"Not pretty."

"They're herding us," she said. "Can't you see it?"

"Hold on," I said, my enthusiasm popping like a balloon. The truth of her words struck me like a cast iron bilge pipe.

I adjusted our flight pattern so we angled away from the Kroerak homeworld. As I did, the response by our pursuers was immediate. With haste, they fired wave after wave of lance weapons, creating a nearly impenetrable curtain through which we could not possibly pass.

"I've got Jonathan on the line," Nick said. "He's talking to Anino, who has sensor access to a few of the ships. He's patching us through."

"Frak, Hoffen, you're in it bad now," Anino said. "I can't reach anyone on those ships."

"What do you mean? I thought Nick said you had sensor access."

"I'm telling you, they're not responding. It's like the crew is asleep at their stations, but with their eyes open," Anino answered.

"Hey, Liam, it's Sendrei," Sendrei said. "How many days before you reach the planet?"

"Eight days, give or take," I said.

"Can you slow them down?"

"Some," I said. "Might be able to stretch it to twelve."

"When you reach the planet, the Kroerak are going to destroy all of you," he said.

"Why not now?" I asked, not really believing him.

"I imagine they want to finish the job all at once," he said. "Believe it or not, they're showing you respect. I suspect they think you'll come up with some plan. So they're using humanity's fleet as bait."

"You're making a shite-pot of assumptions here," I said. "How could you know this?"

"A Kroerak noble controlled my mind when I got too close, Liam," he said. "What if there's something nastier on that planet, something that has a bigger range."

"That can control thousands of minds? That's crazy," I said.

"As crazy as using Munay to draw you to their homeworld so they could put an end to you?" he asked. "That kind of crazy?"

"Yeah," I said. "That's the kind of crazy I'm talking about."

"Liam, listen to me," Tabby said. "You need to jump to this system." An encoded series of numbers sounded and my AI translated it. She was giving me directions to a location in deep space.

"For what?" Anino asked. "You can't help, Masters."

"Where is that?" I asked, not sure what Anino was talking about.

"We can end this. Trust me," she said. "But you have to go now."

For a moment, I just stared at Nick as the battle waged around us. Eight or twelve days of fighting would put a nice dent in the Kroerak forces, but we were already slowing, as Kroerak wised up to our tactics.

"Get Moyo, Perasti Tertiary, on comms," I said. "I'm sure I saw that *Hunting Fog* was still with us."

"Bold Prime, I am honored by your communication," she said formally.

"I need to be quick, Moyo," I said. "We need to jump out of here. Kroerak have set a trap."

"We cannot jump, Bold Prime," she answered. "And we are winning. The Kroerak drop as fleas after a frost."

"I can jump, Moyo," I said. "Mars technicians modified *Hornblower*. The Kroerak have done something to the humans. They're not fighting. I need you to take over the fleet. They're going to herd you to the Kroerak planet, but you need to slow them down. We're going to try something."

"It is cowardly to flee from battle." Her whiskers twitched and I saw her tail flick over her shoulder.

"We aren't running," Marny said, stepping up in front of the screen. "Sister, listen to me. We can't tell you what we're doing. The Kroerak might learn it from you, but you must trust me as I once trusted you."

"Bold Second," Moyo bowed to the screen. "With my kits I would trust you. I will do as you request even if it is my last."

"Nick, set a path to Tabby's location," I said. "Moyo, Perasti Tertiary, I promote you to fleet commander. Fight with honor and may your ancestors sharpen your claws."

"Do not forget about us," Moyo said.

I saw both fear and pride in her eyes as the colors of the world suddenly smeared, as if we'd slid forward in an impressionist painting.

I stumbled back, grabbing for my chair as my head spun. Just as suddenly, the effects of the jump cleared. I looked over to Nick, who was making gagging sounds and then proceeded to vomit onto his console. I thought he'd gotten over that particular reaction but apparently, he'd lost the knack of transitioning to fold-space.

"Frak," he grumbled, opening a cabinet and looking for something to clean his mouth.

Marny stepped toward him. "I've got you."

"Mr. Stolzman, just keep us in the center of that wave," I said. "I guarantee you don't want to get off the edge of it."

"I wasn't sure," Stolzman answered. "My research into fold-space suggested we would create a bubble and should make every attempt to keep it balanced."

"Glad you did your research," I said. "Tabby, you still there?"

"We're all here," she said. "But I'm going to need to ask my friends to stay behind. Ada, Sendrei, Jonathan. You can't come along on this one."

"I suppose you think you can sail this old girl by yourself?" Ada asked. "Remember, you've only got one arm that works and you're having trouble breathing."

"We will accompany her," Jonathan said. "She is right. This is not a journey you would return from and you must stay behind."

"Is that why you had us put on those fold-space engines?" Ada asked. "Did you know this was what was going to happen all along?"

"It was Master Anino who first proposed the idea," Jonathan said. "I am not at liberty to further discuss it, beyond the fact that there is no expectation any will survive."

"You're willing to kill all fourteen hundred thirty-eight of you?" Sendrei asked. "That's not much of a trade."

"We will not perish," he said. "There is some possibility that we will remain trapped for a few years or even millennia, but we are a very resilient species. The fact is, you have little choice. Even now the tranquilizers within the dermal patches I've applied are taking effect. Don't struggle. I've disabled your medical assistant so that you will sleep for a short period. I have so enjoyed your friendships. Be well."

"Tabby?" I asked. "What's going on?"

"I guess, since you put Ada in charge, we're having a mutiny," she said.

FOR SOME STRANGE REASON, I slept well during the four days we traveled in fold-space. I'd always been uneasy in the past, but this time I was relaxed. I suspected it had more to do with the fact that I would soon see Tabby. It was fitting that we would end things together. I'd been willing to sacrifice myself for the destruction of Kroerak for quite some time. It seemed apropos that Tabby and I would do it together.

"If you really think you're leaving us behind like Tabby did Ada and Sendrei," Marny said. "I'm telling you, you've got another think coming."

I chuckled. "Nope. Up to me, you'd head back to Kito and wait for the Kroerak to come in a few years, but I know better than that. No, I'm going to join Tabby and Jonathan on *Intrepid*, and you're likely going to follow us back to the Kroerak homeworld."

"You're awfully sanguine."

"I've just been getting *really* good sleep lately," I said. "There's nothing I can do at this point but play things out."

"All hands, dropping from fold-space in five ... four ... three ..." the AI informed.

I was happy to see that Nick held down his lunch this time. It was progress. A blip on the holo projector showed the presence of another ship. I wasn't a bit surprised to see it was *Intrepid.*

"Marny, the ship is yours," I said, pulling her into a hug. "Give it another thought. You really shouldn't follow us back."

"Not a chance, Cap," she said. "I've played that game before. Not going to happen."

"Fair enough," I said, moving over to Nick. "Nick, you're the best friend a person could ever ask for. It's been a real pleasure growing up with you."

"What are your odds, Liam?" Nick asked.

"No idea," I said, not even a little surprised that he'd likely figured out what was going on. "But I think it's our best chance."

"You want to explain it to me?" Marny asked. "I hate all this secret crap."

"Just have some guesses," Nick said. "I think Liam's not saying anything because he's afraid of tipping off Kroerak."

"You think they can hear us out here?" Marny asked, bewildered.

"I think you'd be surprised at their reach," I said. "Here's to reunions." I held my hand up for a high-five as I walked past. At the last moment, I moved my hand out of the way and allowed my arm to travel around and slap Marny on the butt.

"Seriously, Cap?" she asked, chuckling.

"I can die a happy man, now." I exited the bridge.

Flicking a tear from my cheek, more from the deep feeling of gratitude I had for my friends than any sense of my own mortality, I took the lift down to Deck Four and exited through the airlock closest to *Intrepid.* Feeling eyes on my back, I waved over my shoulder before sliding through the pressure barrier into *Intrepid's* aft hold. I was surprised to find Jonathan there with a full set of tools spread out on the floor. He seemed to be working on two torpedoes.

"Uh. Hi, Jonathan," I said, awkwardly. "What happened to your legs?" The lower half of Jonathan's corporeal form was now a hyper-alloy combat chassis endoskeleton.

"Spring force problem. We should allow Tabitha to explain what is happening," he said.

"Is that it?" I asked, pointing at the tarp-covered torpedoes.

"It is," they answered.

"Okay." I nodded and jogged forward and out of the hold. *Intrepid* had a weird feeling, like the lights weren't up fully in the hallways, or the air was stale, or ... something. But then, it always felt weird to enter a ship that I'd flown before but no longer regularly used.

All thought ended when I saw Tabby floating in the hallway. I ran to her and stopped short. The glow of her eyes was beyond intense as she smiled and reached for me. "You came ..."

"And you're doing that *Lady of the Lake* thing," I said. We'd enjoyed more than one rendition of *Excalibur* together. They all had a creepy, but helpful, mystical woman who floated and bad things tended to happen around her.

"Hug me," she said. "I thought I'd never see you again."

I embraced her and closed my eyes, trying desperately to ignore the feeling of hardened stone beneath the suit. "Does it hurt?" I asked.

"A little," she said. "Iskstar have children, Liam. Did you know that?"

"Like, in you?" I asked.

"Yes," she said. "For the first time in a very long time, they are working on a new child."

"That sounds very polyamorous," I said.

She chuckled, the sound bringing happiness to my heart. "It's different for them. But they have hope, Liam."

"You're okay with this?" I asked. "With us doing this?"

"Would you let me do it on my own?" she asked.

"No."

"I almost skipped stopping here," she said. "Jonathan talked me out of it."

"What do you mean?"

"I'm not really sure I need you for this next part," she said. "Jonathan convinced me you'd come for me, regardless. And if I fail, you'll be dead."

"He's right," I said. "I just had this conversation with Marny and Nick. Speaking of, we need to get going. They're going to try to beat us back."

"They have way too much mass," she said. "We're already moving."

"We are? I didn't feel the transition to fold-space," I said.

"Iskstar use fold-space to communicate," she said. "They like our rings."

"Wildly unrelated ideas," I said.

"Not so. Iskstar take years to communicate incredibly complex emotions and ideas," she said. "Their communications are shared by all, as are their deaths. Our rings allow us to communicate individually. Even though there isn't much information, there's love. They like that."

I sighed. Somewhere along the way, my warrior princess had turned into Yoda. We had a few days and then we were going to simply crash land on the Kroerak homeworld, riding on the back of an Iskstar crystal, powered by a missile engine.

Tabby explained what she had learned about Iskstar. They were a peaceful and trusting species that desired connection with others. One of the first encounters they had was to join with a bug species on their home planet. Initially, like with the Piscivoru, it was a harmless interaction. But over long stretches of time, the bugs evolved into what would become the Kroerak. These bugs, who still carried a part of the Iskstar within, had developed an overwhelming need to consume and they spread like locusts on the galactic winds.

"You know Ada's going to be pissed," Tabby said.

"I slapped Marny's butt," I said. "You know ... when I walked out."

"What'd that feel like?" Tabby asked, eyes boring into me. "I've always wanted to do it, but figured she'd pound me into the dirt."

"Had a glove on," I admitted. "It was kind of a *thought that counts* type of thing."

"Ada kissed me," Tabby confessed.

We were just about to enter local space next to the Kroerak homeworld, yet this was what we chose to talk about in our last moments.

"What's that about?" I asked. "If I'd known that, maybe I would have looked for an upgrade from Marny."

"Careful, sailor," Tabby warned, smiling. "I still have one good arm left. And it was everything and nothing. She was just telling me to return to her and somehow, I did. I can still feel it on my cheek."

"Seriously?"

"Yeah."

"We have arrived," Jonathan said. "Sensors have detected multiple small ships on intercept."

Jonathan had fashioned two chairs between the missiles. The Kroerak homeworld had no atmosphere and we'd impact the surface within a few minutes of taking off, accelerating to our deaths.

"You have returned," a voice in my head said. *"We will give you entire worlds if you turn away now."*

"I think they know we're here," I said. "Someone's talking to me."

"I can hear her too," Tabby said. "You're talking to an ancient one."

"Are you holding my friends in their ships?" I asked.

"I could kill them with a thought," she said, *"but I have not done so. Simply speak your desire. I will deliver it to you."*

My view changed and I suddenly saw Admiral Alderson standing on the bridge of the dreadnaught, *Bukawana.* He simply stood there, not like a statue, but relaxed, as if he were getting ready to bark out his next command. As I watched, blood poured from his nose and ears but still, he said nothing. My view shifted and ran to the rest of the bridge crew, still at their posts. They too had blood running from their eyes, noses, and ears.

"Treaty with me. You will live forever and the infants called humanity will be raised up as gods among the peoples of the universe. Fight me and watch as I destroy those you care for."

Again, my view changed and we were aboard another ship, looking at an admiral I recognized but whose name I couldn't bring to mind.

"Patch," Tabby said. Her voice sounded like it was a thousand kilometers away.

"What?" I asked, just as I felt a small prick on my neck.

"Only room for one, Love," Tabby said, sliding into the forward chair.

"May the genocide of the glorious Kroerak haunt you forever," intoned the disembodied voice of the Kroerak ancient. *"Let the time of humans begin. Such is the nature of the universe."*

"Judgment comes to us all," I murmured as I slid down the wall to the deck and thumbed my ring a final time.

It was through blurry eyes that I watched the missile streak toward the planet's surface. I considered feeling betrayed, but I would have done the same to Tabby under the circumstances. She'd given me a final gift of the last three days and all I felt now was gratitude.

It was almost anti-climactic when the missile disappeared and crashed into the planet. Its surface crystalized into a brilliant blue mass, spidering out from the point of impact, speeding up geometrically as Iskstar took more and more area, faster and faster, finally enveloping the entire planet.

Tears streamed down my face as I felt the loss of my best friend. For a long while, I found I either could not or had no desire to move.

Chapter 23

BREAKING FREE

"Cap, you've got to get up," Marny said. She'd wrapped her fingers around my upper arm and was attempting to pull me from the deck where I lay.

My mind was foggy and I couldn't quite figure out how she'd come to be on *Intrepid.* From my best recollection, *Hornblower* should have been three days behind us. Looking around Marny, I saw the planet that had once been the homeworld of the Kroerak, sparkling the brilliant blue of Iskstar.

"You sure made it here fast," I said, coughing, as my throat was dry. An overwhelming desire for something to drink struck me about the same time a whiff of body odor escaped my grav-suit. That was odd. My suit-liner should have kept me fresh for several days.

"Ten days, Cap," Marny said.

"Ten days, what?" I asked.

"It's been ten days since I last saw you. If I understand correctly, you've been lying on this deck that whole time, with Jonathan doing what they can to keep you alive. The rest of us have been rounding up and putting down the Kroerak fleet ever since they lost contact with their home planet," she said. "Other than that, we've been running rescue missions. Jonathan said you all were managing, although I'm not sure I completely buy his analysis. This was the first chance we had to get back to you."

I accepted her help in getting up and checked my HUD for status. An orange alert warned of stress to my suit's biological systems. I stumbled as I tried to move past Marny and she caught me before I fell.

"I've got it," I said, engaging my grav-suit to provide buoyancy. "What's our status?"

"Confederation Fleet is assembling," Marny said. "They'll be leaving system within twelve hours. Two-thirds of the Mars Protectorate fleet have already left. You should know, though. Everyone on *Bukunawa* was dead, including Alderson. We found a second ship like this."

"The Kroerak?" I asked, although I thought I knew the answer, even though it was more of a feeling than direct knowledge.

"Sir, if I might," Jonathan said, floating into view in his egg-shaped vessel.

"Please."

"We believe you were watching as Tabitha Masters directed the mother crystal found on Mendari to the planet surface below. You no doubt saw the planet's transformation," he said. "It was shortly after this moment that you became less responsive."

"Less responsive?"

"Correct," he said. "You entered some sort of fugue state, neither conscious nor unconscious. It was during this time that the Iskstar left your body and joined with the mother crystal on the planet below."

"Wait, my eyes. Are they glowing?" I asked.

"Negative, Cap," Marny said, handing me a water pouch which I greedily consumed. "Maybe we can walk and talk. I can smell your suit from here."

"Yeah, good idea," I said. The water only served to remind me just how hungry I was, although nothing overrode the desire to free myself from my suit.

"We have learned that Iskstar communicate using fold-space,"

Jonathan said. "This communication is more than just messages, however. They appear to be capable of moving the conscious state as well."

"Not sure why that matters," I said.

"Liam!" Ada yelped, as Marny and I made it around the corner. She was coming from the direction of the forward airlock and I suspected she'd just arrived onboard.

"The mother crystal delivered to the planet's surface would have been insufficient for the transformation we've observed," Jonathan said. "We believe we are witnessing a mass assembly of Iskstar, possibly the entire species, as it comes from the very edges of the great expansion of space."

Ada caught and pulled me into a hug, her wrinkled nose the only indicator of my condition. Jonathan's mention of the crystal being delivered reminded me of something that hadn't penetrated to this point. Tabby had guided the crystal to the planet and known full well she would die in the process. The weight of that knowledge struck me like the weight of a mountain and I sagged against Ada.

"Tabby." I whispered, my throat closing.

"We found her body, Liam," Ada said. "She's on the planet."

"I need to see her," I said.

"Of course," Ada answered. "But you'll shower first."

"The Kroerak," I said. "What about the fleet?"

"Shower," Marny said, nodding sternly at the entrance to my quarters. "We'll fill you in while you're cleaning up." Any other time and I'd have had a smart response, but I had nothing.

"As we've discussed, Kroerak warships require the command of a noble," Jonathan said, as I worked to remove my grav-suit.

The smell wasn't as bad as I'd feared, but I was happy to get the first layer off. I set the suit onto the feed for the suit-freshener and then started removing my suit-liner.

"What we did not realize is that Kroerak nobles receive much of their executive function from higher-ranked Kroerak."

"That doesn't explain what we've seen: the total collapse of the Kroerak fleet," Marny said. "It's like they forgot how to sail their ships.

According to Mshindi Prime, more of the Kroerak fleet was destroyed by friendly fire and collisions than by Confederation fire. When the opposing fleets actually came in contact with each other, it was a slaughter."

"Mshindi Prime?" I asked. "I thought *Thunder Awakes* was destroyed."

"Mshindi's bridge was armored," Marny said. "She and her bridge crew survived."

"That's good. Now turn away," I said, peeling off the remainder of my suit-liner. The hot water from the shower felt good, but the sadness I felt at losing Tabby made me want to tell everyone to leave. I desperately wanted to crawl under my covers and hide.

"The Kroerak nobles appear to have been incapable of functioning without their superiors," Jonathan said. "We believe the executive function provided by Kroerak hierarchy was considerably stronger than is found in human chains of command. It does not appear this was an optional ..."

Jonathan continued talking but I allowed the water falling on my head to drown him out. The price, as usual, was higher than I wanted to pay. The smell of Tabby's soap caught me by surprise and I almost felt her presence. I sobbed as a wave of grief struck me wondering at what our future might have been had we simply ignored Belirand corporation so long ago. If we'd just let well enough alone ... If *I'd* left well enough alone. We could have had a nice life running freight between colonies.

I leaned back against the shower wall and slid to the floor, wrapping my arms around my knees. I wasn't really sure how I was going to move forward.

"Cap, you doing okay in there?" Marny called.

I didn't have an answer for her even though I knew she might come in after me. The fact was, I didn't care. In the end, that's exactly what happened. It was like I was watching from outside my body as Marny's arm reached in and turned off the water. With a large warm towel, she and Ada helped me from the shower.

"You need to eat something," Ada said, concern lacing her voice

I sat on the side of the bed, staring at the floor. "Go away." I'd lost all interest in the talk of Kroerak and Iskstar. I could only feel the loss of Tabby. I wanted to be on my own, not required to think about anything.

"You need to eat something, Cap," Marny said. "You're emaciated."

"Not interested." I slipped under the covers, leaving my towel behind.

"Let's give him some time," Ada said.

The room grew quiet as Ada, Marny, and Jonathan exited. I wasn't sure what to think about the fact that I'd lain on *Intrepid's* deck for ten days, semi-conscious. If I really pushed, I could remember some of what had happened, but the span was mostly a confused jumble. I knew for a fact that the Kroerak were dead – maybe not every warrior on every planet, but without a hierarchy, the generations would cease to breed. I thought back to a book I'd read about destruction of an invasive species and how the character felt so much angst about his role. The only thing I felt was the loss of my best friend. Kroerak were evil and deserved to be destroyed. If anything, I was glad for our participation. It meant Tabby's death was for a greater purpose.

My eyes started to close as I drifted toward sleep. In the weird dimension of existence between wakefulness and sleep, I could almost feel her, and I hugged a pillow and smiled. As I drifted even further, I thumbed my ring, knowing it was now alone in the universe.

Which is why I was startled when I felt two strong bumps in response.

I sat up in bed and flung the covers back, staring at the ring. It was impossible. Tabby was dead. She'd crash-landed on a planet strapped between two missile engines. My mind spun with possibility and I jumped from the bed, stumbling again but pushing through my weakness. It took significant effort to pull on a suit-liner, but I did it. When I bumped the ring again, I got no response. It didn't matter. Ada said they'd found Tabby and I was positive the crystal had throbbed. I picked up my earwig, pushed it into my ear and impatiently waited for it to adhere to my skin.

"Ada, how can we get to the planet's surface?" I asked. "I need to see Tabby right now."

"Liam, you need to rest," she answered. "You're weak. We'll go down in a day or two."

"No," I spat. "Now. I'm coming to the bridge. Does *Intrepid* have enough fuel?"

"Mars Protectorate left a few shuttles behind. We can take one of those," Ada said.

"Cap, I'm serious. Your bios are low and you need to eat," Marny said. "I'm not letting you off this ship without. You read me?"

"Bring as many meal bars as you want," I said. "We're going to the planet's surface if I have to fly there in my grav-suit."

"Forward air-lock," Marny said. "And get that grav-suit on first."

I rolled my eyes and pulled the grav-suit from where Ada had folded it next to the suit-freshener. I tried my ring again and, yet again, received no response. The lack of any communicating bump caused me a pang of concern. Maybe I'd been asleep and dreamed her response? No. I didn't really believe that was the case. I pushed through the hatch and was met by Marny, hustling past me on her way to the galley. She was no doubt fetching food to torture me with.

"She's alive, Marny," I said.

"Cap," she warned. "I've seen the crash site. She's not."

"She is," I said. "I bumped my ring. She answered."

"Statistically unlikely," Jonathan said.

"And possible," I returned.

"There is much we do not understand of Iskstar," Jonathan said.

"See?" I called to Marny's retreating back.

"I hope you're right, Cap."

I half ran, half glided forward to the airlock where a Mars Protectorate shuttle was already docked. When I entered, I found that Ada was already on board and had taken the control seat. I didn't know where we were going so I was just thankful to have her take the stick.

"She answered," I said, holding up my ring hand to Ada.

The look I received was sympathetic. She didn't believe me. I didn't care.

A few minutes later, Marny arrived. "Here," she said, handing me another water pouch and a meal bar.

As it turned out, I was starving and quickly polished off the bar. I looked hungrily back to Marny who shook her head. "Not yet, Cap. Let that sit. You don't want to throw it up."

In the meantime, Ada had detached from *Intrepid* and I got a new view of the skies over the Kroerak homeworld. Hundreds, if not thousands, of derelict ships floated unpowered. Each that I could see had sustained substantial damage.

"Did the battle get this close?" I asked.

"Not really," Marny said. "A lot of Kroerak ships broke off from combat and flew back to the planet. It was like they were looking for help. Of course, that help never came and the Mars Protectorate/Earth fleet took them out.

There was virtually no atmosphere around the planet, which caused me to wonder if the Kroerak had somehow consumed every part of their own home. There were, however, structures across the entire surface. Unlike the hills and towers built from dirt that we'd seen on planet Cradle, these were much more complex and appeared to have required considerably more planning and skill.

Our approach was eerie. There was absolutely nothing moving, nor was there a single ship visible in the sky.

"Is the blue receding?" I asked.

Now that we were closer to the planet, it appeared that the Iskstar crystallization was dimming in some places and in others had disappeared entirely.

"Your observation is correct, Captain," Jonathan answered. "We believe the Iskstar are returning to their points of origin."

"How'd you think they got here?" I asked. "Fold-space? If that's the case, how'd they do it so quickly?"

"Speed through fold-space is directly proportional to mass," Jonathan said. "Theoretically, a mass of zero might allow for infinitely-fast travel."

"If that's the case, then how'd the Iskstar get trapped on Mendari?" Ada asked.

"A mystery we have no answer for," Jonathan answered. "It seems reasonable that the Iskstar should have been able to abandon Mendari before the bomb was ignited. Or certainly, any time after that. Communicating with Iskstar is very difficult. We may never know the answer to this mystery."

"There was radiation on Mendari we couldn't identify," Ada said. "Maybe that was the reason."

"Perhaps," Jonathan said. "It is difficult to know."

I felt the ship settle onto a brilliant dark blue field of crystal. Light from the system's star was so brilliant that my suit had to dim my face-shield so I could see.

"Careful, Cap," Marny said. "We're not sure it's safe to walk on the Iskstar. They might reinfect you."

I opened the hatch and stepped out. "I'll be fine. Give me a few minutes."

The sight of the crash took my breath away. The cylindrical mother crystal was fully intact and resting in the crystal field. Missing were the missile parts Jonathan had fabricated. Propped up next to the mother crystal was the perfect outline of Tabby from the waist up, as if she'd sunk into the very surface of the planet, her right arm raised in triumph.

"Frak, Tabbs," I said to myself. "What'd you get yourself into?"

I walked around to look at her from the front. I wasn't sure what I'd expected, but the perfect, crystalized image of her wasn't it.

"That's messed up," Ada said. I looked around, not expecting her, given Marny's warning. She was floating in her grav-suit, suspended a meter above the surface.

I turned back and approached Tabby. It was clear to me that my ring response had been a fantasy, but it was good that I had come to see her. She'd wanted to save the Iskstar and she'd done it. Even with the minimal atmosphere on the planet, I knew I had to touch her, even if I inadvertently reinvited the Iskstar into my body.

I pulled off my glove and grasped her outstretched hand.

"Cap, careful," Marny said. "I'm not sure she's all that stable."

The familiar sense of Iskstar permeated my body and I was

surrounded by a deep sense of gratitude emanating from the planet. The tinkling sound of a tiny shard of crystal falling to the surface interrupted the moment I shared with the Iskstar.

"I love you, Tabbs," I said, grasping her hand more firmly and staring at her face. She had no expression, but then the crystal obscured most of her features.

A weak thump on my ring nearly caused me to jump out of my grav-suit.

"Marny, Ada, she's in there!" I yelled into comms excitedly. "She just thumped my ring again."

"Cap?" Marny asked.

Suddenly, I knew what had to be done and I looked around for something hard. Of course, there was nothing but crystal terrain. No rocks. Nothing. My hand shot to my side and I pulled the small nano-blade from beneath my waistband. The handle conformed to my hand but I didn't extend the blade.

"What are you doing, Liam?" Ada asked.

I smashed the butt of the weapon into Tabby's chest, the impact causing a shower of small fragments.

"Don't, Cap! That's Tabby. You don't want to desecrate her grave," Marny said, thinking I was acting in grief.

I pulled my arm back for another swing and she caught it, stopping me.

"I'm telling you, Marny, she's alive. I just felt her. I need something to break off this outer skin. Iskstar's been protecting her."

"That's ridiculous, Cap," Marny said. "There's no way."

"Look, since you met me, how many impossible things have we seen?" I asked.

"She's moving." Ada's shocked voice interrupted me, even as more crystal fell away. "He's right."

Marny wasted no time in pulling her bo-staff out and extending it to a meter's length. Together we beat on the crystal surface that gave way, exposing Tabby still in her grav-suit.

"Suit's not operating," Ada said, swooping in. "We need to get her out of it."

"No atmo pressure." I wrapped my arms around Tabby and tried to pull her free.

"Not on my watch," Marny said, pushing me out of the way to swing at the crystal cocoon encasing Tabby's lower body.

"Ada, get the shuttle open. Marny open her grav-suit. We'll pull her out. She can survive the low atmospheric pressure for a few moments. The suit won't hold her."

Neither woman hesitated. Marny opened Tabby's suit, dropping her bo-staff to the ground. Her first attempt to pull Tabby free was unsuccessful. "She's stuck."

A ridge of crystal following the gentle arc of Tabby's bottom seemed to be holding her down. I could see mottling on her skin as the lack of atmospheric pressure started to damage her body. We had precious few moments. With all my strength, I swung Marny's staff across Tabby's bottom. The crystal shattered, flying everywhere. With a single heroic effort, Marny squatted, wrapped her thick arms around Tabby and pulled with all her might. I swung a second time and she popped out.

"Go!" I exclaimed unnecessarily, as Marny sailed more expertly than I might have expected to the shuttle.

"Med kit," I exclaimed, again unnecessarily, as Ada placed dermal medical sensors onto Tabby's skin.

The shuttle lifted and sailed upwards. The medical AI would take about thirty seconds to do its analysis. I closed my eyes and tried to control my breathing.

Ada grabbed my arm and shook me. "Liam. She's alive,"

My eyes flew open and I looked for the AI's analysis, but found nothing. When I looked over to Ada, I saw that she was staring at Tabby, who was looking at me, her eyes unfocused.

"You came for me," she croaked.

"Of course we did," I said and bent to hug her.

"Liam, we have a problem," Ada snapped. "Tabby has significant tissue and organ damage. We need to get her to the medical bay and into the tank immediately."

"Go!" Marny ordered, scooping Tabby from the deck and charging forward through the hatch.

I did my best to keep up, but what little energy hope and one meal bar had given me was gone. I was losing my balance and struggling to control where I was going.

"Captain," Jonathan cut in, as I bounced against the starboard bulkhead, barely making it down the ramp to the lower deck where the medical bay was.

"A little busy just now, Jonathan," I said.

"Time is of the essence," Jonathan answered. "Our analysis suggests the medical suspension device will not be successful in treating the damage caused by Iskstar crystallization."

"Jupiter piss," I said.

"Understandable emotion, but there is an alternative solution," he said as I careened into the medical bay.

"We're losing her." Ada helped Marny strip Tabby's body of the suit-liner. To say they were not gentle with the material would have been an understatement as they used specialized instruments to virtually shred the material. I gasped at the sight of Tabby's marred body. The skin on her legs and left arm was blackened and shriveled, her abdomen covered with hematomas and deep bruising.

I held my breath as Marny and Ada slipped her battered, naked body from the table where they'd been working on her into the tank that was already half-filled with suspension fluid.

"Mask," Marny said, brusquely pulling the oxygen line around the back of Tabby's head and over her nose and mouth.

With the work done, we all wordlessly watched the monitors as nanites were dispatched to stop the decline.

Ada shook her head. "She's not stable. We need to act."

"The medical program will prioritize brain function over all else," Jonathan said. "She is well within the capacity of Anino's medical facility on Irène."

"Done," I said. "Ada, I need you to get us to Irène as fast as possible."

"Liam, that's thirty days," Ada said, turning to the tank and whispering, "Hold on Tabby, we've got you."

"We're transferring crew now," Marny said. "I'll take command of *Hornblower* and get us back to Kito. Mshindi can take care of things here. I just received word of a hostile Strix-flagged fleet entering Mhina space."

"How will you get back in time?" I asked.

Marny smiled. "Maybe you forgot, but we're back in the fold-space business. I can't wait to see their reaction when *Hornblower* pops into the middle of their crap. Nick says if we get cracking, we'll arrive a full day before they do."

"Go get 'em, Marny," I said.

"Damn skippy."

EPILOGUE

I stared into the glass of Tabby's tank as *Intrepid* transitioned to fold-space. With Iskstar gone from my system, the old feelings of nausea had returned. It's hard to rationalize enjoying feeling nauseous, but I did. I guess I'm a control freak and I have no desire to share my body with any other beings, beneficial or otherwise.

The body on the other side of the glass bore few similarities to Tabby. The hair from her head had been removed and what I could still see of her face was severely damaged. For hours, I looked between her and the monitors, hoping for improvement. For the first hour or so, there was improvement as circulation was restored to those parts of her body that weren't necrotic. The medical AI would remove ruined flesh and at a minimum, patch it over. The nanites would even create vascular pathways around the stumps so new flesh would be nourished. It was a time-intensive and painstaking process that would take the entire trip to Irène.

"Liam, it's time to take care of you," Ada said gently from behind me. I hadn't heard her come in.

"I'm fine, Ada," I argued, but didn't resist as she pulled me away from the tank.

THE REMAINDER of the trip was uneventful, aside from Tabby's steady decline. Jonathan assured me that they were monitoring her brain function and that little else mattered. I wanted to believe him, but part of me simply didn't trust anyone with Tabby's wellbeing.

"Transitioning from fold-space in ten seconds." Ada's announcement came over *Intrepid's* public address. "Please brace for possible emergency maneuvers as we're transitioning close to Irène."

I placed my hand on the tank. I'd fully recovered from my own minor ordeal and had spent most of my waking moments in the medical bay next to Tabby.

A moment after transition a warning klaxon sounded. It was a proximity alert and I hustled to grab the safety harness I'd neglected to fasten. Fortunately, the klaxon quieted a moment later.

"Liam, there's a medical team headed in your direction," Ada warned over comms. "They're friendlies."

Just as she finished speaking, two bulky men carrying blaster rifles burst into the medical bay.

"Sir, I need you to step away from the tank and keep your hands where I can see them," the shorter of the two said. With close-cropped hair and clear, focused eyes, it wasn't difficult to identify the man as active military even though he wore what I suspected was a grav-suit without military decoration. If I'd wanted to resist, I had no doubt I'd fail, so I stood up and backed away.

"What's the call here, Sergeant," I said, making a reasonable guess.

"Securing the space for high-value asset," he responded crisply and without hesitation. "Just keep it cool and we'll have no problems."

A moment later, a striking middle-aged, narrow-framed, ebony-skinned woman walked confidently in behind them. She wore a tight smile and immediately made eye contact with me, as if she'd expected to find me here. "Oh, for the love of science, Thor. That's Liam Hoffen. Put your gun down already."

My eyes flicked over to the muscular man and I raised my eyebrows. "Thor?" I asked, genuinely impressed.

He shook his head ever so slightly, indicating that wasn't his name.

"Tabitha Masters," the woman said, having moved into the room and over to where Tabby lay unresponsive in the tank. "I'd hoped we'd get to meet one day."

"You know of her?" I asked, pushing past Thor.

"I can't say too much, Mr. Hoffen. My name is Dorian Anino. I believe you know my brilliant and often annoying son," she said, engaging the drain on the tank. "But yes, I know everything there is to know about your Tabitha Masters, at least from a purely biological perspective. Tell me, is she more aggressive since her surgery at the Mars Veterans' hospital? Outbursts? Rages? Does she hurt you during sex?"

The last question sparked my defensive nature. "I'm not sure how that's your business." Although, it was true. Sometimes Tabby was a little exuberant and I needed patching up afterwards. It wasn't an always thing and I knew she didn't mean to hurt me.

"I'll take that as a yes," she said.

More people gathered in the hallway and two of them entered the rapidly-shrinking medical bay, only these were wearing white lab coats.

"Mars Protectorate doctors are excellent, but they lack finesse. Tabitha Masters is a very rare specimen indeed, but they treated her without the care she needed. Her injury here is a mercy. You might want to look away for this next part. I find it difficult to forget the images of those whom I love in this state. Please, Liam, don't be the hero for two minutes. You'll thank me."

Grudgingly, I turned away as I heard the sound of medical suspension fluid dripping onto the floor and assumed Tabby was being moved. When I turned back, I saw only Anino's back as she disappeared through the door. I started to follow, but was stopped by a heavy hand on my shoulder.

"I go first," Thor said. "You can follow. The Doctor's personal well-being is my only concern. You copy?" I held up and allowed him to pass. His partner allowed me to go next and we proceeded to the airlock behind a procession of four lab-coats and the two bodyguards.

The shuttle we entered was spacious and well-suited to medical purposes. Even as the ship moved, Anino and the other lab-coats worked over Tabby's body, with a visual screen held in place. I appreciated the fact that they'd allowed me to come along. Even without visuals, the sounds of bone crunching and sawing was beyond disturbing. When I cast a look up to Thor, he seemed nonplussed, as if all of this was just another day at the office.

"Hang in there, Mr. Hoffen," Dorian Anino called from over the partition. "We're just about done with the hard stuff."

I stood stock still, staring at the partition while listening to the horrific sounds.

"Drink this," Thor's buddy said, handing me a pouch. "You look like you could use some electrolytes."

I accepted and took a nervous swig. In the background I heard the sounds of a vacuum and the rustling of material being moved. When the curtain was dropped, I was shocked to see Tabby lying on a table with a simple white sheet covering her. Her body was impossibly small, and I realized both of her arms had to be missing in addition to her legs.

"You've ..." I spluttered, finding no words.

An assistant helped Anino remove blood-spattered medical scrubs, trailing her as she approached Liam. "This step in her recovery is rather a grisly one, but it is necessary."

"You couldn't save any of her?" I asked.

"Please sit with me," Dorian said, gesturing to a bench along the inside wall of the shuttle. As we sat, I glimpsed out the window. We were already falling into the atmosphere of what I assumed was Irène, but I didn't feel even the slightest movement within the shuttle.

"It just seems too much," I said.

"Indeed it is," she answered. "I'm about to tell you something that few in the universe know. I figure your current zip code and history with big secrets makes you a minimal risk."

"Zip code?" I asked.

"Not important," she said. "Tabitha Masters is one of the rarest of the rare. Or I should say her body is that. She has what's known as the hero gene. I'm sure you've noticed that the synthetic muscles and ligaments have responded well beyond the expectations you were originally given by Mars Protectorate."

"That's an understatement," I said.

"Unfortunately, those enhancements were improperly calibrated by the well-meaning, but under-trained staff at Mars Veterans Hospital. They should have recognized the markers and alerted my team for Tabitha's original surgery. In life, we rarely get a chance to undo our mistakes. In Tabitha's case, we're getting a fantastic second chance."

"What do you mean rare?" I asked.

"She's what we call a one hundred percenter," Dorian said. "I know of but four people in my long history who have this so-called hero gene at this level of match. Our surgery will restore all of her function and she will once again gain strength, speed and endurance like she did before. Only this time with fewer of the negative effects."

"She wasn't that bad," I said.

"She was a ticking time bomb. But that problem is behind us now and there is no need to dwell on it," Dorian said. "Here's what will happen next. In a few minutes we will land at my medical compound outside the city of Joliot. My medical team will bring Tabitha to the already prepared surgical center where she will undergo her final transformation. The entire surgery will take twenty hours, after which she will be in a rehabilitative medical tank for an additional two weeks. After that, she'll be awakened and we'll run a few tests. All in, you'll be ready for travel two weeks after that."

"I don't know how to repay you," I said.

This brought a kind smile to Dorian's face. "My dear boy, twice you and yours have saved humanity. Consider this a gesture of gratitude and the beginning of a beautiful friendship."

I looked at her quizzically. "You don't want anything? I don't understand. Shoot me straight."

This caused her to chuckle. "A fair statement. You seem to have grasped what so few ever understand. Gifts are rarely free. Allow me to buy or lease a building within your new city, York. Allow us to monitor Tabitha's progress."

"The building is easy. I think you'll need to talk to Tabby about the other," I said.

A building darkened the windows as we landed, throwing the occupants of the shuttle into a burst of activity. "A reasonable request. It was delightful meeting you, Mr. Hoffen."

And just like that, she and the rest of the medical staff were out the door and running across a paved walk to a well-guarded entrance on the building. I started to get up, intending to run after them, when a familiar hand landed on my shoulder.

"We'll take the civilian entrance," Thor said.

"BE VERY quiet as I bring her awake," Dorian said. According to her, the surgery and rehabilitation had gone better than expected.

With considerable anticipation, Ada and I waited as Tabby woke.

"Her brain will require an adjustment period for the new levels of auditory and visual information."

I saw a finger on Tabby's hand twitch and scooped it up into my own. "Tabbs?" I whispered.

"Where am I?" Tabby asked. "Smells like a hospital. Am I dreaming? Are we at Coolidge VA?"

"Tabitha, you're in a private medical facility on Irène," Dorian said. "You've received medical treatment for the injury you received during your mission to save the Iskstar. Do you remember that mission?"

"Of course I remember."

"How about delivering the mother crystal to the planet?" Anino asked. I was surprised at the level of information the woman had about the mission, although with her last name I shouldn't have been.

"No. I just remember finding it on the Mendari planet," she said.

"Good. You may remember more over time."

"Kroerak?" Tabby asked.

"Gone," I said.

"Marny? Nick? Are they okay?" she asked.

"They're fine," I said.

"What about me?" Ada asked.

Tabby smiled and opened her eyes. "I smell your shampoo and hear your heart beating, dearest friend."

"How do you feel?" I asked.

"Amazing." She grasped my hand more firmly and pulled me from my chair.

"Careful!" I said, alarmed that I might hurt her as I fell into her and she wrapped her arms around me.

"Thank you," she said, burying her face into my neck. "I knew you'd find a way." I felt her let go and suddenly Ada was pulled into the mix. The weight distribution was wrong for the bed and we all tumbled to the floor.

"Perhaps we could talk another time," Dorian said. If I hadn't heard the smile in her voice as she left the small room, I might have thought she was offended.

"That didn't hurt?" I asked Tabby as the three of us lay in a knot on the floor.

"Define that," Tabby said. "Falling from the bed is about the least painful thing I've done recently. Really, I feel amazing."

With an evil glint in my eye, I allowed my hands to wander onto her backside. "You sure do," I said, waggling my eyebrows.

"Seriously?" Ada asked. "We're not going there right now. Dogpile etiquette demands no handsy."

Tabby freed her hands and pulled Ada over to her, kissing the side of her face. "If I wasn't spoken for, I'd make a run at you, Ada Chen."

The surprised look on Ada's face was perfect. "What?"

"Same here," I admitted, truthfully.

"Whoa there, big fella," Tabby said, playfully slugging my shoulder. For the first time I could remember, I felt no pain when she did it. She had her control back. "I was mostly joking."

I did my best to feign innocence. "Right. Me too."

"You guys really keep a girl guessing," Ada said. "But on a more serious note, since we all seem to be doing okay, we might have trouble brewing back home."

I scooted off Tabby so I could sit up straight and then pulled her close so I could hold her. She rested her head against me, the short stubble of her hair feeling funny against my skin.

"What kind of trouble? Strix?" I wouldn't be surprised if that were the case. The Strix would absolutely take advantage of our weakened position.

"Mendari," Ada said. "One of our scout ships caught them in a sensor scan."

"Well, frak, what's that about?" I asked.

But of course, that's another story entirely.

GLOSSARY OF NAMES

Liam Hoffen – our hero. With straight black hair and blue eyes, Liam is a lanky one hundred seventy-five centimeters tall, which is a typical tall, thin spacer build. His parents are Silver and Pete Hoffen, who get their own short story in *Big Pete*. Raised as an asteroid miner, Liam's destiny was most definitely in the stars, if not on the other end of a mining pick. Our stories are most often told from Liam's perspective and he, therefore, needs the least introduction.

Nick James – the quick-talking, always-thinking best friend who is usually five moves ahead of everyone and the long-term planner of the team. At 157 cm, Nick is the shortest human member of the crew. He, Tabby, and Liam have been friends since they met in daycare on Colony-40 in Sol's main asteroid belt. The only time Nick has trouble forming complete sentences is around Marny Bertrand, who by his definition is the perfect woman. Nick's only remaining family is a brother, Jack, who now lives on Lèger Nuage. The boys lost their mother during a Red Houzi pirate attack that destroyed their home in the now infamous Battle for Colony-40.

Tabitha Masters – fierce warrior and loyal fiancé of our hero, Liam. Tabby lost most of her limbs when the battle cruiser on which she was training was attacked by the dreadnaught *Bakunawa*. Her body subsequently repaired, she lives for the high adrenaline moments of life and engages life's battles at one hundred percent. Tabby is a lithe, 168 cm tall bundle of impatience.

Marny Bertrand – former Marine from Earth who served in the Great Amazonian War and now serves as guardian of the crew. Liam and Nick recruited Marny from her civilian post on the Ceres orbital station in *Rookie Privateer*. Marny is 180 cm tall, heavily muscled and the self-appointed fitness coordinator — slash torturer — on the ship. Her strategic vigilance has safeguarded the crew through some rather unconventional escapades. She's also extraordinarily fond of Nick.

Ada Chen – ever-optimistic adventurer and expert pilot. Ada was first introduced in *Parley* when Liam and crew rescued her from a lifeboat. Ada's mother, Adela, had ejected the pod from their tug, *Baux-201*, before it was destroyed in a pirate attack. Ada is a 163 cm tall, ebony-skinned beauty and a certified bachelorette. Ada's first love is her crew and her second is sailing into the deep dark.

Jonathan – a collective of 1,438 sentient beings residing in a humanoid body. Communicating as Jonathan, they were initially introduced in *A Matter of Honor* when the crew bumped into Thomas Phillipe Anino. Jonathan is intensely curious about the human condition, specifically how humanity has the capacity to combine skill, chance, and morality to achieve a greater result.

Sendrei Buhari – a full two meters tall, dark skinned and heavily muscled. Sendrei started his military career as a naval officer only to be captured by the Kroerak while on a remote mission. Instead of killing him outright, the Kroerak used him as breeding stock, a decision he's dedicated his life to making them regret.

Felio Species – an alien race of humanoids best identified by its clear mix of human and feline characteristics. Females are dominant in this society. Their central political structure is called the Abasi, a governing group consisting of the most powerful factions, called houses. An imposing, middle-aged female, Adahy Neema, leads

House Mshindi. Her title and name, as is the tradition within houses, is Mshindi First for as long as she holds the position.

Strix Species – A vile alien species that worked their way into power within the Confederation of Planets. Spindly legs, sharp beaks, feathery skin and foul mouthed, most representatives of this species have few friends and seem to be determined to keep it that way.

Aeratroas Region – located in the Dwingeloo galaxy and home to 412 inhabited systems occupying a roughly tubular shape only three hundred parsecs long with a diameter of a hundred parsecs. The region is loosely governed by agreements that make up The Confederation of Planets.

Planet Zuri – located in the Santaloo star system and under loose Abasi control. One hundred fifty standard years ago, Zuri was invaded by Kroerak bugs. It was the start of a bloody, twenty-year war that left the planet in ruins and its population scattered. Most Felio who survived the war abandoned the planet, as it had been seeded with Kroerak spore that continue to periodically hatch and cause havoc.

York Settlement – located on planet Zuri. York is the only known human settlement within the Aeratroas region. The settlement was planted shortly before the start of the Kroerak invasion and survived, only through considerable help from House Mshindi.

ABOUT THE AUTHOR

Jamie McFarlane is happily married, the father of three and lives in Lincoln, Nebraska. He spends his days engaged in a hi-tech career and his nights and weekends writing works of fiction.

Word-of-mouth is crucial for any author to succeed. If you enjoyed this book, please consider leaving a review at Amazon, even if it's only a line or two; it would make all the difference and would be very much appreciated.

FREE DOWNLOAD

If you want to get an automatic email when Jamie's next book is available, please visit http://fickledragon.com/keep-in-touch. Your email address will never be shared and you can unsubscribe at any time.

For more information
www.fickledragon.com
jamie@fickledragon.com

ACKNOWLEDGMENTS

To Diane Greenwood Muir for excellence in editing and fine word-smithery. My wife, Janet, for carefully and kindly pointing out my poor grammatical habits. I cannot imagine working through these projects without you both.

To my beta readers: Carol Greenwood, Kelli Whyte, Barbara Simmons, Linda Baker, Matt Strbjak and Nancy Higgins Quist for wonderful and thoughtful suggestions. It is a joy to work with this intelligent and considerate group of people. Also, to my advanced reading team, you're a zany, fun group of people who I look forward to bouncing ideas off.

Finally, to Elias Stern, cover artist extraordinaire.

ALSO BY JAMIE MCFARLANE

Privateer Tales Series

1. Rookie Privateer
2. Fool Me Once
3. Parley
4. Big Pete
5. Smuggler's Dilemma
6. Cutpurse
7. Out of the Tank
8. Buccaneers
9. A Matter of Honor
10. Give No Quarter
11. Blockade Runner
12. Corsair Menace
13. Pursuit of the Bold
14. Fury of the Bold
15. Judgment of the Bold

Pale Ship Series

1. On a Pale Ship

Witchy World

1. Wizard in a Witchy World

Guardians of Gaeland

Made in the USA
San Bernardino, CA
28 June 2018